i

PIRATES

or

PATRIOTS

L.D. Watson

Watson

Publisher's Note: This is a work of fiction. Names, characters, places, and incidents are a product of the author's imagination. Locales and public names are sometimes used for atmospheric purposes. Any resemblance to actual people, living or dead, or to businesses, companies, events, institutions, or locales is completely coincidental.

Book Layout ©2015 BookDesignTemplates.com

Pirates or Patriots/ L.D.Watson 1st Edition

ISBN 978-0-9910278-6-6

CONTENTS

"I was crucified with Christ and I no longer live but Christ lives in me. The life I live in the body, I live by faith in the Son of God, who loved me and gave himself for me."

Galatians 2:20

Prologue

SANTA ROSA ISLAND,
SPANISH WEST FLORIDA
May 21, 1814

"He's on board sir," the first officer reported.

"Send him in and set sail," Captain Hugh Pigot ordered as he leaned back in his chair and attempted to light his pipe.

"Yes sir," the lieutenant replied as he crisply saluted and exited the captain's ward.

The third generation officer of His Majesty's Navy was impatient to get Major Roberts on board and return to Jamaica. Wars were not won by the idle.

After a longer wait than he preferred, Pigot felt the familiar gentle rocking of the *Orpheus* as the 36-gun frigate began to drift away from the island. Pigot made a mental note to discuss this delay with the first officer just as he heard a knock at the door of his ward, again after a much longer wait than he would have preferred.

"Come in, Major. I don't have all day."

The second thing Captain Pigot observed about Major Francis Lightfoot Roberts as the Marine entered was the odor. Not only did Roberts look like a Yank, he also smelled like one.

His appearance was the first thing Pigot had noted about the junior officer. Major Roberts, like most of His Majesty's spies in West Florida, had discarded his crimson tunic for the filthy rags of the rabble that inhabited the region. Regardless of the mission, it was unseemly for an officer to willingly remove his tunic.

"Major Francis Roberts reporting as ordered, sir," Roberts barked with a click of his heels while standing at attention and staring, as prescribed in His Majesty's Code of Military Conduct, located eight inches above Captain Pigot's head.

"Relax Major." Pigot commanded. "What have you learned?"

Roberts stood less stiff but nowhere near relaxed. A junior marine officer does not relax in the presence of Captain Pigot.

"I have obtained detailed maps of the region sir," Roberts explained, indicating to an armful of rolled maps and charts he carried. "I will have a complete written report within the hour."

"Perhaps you can explain your thoughts to me before putting them on paper."

Roberts breathed a long sigh. He would have preferred to just hand over his report and let Pigot draw his own conclusions.

"The city has no formal defense."

"You've been to the city?" Pigot asked, somewhat impressed.

"Yes sir. Not six days past."

"And?"

"There is a small militia and less than a dozen of their Army regulars. Nothing more," Roberts said with hesitance in his voice.

"Major," Pigot ordered, sensing Roberts' uncertainty, "what exactly did you learn?" Pigot commanded.

"Sir, New Orleans sits on a bend in the river and is about eighty miles upstream," Roberts began as he unrolled one of the charts and laid it across the Captain's desk. "The issue, Sir, is not the military defense of the city. There is none to speak of. The problem is getting our troops to the city."

Pigot studied the chart and asked, "The river?"

"There are hundreds of treacherous and ever-changing sandbars. Navigation is difficult without a pilot familiar with the river, and there are two forts. Fort St. Philip, here," Major Roberts said as he pointed, "and a smaller installation, Fort St. Leon, here at what they call 'English Turn' just below the city. These are minor threats, but given the nature of the river, it would seem advisable that they be destroyed prior to attempting to sail past."

"All of this land to the south and west?" Pigot asked with growing impatience. "It would appear that we could put landing parties almost anywhere."

"Little of it is land, Sir," Roberts replied. "Most of this region is below sea level. Virtually all of it is a mixture of forest and swamp divided up by a maze of small rivers and channels. Almost all travel below the city is done by boat and only then by those well acquainted with the region. A forced march of even a small contingent would be almost futile."

"Are you telling me that New Orleans is impenetrable?" Roberts stiffened back to attention.

"Certainly not, sir," Roberts responded. "The superiority of His Majesty's Marines has been proven throughout the world. I'm simply pointing out that it will be difficult to move an army given the nature of the terrain."

"Surely there are roads?" Pigot asked.

"Only a few, Sir, and those tend to be under water much of the time. If I may, Sir," Roberts said while pointing to the map, "I would suggest staging on these islands to the south of the city."

Pigot studied the map closely.

"Barataria Bay?" Pigot asked. "Your reason, Major?"

"This island, sir, at the mouth of the bay," Roberts said, pointing at the chart. "Grande Terre. The island is a home to a colony of pirates. They virtually control the region below the city. Their smugglers move to and from New Orleans with ease. They use these bayous, as they call them, like highways."

"You believe that these bandits will sell their services?"

"They are," Roberts offered with disgust, "pirates to all nations with no allegiances whatsoever. They're led by a Frenchman, an arrogant chap, who likes to call himself 'The Corsair'."

Pigot looked the Major with obvious recognition in his eyes. "The Corsair?"

"You know of him, sir?"

"Only rumors. Anyone who has sailed the Gulf of Mexico knows of him, Major," Pigot replied with vehemence. "He's a French peasant. A blacksmith, I'm told."

"I understand that he commands quite a fleet - as many as fifty or sixty ships and over a thousand men. In the city he is well spoken of. One might suggest that he is even admired.

"Only Americans would find something admirable in peasant-pirate," Pigot remarked gruffly. "But I see your point, Major. His fleet and smugglers could be of use. Tell me, does this Corsair have a name?"

"Yes sir," Major Roberts replied. "Jean Lafitte."

Chapter One

LIVERPOOL, ENGLAND
May 21, 1814

For the second time, Ephraim Bradford fell face-first in the middle of Church Street. It was only reasonable that he'd fall down with the boots he'd been issued. Granted they were handsome, but they had thick heels and rose up the calf like riding boots, making it almost impossible to run. As a recruit, Ephraim had heard it quoted many times that "His Majesty's soldiers march into battle and march away from battle. Only cowards run." Nevertheless, as all soldiers knew, there are times when a soldier must run, and for young Ephraim Bradford, this was one of those times.

The tall, lanky seventeen-year-old had made his way along the busy street, taking the opportunity to steal a little fruit along the way. Ephraim didn't like stealing from the merchants. His father had been a merchant back in Tenbury Wells, and he knew how much was lost to thieves. More importantly, he knew that if these shop-owners were anything like his father, someone would pay for everything that was stolen. He and his brothers, Llewellyn and Lucian, had paid for many stolen apples over the years. He also knew that his father had been an exceptionally accurate accountant. Ephraim doubted that any of these merchants were so scrupulous.

The 85th Light Foot was all but broke, and a stolen apple was sometimes all the meal he could get. Fighting Napoleon had cost a fortune, and therefore, the soldiers of the Foot often had to supplement their rations.

Finally, Ephraim found his building. Running through the front door and up three flights of stairs, it occurred to him that those miserably painful shoes were exceptionally well suited for climbing steps. The god-awful things might actually prove to be useful if it so happened that that they find themselves fighting a war on a staircase.

At the top, he reached a door and rushed into the tiny flat that was really an attic he shared with his two brothers and a Frenchman named Louis Rose. Louis had negotiated with the owner of the house to let the four of them share the attic in exchange for a handgun the Frenchman had stolen from an officer. The room was terribly small, but it was warm and dry and far better than sleeping on the wharf with the other conscriptions.

Ephraim didn't know much about Louis. At twenty-nine he was considerably older than most of the 85th Foot, and he was both French and Jewish, which was a curiosity to the three Bradfords who had never encountered either in their small village. The brothers came to know him because he had joined the Foot the same day that they had. A sergeant came down from Shropshire recruiting for the infantry and young men started showing up from all over to volunteer.

After their father died, Llewellyn had begun scheming to get them to America where he believed that they would get rich. He reasoned that in the infantry they could earn enough money for the voyage and have some left over to open a business. So the day the sergeant showed up, they sold the shop and joined the legendary 85th King's Light Infantry, known throughout the world as The King's Light Foot.

They'd had no idea how Louis got to Tenbury Wells when they met him. It wasn't until later that they learned that he had served in the French infantry under Napoleon. It seemed odd that a Frenchman would join up to fight his own countrymen, but the sergeant didn't care, so neither did the Bradford brothers. No one else questioned his nationality because, quite honestly, everyone was afraid of him. Louis had a dark, rugged complexion and was taller than most of the Light Foot, except of course for Lucian who was by far the biggest man in the regiment. The thing, though, that had most of the Foot afraid of Louis was his manner. He was stern and confident, and he had a way of looking at people that seemed to make even the Sergeant Major uncomfortable.

Their friendship really took hold when the brothers learned that Louis was trying to make his way to New Spain and had absolutely no intention of dying under the leadership of these British noblemen. The brothers didn't know what Louis had in mind, but they had collectively decided, which meant Llewellyn had decided, that their best hope for the future lay in America and not in Europe. If anyone knew how to get there, it would be Louis Rose.

"We're not going to Gibraltar," Ephraim announced as he burst into the room.

"We know," Llewellyn replied.

"You know? How?" Ephraim asked, both disappointed and dismayed that the news was already out.

"Louis," Lucian said, nodding his head in the general direction of the tall lean Frenchman who stood silently looking out the one window.

Ephraim should have known. Louis seemed to know everything, sometimes even before the officers.

"Does he know where we are going?" The seventeen-year-old asked. In the excitement of learning that they weren't going to Gibraltar, he had not thought to inquire just where they would go instead.

"America," Lucian responded as if it were the worst news possible.

"America! That's wonderful! We'll go to the frontier."

All three heads immediately turned and stared at the boy.

In dismay Ephraim asked, "What's wrong with America?"

The three just looked at him without saying a word. Finally Llewellyn broke the silence and explained, "We're at war in America."

\#

NACOGDOCHES, TEXAS

September 2002

Jeb Bradford reached up to turn the air-conditioner knob. Nothing happened.

"That's just great," he mumbled to himself while pushing the little button on the door to lower the window. The window didn't work on its own, forcing him to awkwardly steer the pickup truck with his left knee while holding the button with his left hand and pushing down on the window with his right hand.

He hadn't really wanted a truck, but in East Texas, men drive pick-ups, and for some reason, which for the life of him he couldn't recall, Jeb let the used car salesman convince him that he needed that particular gas guzzling collection of rusty parts.

At 38, what Jeb really wanted was a BMW roadster, but with three kids, he knew that was out of the question. Not that a pickup was going to be any better for hauling kids, but for some reason, which again he couldn't for the life of him remember, the truck was deemed more practical.

More importantly, Kay approved, which was the real determining factor on all family decisions.

Admittedly, the pick-up was priced right. Of course, now he knew why - the electrical system didn't work.

Steering his partially running pickup into the main gate of the Western Pines Retirement Community, he couldn't help but notice how deserted it became so early in the evening. There wasn't a person in sight. "You don't go to Western Pines for the nightlife," he remarked to himself.

He followed the road past the main building that reminded him of his first dorm at Texas A&M University and pulled to a stop in front of one of a dozen identical cottages. Jeb gathered three plastic grocery bags off of the seat and walked to the front door of the little house. Nailed to the wall on the right side of the door was a wooden placard with a brass plate and an inscription reading, LOUIS C. SHERMAN, COL., U.S.A.A. RETIRED.

After a single knock, and without even thinking about waiting for an answer, Jeb reached for the knob and walked into his uncle's home.

"Uncle Louie?"

There was no answer, and Jeb noted that the television was turned off.

"The man is in his eighties, and he's out chasing skirts. I've got freshmen students with more control of their hormones than this old goat," Jeb said softly as he took the bags into the kitchen.

"I'm not an old goat."

Louie Sherman sprang into the little cottage. It was hard to imagine that at five-foot-four, he was once a distinguished officer and even a hero in the Second World War.

Louie grabbed the remote control off of the coffee table and turned the television on just in time to hear the opening theme to *Monday Night Football*. The Monday night game had become a ritual for Jeb and his "Uncle Louie."

Louis Sherman in reality wasn't his uncle, but rather his father's cousin. Jeb had been brought up calling him "Uncle Louie", and Louie was the closest thing he had to a real uncle, though he had hardly known the man until recent years. Louie had been a career army officer. While Jeb grew up in a Dallas suburb, Louie and his wife Sue had lived all over the world. Sue died only weeks after Jeb's father, E.O., and suddenly, without any warning, Uncle Louie had moved into a retirement community outside of Nacogdoches.

Jeb never asked why the old man had showed up. He assumed that Louie wanted to be around family, and Jeb was his only family. Sue and Louie had no children of their own. Their life had been the Army.

Right away Kay and the kids adopted Louie as if he were their grandfather, which is probably what the old man had expected, and quickly, Jeb and Louie found things in common, such as they both loved watching sports. Soon it became understood that on Monday nights they watched football. Even Kay grew to accept that little fact.

Jeb started taking things out of the bags and putting them into the cabinets. "I got peanut butter and the pickles you like. And, by the way, I put them on a sandwich and tried it like you said. It was disgusting."

"Bring me a beer," Louie replied somewhat gruffly and without taking his eyes off the television.

"Louie, I've told you a hundred times, they will toss you out of here if they find beer in the place. They're really serious about that one," Jeb replied as he walked over to his uncle with a bag of chips and two cans of Diet Dr. Pepper.

"How's a guy supposed to soften up these girls around here without beer?"

"That's probably the point, and they're not girls; they're all over seventy."

Louie took the soft drink and popped it open.

"In the army they would bring you up on charges for treating a man this way," he said as he and Jeb settled on the couch. "Football without beer; it's un-American."

"Kay says I'm to pick you up every Sunday for church and then lunch at our house."

"How about you just pick me up for lunch," Louie suggested.

Jeb looked at him again. They both knew how Kay would respond to that.

"Can we watch football?"

"Of course, but only after we eat. You know Kay," Jeb replied.

"Can I have beer?"

Jeb looked him again. "You'll have to take that one up with her."

The old man just sat there looking at the television. "She'll let me have beer. She's a good girl." Louie took a sip of his soda. "Your old man thought a lot of her."

Jeb didn't respond. He just sat there staring at the game but not really paying any attention to it.

Jeb Bradford had graduated from Texas A&M University, like Uncle Louie, with a degree in engineering. Rather than entering the Army as Louie had, he went to work at a Texas Electric plant outside the little town of Kilgore. It was a good job, and since his parents had retired to his grandfather's old house in the town of Maydelle, he would be fairly close to them.

By age twenty-five, Jeb was miserable. Every morning he had to force himself out of bed and back to the plant. Jeb had always been bright, and because he was really good with mathematics, electrical engineering had seemed a natural and lucrative career path. But four years after taking the job, he found himself sharing a filthy little shed of an office with three other engineers in the corner of an unbelievably noisy power plant watching gauges and trying to find out why one of the generators was constantly overloading.

Finally, in an effort to regain his sanity, he went back to A&M for graduate school. Perhaps, he thought, with a Master's degree he could find some place better to make a living, but in reality he just wanted something to do besides working in that plant.

It was there, working on his Master's when he met Kay. She was a tall, pretty blonde with an uncanny knack for noticing the things Jeb tried to hide from people. Things like, for instance, the fact that he absolutely hated the engineering school. By the end of that first semester, she had him acknowledging that almost anything would be a better choice for his life than engineering.

To be honest, he couldn't recall just why he chose to study American History. Kay was studying education at the time, and one afternoon he picked up one of her textbooks and started reading. Before long, he had read it cover to cover. The fact was that he enjoyed reading about American history, and he no longer enjoyed anything about engineering. So at the beginning of the next semester, his career path changed.

Of course, Jeb's dad blew his top.

"A Master's degree in engineering is worth something. A Master's in history is toilet paper," the older Bradford argued.

It was Kay's presence that settled that argument. To Jeb's parents, she could do no wrong. She convinced them, with little effort, that the two could live just fine on a college professor's income.

So at age twenty-eight, a recently married Jeb Bradford took an opening at Steven F. Austin State University in Nacogdoches, Texas. The money was slightly more than half what he had made at the plant, but Kay got a job teaching Junior High School, and all was well. Actually, it was great. Teaching came naturally to Jeb, and during that time, he managed to get his Ph.D., although he would readily admit that Kay did most of his research and all but wrote his thesis.

Then Rebecca was born, and they decided that Kay should take a year off work to raise the baby. It was tough. They had twice the expenses with half of the income, but they survived. That "year off", of course, turned into two years. Then came Hannah, and it was clear that Kay was becoming a full-time mother, at least for the foreseeable future.

That next year it seemed like all hell broke loose. First Jeb's mother died, and he and Kay found themselves driving the sixty miles to Maydelle three or four times a week to look after his father who was too stubborn to come live with them in Nacogdoches.

Then E.O. Bradford had his first stroke. A large part of his brain ceased functioning, and he required twenty-four hour care. They got him into a facility near their home, but they soon learned that at even the best facilities, family had to be around almost all of the time to make sure that he would get all the care he needed.

The cost was staggering. E.O.'s estate was holding up, but they had no idea how long that would last. So after an all-night discussion, Jeb finally won out, which was possibly the first and only time he'd won an argument in their short marriage. There was just no way that he could make Kay go back to teaching with two girls under age four.

So Jeb went to work as a part-time contractor back at the power plant. It was a forty-mile drive, but he only worked there three days a week, and the pay was great compared to the University.

Then after nine months, E.O. passed away.

A few days after the funeral, Jeb and Kay started getting the bills. With the sale of everything, including the house in Maydelle, they still had about twenty thousand dollars of debt.

Jeb had long suspected, with the girls and all, that he probably wasn't ever leaving the plant, at least not any time soon. This guaranteed it.

"They want me to write a book," Jeb blurted out.

"The school?" Louie asked, realizing that it was a somewhat stupid question.

"They think that the more published authors we have on staff the more credible we appear. You know the story."

"So?"

"I don't know anything about writing," Jeb said, taking a handful of chips. "Kay wrote my thesis. I don't even know what I'd write about."

Louie looked at him like he was an idiot. "You're a history professor. Do the research and write about your family."

"What, that old Texas Ranger?" Jeb asked.

"Grandpa Eli. He'd take up two or three books. But there's a lot more than just him. You could write about Ephraim Bradford or his brothers. They were heroes. Or write about Charlotte," Louie pointed out.

"Charlotte?"

"Charlotte Fuller," The old man explained. "She's the reason your family ended up in Texas."

Jeb took a long sip of his soda and rolled his eyes at his uncle.

"Your old man never told you anything about your family, did he?" Louie asked, with disgust.

"Dad wasn't as good at lying as his kin-folk," Jeb responded with a bit of a smile in his voice.

"You could write a pretty good book about your father," Louie pointed out.

"My father was a truck driver."

Louie began to get angry. "Your father lived. He fought in World War II, and before that he saved my life more than once. As for Charlotte and Ephraim, they were real people. My Grandfather told your dad and me story after story about them. Grandpa must have been my age at the time. We weren't any bigger than your girls."

#

ATLANTIC OCEAN

June 11, 1814

Ephraim was leaning over the side of *The St. Pascal Baylon*. He had tried to hold down a little lunch but to no avail. His new friend, and apparently only friend, Cort, was by his side.

It had seemed like a great adventure to the boy when it all began. They had planned everything carefully. They knew that there would be a muster at sunrise. They also knew that *The St. Pascal Baylon* was to set sail at sunrise. The ship, of course, could be held up for any number of reasons, but the four intrepid soldiers of His Majesty's Infantry were willing to take that chance even though, as they had been informed over and again, desertion was punishable by hanging.

When they got to the docks, there were officers everywhere. Once word got out that the King's Light Foot was headed to America, some colonel, knowing that there would be deserters, ordered that no one be allowed to get on board any ship without proper papers. Since almost no one carried papers, the wharf was covered with drunken sailors who had returned from the pubs to find that they couldn't board their ships.

Louis had made the arrangement the previous day. It cost them everything they had plus two hundred shillings the Frenchman had mysteriously acquired. All they had to do was find a way to get on board without getting caught.

Louis had solved that problem as well. The provosts were checking the docks, but they weren't watching the water. Louis and the boys slipped into the river and swam to the starboard side of the ship. He had suspected that they would have trouble and told one of the ship's mates to be on the lookout for them. Sure enough, a rope came over the side when they got to *The St. Pascal Baylon.*

Of course, that wasn't the end of their troubles. It was mid-morning before the ship's crew could get aboard, and before they could set sail, the Provost Marshal insisted on searching the ship. This meant that the boys, along with Rose and five other renegade members of the 85th Light Foot, had to go over the side again and stay there two more hours.

Finally, as evening approached, they were able to get on the ship and set sail. That's when Ephraim's real troubles began. He was famished when they finally were able to have a meal. Naturally, Ephraim ate far too much. Then someone broke open the rum. Ephraim had never tasted rum.

It was that first night at sea while sitting on deck with his head in his hands that he met Cort. Ephraim's brothers had left him alone at the first heave. Cort, though, saw the young deserter and mercifully brought him some water and sat with him most of the night.

Cort explained that he had been born in Africa but spent his childhood in Spain. After his parents died, he went to sea. He appeared to be about Ephraim's age but confessed that he had no idea how old he really was.

Cort's skin was a deep black. Ephraim had heard that Africans had black skin, but he'd also heard that the Africans were savages. Cort, though dark skinned, was anything but a savage. Frankly, Ephraim didn't know what to think of his new friend.

Although he was around Ephraim's age, Cort seemed twice as old. Aside from English, he spoke Spanish, French, and Portuguese. His English reminded Ephraim of the Reverend Hallowell back in Tenbury Wells. His words were precise and never slurred. He could read and write in all four languages, and though young, he was considered a valuable member of *The St. Pascal Baylon's* crew. In fact, Ephraim had overheard the Captain say that Cort would be a mate before long.

Though Cort spoke English well, he had a great deal of difficulty pronouncing Ephraim's name.

"It's E-phraim," Ephraim would explain. "With the accent on the 'E'."

But as hard as he tried, the young Spaniard could not get it right.

"My brothers sometimes just call me 'E'ph'," the Englishman offered, finally settling on something his new friend could pronounce.

That first week at sea was the worst of Ephraim's life. It was three days before he could get a meal to stay down, and sleep was impossible on those horrible hammocks. On the one night that he did manage to sleep, he awoke the next morning with a stiff back and sore neck.

On the fourth night he made himself a place to sleep in the cargo hold. He had set some fabric bolts on some crates and made a pretty good bed. But late that night they hit some rough sea, and he found himself rolling onto the berth deck. The rough water, of course, re-aggravated his still unsettled stomach and set off a new round of the heaves.

By the end of the week, Ephraim was beginning to eat but still had difficulty holding down full meals. He had also managed to master sleeping in a hammock without too much discomfort. By that point the worst thing about the voyage was the boredom. The group of newly liberated soldiers had nothing to do. Even the sailors had little to occupy their time. The ship's officer often made them do various jobs just to keep them from drinking and fighting.

Ephraim and Cort spent a lot of time talking. Cort confided that he intended to leave the ship when they got to New Spain. He had been to port at Vera Cruz a year before, and the locals had told him that to the north there were vast open lands with prairies and mountains that could be bought for almost nothing. And in the mountains there was gold.

Ephraim and his brothers had heard the stories of gold. That was part of the reason they were going to Mexico; although to be honest, such stories were hardly believable. But he had come to learn that Cort almost always knew what he was talking about. If Cort thought that there was gold in Mexico, it was certainly worth considering.

Cort also helped Ephraim deal with the monotony at sea. One day as Ephraim and Cort were sitting on deck watching the sea roll, Cort asked, "Can you read?"

"A little. Why?" Ephraim replied, which, to Ephraim's embarrassment, was an exaggeration. Though he could, in fact, read, he hated doing it. He had been to school, of course. His father insisted that knowing how to read was essential to being a successful merchant, but the last thing

Ephraim wanted was to become a merchant, so he never really worked at learning to read.

Cort took Ephraim below and opened his footlocker. The box was filled with books. Many were written in languages that Ephraim didn't recognize. In fact, Cort owned almost nothing but books.

Cort pulled one out and handed it to Ephraim, "This is one of my favorites. It's all about Julius Caesar and the Roman Empire," he said. "It will give you something to do. I like to read on deck in the morning when it's cool."

Ephraim accepted the book with genuine appreciation but wasn't sure what to do with it. He had never before even attempted to read an entire book, and though he had, of course, heard of the Romans, he had no idea who Julius Caesar was.

It was difficult at first, but the boy dove into the book. Cort, naturally, knew that Eph would have trouble reading, but he didn't let on. This was the way he had learned to read and with that same book.

Ephraim was soon fascinated. Before long he and Cort were having long talks about the Romans. Cort told how he'd gone ashore at Naples and seen Mount Vesuvius and the ruins at Pompeii.

One morning as they were on deck talking about Caesar, Louis heard them and joined in. He told of seeing Rome and Venice. He explained that the Romans had built most of the highways of Europe, and that even London was once a Roman city.

By now Ephraim and his brothers had heard a lot of stories from Louis but had no idea what to believe. It was clear that he knew his way around the army, but it seemed so unlikely that he had once been an important officer under Napoleon.

He claimed that, though brilliant, Napoleon was next to crazy. He thought of himself as a reincarnation of Julius Caesar and wanted to conquer the world. Louis said that he and a number of other officers had come to the conclusion after the Battle of Leipzig that sooner or later the French army would be completely destroyed. If not, there would be a revolution, and he and his officers would end up on a guillotine.

Louis told them that he watched most of his command die at Leipzig. He said it wasn't just hundreds but thousands that died, and all because of foolish generals. Ephraim wasn't sure if he could believe the story, but he and everyone alive had heard of Napoleon's defeat at Leipzig. They also knew that it had happened only a few months before they had met Louis marching with the Light Foot on the meadows of Shropshire.

Then, as Louis Rose was telling all about his hardly believable adventures in Italy, something happened that confirmed just about everything he had told them.

Ephraim had been so captivated by the Frenchman's stories that he had not noticed that there was a commotion stirring on the ship. Ever aware, Cort suddenly and without any explanation leaped to his feet and scurried up the mainsail mast. Almost immediately, every crewman was running to position.

"What's going on?" Ephraim asked Rose casually and without any sense of concern.

Rose, staring off into the distance answered, "Another ship."

Ephraim and Rose watched as weapons were passed out to the entire crew. Suddenly, Lucian and Llewellyn appeared behind Ephraim.

"Who are they?" Llewellyn asked Rose.

"Privateers," Louis replied.

The three brothers looked at him as if he were speaking French.

"Commissioned pirates," he explained. "Napoleon would hire them to attack the English and Prussian merchant ships."

"Will they attack us?" Ephraim asked, suddenly realizing that they might be in real danger.

"I don't know," Rose answered and then sprinted up the steps to the quarterdeck where Captain Capillas, *The St. Pascal Baylon*'s commander, stood with his eyes fixed on the mysterious ship in the distance.

"Sir, I have myself and eight soldiers of His Majesty's Infantry at your disposal. If you provide arms, I will be pleased to put my men under your command," the Frenchman offered.

"We are obliged," the Captain replied in precise English without taking his eyes off of the distant ship.

After a moment the Captain looked Rose over and asked, "Captain?"

"Lieutenant, 82e Regiment d'Infanterie de Ligne," Rose replied.

Captain Capillas wasn't surprised. He'd seen the likes of Rose before. He was much more professional and confident than the group of rabble with him. Mercenaries, deserters, and all sorts of criminals were regular passengers on *The St. Pascal Baylon*. Professional soldiers, though, were rare, and usually on board for a reason.

"Wanted?" The Captain asked.

"Someone killed an incompetent colonel at Leipzig," Rose responded without the slightest hint of remorse or, for that matter, concern that he could be put in irons.

The Captain just stared out at the ship that was now making a long pass about a half-mile off the port side.

"From what I've heard, there were a number of officers who needed murdering during that one," the Captain responded.

"Do you know who they are?"

"He's flying Cartagena." The Captain replied. "They're probably out of Grande Terre."

"Grande Terre?" Rose asked.

"The Corsair, Jean Lafitte. Grande Terre is his island south of New Orleans in Barataria Bay," the Captain replied, somewhat casually under the circumstances. "Your men will not be needed, Lieutenant. His ship is much faster and better armed than we. A fight would be futile. My men were issued weapons but not powder. I want them to know that we can defend ourselves, but I don't want any accidents."

"The Corsair knows that he has us out gunned. He has no more desire for a fight than we. Men die in fights. They just want our cargo. I'll negotiate. They will take what they want and then leave us to go home."

"As you wish, Captain. Would you prefer that I take my men below?" Rose asked.

"No. Now that I think about it, issue them weapons and have them stand at attention on deck," The Captain commanded.

"Yes Sir," Rose replied.

The Captain turned to face the ship's mate who was standing behind the commander. "Go with the Lieutenant," he ordered.

Rose made a military about-face and returned to Ephraim and the brothers, now joined by the other five deserters from the King's infantry. All were wondering what their role was to be in the coming naval battle.

"I've just become your new commander. Make two ranks and stand here at attention until told to do otherwise," Rose ordered with an authoritative tone that surprised all of them.

He then turned to the ship's mate. "Issue rifles to all of my men just as you have your own," Rose ordered.

One of the former members of the 85th looked at the Frenchman, and in total defiance announced, "You're not my commander."

Suddenly, before their eyes, their good friend, Louis Rose, changed from being a quiet, affable Frenchman into a confident and seasoned commander.

"You will do what I tell you, when I tell you, or you will die where you stand. Is that understood?" blasted their new Lieutenant in a voice that got the attention of everyone on the deck, including Captain Capillas.

A few moments later Ephraim and what was now a nine man detachment of the King's 85th Infantry stood at full attention with their backs to the starboard side of the ship staring straight ahead at shoulder-arms behind Lieutenant Louis Rose of Napoleon's 82e Regiment d'Infanterie de Ligne while a ship loaded with pirates heaved-to along the port side *The St. Pascal Baylon.*

Ephraim didn't know what to think. He was terrified to move because his friend Louis, who only moments before had been telling pleasant stories about his adventures in Italy, might shoot him for breaking rank, and he had no doubt that the Frenchman would do just that.

Of course, he was even more afraid that he was about to be run through with a saber or keelhauled by a pirate. Facing a ship of buccaneers and being handed a rifle without so much as a speck of powder was about the stupidest thing he'd ever imagined.

Not that they would be a lot of use should the shooting start. The 85th had been badly depleted fighting Napoleon, and there was desperate need for recruits. Ephraim and the others had gotten only eight weeks to train on the fields of lower Shropshire. Even then they hardly fired their rifles.

They practiced firing and loading their weapons for days at a time, and they drilled until they were about to drop. But the King's powder was needed in the war, so they only truly shot their rifles one time. Each man was given enough powder to fire three rounds. Lucian was a good shot. He'd hit the cutout of a fat little man in a blue uniform that someone said was Napoleon with two of his shots. Of course, Louis hit it with all three. Ephraim and Llewellyn missed it completely, but then so did most of the regiment, so there was no shame.

He glanced up the mast at Cort, who was apparently there to signal the Captain as to what was happening on board the other ship. Cort watched the pirates as they tossed hooks and pulled their ship next to *The St. Pascal Baylon*. Occasionally he looked at the Captain and made some sort of signal with his hands. Then, for only a second, he looked down at Ephraim who was desperately watching him for some indication that they might survive. Cort just shrugged his shoulders.

That, of course, wasn't any help at all to Ephraim. He wanted to know if they were about to die. He had heard stories of pirates all of his life, and those stories never ended well. Usually, someone "walked the plank" or was dragged behind a ship. All of this might have been fascinating if it were in one of Cort's books, but standing on deck with an empty rifle while a bunch of cutthroats sharpened their sabers wasn't particularly entertaining.

In complete terror, Ephraim watched as the pirate ship, the *Tigre*, was tied on to *The St. Pascal Baylon*. Then he got his first good look at the pirate crew. Peculiarly, they looked nothing like he had heard. None had eye-patches or peg legs. In fact, they looked just like many of the seamen Ephraim had seen on the wharf at Liverpool. Frankly, they looked better. None of the pirates had torn or tattered clothes.

Some were clean-shaven and were dressed almost as if they were headed to Sunday meeting.

Then their captain appeared. He was somewhat short and squarely built. His skin was fair, and Ephraim could see that his hands were as perfectly manicured as that of old colonel what's-his-name from the Kings Light Foot. But what surprised Ephraim most was the man's uniform. The pirate looked as if he had just stepped out of the tailor shop on Church Street. His blouse was white silk, and his coat was crisply pressed, light blue, with some sort of gold shoulder boards with gold tassels. Surely they held some military significance, but they reminded Ephraim of the things his mother made to hold back the window curtains. This captain, quite frankly, looked a lot more like the way a ship's captain should look than the Spaniard commanding *The St. Pascal Baylon*.

The pirate captain stood at crisp attention, saluted, and in a heavy French accent shouted, "Captain, Dominique Youx, requesting permission to come aboard, sir."

"Permission granted," Ephraim heard from Captain Capillas from the bridge.

Captain Youx stepped up on the gunwale of the pirate ship and casually leaped on to the deck of *The St. Pascal Baylon* with the comfort of a man who had done this many times. Then, just before he turned to go up the steps to the bridge, he paused for a long moment looking intently at Louis. Rose, though, showed no response. Like the seasoned officer that Ephraim now realized he was, Louis held at full attention. The man could have been his brother, and Lieutenant Louis Rose would not have shown any indication whatsoever.

Ephraim looked up at Cort, who was now sitting, somewhat relaxed, on the mast. He looked down at Ephraim with a slight smile. Suddenly, the young former soldier felt a rush of relief. If Cort had any concern at all he certainly wouldn't have a smile on his face.

For what seemed like an eternity, the young former soldier stood at attention. He could hear soft voices from the bridge but nothing he understood. He occasionally glanced up at Cort, who was all but asleep on the mast.

"What on earth can be going on?" he continually asked himself.

Finally, he heard Captain Capillas voice. "Lieutenant Rose, would you please order your command to their accommodations and then report to the bridge?"

Louis immediately made an about face, and with nothing more than a nod of the head sent the others below. The fact was that all of them, including Ephraim, wanted off that deck as soon as possible.

Below, of course, there was a considerable amount of discussion as to what had taken place. No one offered a sensible explanation, but all agreed that it was safer below than on deck holding an empty weapon. Llewellyn, as he so often did, seemed to have the best handle on the situation.

"We were nothing more than a show of force," he said. "The Captain knew that these pirates wouldn't start shooting if they could see that we could defend ourselves."

"Then why didn't he give us powder?" asked the loudmouth deserter that Louis a few minutes before verbally disemboweled.

"He obviously didn't want us to start it," Llewellyn replied.

"That Captain and your French friend almost got all of us killed," the loud mouth responded.

"Well, they didn't now, did they?" Lucian interjected somewhat forcefully and silenced the room.

Suddenly, Cort rushed into the hold and motioned for Ephraim to come with him. The boy looked at his brothers, who were almost in a standoff with the other deserters, and walked out, unnoticed. He followed his friend to the crew quarters.

"Take me with you," the young Spaniard demanded.

Ephraim just looked at Cort, not knowing how to respond.

"You're going on the *Tigre* with the Frenchman. Take me with you," he said again, this time more of a request than a demand.

Ephraim had no idea how to reply. He watched Cort begin stuffing some books into a duffle bag. Then said, "Look, I don't know what you think you heard up there, but we're not going on that pirate ship. We're going to New Spain with you."

"This ship is going back to England. The privateers are taking most of the cargo."

"Ephraim," the two heard from the passageway. Suddenly, Lucian appeared. "Come on, we're going."

"Going where?" Ephraim asked as he followed his brother back to the cargo hold with Cort in tow.

"Louis made some sort of deal. We're going with these pirates. Otherwise we have to back to England where we'll be hung for desertion."

Oddly, the logic of the situation made some sense. But Ephraim still had no desire to spend a few weeks at sea with these pirates even if they didn't look like the criminals he had long imagined.

"Are you sure about this?" He asked his brother as they entered the cargo hold.

Suddenly, Ephraim was face to face with Louis Rose.

"It's okay," he said to the boy warmly. "We'll have to work off our passage when we get there, but we'll be safe," he reassured the boy.

"Are they going to New Spain?" Ephraim asked.

"New Orleans. It's close to Mexico." Rose responded.

Then Ephraim realized that Cort was right behind him.

"Cort wants to come."

Louis took a long look at the young Spaniard. "Are you sure?"

For the first time since Ephraim had known him, Cort, who was always confident, showed a little fear and hesitation on his face. He then nodded at the French Lieutenant.

"Come on," Rose replied and then looked at the five other members of the 85th Light Foot.

"We've decided to stay. We would rather take our chances back in England than work for those thieves," said the loudmouth leader of the group.

"Your choice," Louis replied.

With that he turned and headed up from the hold, followed by Llewellyn, Lucian, Ephraim, and Cort.

Chapter Two

GULF OF MEXICO
June 11, 1814

Ephraim leaned back against the taffrail of the *Tigre*, desperately fighting the temptation to doze off in the afternoon sun. He could hardly believe how hot it was. He'd never experienced such heat back in Tenbury Wells. He could always go below, out of the sun, but the heat was worse there. At least on deck there was fresh air and the hint of a breeze. But again, as Ephraim had learned a week before, on deck he ran the risk of falling asleep only to awaken with bright red, blistered skin.

Cort had warned him that the sun at sea was harsh on the skin, so Ephraim, having learned to heed Cort's advice, chose a spot in the shadow of a sail. His blouse was sweat-soaked, so he took it off to let it dry. Naturally, after lying there reading for only a few minutes, he fell asleep only to awaken sometime later burning in the bright sun.

For days he could hardly move. The ship's cook made a lotion that soothed the pain, but he didn't dare put on his blouse, which meant that he didn't dare go up to the deck. So he suffered below where the air felt so heavy that he could hardly breathe.

Now he knew better than to remove his blouse, but staying awake was another issue. There was something about the heat and sun that just made it almost impossible to keep his eyes open.

In the rush to board the *Tigre*, Cort had managed to get quite a number of his books, but, unfortunately for Ephraim, the only one that was written in English was the book he'd read about Julius Caesar.

During one of those days below deck with nothing to do but sweat, the cook handed him a Bible. Ephraim, of course, had seen plenty of Bibles. The Reverend Hallowell held his against his chest like it was part of his coat, and Ephraim's father kept one proudly displayed in the great-room of their house. Frankly, there seemed no need to read it. He and his brothers had heard enough of Reverend Hallowell's sermons to be more than idly familiar with every "thou shalt not" between the book's covers.

So when the cook handed it to him, he really didn't care much about reading the thing. Still, the man was nice enough to give it to Ephraim, which made the boy feel somewhat obligated.

It didn't really seem odd that a pirate would have a Bible until later that day when Lucian made a joke about it. After only a couple of days on board, Ephraim had ceased thinking of these men as pirates. This crew seemed like regular sailors. They were a rough bunch, as sailors tended to be, but everyone was quite friendly. Most of this crew spoke English, so Ephraim was able to converse with them freely, unlike the sailors on board *The St. Pascal Baylon*.

These men made it clear from the very beginning that they were privateers and not pirates. They operated under the command of Captain Jean Lafitte. In their opinion they were taking part in a war against the Spanish and English. Of course, their real motive was profit, but they considered their business legal and even patriotic. They sailed under the flag of Cartagena and considered themselves to be agents fighting for Cartagena's independence from Spain. Their part in the war was to take cargo from ships supplying to Spanish lands. The cargo would be taken to an island called Grande Terre in Barataria Bay, eighty miles south of New Orleans. The goods would then be smuggled into the city and sold. Every seaman got a share, which was a business to them and nothing else.

Fully awake, Ephraim picked up the Bible and began to read again. Oddly, it didn't seem anything like the book from which the Reverend Hallowell read, which naturally made Ephraim wonder if there were possibly two different kinds of Bibles. The book that the Reverend Hallowell used was a collection of things that good people don't do. Good people don't drink, they don't steal, and they don't lie. Most important of all, good men don't look lustfully at women, which was certainly going to condemn Ephraim to Hell.

This Bible was nothing like the Reverend Hallowell's. This one seemed to be just a bunch of stories. Though there were long sections that were really boring, there were other sections that seemed every bit as interesting as Cort's book about Julius Caesar.

Just as Ephraim was settling back into a story about a guy named Joseph, Cort sat down next to him.

"Is that a good book?"

Ephraim was a little dumbstruck by the question. Of course the Bible is good. It has to be good. Everyone knows that the Bible is good. It would be a sin to think otherwise. A question like that would get a thirty minute lecture from the Reverend Hallowell, not to mention eternal damnation for asking it in the first place.

Then it dawned on Ephraim that Cort didn't grow up around someone like the Reverend Hallowell.

"You've never seen a Bible?"

"No. I've heard of it. But I've never seen one."

Ephraim wasn't sure how to respond. He and Cort came from two totally different worlds.

"Honestly, I've never read it myself, until now. It's pretty good," he managed to say, although feeling somewhat blasphemous.

As the two leaned back in the shade, Cort looked across the deck to where Louis was lining up a group of the Tigre's sailors and barking orders. All of the sailors were holding rifles at left-shoulder-arms, just like they would on a military parade ground.

"They are at it again," Cort observed.

"Twice a day. Just like we did on the fields of Shropshire."

Louis had the sailors lined up on the starboard side of the ship in two staggered rows with each sailor one arm's length apart. On his command the first row stepped forward to the side of the ship, knelt, and took aim. Then Louis yelled "fire" and a volley of musket balls burst into the open sea. He then yelled, "Change ranks!" The front row would back up, and the second row of sailors would step forward, kneel, and take aim, just as the previous row had done.

When he boarded the Tigre, Ephraim learned, as he had suspected, that Louis Rose and Captain Youx knew one another. Youx had been an officer on the ship that had carried Rose and his command to Italy. The two had become friends, which was why he invited Rose, along with Ephraim and the others, to come to New Orleans.

A year earlier, Captain Youx had left the French Navy and become the Captain of the Tigre. Being a privateer, he reasoned, was little different than the navy; only now he chose who to fight and why. More importantly, it was profitable.

Plus, in their opinion, it was legal. They avoided American ships, and thus far the American Navy paid little attention to them, even though the Americans did consider them to be pirates and smugglers. New Orleans was a long way from the rest of America, and very few people in New Orleans considered themselves to be Americans. Also, the city had trouble getting goods, so the authorities in New Orleans turned a blind eye to the operation. In fact, the people of New Orleans appreciated what Lafitte's privateers did for them considerably more than they appreciated what the United States Government did for them.

Since boarding the *Tigre*, Ephraim hadn't seen a lot of Louis. The Frenchman immediately moved into the ship's First Officer's quarters while the brothers slept in the galley. This, at first, didn't sit well with the First Officer, but he soon realized that Rose was an officer of some significance and was to have an important job on ship. That same day, Rose explained to Ephraim that he was now an officer. In order to get the respect of the crew, he wouldn't be able to eat and sleep in the hold with the rest of them.

As it turned out, the *Tigre's* crew was less prepared for battle than The St. Pascal Baylon's crew had been. These were smugglers and merchant crewmen who had joined up with Captain Youx for money. They all knew how to shoot a weapon, but few, if any, had even the slightest military training. Captain Youx tried to avoid ships that were prepared to fight. Fortunately, he out-gunned and out maneuvered most merchant ships. The *Tigre* was a fast schooner, and the ships he raided were loaded down with cargo and usually surrendered without a fight.

The Captain knew all about handling a ship in combat, but training his men to handle rifles and cannons was something altogether different. Lieutenant Rose, conversely, was a professional soldier and knew all about handling weapons and men.

Ephraim enjoyed watching the drills, partially because he was not involved, but mostly because it was downright entertaining. At first not one of these sailors could follow the simplest of commands. He wondered if he and his brothers had looked that ridiculous on the meadows of Shropshire.

One of these sailors actually dropped his rifle. He was a really large rough-looking fellow named Theo. The Captain had told all of the sailors that anyone not willing to accept Lieutenant Rose's orders would be tossed off the ship. Theo was bordering on it. He had challenged Louis' authority on a number of occasions. Then on the second day of drills when he dropped his rifle, Louis got in Theo's face and started yelling. Theo, who was taller and easily fifty pounds heavier than Rose said something that Ephraim couldn't quite hear but apparently involved Louis' mother.

Louis grabbed the larger man by the collar of his blouse and somehow flipped Theo off his feet. A moment later, Theo was lying on his back on the center of the ship's deck. Then Rose, with cat-like speed, pulled a handgun from his belt and put the barrel into Theo's mouth.

Everyone on deck, including Ephraim, froze. The look on Louis' face was nothing short of rage. Then Rose said something softly to Theo and let go of him. Ephraim asked around, but no one had heard what the Frenchman said. All anyone knew was that from that moment on, Theo became Louis' best soldier. After a week, the large man even began taking over drills for Louis.

#

Two weeks after the episode with Theo, Ephraim, Cort, Lucian, and Llewellyn were on deck taking an afternoon "siesta". This made sense to Ephraim because he couldn't manage to keep his eyes open that time of day anyway. Suddenly, they were all awakened when someone yelled, "Ship!"

Instantly, the *Tigre* was alive with activity. Sailors were running in every direction. Louis appeared next to Ephraim, who was anxiously looking to see the ship. Rose was perfectly calm as he always seemed to be while he watched Theo take command of his unit.

"The Captain seems to want to take this one on even though his men aren't ready. I want all of you to take arms and position yourselves on the afterdeck. If shooting starts, remember your training. Make two rows and wait for your orders. Stay in position for your first volley. Then keep low and continue firing alternately. I'm going to check the heavy guns. I'll be back," he said as he started off.

Ephraim looked at his brothers, unsure of what to do.

"Come on," Llewellyn ordered.

They went to the armorer, who handed out rifles, powder, and ammunition. Then the three brothers, followed by Cort, ran to the afterdeck and took position. In the distance they could now see a ship getting closer.

On the main deck, Theo was positioning his command between Ephraim and the *Tigre's* heavy guns. He barked orders, Ephraim thought, with more vigor than the master sergeant of the Light Foot.

Suddenly, Ephraim saw a burst of flame from one of the guns on the approaching ship, and a moment later he heard a loud booming sound followed by a whistling noise.

Ephraim looked at Cort for some sort of explanation, not realizing what had just happened. Then the whistling noise grew louder, and there was large splash behind the *Tigre*. Ephraim immediately realized that they had been fired upon.

He ducked low, clutching his rifle. He was almost lying on deck when he heard a second and third shot fired from the approaching vessel. Cort, as well as his brothers, continued to kneel in firing position.

Then Ephraim heard someone shout, "Fire one, Fire two!"

Two booms came from the main deck, and Ephraim felt the Tigre shudder as the pirates began to return fire.

Ephraim got back to one knee and looked across at the other ship. It had been hit twice. Then there were more bursts from both ships. Finally, one hit the Tigre and the schooner shook and rolled. Ephraim again ducked back down.

Rose suddenly appeared and knelt to Ephraim's left.

"Hold your position, soldier, and you'll be fine. They're just feeling us out," he said with a calm, reassuring tone.

Ephraim felt himself returning to position even though every instinct told him to keep his head below. It may have been Louis' confidence or possibly just blind will, but despite the terror raging through his soul, he knelt between Cort and Louis and peered over the side as the ship came within rifle range.

"Hold fire; take aim!" Louis yelled, loud enough to be heard, not only by those on the *Tigre* but by the sailors on the other ship as well.

Ephraim heard Theo echo Louis's command.

"Front ranks, ready. Fire!" Rose yelled and a burst of gunfire exploded from the rifles on the *Tigre*.

Ephraim wasn't sure if he intended to fire his weapon or if he had just pulled the trigger from a nervous reaction to Louis yelling, but his rifle went off, sending a musket ball in the general direction of the other ship. He later realized that he had closed his eyes and had no idea if his shot had hit anything.

From reflex or possibly his training, he backed up and began to reload while Lucian and Llewellyn moved forward and took aim.

"Second ranks, take aim. Fire!" Rose commanded, echoed needlessly by Theo on the next deck over.

"Begin firing at will," Louis ordered as Ephraim and Cort moved back into position.

Ephraim was surprised at how close the two ships now were. He could see sailors lying all over the deck. To his right Cort fired another shot and began to reload. On his left, Rose did the same. Then his two brothers began to fire.

He tried to aim at something, but all he could see was commotion on the other ship. There were sailors running in all directions. It looked like total chaos. Ephraim could see one sailor clearly taking aim when he suddenly took a hit from someone on the *Tigre* and fell back with a stunned look on his face.

Ephraim fired a second shot, still not sure if he had hit anything. With the ships so close he could easily have shot someone, but again he had closed his eyes

He leaned back to reload, but when he returned to position, most of the firing had stopped. Sailors from the *Tigre* had tossed ropes across the bow and pulled the two ships together.

He and the others held their fire as the *Tigre's* crew began leaping over onto the other ship. The pirates then started shooting and slashing with daggers and sabers. Ephraim watched in horror as a man's head was cut from ear to ear.

He looked to his left where Rose stood watching the spectacle with a look of both vehemence and disgust.

Until now Ephraim couldn't understand why Louis had left the French army. He had been an officer and lived adventures all over Europe. But suddenly, seeing the look on the other soldier's face, Ephraim realized that his friend Louis Rose had seen this sort of thing before.

Ephraim looked over at Cort, who was watching with dismay. To Ephraim, Cort appeared to always know what to do. But at that moment the young Spaniard looked as frightened and shocked as he.

Ephraim looked back at Rose who muttered, "This is why you marched and drilled on the fields of Shropshire. An army without discipline is nothing but rabble."

Ephraim looked back at the other ship and then at Llewellyn and Lucian. Llewellyn was seated on the taffrail with no emotion. He seemed almost unaffected by the events.

Lucian conversely was sitting on the deck with his rifle between his knees staring at the other ship, but his eyes didn't seem to be focused on anything.

Ephraim heard a whistle blow and looked back across at the other ship. The *Tigre's* first officer was bringing order to the rampage. Then Captain Youx crossed over to meet the other ship's commander.

As things calmed, Ephraim sat down next to Lucian.

"Are you okay?"

"I killed a man."

"Are you sure?" Ephraim asked, suddenly realizing that he could have done the same but would never know.

"I could see his eyes. I can still see his eyes. He was a scared as I was. He couldn't have been much older than you. I just pulled my trigger. I didn't even think about it. I just pulled the trigger and his head burst open," Lucian said in a tone of despair.

"It could have been Cort or even me. Anyone could have fired that shot." Ephraim replied, trying to help his brother but knowing it was to no avail.

Lucian looked at his younger brother with emptiness in his eyes.

"It was me," he said softly.

Ephraim looked over at the other ship. The *Tigre's* sailors were beginning to gather their rewards.

Llewellyn got off of the rail and ordered, "Get up boys. We'll have to help."

Chapter 3

July 11, 1814

When Charlotte Fuller was nine years old, she attended the wedding of her cousin, Agnes Worthington. It was the first wedding the young girl had witnessed, and it was all she had imagined. Charlotte recalled, however, that Agnes was a horribly bitter young woman who seemed to hate just about everyone, including her groom, Mr. Martin Waddington. Charlotte couldn't understand why Agnes treated Mr. Waddington so poorly. He was a handsome and kind young man and certainly way too good for the likes of Agnes Worthington.

That wedding was one of Charlotte Fuller's favorite memories in a life with few pleasant memories. Agnes was beautiful in her long white gown, and it was springtime so the New Antioch Baptist Church was filled with flowers. Afterwards there was a huge feast under the white-ash and hickory trees on the long wooden tables usually reserved for the annual fall homecoming.

All of Randallstown showed up that day. The women brought their best pies and cakes, and even Pastor Pleasanton, who almost never had anything nice to say, remarked at how pleased he was that everyone had been so kind to make such a fuss over Agnes' wedding. As Charlotte saw it, the reason everybody made such a big deal out of Agnes' wedding was that they all liked Mr. Martin Waddington and wanted him to have one good day to remember before spending the rest of his life in the miserable company of Agnes Worthington Waddington.

Nevertheless, Charlotte always remembered that day fondly. The church was beautiful, and even Agnes, as wretched as she was, looked lovely. Throughout her childhood Charlotte dreamed that she would have just such a wedding day.

That was seven years before Charlotte's father died and before her mother married Mr. Eliphalet Rhodes and before they moved to Baltimore to live with Mr. Rhodes and his mother.

Mrs. Rhodes, Charlotte decided, was the only human being on earth that was less likeable than Agnes Worthington Waddington. She had made it clear from the day Charlotte's mother married Mr. Rhodes that Charlotte was not welcome in her house. More than once the woman commented that there was not room for the old-maid daughter of her son's wife under her roof.

Of course, Charlotte really didn't have any choice in the matter of marriage. No one had come calling. Her mother insisted that it was because she was so thin and demanded that Charlotte eat as much as she could possibly hold because, as everyone knows, men prefer girls that look healthy enough to bear children and put in a good day's work.

Frankly, Charlotte had few options. Back in Randallstown there just wasn't anyone to marry. The only boys close to her age were the Wisner brothers. There were at least nine Wisner boys, which gave her several to choose from, and Charlotte had noticed Payton Wisner looking at her on a number of occasions, but her mother refused to allow Charlotte to ever speak to any of the Wisners. Her mother had known the Wisner family all of her life, and as long as she could remember not a single Wisner had ever set foot through the door of the Randallstown New Antioch Baptist Church. There was just no way that Charlotte would be allowed to marry a man who was not a baptized-by-immersion Christian.

That rule, of course, did not apply when Charlotte's mother had married Mr. Rhodes. He and his mother were Presbyterians, and though technically Christians, they didn't believe in immersion baptism. More importantly, Mr. Rhodes almost never attended church, a fact which, if Charlotte's mother had known before marrying the man, might have changed the course of Charlotte's life.

Mr. Rhodes was also somewhat foul spoken and drank to excess almost every night. Charlotte's mother naturally detested those habits, but she was now his wife and would therefore find a way to tolerate his poor behavior.

About two weeks after her mother's wedding day and a week before Charlotte's seventeenth birthday, Mr. Rhodes came stumbling home from a tavern and entered Charlotte's bedroom by mistake. At least, at the time, she thought it was a mistake. Fortunately the bumbling fool, as she began to think of him, was so drunk that he didn't succeed in what he attempted, but he did make quite a commotion. When she tried to fight him off, he hit her several times before passing out on top of her. With effort she managed to get out of the bed and slip downstairs where she spent the night on a chair.

With his own mother in the very next room and her mother just down the hall, Charlotte knew that there would be all sorts of questions to be addressed the following morning, and she had no idea how to answer any of them. How was she to explain what her mother's new husband had tried to do? Did he even know where he was and what he was doing? Though Charlotte was pretty sure that the answer to both questions was a definite "yes," his condition was clearly such that one might wonder.

To her dismay, as Charlotte helped with breakfast, not a single word was uttered to suggest that anyone but she knew about the previous night's escapade. Her mother didn't even ask how she got the bruises on her face. Still, although Mrs. Rhodes didn't say anything, she made it clear from the looks she gave Charlotte that she knew exactly what had happened and just who was to blame.

If Charlotte had any doubts as to Mr. Rhodes' intentions, they were clarified the following night. Unfortunately, this time, he was not so drunk and thus he was much more successful, and there was also no question as to whether or not her mother and Mrs. Rhodes were aware of the incident though neither responded to Charlotte's screams in protest.

The next morning, while Mr. Rhodes slept, the three women had a long discussion about the matter. Actually the discussion was between Mrs. Rhodes and Charlotte's mother because Charlotte's opinions were deemed unworthy of consideration once Charlotte claimed to be an unwilling participant in the previous night's escapade, despite the bruises.

Mrs. Rhodes maintained that Charlotte had been trying to get her son's affections from the moment she had moved into his house and, judging by the girl's behavior, she would not have been surprised if half the men in Baltimore hadn't been slipping in the door while the family slept. Though Charlotte's mother stopped short of blaming Charlotte for the incident, she made no effort to stand in her daughter's defense. More importantly, she agreed that Charlotte had no business sleeping in the Rhodes' house and would soon need to find a husband of her own.

So rather than kicking her daughter out of the house altogether, Charlotte's mother agreed that, until a proper husband could be found, Charlotte would sleep in the shed behind the house and thus provide an immediate solution to the problem child's immoral attraction to Mr. Rhodes.

This "solution," of course, only served to make Mr. Rhodes' nocturnal visits to his stepdaughter less obstructed. He would simply stop by the shed on his way home from the tavern. Charlotte's protests, if not unheard, were certainly much more easily ignored.

That following Sunday, Charlotte's mother all but solved the "Charlotte problem," as Mrs. Rhodes liked to refer to it, when she introduced her daughter to Mr. Benjamin Whitechapel.

Mr. Whitechapel, who was well over forty and a good three years older than Charlotte's mother, was recently widowed and apparently quite wealthy, having inherited a vast land grant from his recently departed brother in Louisiana, or possibly Mexico, or Texas, depending upon whom you asked. Most importantly, though, he was a deacon in the Chesapeake Bay Presbyterian Church and therefore was an excellent choice of husband for young Charlotte.

For his part, Mr. Whitechapel welcomed the idea of marrying Charlotte. This was mostly because she was young and pretty but also because he was alone, having lost his wife only a few months earlier, the result of an accidental fall down a flight of stairs. Of course, only he knew that he had hit his wife a little too hard, and she had stumbled backwards and fallen down the stairs. It was her fault, really. She knew better than to pester him when he'd been drinking. A man, he reasoned, could not be held accountable for how hard he hits his wife when he's drunk.

Fortunately, the good people of Chesapeake Bay Presbyterian had been sensitive and comforting in his loss, unlike those busybodies back in Philadelphia after the unfortunate and coincidentally accidental death of his first wife.

To be perfectly honest, he couldn't remember exactly how she had died. He had been drunk at the time, as he recalled, and when he awoke the next morning, she was lying on the floor deader than George Washington. That was back in Philadelphia, and since the magistrate could find no sign of any crime committed there were no charges brought against him, which was only reasonable since he had done nothing wrong. Still, the gossips of that ridiculous town blamed him because her face and arms had some bruises, but as he told the magistrate, those probably happened when she fell. Nevertheless, though he clearly was not responsible, the meddling gossips forced him to move to Baltimore and begin a new life.

Starting over was tough, especially since he had no money, which, as he recalled, had been the reason for a quarrel the very night his first wife had mysteriously died. Success had evaded Whitechapel all of his life, but still, in Baltimore, he had managed to rise to a position of some respect, though financial prosperity was never forthcoming. The truth of the matter was that Benjamin Whitechapel was flat broke. Actually, he was worse than broke, as his creditors would attest.

Then in late spring he had received a letter from an old friend now living in a town in northern Mexico called Nacogdoches. The letter told of vast lands in the west and that there was talk that the Spanish government was considering opening portions to colonization. The friend suggested that a man of enterprise could get rich by simply paying off the right officials and starting a colony.

It seemed a great idea but for one problem. Whitechapel didn't have any money. Still, he was enterprising. He knew, for instance, that Mr. Mulholland, the postal clerk, and more importantly Mrs. Mulholland, who were both members of Chesapeake Bay Presbyterian Church, were notorious gossips and had, even before giving him the letter, let word out that Mr. Whitechapel had received a communication from Mexico. Such letters were not common in Baltimore, and surely by the next deacon's meeting he would be asked about it.

He was up half the night concocting his story. First his brother, whom he hadn't heard from in years, had acquired thousands of acres in the Spanish province of Texas. Then he would explain that the brother had suddenly died, leaving everything to Benjamin. Naturally Ben had to go to Mexico to claim his lands and pay whatever taxes were due.

The next part would be tricky. He couldn't let anyone know that he was flat broke. His solution was to say that to claim his inheritance in Mexico he had to get there as soon as possible, but since most of his holdings were back home in Philadelphia he would have to go there first, sell his businesses, and then go to Mexico. This, of course, would take time and possibly make him too late since the Spanish officials were clamoring to steal his lands. Everyone, of course, knew how corrupt Spanish officials were.

Naturally, no one in Baltimore knew that he had neither a brother nor any business holdings in Philadelphia. But since he was a deacon at Chesapeake Bay Presbyterian Church and chairman of the church committee on committees, it was unlikely anyone would bother to check up on his story.

The plan worked like a charm. Half the deacons at the Chesapeake Bay Presbyterian Church were offering cash money to "help" him in his time of need. In exchange, he would sell a couple of thousand acres and repay his "brothers" two or three times their investment.

The idea of stealing the money never really entered his mind. He simply intended to use it to make the necessary pay-offs. In a year or two when he had multiplied their "investment" many times over, he would triumphantly return to Baltimore and give his brothers in Christ the reward they deserved. He would even give Chesapeake Bay Presbyterian a sizable donation. Possibly, if his colonization plan worked as well as expected, and there was no reason why it wouldn't, he would build Chesapeake Bay Presbyterian a new church. That should easily put a stop to any chatterboxes who might try to suggest that Benjamin Whitechapel had done anything less than honorable with their money.

One week to the day after Charlotte first laid eyes on Mr. Whitechapel, she sat red-faced at Sunday dinner listening to her mother and Mrs. Rhodes ramble on and on about how fine a wife Charlotte was going to make some lucky man. Charlotte, he was told, made the potato salad. Charlotte made the stuffing. Charlotte baked the ham, and Charlotte also made the bread pudding. None of this nonsense, of course, possessed even an ounce of truth, since Mrs. Rhodes never let Charlotte near the kitchen while she cooked Sunday dinner.

They did mention that Charlotte was the best seamstress in the house, which was in fact true, but contrary to what Mr. Whitechapel was told, she did not make the window curtains or the tablecloth, or the covers on the chairs in the sitting room.

Over coffee, Charlotte's mother and Mrs. Rhodes discussed Charlotte's "lovely" blonde hair, and then Mrs. Rhodes, to Charlotte's utter humiliation, added, "Don't be put off by her small bosoms, she's still young. She'll be quite plump once she fills out."

So two weeks later, on July 11, 1814, standing on the waterfront next to the merchant ship, The *New Amsterdam*, Charlotte Fuller took her vows. There was no chapel filled with flowers and candles, and there was not a celebration banquet under white-ash and hickory trees, and there was not a handsome young groom. Rather, Charlotte held a single rose, and the fat bellied old man beside her smelled of tobacco and alcohol.

Thus the reality of Charlotte's wedding day held little resemblance to the dreams she had as a child.

#

NACOGDOCHES, TEXAS
September 2002

"Damn," Uncle Louie mumbled, as he parked himself on Jeb's couch while simultaneously popping the top off a can of Diet Dr. Pepper and glaring at his nephew.

Jeb smiled somewhat smugly at the sight of his uncle.

"The remote's on the end-table," he motioned as he turned and gathered dishes off the enormous dining-room table.

Jeb hated that table and hadn't liked the idea of bringing it home. It had been his mother's and his grandmother's before that. The thing was made of maple and was enormous and weighed at least as much as an elephant, but Kay wanted it, and, as with most things, what Kay wanted, Kay got. So after his dad died, the table came home.

Actually, he couldn't really complain. The table cost nothing. But he really didn't see the need for a dining-room table; they only used it when they had company, a category of which Uncle Louie apparently held membership. In truth, the house was pretty well furnished and cost Jeb very little. He was really proud of Kay for that. She dug through every flea market and junk store in East Texas, and as a result, the place looked great.

He had argued against the house. It was almost a hundred years old, and of course, had "old house problems." Right off the bat he'd had to replace the air conditioning and put insulation in places that had never had any. But Kay had fallen in love with it the instant she saw it, and it was considerably less expensive than most houses of its size.

The truth of the matter was that the house had proven to be an excellent investment. He could easily sell it for a third more than he had given for it. Of course, Kay wasn't about to let that happen.

The only real problem with the place, aside from bad plumbing and the fact that it was impossible to keep cool, was that Kay never quit changing it. For the first time in the four years that they had lived there, she had no project going. More importantly, for the first time in the four years that they lived there, Jeb was able to come home without having to build shelves or paint a door or plaster a wall. Life was finally at peace, which would soon change since Kay announced at lunch that she was going to paint the kitchen. Naturally, this meant that Jeb was going to paint the kitchen. Her projects somehow always became "their" projects.

This would be at least the fourth time she had painted the kitchen. It had been red and then it was purple at one point, though she called it something else. It was also black for a while which seemed really weird, but he eventually got used to it.

Jeb took a handful of dishes from the dining room to the kitchen but stopped in the doorway. For a moment he just watched his wife who had her back to him scraping food off dishes and putting them into the dishwasher.

Looking at Kay he couldn't help but think how lucky he was to have married her. She'd never once complained about their finances. She considered finding clothes on sale an adventure, not a necessity, and frankly, her figure had hardly changed since college. Her hair was shorter, as seemed to be the case with young mothers. But hair aside, she hadn't changed at all despite giving birth to three daughters.

"Are you going to bring those dishes over here, or are you just going to stand there checking out my butt?" She asked with a tone that would have annoyed Jeb if not for a hint of playfulness that only he would ever detect.

He walked over and set the dishes in the sink, thinking how really irritating it was that she always seemed to know what was on his mind.

Through the kitchen window he saw the girls playing outside.

"You're evil," Kay said flatly.

"What?" Jeb responded, trying to maintain innocence.

"I got two six-packs, and you hid them out in the garage," she said with annoyance.

"Relax, I'll get him one at halftime," Jeb responded. "If he started drinking them now, he'd be drunk by the time I take him home, and he's likely to molest all those old women and half the nurses."

"He will not," Kay said flatly.

"We agreed. One beer is all he gets." Jeb insisted.

"I know, but I still think that it's mean of you to let him think that I didn't get him any," she scolded. "And don't give me that nonsense about limiting him to just one. You just enjoy pestering him."

Jeb just smiled, knowing that she was right.

"You're wrong about the old ladies and nurses, too."

Jeb looked at her, realizing that there was something up.

"He has a girlfriend," she added, somewhat proud that she once again was aware of something that had completely escaped her husband's notice.

"No way."

She just looked at Jeb and confidently nodded.

"When did he tell you?"

"The girls and I stopped by to see him Friday after school," Kay told him. "They were on the couch watching *Oprah*."

Jeb was stunned. Then suddenly he began to laugh.

"The Iron Colonel was watching *Oprah*?"

"Hush," Kay demanded, smiling. And then she ordered, "don't you dare say anything!"

"How old is she?" He asked, still trying not to laugh.

She looked at him, hesitating to speak. "He told me that she's seventy-two."

"My God, he's a cradle-robber."

"I mean it, Jeb."

Jeb was still partly laughing, but he'd long since learned what lines he could and could not cross. He looked at her for a long minute and then headed out toward the garage.

"I won't say a thing," he said heading out the door. "But news like this deserves a beer."

#

GULF OF MEXICO
July 11, 1814

Ephraim and Cort watched as the sailors of the *Tigre* gently pulled the ship to the dock at Grande Terre Island. Cort explained that this sort of thing was not easy and that the Captain Youx was an excellent pilot.

"Those are sandbars," he said, pointing. "I've seen many ships stuck."

The *Tigre* was riding heavy from all of the cargo collected. Llewellyn, naturally, had kept an exact account of what was taken, a habit acquired from years of working for their father. He said that there were two hundred bolts of cloth and a hundred bolts of valuable silk. There were also almost two hundred sacks of flour, which according to one of the crewmen, was sometimes more valuable than silk in New Orleans.

After the battle with the merchant ship, Captain Youx saw Llewellyn writing in his ledger and not helping with the work, so he inquired as to what the young Briton was doing. Llewellyn explained that he had not seen anyone keeping inventory and that it only made sense for someone to make a record of the cargo on board.

"No business can succeed without accurate accounting," he explained, echoing a phrase their father quoted almost daily.

Captain Youx was so impressed with Llewellyn's accounting that the brothers spent most of their voyage inventorying the ship's hold.

Grande Terre was not at all what Ephraim had expected. From the moment he had boarded the *Tigre*, he'd been hearing stories from the crew about the great Captain Lafitte and his pirate island and expected some kind of paradise. The truth of the matter was that you could hardly call it an island at all. From what Ephraim could tell, it was nothing more than a sandbar with a few trees and buildings. It was so tiny and flat that he could easily see across it.

Despite its size the place appeared to be quite an amazing operation. There were three large buildings that a sailor told him were warehouses. There was also a little strip of buildings that made up, for all practical purposes, a small town. One building was a store for the seamen, and another was a bunkhouse. There was also a tavern with what was described as a "house of pleasure." There was even a hotel for visitors.

On the far side of the island was a small dock for citizens of New Orleans. Apparently it was not unusual for storekeepers to come out to Grand Terre to get a first look at whatever goods had come in.

The focal point of the island, though, was the house. Ephraim had never seen anything like it. There was nothing so big in all of Tenbury Wells, not even Reverend Hallowell's church. The house was whitewashed wood and had two stories with an extremely wide, gently sloping roof. There was a porch that went all the way around the first floor and a balcony doing the same on the second story. From what he could tell, the front and sides were at least as long as the *Tigre*, and he counted four chimneys, though he couldn't quite see the point considering the miserable heat.

Llewellyn was the first to remark about the efficiency of the place. The moment they were sighted, activity began. First, a boat came out to help guide the *Tigre* to the dock. Then when they got to the pier, there were five or six men waiting to tie the ship to the dock and begin offloading.

Wagons quickly arrived to carry cargo to the warehouses, and at least fifty men showed up to help. The men made a long line down the dock from the wagons to the ship. They then simply handed the cargo from man to man until it all went from the hold of the ship to the wagon. As soon as a wagon was full, it went to a warehouse, where it was offloaded in the same manner.

Then Ephraim saw him. There was no mistaking the man. This was no average sailor. Ephraim had heard all sorts of stories about the great Jean Lafitte, but nothing he had been told accurately described the man walking toward the ship. The crewmen called him the "Bos" and spoke of him with reverence as if he were a king or a prince. His ships roamed freely throughout all of the Gulf of Mexico and half of the Atlantic Ocean, and his smugglers controlled the lower Mississippi River. He had command of fifty ships and over a thousand men.

Ephraim watched in awe as the leader of this band made his way down the dock to the *Tigre*. Unlike Captain Youx, Ephraim thought, this man looked like a pirate. He was taller than most of the men on the docks, and he wore a black wide-brimmed hat and had on high-waisted, black trousers with high- raised boots much like the ones Ephraim had seen on the men of the 35th King's Calvary. He wore a white, silk shirt buttoned up high, and despite the heat he wore a long black silk coat that split in the back for riding.

He had long, curly hair that billowed out from under the hat, and although most of his face was closely shaven, he wore a long mustache that was waxed and curled at the ends.

Though the mustache was unusual, it did not compare to the way his dark eyes contrasted with his fair complexion. The eyes seemed piercing, making him look ruthless, the way, Ephraim thought, a real pirate should look.

Ephraim watched as Lafitte approached the ship. Captain Youx proudly marched down the gangplank, followed by Louis Rose. He couldn't hear their conversation, but he could easily see what was happening. There was something comical about Youx, who was short and stocky standing between the two much taller men.

Lafitte warmly greeted his Captain, and Youx introduced Rose. Louis, Ephraim could tell, was cautiously sizing up the great pirate. He was careful not to do anything to offend the man, but Ephraim could also tell that Louis was nowhere near as impressed with the great Jean Lafitte as everyone else seemed to be. For his part, the pirate king of Barataria seemed extremely impressed with Rose.

Finally, Louis saluted the pirate, made an about-face, and returned to the *Tigre*.

Rose walked somewhat stiffly and militarily over to Ephraim and Cort who had since been joined by Lucian and Llewellyn.

"Monsieur Lafitte would like to meet the four of you," he said. "Captain Youx told him that you're skilled at accounting and merchandising. We will all have to work off our passage. I suspect that he intends to have the three of you inventory his warehouses."

"What about you?" Ephraim asked.

"I'm to spend the next two months training and drilling his men. He wants all of his ships to be trained to fight. He's a bit paranoid. He thinks that the local Governor will someday attack his island and steal his merchandise," Louis explained.

"What about me?" Cort asked.

Louis looked at the young Spaniard with an odd sensitivity that Ephraim found unique to the Frenchman.

"I want you to stick with me," Rose replied. "I told them that you were a sergeant in the Spanish Army. These fools will never know the difference."

"I don't know how to be a sergeant." Cort responded.

"You learn quickly. I'll teach you to be the drill sergeant. Besides, if these barbarians don't think that you're important, they'll sell you for a slave," he said with a nod in the direction of the line of dockworkers.

Suddenly, Ephraim realized that all of the men offloading the *Tigre* were slaves. He had noticed that they were all black men, but it never entered his mind that these men were slaves. As he watched, he saw that all had worn-out and tattered clothes, and some had scarred backs.

"I thought that it wasn't legal here?" Lucian asked.

"It's not legal in New Spain," Rose answered adding, "but these Americans are backward."

Ephraim watched the work with a sense of disgust. He looked at his friend Cort, whose face was staunch and without emotion.

Rose then added, "Many of Lafitte's Captains make a lot of money by purchasing slaves in the Caribbean and selling them here for a tremendous profit."

"That's..." Ephraim paused, searching for a word.

"Barbaric," Rose finished.

#

A few minutes later the three brothers, along with Rose and Cort, were following Captain Youx to the porch of the main house. Captain Lafitte was reclining on a cushioned chair behind a large, round table. He had his hat and coat off in accommodation of the already stifling heat. A black servant woman was hovering around, pouring coffee, and setting out dishes.

Just as he reached the steps to the porch, Captain Youx pronounced, "Captain Lafitte, these are the Englishmen I told you about. Llewellyn, Lucian, and the young one is Ephraim Bradford."

"Please, join me for breakfast, all of you," the pirate said, motioning with his hand for all of them to be seated at his table.

Ephraim was a little surprised the first time he heard the man's voice. There was a high, almost feminine pitch to it, and his accent was not at all what Ephraim expected. There was a hint of French in the sound of it, but there was also an attempt to sound British, like the officers of the King's Light Foot. It reminded Ephraim of when one of the recruits would mock the officers. The silly sound of it would make everyone laugh.

Ephraim realized, of course that Lafitte was not trying to be humorous. Lafitte was seriously attempting to sound like a refined English gentleman.

Upon reaching the table the three brothers and Cort were stunned by the amount of food laid out. There was a massive pile of bacon and an equally large pile of sausage. There were bowls of fruit and beans and potatoes, and there were huge stacks of pastries. At each setting there was a crystal glass of water and finely polished silver utensils.

Following Captain Youx's lead, Rose, Cort, and the brothers seated themselves.

Lafitte motioned with his hand as he filled his plate with potatoes and bacon. "Please, gentlemen take what you want. If there is anything else you require Margaret will prepare it for you."

The servant woman smiled broadly and added, "You boys just tell me what you want, and I'll be happy to make it."

The four were dumbfounded. They couldn't possibly imagine wanting any more than that was before them.

"This will be fine, thank you," Llewellyn said, as Lucian and Ephraim nodded in agreement.

The young Englishmen began filling their plates, not really sure how to properly behave.

Lafitte smiled as he watched the awkwardness of the young men.

"I shouldn't tell you this, but I was born in a tiny village in the Pyrenees near Spain," he said. "I was once a blacksmith by trade."

"And not a very good one," Margaret added as she walked into the house.

Ephraim watched the woman and wondered if she had been a slave all of her life.

Then Lafitte, almost as if he could hear Ephraim's thoughts, added with conviction, "Margaret is not a slave."

Ephraim looked up at Lafitte feeling like a little boy having been caught stealing cookies. The man's dark eyes are fixed on him. The intensity was almost piercing.

"I'm sorry, sir. I meant no offense," Ephraim said somewhat feebly, feeling Llewellyn's condescending glare.

"Europeans are always shocked by the practice. I personally refused to own one. Margaret is my housekeeper. I was lucky to find her. She's taken care of me for over ten years now," he explained.

Ephraim couldn't help but be dismayed by the man. He spoke as if he had distain for the practice but collected profit from it.

Then, changing the subject, Lafitte asked, "I understand that you are merchants?"

"Our father operated a shop in our village. He taught us the trade." Llewellyn answered.

"You are good accountants, as well?"

"They made detailed inventory of the cargo of my *Tigre*," Youx answered with an obvious pride in having discovered the three.

"Your Lieutenant said that you are willing to work off your passage?"

"Yes sir," all three Englishmen answered almost in unison.

"I'd like the three of you to make an inventory of the contents of my warehouses," he said. "I have five on the islands and one more in New Orleans. I would also welcome any ideas you might have in moving the merchandise. My men are inept at selling. Not to mention that they are, by trade, thieves and have a tendency to behave as such.

"We sell a few things here, but most of our goods are sold in an outdoor market next to the St. Louis Cathedral in the city."

"Why don't you sell outside the city?" Lucian asked somewhat timidly for a man of his size.

"What do you have in mind?" Lafitte asked glancing over at Youx, who was beaming with pride.

"Every summer our father would hold an event to help reduce inventory. We would go to all the neighboring townships and pass out pamphlets, and then we'd set up tents in a field near our Village. People would come for miles. It became known as Bradford's Summer Bazaar," Lucian explained.

Lafitte looked at Captain Youx, who was still smiling like a proud father.

"The Temple."

"It's perfect," responded Youx.

The three brothers looked inquisitively at the privateer.

"There is an ancient Indian settlement south of the city. We call it The Temple. Everyone knows the place," Lafitte explained.

He looked at Lucian. "I must apologize, sir. I've forgotten your name."

"It's Lucian, sir".

"Lucian, you are now in charge of Captain Lafitte's Bazaar. You can have as many men as you require."

He then looked at Llewellyn. "Llewellyn?" he asked.

"Yes sir."

"Captain Youx said that you are a great organizer. I'd like you to oversee inventory on the islands. It will be a sizable task. I also want you to take charge of our supply network. Things tend to disappear in transit to the city."

He then turned to Ephraim. "Ephraim, I'd like you to go to New Orleans. "The warehouse there tends to 'lose' things. Also, I'd like you to watch over 'Pirate's Alley'. Can you handle that?"

"Yes sir," Ephraim responded, excited that he would be spending time in the city and not on this miserable sandbar.

"But, first, enjoy your breakfast.

.

Chapter 4

NACOGDOCHES, TEXAS
Sept 2002

Jeb waited patiently in the paint department of the massive home improvement center as the clerk handed him his fifth gallon of freshly mixed "Hawaii Blue" along with two fresh brushes and four new rollers.

"Come back, Mr. Bradford," the clerk said cheerfully as Jeb started to push his cart away.

"I'm sure I will," he responded, somewhat embarrassed that he had been there so many times in the past few years that the clerk not only recognized his face but also knew him by name.

He pushed the cart over to the window section where Kay was busy looking at window blinds with baby Melissa in her arms.

"No," he said flatly.

"No, what?" She asked.

"We can't afford blinds. You blew the budget on five gallons of Hawaii Blue," he responded.

She looked at him with annoyance. "It's 'Blue Hawaiian Sunset,' and I know that we can't afford blinds right now."

"Are you ever going to finish this house?" He asked with genuine interest.

"Nope," Kay answered without an even moment's hesitation, and then she turned and headed for the front of the store.

Jeb just grunted and followed, knowing that he'd been beaten.

"I think you should write the book," she said matter-of-factly.

Jeb stopped walking. It always annoyed him that she seemed able to read his mind, but how could she possibly know about the school wanting him to write a book?

"I took Uncle Louie and Rachel out for lunch," she explained without stopping but clearly knowing his thoughts.

He followed along behind her, making no real attempt to catch up.

"I haven't got the time to write a book, and even if I did, what am I going to write?"

Kay looked over her shoulder. "Write your Uncle's stories," she suggested, though to Jeb it sounded more like an order.

"You know that he makes those stories up, don't you?"

"They're not all lies. You're a historian. Do the research. I think they're great stories, Lucian and Charlotte and Ephraim. And besides, how do you know they aren't true?" she said convincingly.

He pushed ahead and caught up with her. "When did he tell you any of those?"

"He tells them to the girls all the time. They love them," Kay answered.

Jeb stopped again. "You let that old man tell my daughters that their great, great, great, great grandmother was a whore?" Jeb responded, a little too loudly.

"Hush" she said, looking around. "He didn't use that word, but, well, yeah. It's romantic, and they loved hearing it."

"I don't have time to write."

"I've already worked out your schedule. You'll have two hours every night in your study after the girls are in bed. You'll have Monday nights off for football, of course."

"Thank you," he said with a bit of sarcasm. Then he added, after a moment's thought, "What study?"

"We're converting the attic, so you'll be ready to start work on Tuesday," she answered and walked off to the cashier.

As she left Jeb mumbled, "God, please don't let her paint my study "Hawaiian Sunset Blue."

#

WAREHOUSE DISTRICT,
NEW ORLEANS
July 26, 1814

Ephraim briskly made his way through the New Orleans warehouse district. The Bos' warehouse was on Tchoupitoulas Street, which was a long walk from Pirate's Alley. Although there were wagons that made the trip a couple of times a day to keep the Alley supplied, Ephraim almost never managed to hitch a ride on one because he was constantly trying to figure out what had happened to twenty sacks of flour or a dozen cases of wine.

Taking on the warehouse was quite a task. Ephraim had learned accounting in his father's tiny shop, but that was totally different. This warehouse was at least a hundred feet long, and the Bos was right about his men. Not only were they thieves, they were stupid thieves. They would take something and try to sell it on the street out front.

When Ephraim first arrived, the place was a mess. The Bos' men would dump wagonloads of goods in the middle of the floor. No one would bother to make any record of what was in stock.

The first two weeks were impossible. He spent all of his days and most of his nights in the warehouse. The workmen were naturally no help. First of all they didn't like the idea of working for a boy, and especially not an English boy. Apparently, though pirates and thieves, Lafitte's men were patriots.

Their leader was a fat, gruff fellow named Al who spoke an odd language that was a mixture French, English, Spanish, and something else, none of which Ephraim could understand. The only thing that Ephraim really did understand was that the warehouse belonged to Al and there was no way in hell that he would ever take orders from some British "pup". Help finally came about a week after taking over when the Bos himself walked in.

When Lafitte was in New Orleans, it seemed like the bustling city stopped moving. He traveled on a large open carriage, pulled by two massive horses. That sight alone would have caught a lot of attention. Everybody with wealth and position in New Orleans traveled in an open carriage, but no one traveled as spectacularly as Captain Lafitte.

His mere presence could stop traffic. Everyone in the city knew who he was, and almost everyone respected him. The ladies loved him and the men feared him.

Early on, Ephraim noticed that there was just something commanding about Lafitte. First of all, he was taller than most men. His fashionable coats with the long tail made him look distinguished, and then there was the hat. Ephraim had seen a lot of hats. They sold all sorts in the shop back in Tenbury Wells, but he had never seen anything like the big, black, broad-brimmed hats that the Bos would wear. On most men, a hat like that would be comical, but Jean Lafitte looked like a prince.

The Governor was one of the few who didn't respect the Bos. The Governor's Office was practically next door to Pirate's Alley, and the Governor was known to come through to show his disgust. Governor Claiborne hated Lafitte and made no effort to hide it. The papers often quoted him as saying that The Alley was illegal, and everyone there should be put in the calaboose. It was a week before Ephraim learned that the calaboose was a jail.

Ephraim couldn't help noticing how opposite Lafitte and Governor Claiborne were. Where the Bos was tall and distinguished looking, the Governor was average, if not downright short, and was as dignified as a potbelly pig. He looked to Ephraim like a man of position who tried very hard be respected but couldn't manage it. The Bos, conversely, got respect for his looks but couldn't for the life of him get respect for his position.

The day Lafitte came into the warehouse, his "look" saved Ephraim's life. The young Englishman had worked the entire week trying to make order of the place yet couldn't even get shelves built. To make matters worse, he had just gotten things relatively organized when, while taking a lunch break, two wagonloads had been dumped on the floor even though he had just given instructions that it not be done.

When the Bos walked into the warehouse, Ephraim had his back to the door and was in the process of ordering Al to clean up the mess. At that point, Al had had just about enough of the Englishman and was going to beat him senseless.

The night before, Ephraim had decided that sooner or later he was going to take a beating. If Al and the boys didn't do it, the Bos surely would when he found out what a mess the warehouse was. The way Ephraim saw it, Al probably wouldn't kill him because the Bos would eventually want to know what happened to the young Englishman who was supposed to organize the warehouse. Al, though lazy and stupid, certainly wouldn't want it to get back to Lafitte that the man he had sent was found floating down the river with his hands and feet tied.

So when Ephraim stood face to face with Al, he knew what was coming but had decided that it was a lot better to take it from this little fat slob than risk setting off the Bos' famous temper.

Ephraim was stunned when, after ordering Al to sort the merchandise, Al said in clear and precise English, "Yes sir, right away."

Ephraim couldn't think of a way to respond. This was the last thing he expected from Al. Usually when he and Al got into it, the little fat man turned his back and expelled gas.

It was only after Lafitte spoke that Ephraim realized that the King of Barataria Bay was standing right behind him, paying witness to the young Englishman's plea.

From that moment on, his job got a lot easier. Shelves that he had been trying to get built for a week were in place the next day. The practice of unloading wagons wherever convenient immediately halted. Wagons were offloaded onto carts, and merchandise was sorted, inventoried, categorized, catalogued, and placed appropriately on the shelves, and more importantly, Ephraim's orders were obeyed without question or hesitation.

This change in behavior had nothing to do with anyone fearing or respecting Ephraim, and he knew it. As it turned out, Llewellyn and Lucian were having similar problems with their operations. When the Bos showed up in the warehouse on Grande Terre, he found Llewellyn stacking sacks of flour while his men were sleeping.

That episode almost cost a man his life. The Bos went into one of his notorious rages. Ephraim had yet to see one of these tirades, but he had heard plenty about them.

The Bos had never set foot in the New Orleans warehouse. So naturally, Al and his men were shocked at his presence. More importantly, they were as awed and fearful of the man as anyone.

To ensure that there would be no further problems, the Bos ordered that several times a week his personal bodyguard, an enormous Englishman known throughout New Orleans as "the Major," pay Ephraim a visit. No one knew when the Major would show up, but everyone knew why. The last thing anyone wanted was to have the Major angry.

To Ephraim, the Major was a curious sort. Back home Lucian was easily the largest man in Tenbury Wells and probably in all of Worcestershire. But the Major was so large that he made Lucian look quite average. To appear even more menacing, he wore a military uniform with shoulder boards like the officers of the 85th, and though most people would never notice, Ephraim knew that he carried two handguns in a leather holster under his coat.

When not coming into town to check on Ephraim, the Major was thought to almost always be near Lafitte's side. He drove the Bos' carriage and was always a step or two behind when the Bos walked the street.

The man almost never spoke audibly but rather grunted a lot. About all anyone knew about him was that he had been with the Bos for years and helped to look after the Bos' interest. The one thing everyone did know about him was that he had no problem with severely hurting anyone who got in his way.

Usually when the Major came into the warehouse, Ephraim would say "hello," and invite him into the office for some coffee. In response, the Major would simply grunt and walk away. Then one rainy afternoon, like usual, Ephraim invited the big Englishman into his office. Surprising everyone, The Major responded by saying in a heavy British accent, "Thank you, Mr. Bradford. I would like some coffee if you would be so kind."

As it turned out, he was quite a pleasant and talkative fellow. The silent demeanor preserved an image that he found useful serving the Bos. Ephraim learned that the Major's real name was Reginald Blankenship, and he came from a town in Shropshire just a little north of Tenbury Wells.

When he was twelve, The Major's parents died from fever and he went to live with his sister and her husband. His sister's husband saw Reggie as nothing more than a farmhand, and because of his size, Reggie was expected to do the work of a grown man. The brother-in-law would take a stick and beat the lad when he was caught napping or if he didn't do as much work as expected.

His sister was not any better. She saw no reason to cook or clean for her little brother, and so after a day in the fields, Reggie was left to fend for himself. He was welcome to sleep in the barn and eat vegetables from the bins, but of course, he often had to eat them raw because he was not allowed to make a fire in the barn.

One day he went into the field to dig up carrots and found that the entire crop had been infested. When he came back with only half a bushel, his brother-in-law started beating him with the stick. Reggie finally had enough, and the next day, twelve year old Reginald Blankenship headed for

Liverpool. Within a week he had a job on a merchant ship. He wasn't much of a sailor and bounced from ship to ship until finally, off the coast of France, he met Lafitte. The Bos was on his way to becoming a Captain, and Reggie became his apprentice.

Though hardly anyone knew it, the Major had a wife and two daughters in the city. He spent most of his nights with them and only went to the island when necessary.

From that first day Ephraim and Reggie, a name Ephraim tried to use only when the two were alone, began taking a nice long coffee break when the Major paid his visits to the warehouse. Oddly, Ephraim's only friend in the city turned out to be the man that most people in New Orleans feared.

Reggie's visits and the coffee were the best part of his job, though the coffee took some time getting accustomed to. The coffee in New Orleans was notoriously strong and addicting. Everyone took breaks for a cup, and coffeehouses were on every corner. Ephraim and Reggie made an effort to visit most of them.

Being seen with Reggie changed things considerably for the young Englishman. Word got out all over New Orleans that Ephraim worked for Jean Lafitte and called the Major by name, which made for quite a bit of discussion in coffeehouses and saloons since no one knew the Major had a name. It wasn't long before Ephraim was able to walk into any restaurant in town and be treated to a free meal.

Ephraim took very little advantage of his newfound importance. He had a few places that he really liked to eat, but in return, he let the restaurant owners come down to the warehouse and purchase spirits and produce directly from him rather than waiting for it to get to the Alley. He still charged them full price, but they were guaranteed necessities that were sometimes in short supply.

This practice escalated, and before long most of the finer restaurants took advantage of his generosity, which turned out to be good for everyone. The merchants on the Alley often charged outrageous prices when something was in short supply. That was profitable for a time, but when goods were plentiful, like a few weeks earlier when boat loads of sugar were coming down river, prices dropped through the floor. For a while the people on the Alley couldn't give it away. However, by letting the restaurant owners come by the warehouse each morning and get what they wanted, Ephraim didn't need to worry so much about the ups and downs of the market. The restaurant owners were willing to pay a little more than street value in order to get what they needed without having to fight the crowds on the Alley. More importantly, they realized that Ephraim was fair. When flour jumped to a dollar a sack on the Alley, Ephraim sold it to them for thirty-cents. This meant that the restaurant owners never had to raise their prices to make up for the higher costs. Ephraim, on the other hand, had nearly every restaurant owner in New Orleans coming by his warehouse each morning rather than waiting to see if they could get a better price elsewhere. This resulted in good sales every single day regardless of the market value. Lafitte himself even came to the warehouse once to show his appreciation for the way Ephraim was managing things. Restaurant owners had been approaching him on the street to thank him for sending Ephraim to run his business.

But Ephraim, of course, wasn't just in charge of the warehouse. He had to take care of business in Pirate's Alley as well, and the Alley had a set of issues all of its own.

The Alley was one of those places in New Orleans that neither qualified as a street nor an alley. Officially it was a street named "Orleans Alley." It was so narrow that it could hardly be used as anything other than a walkway between

Charters Street to Royal Street. But somewhere along the way this narrow, brick path had become the city's most notorious marketplace.

On one side was the enormous St. Louis Cathedral, and on the other stood the old Spanish Governor's palace called the Cabildo and an old Spanish Dungeon, which Ephraim thought made it a very odd place to be selling stolen merchandise.

For over a hundred years, thieves had been selling their wares along the Alley as if they were respectable merchants. It was often remarked, somewhat tongue-in-cheek, but with way too much truth to be comfortable, that if you came home one night and your jewelry were missing, you could go to the Alley the next day and buy it back.

Ephraim, quite frankly, was completely taken aback by the place. From one end to the other, vendors had tables set up selling everything from flour to furniture. There was often so much merchandise that customers had to step over it to get past, and if what you were looking for wasn't on one of the tables, there were any number of vendors walking from one end of the Alley to the other with their arms loaded down with clothing and jewelry, most of which had been stolen the previous night. Should a buyer get hungry, at either end of the Alley someone was selling deep fried chicken and baked goods along, of course, with beer.

With a good afternoon turnout, a vendor couldn't keep track of his own merchandise. Thieves would regularly steal from a table at one end of the Alley and sell it at the other end. For Lafitte it was even worse. His own vendors stole more than the street thieves. It was not at all unusual for the vendors to keep fifty percent or more for themselves, and with no accounting, the Bos had no way of knowing how badly he was being robbed.

For the first couple of weeks, regardless of what was going on at the warehouse, vendors on the Alley showed absolutely no respect for Ephraim. Then one day the Bos came into Pirate's Alley. Ephraim was making one of his regular walkthroughs, not that it would help much, but hoping he could possibly catch some of the thieves in the act.

When the Bos and the Major stepped off the white carriage at Royal Street and walked into the Alley, it was as if Moses had parted the Red Sea. The Alley, which was normally almost impossible to negotiate, suddenly had a clear channel.

Lafitte, with Reggie in tow, walked directly to Ephraim, put his arm around the boy, and began chatting. The two, with Reggie behind them, walked from one end of the Alley to the other, stopping to talk to all the vendors and customers.

There was not a person on the Alley who didn't have admiration or fear of the Bos. The decent people of New Orleans may or may not have really respected Lafitte. After all, he was a pirate, but they still treated him as if he were a prince.

For the thieves, vendors, and street people of the Quarter, it was entirely different. These weren't the people who lived in the Garden District. These people lived in sheds in alleyways, scraping and fighting for what little they had, and though he wore the clothes of a gentleman, Jean Lafitte was one of them. They knew his story. He'd grown up penniless and worked his way up. Rumor was that he once had a blacksmith shop only a few blocks away.

Being seen with Lafitte that day didn't change much with the vendors. They still pocketed as much as they could get away with. The vendors were thieves, and a thief will behave like a thief, yet the Bos' visit certainly changed the way the vendors and everyone else on the Alley looked at Ephraim. The kid may have been a young Brit, but if Jean Lafitte considered this young Englishman to be a man of importance, than they should as well.

#

NACOGDOCHES, TEXAS
September 2002

Jeb was sitting on his Uncle's couch, holding a Diet Dr. Pepper and staring at the television. Beside him, Louie fiddled with the television's remote control.

"The problem with these new TVs is that they put too many channels in them." Louie remarked.

Jeb glanced over at his elderly uncle for a long moment and finally responded, "The channels aren't in the TV, you know."

"So where are they, Mr. Know-it-all?" Louie responded.

Jeb wondered if there was any use at all in trying to teach technology to a man who could remember Herbert Hoover. Then it hit Jeb that this man beside him was born during the First World War and could probably remember the day that Charles Lindbergh had crossed the Atlantic.

He took the remote from his uncle's hand. "Here, give me that. The game is on twelve. You were on one-thirty-eight."

"A hundred and thirty-eight channels; TV was better when we just had four."

Jeb couldn't resist the opportunity. "I hear that you're a big fan of *Oprah*."

Louie glared at him and then asked, "So what if I am? What business is that of yours?"

"None," Jeb replied, with an evil smile.

"There's good information on *Oprah*," Louie fumed. "She's a great American."

"I'm sure she is."

"A man can do a lot worse with his time than watching her show."

"I'm sure a man can," Jeb replied with just a slight hint of sarcasm in his voice.

"Do you have a problem?" Louis asked, now a little heated.

"I just heard that you like *Oprah*, that's all," Jeb replied teasingly.

"You've barely said anything since you got here. And now you're riding me for what I watch on television?"

Jeb sat silent a moment and took a sip from his soft drink.

"You've been filling my wife's head with stuff that she doesn't need. Right this minute she's painting my attic. This afternoon she bought a desk. A desk that I can't afford, I might add. And one I'm going to have to lug up those stairs."

"And this has something to do with me?" The old man asked with an innocent grin.

"You know damn well what I'm talking about. She thinks that I'm going to write a book, thanks to you."

Louie looked at Jeb and laughed. "Oh, you're going to write that book. Boy, she turned into a little fireball when I told her about it."

"That's my point. It isn't your job to mention things like that to her."

"I had to. You sure weren't going to tell her."

"Arguing with you is like talking to the wall," Jeb said in complete defeat. Then he added, "and there is no book! She's made a schedule. When I get home every night I'm to eat dinner, say goodnight to the girls, and go to work on a book that doesn't exist."

"It sounds like you'll get a few hours of peace and quiet. What's wrong with that?"

"I thought that at first, but you know Kay. She'll be checking my progress."

Louie laughed a little. "Yeah, she's a determined little thing."

Jeb looked over at his uncle. "Last week you said something that has had me a little bugged."

"What's that?" Louie asked.

"I said that my old man was just a simple truck driver, and you said that he had 'lived,' like he was some kind of Hemingway or something."

"I don't know much about Hemingway, but your dad did a lot in his time. When he settled down, it was because he loved your mother. He became a truck driver to put food in your belly. If you ask me, he had a pretty good life," the old man said with a bit of anger in his voice.

"Don't get hot with me, old man," Jeb responded. "I just wanted to know a little about my father."

Louie looked at his nephew for a long moment then asked, "What do you know?"

"That he'd come home from a week on the road and plop down in front of the TV and watch *Gunsmoke*," Jeb answered, and then added, "that's it."

Louie sat for a long moment and then asked, "What do you know about Eli?"

"Not much. He was your grandfather. I can faintly remember grandpa telling stories when I was really little. I must have been five or six when grandpa died."

Louie's mood turned serious. "Your old man didn't want you doing any of the stuff that we did. We used to sit and listen to old Eli's yarns about his life and Ephraim's. Ephraim was his father. Pretty soon we were looking for adventures of our own. I think that your old man knew that we were really lucky to be alive. We couldn't help it though. Eli's stories were captivating. He was the reason I went into the Army. He fought in the Civil War you know. We used to sit at his feet and listen to his stories until we fell asleep."

"I had no idea," Jeb said and then thought to himself, *this man actually knew someone who was in the Civil War.*

"What sort of things did you get into?"

"We got in a shootout with Bonnie and Clyde," the man said, almost matter-of-factly.

"You're so full of crap," Jeb responded, clearly not buying it.

"We were seventeen years old." Louie began. "We heard that Frank Hamer was after them. You know who he was?"

Jeb shook his head.

"At the time he was the most famous Ranger in Texas, maybe the most famous man in Texas. Everybody knew who he was. We took off and hooked up with him and his posse down in Crockett. We lied and told him that Eli had sent us. Of course, Eli didn't know anything about it. Neither did our parents.

"He was a little reluctant to deputize us but took us on out of respect for Eli. Eli Bradford was a legend among the Texas Rangers. Hamer got a tip that the Barrow Gang would come to Gibsland, Louisiana. One of their gang, a guy named Melvin, grew up there," Louie explained.

Jeb saw that the old man was getting teary-eyed and knew that as outlandish as it sounded, Uncle Louie believed what he was saying.

"Hamer had us set up on the side of the road near town. He tied Melvin's father to a tree and put the old man's truck in a ditch with a wheel off. He knew that they would recognize the man's truck and slow down. Finally at about nine in the morning, we heard Clyde's big V8 rolling down the highway. When Clyde got close, Hamer stood up, looked straight at Clyde, drew his pistol, and started shooting. Then we all opened fire. There were six of us. Each man had a rifle, a handgun, and shotgun. We started with the rifles. The car kept rolling down the road and into a ditch. When the rifles were empty, we dropped them, and grabbed the shotguns and ran up to the car, and just kept shooting.

"They were a bloody mess," the old man continued. "I've been in three wars, and I've still never seen anything as terrible as what we did to those two kids. I don't know if it was the excitement or what, but we all just kept shooting. Hell, they were barely older than your dad and me. Bonnie wasn't even wanted for anything serious. I can still hear her screaming. She probably had twenty bullets in her, and she was still screaming. I put four or five shots in that girl myself."

Jeb just sat there stunned. He didn't for a moment believe that his father actually helped put an end to the famed Bonnie Parker and Clyde Barrow, but there was no doubt that Louie believed it.

"What did you two do after that?" Jeb asked.

"We both threw up."

Jeb looked at him, half believing it.

"Hamer ordered the two of us and a couple of Sheriffs deputies from Dallas to keep watch while he went into town to phone in his report. Pretty soon people from all over started showing up to take pictures. It was horrible. We had to fight them off. Some people got locks of Bonnie's hair and pieces of her dress. A few even saved their blood. One fellow tried to cut off Clyde's ear. Your old man almost shot that guy.

"When Hamer came back, your dad and me jumped in the car and took off. I can still remember Hamer yelling at us as we drove away. He was so pissed that he refused to mention our names to the press.

"That was the longest drive of my life. It was like death was in the car with us. We were halfway home before either of us said a word. We promised never to tell anyone about it. Both of us wanted that memory out of our minds. I had nightmares for weeks. I kept waking up, seeing her face all shot up," Louie explained. "I've never talked about it. Not until this minute."

\#

Jeb climbed the last step to his attic. "This is going to get really old," he mumbled to himself.

There was a light coming out from under the door, and he heard K.C. and The Sunshine Band playing on Kay's old jambox. When he walked in, she was putting the finishing touches on the "study." She had on a pair of faded blue denim bibbed overalls with a red bandana tied in her hair. He looked around the room. There were paint cans and drop cloths everywhere. In the corner the baby was curled up asleep on a makeshift crib that Kay had fashioned out of a drawer and some blankets.

"What do you think?" She asked, not bothering to turn around.

Jeb didn't say a word. He just walked up from behind and wrapped his arms around his wife and held her.

"What's wrong?"

"Nothing," he lied.

"You're lying," Kay replied, sensing his mood.

"I spent twenty years under my father's roof, and now I'm finding out that I hardly know anything about the man."

"Are you okay?"

"Yeah. Louie..." Jeb paused searching for some words. "Some of those stories might be true."

"I know."

"Let's go to bed."

"Get the baby," Kay answered.

Jeb reluctantly let go of her, although for a moment he had other thoughts. Kay started closing paint cans, and Jeb turned to pick up, Melissa who was so dead asleep that she was limp. He couldn't help but wonder why babies always feel so much heavier when they are asleep.

Kay looked at him as they headed out the door. "No fooling around tonight. You need your rest."

"How come?" he asked with a bit of a grin.

"Because I want five pages out of you by the end of the week," Kay demanded.

"I hate this book."

Chapter 5

NEW ORLEANS, LOUSIANA
August 3, 1814

When Charlotte Whitechapel stepped off of the *New Amsterdam*, she was awkwardly carrying two large heavy bags, one small bag, and a little brown case. One bag had all of her clothes and personal items, which amounted to three dresses, some undergarments, a hairbrush, a mirror set, a pair of shoes, and a Holy Bible. The large bag consisted of Mr. Whitechapel's clothes. The smaller bag carried all of his personal items, of which there were many, and the little brown case held a number of paper bank notes and some gold coins that, according to Mr. Whitechapel, equaled about ten thousand dollars.

Charlotte was uncomfortable walking into the city with such a sum of money, but it just couldn't be helped. She could only hope that no one would pay any attention to her.

She only knew about the money because the first night on ship while they took dinner her idiot husband got drunk and began to brag to the Captain, the First Officer, and anyone else listening about his wealth and how he planned to invest the money in Texican lands. He explained all about how he had let the deacons of Chesapeake Bay Presbyterian Church think that he needed quick cash to pay taxes on his inheritance from his brother in Mexico. They loaned him the money so he could go to Mexico and sell the land. Then he would repay their investment many times over. Actually, he had no lands but intended to start a colony. It would take several months or even a year or two, but he would be rich before he was finished. Of course, if he ever got back to Baltimore, he would repay his "investors," he'd say with a laugh in his voice.

Charlotte didn't know much about money or investing, but she was beginning to suspect that Mr. Whitechapel knew even less. She did know that what he had done to those poor men at Chesapeake Bay Presbyterian Church was practically the same as theft, and more importantly, she knew that it wasn't smart to brag about having a case full of money to a bunch of strangers.

That was just one of a number of stupid things the man had done. From the moment he boarded the ship he acted like a fool. Before they had even left Baltimore, he approached the captain, and without so much as introducing himself he ordered, "Captain, my wife and I expect coffee in our cabin at seven each morning."

The Captain just laughed, of course, and replied that there would be plenty of coffee in the galley should he and Mrs. Whitechapel desire.

At that Mr. Whitechapel became so belligerent and demanding that for a moment Charlotte thought that the Captain might just push him over the side. In fact, it was only the interference of the ship's First Officer that prevented that very thing from happening. Quite frankly, what calmed Mr. Whitechapel down and kept him from being thrown overboard was the First Officer telling him that he could get his coffee in the galley like everyone else or he could remain in Baltimore.

Next came dinner, where he talked endlessly about his wealth while drinking until he was almost ill. This, of course, was Charlotte's wedding night. Charlotte knew what was expected of her, thanks partially to her mother's warnings, but mostly because of her stepfather. So immediately after dinner, she politely excused herself from the Captain's table and went to their cabin. Mr. Whitechapel wasn't the man she would have chosen for a husband and certainly not the man she would have chosen for what was about to happen, but they were married, and she was resolved to do her best to be a good and dutiful wife.

When he came stumbling into the room, she immediately got out of bed to help her newly betrothed, who would have had difficulty walking in broad daylight, let alone in the dark on rolling seas. His reaction was to push her aside saying, in a voice much too loud for her comfort, that he was not a child and had no need for her assistance.

As she fell back from his push, he tumbled to the floor, landing on his face with such a crash that she thought he surely must have broken his skull. She immediately, of course, tried to help him up, but he began to shout curses at her and then fell on the bed and started to regurgitate, followed by falling into such a deep sleep that he didn't even stir while she cleaned him.

So Charlotte Fuller Whitechapel spent her wedding night curled up on the floor of a little cabin trying her best to ignore the foul stench of her beloved's vomit.

The following day Mr. Whitechapel slept late, which made Charlotte wonder why he had insisted on coffee early. She went to the galley and brought him a cup, but he didn't wake until late morning and only grunted when she offered it to him. When night came, he once again drank himself ill and vomited himself to sleep. At one point, Charlotte began to wonder how he had gotten so fat if he did this every night.

After their noon meal on the third day at sea, Mr. Whitechapel informed Charlotte that he intended to come to her after their dinner. She spent the rest of that day in a state of nervous dread. For the two previous days she had enjoyed the rolling of the sea and the fresh sea air, but this day she could only think of her foul-smelling, bristly-faced husband. It was then that it occurred to her that, given his overall loathsomeness, cleaning her husband's vomit was a significantly more preferable wifely chore than anything she expected to happen later that evening.

That night, Charlotte again politely excused herself early from dinner. Like before, Mr. Whitechapel had been drinking, and she quietly hoped that God would have mercy and all she would have to do was clean up his vomit. But she knew that sooner or later this night would come, so she may as well get accustomed to the idea. Therefore, she put on her sleeping gown and lay in bed waiting patiently for her husband.

When she awoke the following morning, Charlotte felt more rested than she had since boarding the ship. For the first time, she had gotten a good night's sleep, and more importantly, she got to sleep on the bed and not on the floor. Better still, she didn't have to clean her husband's vomit.

Obviously, Charlotte realized, Mr. Whitechapel had gotten drunk and passed out at the Captain's table. Quickly, she got herself dressed and went to the Captain's wardroom to gather her husband and hopefully clean him before he was seen.

When she got to the ward, her husband was nowhere to be found. She then sought out the First Officer and asked about Mr. Whitechapel. The First Officer informed her that her husband had gotten excessively drunk the previous night and was last seen stumbling back to his room.

Immediately, he ordered that the *New Amsterdam* be searched. It was then confirmed that he was not on the ship, and as the First Officer suspected, poor Mr. Whitechapel must have fallen overboard sometime in the night.

Right away the Captain came to Charlotte and offered his deepest sympathies. He assured her that in Mr. Whitechapel's condition, he felt no pain and probably never knew what happened.

That afternoon the officers and crew held a memorial service. The Captain read a few words from the Bible, and all of the officers and crew came to Charlotte to offer their sympathies. They all said what a good man he was and how sad it was that he had to go. Of course, if they had known him, they would have known that he was not a good man, and though it's true that it might be a sad thing that he had to go, in all honesty, she just wasn't sure.

The truth was that Charlotte had trouble being sad at her husband's passing. He was foul, belligerent, and she suspected that he was a thief. Of course, being the grieving wife, she couldn't let it be known, but the fact of the matter was that she had never liked the idea of marrying the man. Now that he was gone she just couldn't bring herself to be sad for him. As a matter of fact, she felt relieved.

Naturally, though, that feeling of relief was coupled with a horrible feeling of shame. After all, he was her husband. Of course, she wasn't actually happy that he was dead. She was just happy that she wasn't going to be spending the rest of her life cleaning up his vomit. That thought might be a sin, now that she thought about it. A good wife is supposed to take care of her husband and clean up after him, and she should love him even if he wasn't always nice to her. She just wasn't sure that applied to husbands who drank, beat their wives, and vomited themselves to sleep.

Unfortunately, being out of a hopelessly miserable marriage presented a whole new set of problems for Charlotte. She was now alone on a ship somewhere in the middle of an ocean and had no idea what she was to do. The ship was going to New Orleans, and she didn't even know where New Orleans was. She could probably book passage back to Baltimore, but what would she do there? Her mother surely didn't want her back. Frankly, her mother went to a great deal of effort to get rid of her.

There was also the issue of the money. What was she going to do with it? Sooner or later the deacons of Chesapeake Bay Presbyterian Church were going to come after it, and that idiot had bragged to everyone on the ship about it. Charlotte had seen plenty of sailors in Baltimore, and though these men on the *New Amsterdam* seemed to be relatively nice, she was well aware that sailors in general were not the sorts that you trusted with ten thousand dollars, and she didn't want to think about what they might do to her while they were taking it.

As if he had been reading her mind, the captain came over to Charlotte after the memorial and took her aside and assured her that she would be safe on board the ship. Charlotte appreciated his kindness, but the fact was that she didn't trust him any more than she trusted the rest of the crew. For all she knew, he ordered someone to shove Mr. Whitechapel off the side so he could take the money. As the Captain was speaking, she realized that it might be just a matter of time before someone shoved her off the *New Amsterdam.*

Charlotte suddenly hated Mr. Whitechapel. "How stupid can a man possibly be?" she thought to herself.

Then it occurred to her that she had no business feeling guilty that Mr. Whitechapel was dead. He was a terrible person, and his death was his own fault. What's more, he had taken all of that money from those poor men at Chesapeake Bay Presbyterian Church, and now he had left it with her, which would probably get her killed.

For the next few days Charlotte barely stepped out of her cabin except for a few minutes each day for some fresh air. But each time she went out she worried about the money, and even worse, the looks she got from the ship's crew. Being the only woman on board was issue enough, but knowing that on the deck below was all that money terrified her.

In all honesty she had no idea what she would do if one of the sailors chose to come into her room. She supposed that she could scream, and perhaps the Captain might send someone or possibly come down himself and do something about it. He did seem like a respectable man and was probably true to his word. Then again, Mr. Eliphalet Rhodes and Mr. Benjamin Whitechapel seemed like respectable men, and look at what they turned out to be.

Spending all of her days in that tiny room with the lingering smell of Mr. Whitechapel's vomit gave Charlotte a great deal of time to think about her future. It frightened her to think that she was alone and had no family to which to return. Baltimore was certainly not an option. Mr. Rhodes would unquestionably welcome her back, but that prospect wasn't particularly appealing to Charlotte. Even if her mother did love her enough to show some sympathy for her situation and allow her return, which Charlotte was somewhat doubtful, there was no chance Mrs. Rhodes was going to welcome her into the house. The "trollop," as Charlotte had overheard herself being referred to, was out of their lives.

Frankly, Charlotte didn't relish the idea of another long sea voyage either. Even without the smell, sitting in that little room for days on end guarding that fool's money was just about as miserable as anything she could think of, save of course, being married to the fool.

Still, there was the problem of the money. It was "borrowed," and Mr. Whitechapel had emphasized the word "borrowed" in such a way that he made it clear that he was hardly concerned with repaying it. Still, borrowed or stolen, it didn't really belong to Mr. Whitechapel, and thus it didn't belong to her. Surely, someone would eventually come looking for it.

As a young girl in Randallstown, Charlotte's father had warned her many times that she shouldn't trust banks. In fact, she could recall many Sunday afternoons listening to the men discussing politics and crooked bankers. She had long since come to the conclusion that the two things that most raised the angst of the men of Randallstown, Maryland were crooked bankers and liberal politicians, although she had to concede that her father was also not particularly fond of newspaper editors, lawyers, or the Reverend Pleasanton at the New Antioch Baptist Church. The latter because he'd once had the audacity to suggest that drinking enough spirits to get drunk was a sin. That assertion caused such a stir that half the church, her father included, threatened to become Presbyterians or even, God forbid, Methodists who, according to Charlotte's father, had more sensible views about such things than the liberal Baptist.

But one thing she noticed at a very young age was that men such as her father, who never had any money, hated banks and thought that all bankers were crooks. Yet it seemed that the people using the banks were people with lots of money. This led her to believe that it was entirely possible that rich people knew more about banks than her father and his friends. After all, why would people with a lot to lose trust bankers with their money if, as her father often remarked, "Everyone knows that all bankers are crooks?"

So Charlotte's plan was to get off the boat at New Orleans and look for the nearest bank to put all of the money in. At least then she wouldn't be walking around afraid that someone was going to kill her. If the banker did steal the money, she could at least prove to the "investors" that she tried to protect the money that her late husband had taken.

She had nothing to worry about, because she had thirty dollars of her own that she had been saving since she was a child. Mrs. Whitwell taught her to save her money, and quite frankly, there wasn't much in Randallstown to spend it on. So whenever she earned any money, which usually meant sewing for Mrs. Whitwell, she saved it. Mrs. Whitwell was far from being the nicest woman in Randallstown, which is why most of her sewing work fell to Charlotte. Charlotte was not a bad seamstress, but she was not nearly as good as many of the other ladies. But none of those ladies would so much as speak to Mrs. Whitwell, let alone work for her.

Mrs. Whitwell had a nice home in a valley next to Windsor Mill Creek. Years ago, long before Charlotte was born, she had been married. However, her husband went off to fight in General Washington's war, "and got himself killed by the British." Mrs. Whitwell had managed all through their marriage to save a little money on the side, and after her husband died she used her money to buy most of the land that eventually became Randallstown. Each year she would sell a little more land, and as a result, she always had money to live on. The way she saw it, the land and money would run out about the same time she did.

Once when Charlotte was over at her house taking measurements for a dress, Mrs. Whitwell told her that she should always save her money. "A girl needs a little money of her own because she can never know when she will need it. Don't expect a man to be able to take care of you. Men are stupid with their money, always buying wine and fancy topcoats and such. And, worse still, they think that they need to go off and fight in wars."

So as Charlotte stepped off of the *New Amsterdam* into the busy city of New Orleans, she thought of Mrs. Whitwell's advice and how right she had been and how glad Charlotte was that she had saved her thirty dollars. Mrs. Whitwell may not have been a very pleasant woman, but she was probably the smartest person Charlotte had ever met.

New Orleans was a bustling place like she had never seen. The streets near the river were full of people. Many were Negro slaves. Charlotte hadn't been brought up around slaves, although there were many in Baltimore. Slave owning was quite a topic of debate among the men after Sunday dinner. Her father believed that slavery only existed so that rich liberals could keep from paying poor people to pick cotton and tobacco. He also didn't like the abolitionists because he thought they were all a bunch of northern liberals trying to take away their rights.

Charlotte often wondered what her father would have thought about slavery if he had been rich.

She stopped for a moment watching a long row of black men offloading a river barge. They were all sweat-soaked from the heavy work and the terrible humidity. Oddly, most of them were singing. It was a religious song, but it was somehow very sad. She watched one particular man, and for the first time she wondered if he liked being a slave. Surely, he didn't. It seemed shameful that the thought had never before entered her mind. There had been endless Sunday afternoon discussions of the politics and banks and the right of slavery, but no one ever mentioned the rights of the slaves.

Charlotte awkwardly made her way up the street. It was very difficult, not just because she was carrying four bags but also because of all of the activity. There were so many giant bales of cotton that it was difficult for her to walk through the street. She couldn't imagine how someone managed to get a wagon through, yet it seemed that there were wagons everywhere.

Charlotte had no idea where to find a bank, but she was sure that there wasn't one along the river. More importantly, she needed to get away from that crowded street. She turned up two blocks into an area of warehouses, which was still busy, but far less than by the riverfront.

She looked up and down the street for someone whom she could ask directions and finally spotted a lady selling fried potatoes. The lady pointed up the street and mumbled something in what seemed like the oddest language Charlotte had ever heard. Charlotte, not knowing what to do simply thanked the woman and headed in the direction that the lady pointed.

Then suddenly, she saw a young man staring at her. She had seen him right before stopping to ask the lady with the strange language for directions. He had been rushing up the street as if he was in a terrible hurry. Now he was just standing there like a statue staring at her.

She tried to ignore him and go on up the street, but she couldn't help but look back, partly because he looked sort of silly standing there staring at her and partly because she feared he was about to come steal her money.

Sure enough, he was still staring, but now he was moving more slowly than before and well behind her. This frightened Charlotte a little, and she picked up her pace. She looked back and saw him again, but as she turned her head, he quickly looked away as if he didn't want her to know he was watching her.

Before she was just concerned, but now she was frightened.

Charlotte looked back one more time and saw that he had once again looked away like he was afraid she would see him. It seemed strange because he didn't look like a thief. He looked like a nice young man, actually. In fact, she had to fight the temptation to look at him because frankly, he was sort of nice-looking.

Finally, she came to a really wide, busy street where she felt safe, but just as she was about to turn the corner, out of some uncontrollable impulse she looked back at him one more time.

Charlotte, you fool.

He was running right at her. She immediately turned to run when her feet flew out from under her, and she fell hard to the ground. Then she saw two of the sailors from the *New Amsterdam.* Kicking and screaming, she realized that a third man had picked her up from behind and thrown her down. Then, without warning the young man who had been staring at her fell hard to the ground next to her.

Out of the corner of her eye, Charlotte saw three sailors running up the wide street with all of her bags.

The young man quickly sat up and asked, "Are you alright?"

Charlotte just looked at him and nodded as she awkwardly tried to sit up.

Then he leaped to his feet and ran off behind the three sailors who were now at least a block up the street. The young man crossed the wide street, turned a corner, and disappeared.

A few people had gathered, and a nice, well-dressed lady helped Charlotte to her feet. The lady said something, but Charlotte was so shaken that she didn't hear her. She just nodded and stared. All she could think was that the nice-looking young man had, sure enough, turned out to be a thief.

It then hit her that the three sailors and the nice looking young man had just left with the little brown case.

While she was standing there wondering what to do, the nice looking young man approached from behind holding one of Mr. Whitechapel's bags.

"I'm sorry. I lost them," he said.

Charlotte just stared at him, not sure what just happened or why he was handing her Mr. Whitechapel's bag right after he had stolen it. Then it dawned her that she was just staring at him because he was nicer-looking than she had thought, even if he was a thief. But why would a thief bring Mr. Whitechapel's bag back?

"I have to go," she said, reaching for the bag and growing more and more terrified of the nice looking young man.

"Where are you going? I can help you get there," he responded.

Charlotte turned quickly and headed away.

"I have to go," was all she could think to say as she headed up the wide street.

She looked back one more time, and he was still standing there staring at her with a sad little boy's look on his face.

Then while rushing up the street she realized that the nice-looking young man wasn't one of the thieves, but rather, had tried to help her. That was why he brought the bag back.

Charlotte, now a couple of blocks away, looked back one more time at the sad looking young man and wondered, *Why does he keep staring at me?*

#

TCHOUPITOULAS STREET,
NEW ORLEANS

August 3, 1814

Ephraim was briskly making his way through the New Orleans warehouse district. The difficulties he'd had with the vendors had improved, but of course they were still thieves. When Ephraim began working for the Bos, each vendor was paid a dollar a day. That was a healthy sum, but nothing compared to what they were pocketing on the side. Ephraim's solution was to pay on a commission. The more they sold, the more they made.

The vendors really didn't mind the plan so much. They knew that Ephraim was keeping an inventory, and they all feared what would happen if he told the Major that they were skimming. This way they made good money and had nothing to fear, and the fact that Ephraim had worked it out with them rather than reporting their sales methods to the Bos said a lot about the young Englishman.

Yet just because they trusted him didn't mean that he trusted them. The vendors were still thieves, which meant that Ephraim needed to keep an eye on them. So at least twice a day Ephraim had to make the walk from the warehouse district past the Cabildo to the Alley. Most days, when he finally got to the Alley he was exhausted, and his feet were sore.

Every day for the past week or so it had rained in the afternoon. For once, though, it wasn't raining. So, muggy heat notwithstanding, for the first time in weeks Ephraim made the long walk up Tchoupitoulas Street in dry clothes.

Then suddenly he froze. It was as if his legs refused to work, and all he could do was just stand there and stare. About a half block ahead at the corner of Tchoupitoulas Street and Poydras Street was the most beautiful girl Ephraim had ever seen. She had long blonde hair and fair skin that seemed terribly out of place among people who spend all of their time working out in the sun. She was tiny and awkwardly trying to hold four bags that were so big they made her look hardly more than a child.

It was not until she looked over at Ephraim that he realized that he had been standing there staring at her like some sort of fool. Finally she took off up Tchoupitoulas toward Canal Street. Ephraim eventually regained control of his legs and began to head up the street a few yards behind her.

After a few steps she turned and looked back at him. Out of reflex he looked down at his feet as if there was something very important that they had to say to him.

You idiot.

A moment later she looked at him again. Again, like a schoolboy he looked down.

Why do I keep looking at my feet?

When he looked up this time, there were three men rushing across the street right at the girl. Instinctively, Ephraim broke into a run just as the girl looked back again. The largest of the men grabbed the girl from behind, causing her to lose all of her bags. The other two men grabbed her things as the large man tossed the girl to the ground as if she were a toy.

When Ephraim got to the three men, he realized he had no idea what to do. That problem was solved, however, when one of the men knocked him in the face with one of the girl's bags.

Ephraim fell violently to the ground next to the blonde girl, hardly realizing what had just happened to him.

As he tried to sit up and regain his senses, he heard the three men running away with the girl's belongings. He quickly looked over at the girl, who was still lying on the ground.

"Are you alright?" he asked.

The girl just nodded. Then Ephraim caught a glimpse of one of the three men running up Canal Street. He leaped to his feet and took off after the man, again not knowing what on earth he intended to do.

Ephraim rounded the corner at Bourbon Street and had just about caught the man when the thief suddenly turned around and tossed a bag in Ephraim's face. Ephraim, again, fell hard to the ground. When he got to his feet again, the thief had disappeared into the Quarter. Ephraim looked around for a moment and finally picked up the girl's bag, and headed back to Canal Street.

When Ephraim got back, the girl was on her feet, and some people were helping her. She was so beautiful that Ephraim couldn't help but stare.

"I'm sorry; I lost them," he told her, unable to think of anything else to say.

The girl reached for the bag, and for the first time Ephraim got a close look at her face. She was even more beautiful than he had previously thought.

"I have to go," she said.

"Where are you going? I can help you get there," he said, not knowing how the words came out of his mouth.

She turned quickly and headed away.

"I have to go," is all she said as she headed up Canal Street.

Ephraim just stood there watching her go and feeling completely helpless. He wanted to speak, to desperately beg her to stay, but his mouth didn't have any words. All he could do was watch her walk away.

Chapter 6

CHARTRES STREET,
NEW ORLEANS
August 3, 1814

Charlotte rushed away from the nice-looking young man clutching Mr. Whitechapel's bag as if it were her most valued possession. The truth of the matter was that the bag she held wasn't just her most valued position; it was her only possession. As she turned a corner, she glanced back one last time at the handsome young man. He was still staring at her.

She paused for a moment, looking back at him.

He can't be a thief.

Then, still frightened and shaken, she rushed away up another narrow little street. Clutching the bag close to her chest, she looked around wondering which way to go as she came to the realization that she was a long way from home and knew no one except the young man who may or may not have been a thief.

"My money!" Charlotte suddenly said out loud.

Hurrying, she found a little sidewalk café and sat down. She looked around to make sure that no one was watching her and then began digging through Mr. Whitechapel's bag.

"Surely he kept some personal money in there," she whispered.

In the bag she found combs, hairbrushes, and perfume, but no money. It occurred to her that the man her mother insisted would take care of her because of his wealth was actually flat broke.

She sat for a moment looking up and down the little street as people all around were busily going about their day. Despair and loneliness began to creep upon her, and tears started to swell in her eyes. Out of sheer will, she forced them back.

Charlotte, stop it! Crying is not going to help one bit.

A waiter walked up to Charlotte and asked, "Would you like some coffee?"

She was startled by his sudden presence and instinctively nodded, and then stopped. "I mean no thank you. I have to go," she said as she grabbed Mr. Whitechapel's bag and hurried away.

#

After watching the blonde-haired girl turn up Chartres Street, Ephraim finished his walk to the Alley, though he was no longer in a hurry. He just couldn't get the picture of that little blonde girl out of his mind. She looked so helpless and alone.

When he finally got to the Alley, Reggie was waiting for him. Ephraim approached the man whom he now thought of as a friend and said, "Hi, Reggie. What brings you here?"

"The Bos has business. Do you have time to take some coffee?" the Major asked.

Ephraim had long since figured out that the Bos' "business" usually meant that he was with a lady, and thus Reggie had some time on his hands. The Bos often had "business" in the city.

"Certainly," Ephraim replied. It was a lie, of course. Ephraim had much to do, but he couldn't say "no" to Reggie. Ephraim may well have been the only person in New Orleans who didn't fear saying "no" to the Major. Yet he couldn't do so because he'd grown quite fond of the man.

The two began to stroll to a little café at the corner of Royal and Toulouse Streets where they had, on occasion, taken lunch.

"Your brothers are doing well on the island," Reggie remarked.

"That doesn't surprise me," Ephraim replied.

"When was the last time you were there?" Reggie asked.

Ephraim had to think a moment. "Over a month, I think."

"Your oldest brother..." Reggie paused, searching for a name.

"Llewellyn," Ephraim finished.

"He has organized everything." Reggie continued. "He and the Bos have breakfast together almost every morning. The Bos has put him in charge of the enterprise."

Ephraim smiled, "I'm sure Llewellyn loves that. There's nothing he likes more than being in charge."

The two arrived at the café and sat down at a table on the sidewalk. The waiter, who immediately recognized Ephraim, quickly brought them two cups of coffee.

Reggie took a long sip and then added dryly, "Lucian has made quite a business out of the 'Bazaar'. Over a thousand people came out last week."

"You don't sound all that happy. Isn't business going well?" Ephraim asked.

"There's trouble brewing. Do you know the Governor?" Reggie asked.

"I've seen him," Ephraim replied.

"He wants to put the Bos out of business," Reggie explained. "The Bos won't be coming into town any more. He is trying to clean things up. We're moving out of the slave business entirely. Any ships that bring in slaves will be turned over to the Bowie brothers down the coast. Lucian worked out the deal. He and the youngest Bowie have become close."

Ephraim was surprised. "I've heard that they're dangerous men."

"They're stupid. I don't know about dangerous. They get into fights when they don't need to. That's stupid," Reggie answered.

"So can the Governor put us out of business?" Ephraim asked, suddenly realizing that the business was as much his as anyone's.

"I don't know," the Major replied. "A while back he put a bounty of five hundred American dollars for the Bos' head. The Bos responded by posting handbills offering a thousand dollars for Governor Claiborne's head."

Ephraim smiled. The Bos had an answer to everything.

"But even if the Governor can't stop us," Reggie continued, "the British will."

"The British?"

"We're at war, you know."

"I know, but I thought the war was up North."

"They're trying to blockade the Gulf of Mexico. There is news that they are amassing troops in Jamaica. It's only a matter of time before they send troops here. New Orleans is too important. You've seen what comes down that river. There's nothing our countrymen would like more than to get their hands on all of that cotton and sugar."

"War," Ephraim remarked. "It's hard to imagine."

Reggie looked at his young friend, "You know that is the reason the Bos has Lieutenant Rose training the men to fight like soldiers? At some point we will encounter British gunships."

Reggie paused for a sip of coffee and then continued, "I sent my family up river this morning. My wife's sister lives in Baton Rouge."

Ephraim sat there for moment thinking about what would happen to New Orleans if the British invaded. What would he do? Would he fight his own country? Then another thought entered his mind. "What will that blonde girl do? Does she know that there might be a war?" Ephraim asked himself.

"Lieutenant Rose and his Spanish Sergeant are doing a fine job training the crewman," Reggie said.

"Spanish Sergeant?" Ephraim asked and then recalled, "You mean Cort?"

"He's an interesting young man. He's quite intelligent. He and the Lieutenant spend a lot of time together. They chat in different languages."

Ephraim smiled. Cort was the smartest person he had ever known, except for maybe Louis. It didn't surprise him that Cort and Louis had become close friends.

"He and Lieutenant Rose are planning to go up river and then head west into Texas soon."

"Do you know when they are going?" Ephraim asked anxiously.

"No, but they're going soon. The Lieutenant is the one who figured out the British plan. He thinks that the purpose of the blockade is to prepare for an invasion."

"I hope to see them before they leave."

"I'll tell them. I'm going to the island tonight."

#

NACOGDOCHES, TEXAS
September 2002

Jeb sat staring at a blank computer screen. Even after the painting was finished, it had taken two full evenings getting the office/attic in an order that met Kay's satisfaction. It struck Jeb as somewhat humorous that it was to be his office, and quite frankly, he couldn't care less which pictures of the girls were on the walls or where to put the desk. But for some reason that Jeb couldn't begin to understand, all of these things were of tremendous importance to Kay.

If it had truly been his office, he would have a television up there, but that suggestion surely didn't fly. She wasn't about to buy the argument that he'd just use it to watch the News. She almost conceded, but only under the condition that they drop their subscription to ESPN. Of course, that defeated the very purpose of having a TV, of which, naturally, she was well aware.

When he finally sat down and started to think about the book, his mind was empty. All he could really think about was the possibility that the story Uncle Louie had told a few nights earlier might have been true.

Jeb sat for a few minutes thinking about the old man's story. Then, on impulse, he typed the names Bonnie and Clyde into Google. There were thousands of results. He scrolled through and stopped here and there. Then he hit an article from the *Longview Texas Herald* dated May 24, 1934. Jeb skimmed it, looking for, though not really expecting to see, his father's name. The article described the ambush almost exactly as Uncle Louie had and ended with the notation:

> *Along with Captain Hamer were*
> *two Dallas County Sheriff's Deputies,*

Bob Alcorn and Ted Hinton,
Texas Ranger B.M. Gault, Louisiana
State Troopers Henderson Jordan
and Prentiss Oakley, and two young
deputies who are not yet identified.

Jeb was staring at the when Kay walked into the study. Without saying a word, she sat down on the desk next to the computer keyboard.

"You're not getting anywhere are you?" She asked.

"Nope."

"You will," she said, reassuringly.

"Let's see. My job has all but required me to write a book, or I could possibly get fired. I have no experience in writing, and I have no idea of what to write. I've got no plan, and to be honest, I don't even know how to begin. I should have it done in no time," he said sarcastically.

Kay just sat patiently, looking at him. She knew that he was just venting some frustration. She also knew that he really wanted to do this. He just didn't know how to get started.

"My father helped capture Bonnie and Clyde," he said and then added, "Let me correct that. He helped kill Bonnie and Clyde."

"Uncle Louie hasn't told me that one," she said empathetically.

Jeb pointed at the computer screen and Kay turned to read it.

"The 'two deputies not yet identified' are Dad and Uncle Louie."

"You believe this one?" Kay asked.

"He would have had to do some serious research to have known about the two unidentified deputies. He sure didn't use the Internet. He doesn't even know that there is an Internet. I know that it seems crazy, but there was something in Louie's voice when he told me the story. For a minute there I thought he was going to break down and cry."

"That isn't what's bothering you."

"Dad never mentioned that story. Don't you think that's a little odd? This is pretty big, don't you think? Shouldn't he have said something about it? He was forty-something when I came along. The man lived a whole life before I was born that I know nothing about."

Kay turned around and shut down the computer and then looked at Jeb and said, "Come on. It's time for bed."

"You're letting me quit early?"

"You've done enough for tonight. Besides, the girls are asleep." She said with a smile.

Jeb's eyes lit up, sensing a hint.

"All three?"

Kay took his hand and led him out of the office.

"Yep," she said with a smile. "But you still owe me five pages."

#

MISSISSIPPI RIVERFRONT,
NEW ORLEANS
August 5, 1814

Charlotte's first two nights in New Orleans were the worst of her life. She walked the streets trying to make some sort of plan, but by nightfall she had nothing. At one point she considered returning to the *New Amsterdam,* but she feared seeing any of those sailors again. For all she knew, the captain had sent those men to steal her bags. Finally, in an old building near a park by the river she found a spot under an arch by the front door. The spot was somewhat covered and she thought she could curl up for the night, but late in the evening a rather large woman arrived with her two friends claiming that it was their spot and insisted that if Charlotte didn't leave immediately they would kill her.

Charlotte didn't, at the time, think that they would actually kill her for a spot on a building's porch, but by night's end she realized that there were people on the streets who would do just about anything. The park, *Place d'Armes* as it was called, sat between the church and the river. During the day it was a quiet, peaceful place where Charlotte had sat and rested her feet, but right after dark the park became alive with a different kind of activity. There were dozens, if not hundreds in New Orleans who, like Charlotte, had no place to go, and they all seemed to show up at the *Place d'Armes*.

Among those wandering the park were a number of prostitutes. Charlotte had of course, heard of prostitutes. Back home in Randallstown, Anna-Ruth, Charlotte's best friend, had told her stories about the prostitutes she'd seen while visiting her aunt in Philadelphia, but those were just stories. Growing up in Maryland, Charlotte never had an occasion to actually witness such a thing. Even after her father died and she and her mother moved to Baltimore, she never saw anything like what took place in the *Place d'Armes* in New Orleans.

Terrified of the prostitutes and sailors and dockworkers and everyone else in the *Place d'Armes*, Charlotte began to walk the dark narrow streets of what the locals called "the Quarter." Finally, after she had walked until she was completely exhausted, she found a stoop that had no one sleeping on it. There she sat through the night, huddled in a shadow, clutching Mr. Whitechapel's bag, too terrified to sleep.

The next morning Charlotte set her mind on accomplishing two tasks. The first was to find a job, and the second was to find some place to sleep. Any place would do as long as it was indoors and away from the streets of this city. She could cook, sort of, and she could sew. Surely there were people in this city that needed those things.

There was a third task. She hadn't eaten since stepping off the *New Amsterdam,* but food was of lesser importance. She had sat through many sermons and knew all too well that Jesus went forty days without food. Reverend Pleasanton at New Antioch Baptist Church in Randallstown had even preached that the congregation should fast for a week and give the food that they would have eaten to the poor. Of course, as Charlotte's father pointed out, not eating was easy for the Reverend, who was as fat as a pig and could easily last a month or more.

Still, Charlotte supposed, if Jesus could go forty days without food, she could make it a day or two.

She knocked on what seemed like every door in the city. The first thing she learned about New Orleans was that the people who could afford a cook or a seamstress owned slaves to do those chores. By midday she began to realize that there were few, if any, jobs for a woman. By mid-afternoon the second task had become her priority. She looked everywhere and even asked people if she could sleep in their shed or stoop, only to be turned away.

Late in the afternoon she found a place. Along the river near where the *New Amsterdam* had docked, there were dozens of bales of cotton waiting to be loaded onto a ship. At night they were often covered with tent cloth to protect them from dew and rain. When no one was watching, she managed to press a little gap between two bails. It wasn't a big space, but it was soft and covered, and most importantly, she would be out of sight.

After dark she came back and slipped into her little bed. She was hungry and thirsty, but at least she had a dry place to sleep that was relatively safe.

Late in the night she heard a sound that startled her out of a deep sleep. Outside her little nook she heard voices. She didn't understand anything said, but peeking out, she could faintly see three men. Though she couldn't see them well or understand them, she could tell that they were quarreling. When one of the men pulled a gun out of his coat, the tallest of the three quickly drew what looked like a butcher's knife and sliced the man's hand at the wrist so deeply that the hand dangled from his arm.

The man grasped the dangling hand with his other hand and ran up the docks, screaming in agony.

As he ran the tall man coldly shouted, "If you ever draw on me again, I'll cut off your other hand."

Charlotte lay frozen as she watched the spectacle. The tall man then came over to the cotton bails right next to where she lay cuddled in the darkness and began wiping the blood off of his knife.

When he had finished, the man with him said, "Let's get out of here, Jim. I'm hungry."

For a second night, Charlotte lay in terror, too afraid to sleep.

#

PIRATE'S ALLEY,
NEW ORLEANS
August 10, 1814

Ephraim was making an early visit to the Alley. It was cooler in the morning, which usually brought out a large crowd. But this morning the place was almost empty. In all the time he had been in New Orleans, he had never seen it so vacant. The tables were there and the vendors were all in place, but there was almost no one shopping.

At first he didn't know what to think of this, but then at the far end of the Alley he saw the reason. Standing in the middle of the passage, looking at the tables of stolen goods was a short fat man in a poorly tailored topcoat followed by a four-man entourage. Governor William C. C. Claiborne had come to Pirate's Alley.

Ephraim hesitated at first. This was the Governor, and from what Reggie had said, he was not going to be particularly friendly. But for some odd reason he couldn't quite put his finger on, Ephraim wasn't afraid of the man. Governor Claiborne stormed around like he was the King himself, but in reality he was about as un-intimidating as any man as Ephraim had seen. Everyone in the city thought the same as Ephraim did. The newspapers were full of cartoons making light of his ill-fitting suits and arrogant demeanor.

So in what he later thought of as an uncharacteristic act of courage, Ephraim walked right up to the man. Immediately, one of the little band of minions stepped between him and Claiborne.

"May I help you find something, Governor?" Ephraim asked.

The man between Ephraim and Claiborne put his hand out to stop Ephraim from approaching.

"This is government business, son," the man informed Ephraim.

"Wait a minute, Farnsworth," Governor Claiborne said firmly.

The man let his hand down and the Governor walked up to Ephraim.

"You're the young man I've been hearing about, aren't you?" the Governor asked.

Ephraim wasn't sure how to respond. He was clearly a criminal selling stolen goods, and he had just marched up the Governor of the State of Louisiana like some fool. He felt a knot forming in his stomach.

"You are the Englishman who recently took over management of this illegal marketplace for that thief, Jean Lafitte?" Claiborne continued.

Again Ephraim just stood silent. There just simply weren't any words. In one sentence Claiborne had called Lafitte a thief and accused Ephraim of working for the man, which in effect, made Ephraim a thief. This was a man whose sworn duty was to uphold the law. Governor Claiborne might be an arrogant little man who looked silly in his badly fitting clothes, but he was the Governor.

The thing that really kept Ephraim from finding any words was that the annoying little man happened to be right. Lafitte was a thief, and Ephraim worked for him.

"What's the matter, boy? Nothing to say for yourself?"

Ephraim stood there silently for a long moment and then looked at the arrogant little man and remembered something his father often said when people were hanging around in the store and not buying anything.

"We've no time for loiterers. If you need something, buy it. Otherwise, please move on."

Claiborne's eyes widened and almost exploded from his head. He was clearly not accustomed to being spoken to in such a manner. Still, though visibly boiling on the inside, the man was unable to find a way to respond.

"You've not heard the last of me, Englishman," the Governor finally blurted.

With that the little fat man turned around and stormed out of the Alley, followed by his four attendants.

Ephraim stood nervously watching as the Governor and his entourage marched away, the knot in his stomach not yet beginning to relax. He couldn't imagine what had made him say those words. They simply erupted as if he had no control.

Then Ephraim turned around and saw business begin returning to normal.

#

FRENCH QUARTER, NEW ORLEANS
August 16, 1814

After the man was almost killed right in front of her, Charlotte found it impossible to sleep. If she did doze, she would have a nightmare and awaken with the fear that the man holding the knife was right outside her little bedroom of cotton bales.

Still, terror and lack of sleep were not her worst problem. Going without food and water had made her weak. With each passing moment, the desperation of her situation became more real.

Rain would gather on the tent material under which she slept, and she managed to keep some in the bottles Mr. Whitechapel had in his bag. The bottles had contained bourbon and perfume and hair tonic. She emptied them out, having no use for such things and filled the bottles with the water. It tasted terrible, but in the New Orleans summer heat, any water was better than none.

Food was another issue. She had learned that one of the churches gave out food each Wednesday. When she had arrived, there was already an enormous crowd of hungry people. Of course, Charlotte was so far back in line that most of the food was gone before she got to it. Still, a little was better than none at all.

The following week, she got there really early. The food wasn't anything special. It was mostly leftovers that the restaurants would have thrown out. But at this point, that didn't bother Charlotte. It was a matter of surviving now.

She kept knocking on doors in search of work, but everywhere she went, she was turned away. Either they had slaves to do the work or they preferred to use men. She'd lost count of the number of times she was told that a pretty girl like her should find a husband.

Eventually she started going to the saloons. She had previously avoided those places. Although she had never actually been in one, she had a pretty good idea what went on inside, and she was sure that they were dangerous. She reasoned though, if she could survive living on the docks, she surely could survive working in a saloon.

The first one she went into looked terrifying even in the daylight. The place was dark and filthy, and even though it was still early in the day, there were at least twenty men inside drinking. The place frightened her so much that she turned and hurried out before even speaking to anyone.

She continued to walk Bourbon Street hoping to find a place that looked clean. Eventually she came to a saloon named Cheri Royal. She couldn't tell much about the place from the outside, but it seemed nicer than the others, so she slowly looked in the door. There was a large room full of tables with a bar running down one side. In the back there were a couple of men at one of the tables. One man wore an apron, and the other had on a coat and tie.

Charlotte gathered her courage and, clutching Mr. Whitechapel's bag, walked up to the man in the apron.

"Please, sir. I'm looking for work. I can wash dishes and clean floors. Please, I desperately need work." She said.

The man in the apron smiled at her and pointed at his companion. It was the first smile she had seen in the city since the nice-looking young man who had returned Mr. Whitechapel's bag.

She turned to look at the other man. Although he was well dressed, there was something frightening about his eyes.

"My name is Hamilton," he said. "This is my place."

"I'm terribly sorry, sir," Charlotte said meekly.

"It's okay, girl. I'm happy that I don't look like a saloon keeper," he replied. Then he looked at the other man. "What do you think, Jeth? Can we use a girl like this?"

The man in the apron looked Charlotte up and down. Suddenly, his smile no longer looked so nice to her.

"I think we can put her to work," Jeth responded. "What's your name, girl?"

"Charlotte sir," she replied with both apprehension and excitement in her voice.

"Well, Charlotte, there's a bucket of dishes out back. Get to work," Hamilton ordered with a smile.

#

Charlotte spent the rest of the morning scrubbing dishes. The bucket was a large tin drum, and there must have been a hundred plates and glasses in it. The back of the saloon opened into a courtyard that connected several of the other saloons. There were all sorts of women out there. Some were doing dishes. Others just sat, drinking and staring at Charlotte.

No one spoke to her, which was just fine with Charlotte, who really didn't want to meet any of these people. She was just happy to be working. Granted, Mr. Hamilton and Jeth frightened her some, but she wasn't the same girl she had been when she stepped off the *New Amsterdam*. She had grown stronger, and she now had a job and was making some money. That's all that was important to her.

When she finished, she carried the dishes into the kitchen and stacked them neatly. She then took a rag and began cleaning. The place was filthy. After about an hour of work, Jeth came to the kitchen door.

"Charlotte, will you come out here?" He asked.

"Yes sir," she replied, proud of her work.

Charlotte cleaned herself off and walked into the main room of the saloon. Hamilton was sitting at the same table, but this time he was with a woman. Charlotte noticed for the first time that there was a staircase running down the wall opposite from the bar. For some reason she had not seen it when she came in. There were two more women walking down the stairs. All three looked as if they had just awakened for the day, even though it was well past noon.

Charlotte then realized what sort of place this was. She remembered the women she had seen in the park on her first night in New Orleans. These women were cleaner, but they had the same hard look about them. Charlotte caught herself staring at one of the women coming down the stairs. She could have been Charlotte's age or ten years older. It was impossible to tell which. Charlotte wondered what she must look like to these women.

As she came in Hamilton turned his attention to her.

"Come over here, Charlotte," he said.

Hesitantly she walked over to him.

"Charlotte," he explained. "This is Dianna. She's going to get you some clean clothes and show you your room."

"Hello, Charlotte." Dianna said, partially smiling.

Charlotte froze. She wanted to speak but couldn't think of any words. She just stood there staring at Dianna's cold eyes.

Finally, she looked at Hamilton and said, "Sir, I. I..."

"You don't think that all you will do here is wash dishes, do you?" He asked with a smile.

Charlotte felt a churning feeling in the pit of her stomach. If there was enough food in there, she would surely vomit. She started to speak, and suddenly without her even thinking, she turned and ran out the door. She could hear the women laughing as she hurried up the street.

About a block up Bourbon Street, she turned a corner and stopped. Tears were now flowing down for the first time since this nightmare began. Then, as suddenly as the tears began, they stopped.

Frozen against a wall it dawned on her that she had left her only possession behind. As useless as it was, Mr. Whitechapel's bag was her only connection to her past and her home in Maryland.

#

NACOGDOCHES, TEXAS
September 2002

Jeb sat on his couch holding the TV remote. Uncle Louie was on an armchair beside him holding a can of Coors beer. He held the can up at his nephew.

"Are you sure that you won't have one? A game just isn't a game without a beer," The older man remarked.

"Kay doesn't like for me to drink in front of the girls," Jeb replied.

"She lets me."

"You're not the Daddy," Jeb retorted.

Louie took a long sip of his beer, watching as his nephew stared at the television.

"What's bugging you?"

"Nothing," Jeb replied innocently.

"Bull. Something's got up your shorts. What is it?" Louie demanded.

Jeb was getting annoyed. It was bad enough that Kay could read his mind, now he had to deal with this old goat.

"Nothing's wrong!" Jeb blasted.

Louie just stared at him.

"Crap. You're an annoying old man. Do you know that?" Jeb said, breaking a bit of a smile.

"Yep. And I'm pretty good at it," the old man answered. "So what are you so bent out of shape about?"

Jeb hesitated a long minute, looking at the television.

"Is any of that stuff you're always telling true?" Jeb asked with sincerity in his voice.

"What stuff?"

"You know what I mean, all those tall tales," Jeb began, "and I want the truth. I remember Grandpa telling about Eli and Ephraim too, but Dad used to tell me that they were just old wives tales. And that one about Bonnie and Clyde, if it's just a yarn, tell me now."

"You really look like your Pop when you're angry," Louie said, trying to steer things a different direction.

"Leave my dad out of this."

"Your dad is the center of this. You're mad at him, and you're taking it out on me."

Jeb was getting angrier and angrier.

"Just answer the question!"

"Me and your Daddy shot Bonnie Parker dead. I can tell you that for a fact because I was there, holding a shotgun, and that's no tall tale." The old man answered. "Your grandfather heard the rest of the stories from my grandfather, and I believe every word. As I live and breathe, I have not made up one thing."

Jeb sat there taking it in and then took the beer from his uncle's hand and finished it off. He then got up from the couch and walked into the kitchen. A moment later he returned with two more cans of beer.

"I want to know everything you know," he said. "Ephraim, Lucian, Charlotte, all of it. And I especially want to know everything you can tell me about my father."

Chapter 7

NEW ORLEANS

August 24, 1814

It had been three full weeks since Charlotte began life on the streets. In that time she'd had only two full meals. For several days the courage and determination that had kept her driven was slowly giving way to despair.

After her experience at Cheri Royal, she returned to the riverfront only to find that her little home between the two cotton bales had been shipped downstream. She had spent the rest of that day wandering the streets in hopes of finding a place to sleep. Eventually, she ended up back at the *Place d'Armes*.

Her perspective of the things that had transpired each night in that little park had changed. Those women were no different than she. They were just people trying to survive. In a city full of wealth, they were starving and doing the only things the city would let them do. The thought that she had once looked down upon such women shamed her.

And the knowledge that she was little different than these women frightened her.

Each night she would find a place to curl up beneath a bench, and each night she would see a sailor beat some girl because she had done something that displeased him. But as Charlotte saw, there were much worse men in the park. These men would come around and take the money the ladies had made from the sailors. Sometimes they would beat the women if they hadn't earned enough. Sometimes they would beat the women for no reason at all. They just wanted the women to know who was boss. If that wasn't enough, often the women would fight and beat one another. Sometimes sailors would laugh and place bets. The loser usually had her money stolen. This resulted in her being beaten again by the man who came for her money.

So far, Charlotte had been successful at remaining hidden from all those who wandered in the *Place d'Armes*. Most nights she would stay awake for several hours. Late in the night the activity would lighten up, and she would be able to go to sleep. Her worst fear, of course, was that she would be discovered. If one of the women found her, she knew that they would beat her. She refused to think about what would happen if one of the men found her.

Charlotte always woke with the sun and got as far from the *Place d'Armes* as she could. Most days she searched the streets for something to eat. But this was Wednesday, and on Wednesday the little church handed out food. She wasn't going to miss out this time. She arrived at the church just as the sun was coming up. There were already several people in line, but she was early enough to get near the front. By late morning there were more than a hundred people waiting for handouts.

It was an exceptionally hot and humid day, and as the sun burned down from overhead, the hungry people in line started to become irritable. By mid-day many were becoming quite angry.

Finally at around half past noon, the door opened. But this time instead of some ladies coming out to set up tables, a man came through the door. He stood there silently, looking out at the crowd of hungry men and women.

Charlotte was near enough to the door to see his face. She watched intently as fear swelled up inside her. Something was wrong. She could feel it just as every other starving person in that line could feel it. This was not the way it was usually done.

The man had tears in his eyes as he looked out at the people in that line. He could see the desperation on their faces, and he knew that what he had to say was the worst news these people could possibly hear.

"I'm sorry," he began. "We have no food today."

Some of the crowd began to shout and curse as Charlotte watched the teary-eyed man. He trembled with sadness as he looked out at the hungry group. Looking around, she began to fear the angry crowd, but she was more afraid of what that news meant.

"We rely on donations," the man explained with such sadness that he was oblivious to the anger coming from the crowd.

This truly hurt the man. He understood that the anger was nothing but disappointment of people who desperately needed nourishment.

"We simply haven't any food. I'm terribly sorry. Please come back next week," the man said and then retreated into the church and closed the door.

Some of the women in the line ran to the door and began to pound on it. There were several children, and Charlotte could see that some of the smaller children were little more than skin and bones. She wondered if there had been children like that in Baltimore or Randallstown and she had been too consumed with her life to notice. The truth was that she had been standing in line next to these little ones all morning and had been so anxious to get something to eat that she had not realized that these babies were living a plight far worse than hers.

One woman with two small children ran to the door of the church, holding her little ones by the hand. Screaming and crying, she begged for someone to open the door and take her kids. Tears ran down Charlotte's face as she watched the woman who was willing to give up her children if only someone would give them something to eat.

Trembling, Charlotte turned and walked away. After only a few steps she began to stumble, realizing that the strength that gotten her there was the anticipation of food. Now that hope was gone, each step felt as if she was carrying two or three times her weight.

About a block up from the church, she sat down on a stoop to rest. The little hope that had existed in her life had left her. She sat watching the hungry people slowly move up the street to begin a futile search for food. At the church the lady with the children sat crying, her wails echoing between the buildings. Standing across the street, Charlotte saw one of the prostitutes from the *Place d'Armes.* The woman's face was bruised and her dress was tattered. In the daylight Charlotte could see that she too was barely surviving.

Charlotte could feel her heart beginning to pound, her head to ache from lack of food, and her knees to shake uncontrollably. As she sat there, she thought about what her life had become and how it had been almost a month since she'd had a bath or felt a brush in her hair. It occurred to her that the very best that she had to hope for was a weekly meal from a church that sometimes had no meal to give.

"Hello, Charlotte," a voice said.

Startled, Charlotte looked up at the man standing next to her.

"No food this week?" The man asked.

Charlotte looked at him and shook her head.

"You know, it's just a matter of time before you starve," he said and then added, "come on, I'll buy you something to eat."

Charlotte watched as he reached out to her. For a moment she just looked at the hand. Then finally she took hold of it and stood. Out of sheer will, she kept herself from trembling as she and Hamilton walked away.

#

A week after having lunch with Mr. Hamilton, Charlotte took a long stroll down Canal Street. She'd eaten, bathed, and wore a fresh new dress. Yet she felt every bit as miserable as she had when she was starved.

When Mr. Hamilton bought her lunch, it almost made her ill. It had been so long since she had a decent meal that the food made her weak. But what really made her sick was the knowledge of what price she would pay for each bite. Of course, at that point it made little difference. She had lost the battle. She now belonged to Mr. Hamilton and the Cheri Royal. New clothes, a bath, and a few good meals may have made her look better on the outside, but in the pit of her stomach, Charlotte knew that her life had been taken and she would never get it back.

She reasoned, if this was to be her life, then she could have done much worse than the Cheri Royal. In fact, it was a clean place, and her room was nice, with a big, soft bed, plus the prices there were relatively high which meant that the customers tended to be somewhat wealthy and clean. Most importantly, Mr. Hamilton didn't tolerate customers beating the ladies. He said that bruises were bad for business.

On her first night at Cheri Royal, Charlotte was sitting at a table with Dianna and two businessmen when they heard screaming from upstairs. Immediately, Jeth, the man who ran the bar, went running up the stairs with a club in his hand. Within moments a half-dressed man came falling down the staircase with blood streaming from his face.

"Jeth likes to make a big show," Dianna later explained, "so everyone knows what happens when someone hurts one of our ladies."

Dianna was the boss of the ladies and spent most of that first evening showing Charlotte how things were done. It surprised Charlotte how many rules there were. Things like keeping your room clean, how to treat the customers, how to wear your hair, and how to walk. Most importantly she told Charlotte what happened if you broke the rules.

"It's simple," she said. "Jeth will take you for a ride into the bayous and leave you for the snakes and alligators."

Hamilton encouraged the ladies to get out during the day. He said that it was healthy for them to get sunlight, and more importantly, it was good for business for them to be seen. Since there was little else to do, Charlotte began taking an afternoon stroll.

The city looked different to her now. Before, it had been this frightening place where there were so many different languages and rough looking people. But now she was no longer the same. She was hardened. As she strolled through the city, she looked and dressed like any of the finer women of New Orleans, but she wasn't one of them. She had lived on the docks under a tent cloth and in the *Place d'Armes* under a bench. Charlotte knew a side of the city that the other ladies walking Canal Street never saw.

That afternoon she walked to the *Place d'Armes* and sat on the bench under which she had spent so many nights. The park was different in the daylight. There was a different crowd of people. Birds would land and eat crumbs tossed there by children. Ladies in beautiful dresses walked arm and arm with men in silk coats.

Then she watched closely as one of the couples walked passed. The girl was about Charlotte's age and wore a wide-brimmed hat with a scarf wrapped over it that tied tightly under her chin. The young man walked proudly with her holding to his arm. The two were in love.

A cold feeling swept over her as she realized that she was no longer Charlotte from Randallstown. She would never stroll through a park arm and arm with a beau. She was now one of "Lovely Ladies of Cheri Royal".

Saddened, but determined to make the best of her new life, she stood and walked up toward the church at the end of the park. Dianna had told her that there was a market there run by the Monsieur Lafitte's pirates. She said that everyone in New Orleans shopped there and that they always had the best of everything. Charlotte really didn't' want anything. She had plans for what little money she got from the Cheri Royal, but it had been such a long time since she had walked through a market that she decided to head that direction.

It was a beautiful day, and there were many people about. The market was actually a long alleyway that was almost packed full of people. She wandered through the crowded passage like everyone else, looking at the tables where the pirates sold everything from jewelry to clothes to furniture. She paused for a moment and looked at a stack of ladies' hats. She'd once owned a wide straw hat that tied tightly under her chin. She stood there looking at the hats, thinking about a past she would never see again when someone suddenly bumped hard into her from behind, almost knocking her onto the table and causing her to push all the hats onto the ground.

"I'm terribly sorry. Let me get those things," she heard from behind her while she pushed herself up from the table.

When she managed to get herself upright she looked down to see someone gathering up the hats.

#

Ephraim stood up, feeling like an idiot. As many times as he had negotiated that Alley, he should have known better than to ever take a step backwards. But for some reason, which now escaped him, he had backed up and almost knocked some poor lady over one of the tables right in the middle of the Alley. If this had been Father's store, he would be spending the rest of the day on his knees scrubbing the floor. As he stood with his hands full of ladies' hats, he realized that he was looking eye to eye with the young blonde girl who had been on his mind for quite some time.

"You," he blurted out.

Charlotte couldn't help looking into his eyes. There was something soft and warm about them. He looked so innocent and genuinely happy to see her, and although he was a complete and total stranger, she felt that she was face to face with her dearest friend. After weeks of loneliness and despair, she was looking into friendly eyes. For a moment in time she felt like Charlotte from Randallstown, looking at boy with whom she belonged. She found herself fighting the urge to leap into his arms and hug him.

Then suddenly she felt that cold feeling that had been lurking in the back of her stomach and realized that she was anything but the innocent girl from Maryland he had met some weeks before. He was a handsome young man with a warm smile and dark eyes, and she was one of the "Lovely Ladies of the Cheri Royal."

"Excuse me, I must go," she said as she turned to hurry away.

The crowd, of course, made movement almost impossible, and he touched her arm to stop her.

"Please wait," she heard him beg.

She looked at him, trying not to stare at his eyes.

"I must go," Charlotte responded.

"Please, I'm so sorry that I knocked you down." he said.

"I'm all right. I must go," Charlotte replied and headed out of the Alley.

She was almost frantic as she rushed out to Royal Street. Trying to get her bearings, she looked to her right and then the left. Finally deciding to go to the right, she turned and ran directly into the young man, having not realized that he'd followed her up the alley.

"Please don't run away," Ephraim begged. "I've been looking for you all over town."

Every instinct within her told her to run, but as she looked at his eyes she saw a longing in them. Somewhere deep inside she felt the same longing. She had sensed that same longing that day those men stole her things. It was, she realized, her own feelings and not him that she had run from that horrible day.

This young man is no thief.

"I felt terrible for not getting your things back. I hope that it wasn't a hardship?" Ephraim asked.

"Oh, those things were not important," she lied.

Ephraim stared at her, trying to say something, but his mind had suddenly become empty.

He was obviously searching for words. Somehow he looked like a little boy. She saw that he was trembling, and it made her smile.

"I'm new to New Orleans and I really haven't any friends here. Would you walk with me?" he asked. "I'll take you anywhere you'd like to go."

Charlotte could see that he was beginning to blush, and it made her smile even more. He's just a little boy, she said to herself. She knew that it would crush him if she said "no".

"I suppose you can come with me," she said hesitantly. "I need to go up the street. My name is Charlotte Fuller."

"I'm Ephraim Bradford," he replied.

The two headed up Royal Street. At first neither spoke. They were both searching for something to say, but for some reason there was nothing uncomfortable about it. Finally, Charlotte broke the silence.

"You're new to New Orleans?"

"I've been here a couple of months."

"You're British?"

"We're from a little village in Worcestershire, just south of Shropshire. Tenbury Wells. It's in the middle of the country."

"We?" She asked

"I came here with my family," he paused for a moment, then added, "but they don't live in the city. What about you?"

Charlotte's mind was suddenly racing to find a way to explain. Finally, she settled on the truth but tried to be somewhat vague.

"I had just gotten off the boat from Baltimore when those men stole my things."

"That must have been terrible."

"Oh, I'm okay," she said assuredly.

She was suddenly ashamed. There was something about his innocence and honesty that made it painful for her to lie to him. Still, she knew that she couldn't tell him the truth, and that pained her even more.

Charlotte what are you doing here? Why don't you go home now?

Suddenly, they encountered a little old lady walking on the sidewalk with a cane in her hand. Ephraim was so transfixed on Charlotte that he hadn't notice the woman. Trying to step around the woman he stumbled and almost fell on top of her. Charlotte laughed out loud at his awkward attempt to keep from falling on his face and realized that he had been as nervous as a kitten the entire time.

"I'm so sorry, ma'am," he said to the woman.

"You should watch yourself, young man," the old woman scolded. "You could hurt someone."

Charlotte began to giggle and started walking away to keep the woman from seeing her laugh. Seeing the look in her eyes caused Ephraim to giggle as well.

"I will. I promise. Again, I'm so sorry," he said, trying not to laugh as he attempted to get away from the woman and catch Charlotte.

"It's not funny, young man," the woman yelled as Ephraim fled.

"That was cruel," he said to Charlotte as he caught up.

"I couldn't just stand there and watch. I thought she was going to beat you with that cane," she replied.

They were both laughing and realized that, for reasons that neither quite understood, they were almost instantly very comfortable together.

The two walked a little further. Neither really felt the need to talk. They were both just glad to have found someone friendly in this lonely city.

"You said that you're from Baltimore?"

"Well, actually, a little town near there called Randallstown. After my father died, my mother married a man in Baltimore, but I didn't live there long."

"My father died," Ephraim said, becoming much more serious. "Last fall, he came down with a fever."

She stopped and looked sensitively into his eyes.

"My father came down with a fever last October," she said softly.

Ephraim's heart was pounding as he stood there looking down into her eyes. There was a hint of moisture in them, and he knew that she was feeling the same combination of emotions that were surging through him. He had this urge to wrap his arms around her and hold her, somehow sensing that she wanted him to.

Charlotte, catching herself with an unanticipated desire to reach out to him, suddenly turned and started up the street. Ephraim followed without saying a word. The silence had now become very awkward, and he again started searching his mind for something to say.

"Do you have family in Baltimore?" he blurted.

She stopped walking for a moment as she returned to her reality. A few weeks earlier she would have said, "yes," and she would have told him about her mother and her home in Randallstown, but now she had no words. Back in Baltimore was Mr. Rhodes who had abused her and hurt her badly. Because of him her mother and Mrs. Rhodes had sent her off with a stranger who turned out to be a swindler. A man who got himself killed and got her robbed, leaving her alone to starve. Because of them she had become one of the "Lovely Ladies of Cheri Royal."

Now she was walking with a nice young man who might have wanted to marry her if she hadn't become what they'd made her into.

As she began to walk again, a sad, sick feeling covered her like a blanket. She no longer loved or hated her mother or her home. She didn't feel anything for them, but she did care for this young man named Ephraim Bradford, and she so badly didn't want to hurt him.

"Did I say something wrong?" he asked.

Charlotte looked at him with some confusion and then said with almost no emotion, "I don't have a family."

Ephraim sensed that there was much that she wasn't telling him. When he mentioned family, something touched her deep inside, but he knew better than to ask. There was pain in her eyes - the kind of pain that you feel in your heart.

The two turned up Esplanade Avenue and stopped in front of the little church Charlotte had come to for food.

"Wait right here. I'll only be a minute," she said.

Charlotte went up the steps and knocked on the door. After a moment a man opened it. He was the same man who had tearfully told the crowd of hungry people that there was no food a week before.

"Sir, is this the church that gives out food each week?" she asked, innocently.

The man looked closely at her. He sensed something about her. Though she wore a fine dress, she was not as she appeared.

"Yes ma'am. Each Wednesday," he replied cautiously.

Charlotte reached into her purse and brought out some coins and handed them to the man.

"Would you please use these to help buy food?" She asked.

The man looked at the coins and then looked closely at her. When their eyes met, he knew exactly where the money came from and why she was there. There were many girls like her in this city, though none had ever returned. He smiled and took the coins.

"Of course," the man said. Then he added, "God has not forgotten you."

Charlotte looked at him, suddenly reminded of who she was. She quickly turned and headed down the steps.

"Thank, you. I'll be back next week," she said returning to Ephraim.

The man watched as she and Ephraim turned and walk away.

Ephraim didn't know what to think. How many girls go to churches to give money to feed people? Surely she's very wealthy, he thought. He suddenly got a sinking feeling. A wealthy young woman like her would have nothing to do with someone like him, and if she ever found out that he worked for Mr. Lafitte, she would not even talk to him.

They approached a corner, and Charlotte stopped.

"I have to be going now. Thank you. I enjoyed our walk, Mr. Bradford," she said.

"I'll be glad to walk you home."

"That's okay. I'm just going up the next block," she said with a smile that made him feel helpless.

"Can we walk again sometime?" he asked, unable to think of anything else to say.

Charlotte was prepared to say a firm "no," having anticipated that he would ask, but when she saw the lonely look on his face she couldn't.

"Perhaps," she replied.

"Tomorrow?"

"No, not tomorrow," she responded. Proud that she had managed to put him off.

"This weekend then. Saturday. Coffee?" He insisted with smile that made her smile broadly in return.

Charlotte, don't do it.

She shook her head.

"Monday," he said pleading. "I'll be at the Pearl Café on Canal Street."

Smiling, Charlotte turned and crossed Royal.

"Maybe," she said as she hurried away.

"I'll be there at eleven," he said, confirming.

Charlotte looked back one more time as she rushed away and saw the smile on his face. She couldn't help thinking how much he looked like a little boy.

"Tuesday?" he begged, knowing he'd won.

"Okay Tuesday, at eleven," she heard herself say.

As she hurried away, Charlotte felt something that she hadn't felt in a while. Then she realized that she too was smiling, and it dawned on her that for the first time in as long as she could remember, she was happy.

#

About an hour later Ephraim strolled up Tchoupitoulas Street and into the warehouse. Fortunately, there hadn't been much going on that he needed to keep an eye on. When he opened the door to his little office, he saw Lucian sitting in his chair with his large feet on the table that Ephraim used as a makeshift desk. Opposite him, Llewellyn was in the only other chair taking a sip from a bottle of Jamaican Rum.

"Welcome back to work, little brother," Lucian said as Llewellyn handed him the bottle.

"Luc, Llewellyn", Ephraim said truly happy to see his brothers, although he knew that there were other reasons he was in such high spirits.

"Well, he does remember us. That's a good sign," Llewellyn said sarcastically.

Ephraim looked at his brother, a little confused.

"Our older sibling is suggesting that since you've become so important, you might not remember your less significant family members," Lucian explained.

Ephraim still wasn't following them.

"What are you talking about?"

Lucian took a swig from the bottle and handed it to Llewellyn. Ephraim could tell that they were both a little bit drunk.

"He still isn't catching on, big brother," Lucian said to Llewellyn.

"We just thought that a man important enough to tell the Governor of Louisiana to 'buy something or move on' might be too important for peasants such as the two of us," Llewellyn explained.

Ephraim froze, realizing that they had heard about the encounter with the Governor.

"I do believe that our little brother is blushing," Lucian said.,

"That's not blush, little brother. That's pure terror," Llewellyn corrected.

"Oh, my god. I can't believe you two heard about that. The Bos must be furious," Ephraim said.

"The entire state heard about it. You're a hero. Everybody hates that man," Lucian told him.

"That's why we're here. The Bos wants us to take you back. He's going to chop you up and feed you to the alligators," Llewellyn told him.

Ephraim just looked at Llewellyn in fear but knowing that something was up.

"Relax, Eph," Lucian said. "The Bos almost laughed his mustache off, but he did send us to bring you back to the island. He thinks that the governor is going to shut down the Alley."

#

NACOGDOCHES, TEXAS
September 2002

It had been a miserable day for Jeb Bradford. He'd had three classes back-to-back starting at eight in the morning, which was almost unheard of in the History department. Teaching three classes was strain enough on his brain, but two of the three were freshmen classes. Freshmen classes, Jeb had long since learned, had a tendency to take twice the effort.

Afterwards, he ran over to the plant, where he had two minor catastrophes that were just large enough to require taking one of the generators off-line. This of course resulted in an extra load on the other two. In ninety-five degree Texas heat, it put quite a strain on the system that ran at near-capacity this time of year. Thus everyone at the plant had been in panic mode most of the afternoon.

So as Jeb turned down Sam Houston Avenue toward his home, all he really wanted to do was eat and fall asleep, but that was not going to happen. His self-appointed editor-n-chief was going to insist that he spend at least two hours in his office writing a book that thus far had only two words: "Chapter One."

Actually, Jeb felt pretty good about the book. He had been spending a lot of time poring over biographies and historical documents from the school library. Stephen F. Austin State University may not have the reputation of Harvard or Princeton, but they had one great library. The truth of the matter was that he had begun to like the peace and quiet and would probably enjoy the research if it wasn't for Kay checking on his progress. But then again, if it was not for her nagging, he would be downstairs watching television rather than upstairs enjoying the quiet.

As Jeb pulled the pickup into the driveway, he saw Kay on the porch with the baby and the girls playing in the front yard. Kay allowed them to play after dinner while there was still daylight. She said that they need the exercise, but Jeb knew that her real reason was to get them worn out right before bedtime. He would never point that out, of course, because she would just tell him that she wanted to make sure that there would be peace and quiet when he came home from work. The woman had an answer for everything.

As he parked and stepped out of the pick-up, Rebecca, who was on the tree swing, yelled, "Watch, Daddy!"

Jeb was partly watching as he began pulling books and stacks of quizzes out of the truck. The tree swing had been Kay's idea, like everything else. She claimed to have had one when she was a little girl and argued that the kids needed one, but Jeb suspected that the real reason was that an old house like this just didn't look right to Kay without a swing hanging from a tree in the front yard.

That swing was a problem in itself. The tree was certainly big enough and strong enough to support a swing. It was a Bois de Arc, and an enormous one at that, and could probably have supported fifty swings. The problem was that the limb that Kay wanted it on was considerably higher than Jeb's ladder. That, of course, required him to climb the tree. Bois de Arcs, Jeb had learned that day, have thorns - long sharp thorns.

Nevertheless, for the girls enjoyment, or more likely for Kay's sense of aesthetics, Jeb risked his life tying ropes to that limb.

"Not too high, sweetheart," Kay yelled as she met her husband at the porch steps.

"Watch me!" Rebecca yelled again.

"I am," Jeb responded like he had a hundred times before as he awkwardly hugged his wife while balancing a dozen books.

Then suddenly he and Kay sensed something. In a way only parents can, they both felt danger. He quickly turned to look at Rebecca as she was swinging forward. In an instant her tiny hands broke free from the ropes. Her little body flipped backward and fell headfirst to the ground.

Later Jeb couldn't recall how he got to his little baby's side. All he could remember was that one moment he was at the porch, and the next moment he was kneeling next to her.

Somehow he fought the urge to pick her up and carry her into the house though he so badly wanted to take her into his arms. The child had fallen at least five feet and landed on her head. There must have been something in the back of his brain that knew what to do in that kind of situation because, as it turned out, he was right to let her lie there.

Kay, who was normally in complete control, was on the edge of panic. Under the circumstances, it was all Jeb could do to keep control of the situation.

#

Thirty minutes later Jeb was sitting in an emergency waiting room next to a sleepy Hannah and holding Missy, who was out for the night. He had made a feeble attempt to be the one to go into the examining room with Rebecca, but Kay had already lost a few battles that night and was not about to lose this one. She was, of course, right. Rebecca needed her mommy there.

Though that seemed reasonable, it didn't help Jeb through the horror. In one instant everything that had seemed important to him had changed. When he had pulled into the driveway, all that he wanted to do was eat dinner and go to sleep. Now all he wanted in the world was to go into that room and hold his little girl and know that all was well.

Right after the fall, one of the neighbors had called for the paramedics. Jeb had to hold Kay back while they tied Rebecca to a board. The memory brought tears to his eyes. This was the part of being a daddy that no one had told him about. How was he supposed to be strong when his little girl might be about to die?

Suddenly he felt a cold chill run through his body. Until that moment he hadn't actually let himself think about death. Up to now he was just being cautious. He was doing what he had to do as a father, but now Rebecca was in serious trouble. The full weight of the situation was beginning to set in. Rebecca might not wake up.

Each second passed like an hour, and all he could think about was how he should have spent more time at home with the kids. He cursed himself for working so much, for hanging that swing, and for not watching her when she called to him. His heart was pounding so hard that it almost hurt, and he wondered how the baby could sleep against his chest. Finally, after an eternity, a nurse came into the room.

"Mr. Bradford, you can come in now," she said.

Jeb wanted to leap to his feet, but he slowly stood and took Hannah's hand and led her through the doors into the examination area. Inside, Kay was standing next to his daughter's bed. Rebecca was flat on her back. Her head was in a contraption of metal rods that somehow prevented her from moving. Her eyes were closed, and she had tubes in her arm. Next to Kay was some sort of machine that monitored Rebecca's heartbeat.

The sight of his daughter like that brought a world of emotions that he hadn't expected. Then he looked at Kay, and their eyes met. Neither said a word. They both felt the same things. He could tell that she was barely holding up, and he desperately wanted to hold her. Deep within he felt a need for strength that he didn't have. The helplessness of the moment tore at his heart. Kay needed him, Hannah and Missy needed him, and most of all, Rebecca needed him, but there was absolutely nothing he could do.

Hannah went directly to her mother, who picked her up into her arms. Oddly, Jeb realized that holding Hannah was exactly what his wife needed. A moment later a doctor came into the little sectioned-off room.

Later, Jeb recalled, the doctor spoke for quite some time. He said a lot of things that neither Jeb nor Kay understood or remembered. There were only two things that had any meaning to him or Kay. Their baby girl had a mild concussion and an upper cervical fracture.

"In layman terms," the doctor said, "she has a broken neck."

Chapter 8

GRAND TERRA ISLAND
September 2, 1814

Ephraim's only clean shirt was already damp with sweat. It seemed impossible, he thought, to keep clean in this place. Back in Tenbury Wells he could wear the same clothes for days without noticing the smell. Of course, the condition of his clothes hadn't bothered him until the day he had taken a walk with Charlotte. Suddenly, he had become quite self-conscious.

It had been a slow trek to Grande Terra. They spent a full day at the Temple sorting new merchandise and arrived at the island just in time to have dinner at the main house with the Bos.

When they climbed the steps to the house, Lafitte was already seated at the table on the veranda sipping wine along with Louis, Reggie, Cort, and Captain Youx. Ephraim didn't know a lot about wine, but he recognized the bottle and knew from his work in the city how much it was worth. The Bos always had the best of everything.

"Welcome," Lafitte said cheerfully to the three as they came to the table. "Please sit."

A black man in a white waiter's coat poured wine for all of them.

"We're having a 'going away' party. Your friends are leaving tomorrow," Lafitte said as he motioned to Louis and Cort.

"You're going?" Ephraim asked Cort.

"Texas!" his friend said with excitement.

"They have been hearing stories of vast prairies of cheap land," the Bos said, somewhat directed at Louis. "Personally I prefer civilization to the wilderness."

"I've seen all of civilization that I need. I look forward to living on a quiet prairie," the Frenchman responded.

"But there are no Comanche raids in civilization," the pirate remarked with a smile.

Lafitte held his glass up in a toast, and all of the others followed.

"To the prairie. May yours be peaceful," he said cheerfully.

Everyone touched glasses and took a sip of the wine. Ephraim and Cort glanced at one another. Both were wondering how they had come to be seated at a fine table drinking French wine and eating from dishes made in China.

"Ephraim, I understand that you had some trouble with Governor Claiborne?" Lafitte asked.

Ephraim looked uncomfortably at Reggie, who was seated next to Lafitte. His friend just smiled and nodded at him. That slight grin was considerably reassuring in that the Major was not known for his smile.

"Ah, yes, sir. He came to the Alley," Ephraim sheepishly replied.

"The way I heard it," Lafitte corrected, "you told His Imminence that you don't tolerate loiterers."

Everyone at the table laughed out loud as Ephraim sat embarrassed but a little proud as well.

"I've been getting reports that Claiborne intends to shut us down soon," Lafitte began. "He wants to raid the warehouse. Llewellyn and I have decided to stop shipments to the city. I want you to slowly sell your inventory and move out of the Alley. We'll see if that makes him happy for a while. In the meantime I want the Bazaar operating every weekend. With the Alley shut down there will be a lot of business out there."

Ephraim nodded at the Bos, but the news was the worst he could have heard. There had been a time when he would have loved closing down the warehouse and leaving New Orleans, but now all he could think about was how he would manage to keep seeing Charlotte if he moved to the island.

"I'd like you to stay on in the city, though," Lafitte continued. "Find a way to keep supplying the restaurants. That is an excellent arrangement you've worked out with them."

Ephraim smiled but tried to conceal it.

"But be prepared for trouble. Claiborne could have you arrested at any time. I'm told that it was almost done that day in the Alley," Lafitte explained.

Ephraim showed little emotion. After that day he had often wondered why he hadn't been arrested.

"Don't worry little brother. They will have a trial before they hang you," Lucian remarked lightly.

"Relax. We have plenty of judges and lawyers our payroll," Reggie commented.

The waiter placed slices of roasted beef on each of their plates.

"We're also going to move off this island," Lafitte went on. "Sooner or later we're going to draw the attention of the American Navy. There is an island off the coast of Texas called Galveztown. I have a home there. I've established a relationship with a group of filibusters who intend to establish Texas as a republic. When that happens, we'll be able to operate business with the Americans as legitimate importers."

"Now gentlemen, unless someone has further business, let us enjoy our dinner," said Lafitte.

With that everyone but Lucian began to eat. He was seated to the Bos' right and could see the dock over Ephraim's shoulder. A small boat approached, and a dozen women stepped off. It was not an uncommon sight. The Bos had ladies brought out regularly to work in the Saloon.

Lucian watched closely as a small, blonde-haired woman stepped off the boat and onto the dock. She was different than the other ladies that had come out. He couldn't exactly tell why, but there was something about the girl that made her look as if she didn't belong with these other women.

Lafitte noticed Lucian wasn't eating and asked, "Is the beef not to your liking?"

"Oh, of course. It's very good, sir," Lucian responded as his attention returned to his meal.

#

Charlotte was terrified as she stepped off of the boat and onto the dock at Grande Terre. She had been told that going to the island was quite safe. Dianna had explained that the pirates were under orders from the "Bos" to be well-behaved, and they always had a lot of money to spend, but her reassurances didn't help. It was the word "pirate" that terrified her. She had visions of eye-patches and wooden legs.

The place, though, wasn't anything like she expected. The first thing she saw as they approached the island was the big house. It was far grander than anything in Randallstown or even in Baltimore, for that matter. She had heard stories about the great Jean Lafitte but had no idea what to expect. She certainly didn't expect him to be living in a place like that.

She could see people seated at a table on the veranda, and one of the girls told her that the man with the long black mustache was Mr. Lafitte. Oddly, he was nowhere near as menacing as she would have thought. He was actually quite nice- looking, even handsome and dashing, in a way. She had heard how many of the more prestigious ladies of New Orleans welcomed his company, and though she previously had dismissed such things as nonsense, she could now see that those stories were probably quite true.

When they reached the saloon, Charlotte saw that it was already crowded with men even though it was not yet dark out. The sailors, or pirates as she kept thinking of them, were eager for company. But it surprised her that they were not a rough and filthy lot. In fact, they were better dressed than most sailors she had seen in New Orleans or on the *New Amsterdam*. She had been told to expect them to have a lot of money, and from the look of them, that seemed to be the case.

Charlotte and the other girls walked in and were seated. Some of the ladies were approached right away and taken upstairs, but Charlotte sat alone for quite some time. This was not unusual for her. The same thing happened at Cheri Royal. It was often well into the night before someone requested her company. Dianna had told her that the men tended to prefer women who were more plump and healthy-looking. She told Charlotte not to worry. After a few weeks of New Orleans cuisine, she would fatten up and be as popular as any of the girls. Charlotte didn't mention that being "as popular as any of the girls" was not one of her goals.

#

After dinner Cort and Ephraim excused themselves and went back to the hotel. Ephraim didn't like knowing that Cort and Louis were leaving, but they had come to America to make homes in the frontier, and it was time for them to go.

Actually, if it was not for Charlotte, Ephraim might have wanted to go as well. It sounded like it would be a hard life, but it would truly be an adventure.

The two talked most of the night. Cort told Ephraim that he had taken to being a soldier. He would have liked to become one, but he had been told that the Americans did not take black men into their ranks. Ephraim assured him that being a soldier was not all that great, and they both recalled that terrible day on the *Tigre*.

Ephraim changed the subject by telling Cort all about Charlotte. It was odd, the friendship they shared. Ephraim would have never mentioned Charlotte to his brothers. They would have teased him and assured him that there was no hope of ever marrying a rich girl like her. If they ever saw her, they would know for sure that he had no hope. She was beautiful and refined and obviously came from a good family. They would laugh at him for being so stupid. A girl like her would not marry a shopkeeper.

Cort, though, was not like his brothers. Cort listened intently, wanting to know every detail about the girl. For Ephraim it was relieving to talk about her. He had wanted to tell someone about her since the day he saw her being robbed.

It was well into the early morning when the two of them finally fell asleep. As his eyes slowly gave way to the night's slumber, Ephraim's thoughts lingered on Charlotte's smile and the anticipation of seeing her again.

#

As Ephraim and Cort were walking to the hotel, Lucian took a stroll across the street to the saloon. He didn't go in there often. Most of the patrons were sailors fresh from several weeks at sea and not the sort of company that he preferred, but he had seen something that had roused his curiosity.

There wasn't much to do in the evenings on the island except go to the saloon, which is why everyone went there. That is, everyone except Lucian, Llewellyn, Louis, and Cort. Most nights the four of them would sit on the veranda of the Hotel and discuss their plans now that they were in America.

Llewellyn had already decided that the Bradford brothers would go to Philadelphia or Baltimore and open a shop like their father's. He reasoned that among the three of them they could make enough money working for Lafitte to invest in a sizable business. He concluded that there was much money to be made in the big cities.

Lucian, however, felt differently. First, there was the war. No one knew how it was going to go. The news had not been good for the Americans, and if the British invaded New Orleans, things could get far worse.

Secondly, and more importantly, Lucian had no desire to go to the either of those big cities. Liverpool was a big city, and he hated it because the place was crowded and smelly. Unlike his two brothers, he loved Tenbury Wells and probably would never have left had it not been for the other two.

Like Louis and Cort, he had heard the stories about the land in Texas. He had also talked to Jim Bowie about Mexico and how the Spanish government welcomed Europeans. Bowie planned to go there himself as soon as he had some money. He believed that the Americans would keep moving west, and Texas would be one of the first places they would begin settling. He suggested, and Lucian thought quite reasonably, that a smart merchant could do well in Texas.

The more he thought about Texas, the more he liked the idea, though he had not yet mentioned it to Llewellyn, and he certainly wouldn't mention that he had discussed his thoughts with the Bowie brothers. Llewellyn didn't trust the Bowies, and for good reason. They were a rough bunch. They were also slave smugglers, which in Llewellyn's opinion, and Lucian's for that matter, put them on the same level as common thieves. There was also a story going around that they had cut a man's hand for not paying a debt.

Still, the Bowies had been to Texas, and their stories were inviting. Lucian had decided to discuss it with Ephraim first. Eph was much more reasonable than Llewellyn. Llewellyn tended to make a decision for the three of them without actually listening to what the other two thought. It was Llewellyn who had decided that they should leave the army. That was something else that Lucian would not have done. He liked the army and felt that he could have been a good soldier. It was only when he shot that man while on the *Tigre* that he began to have second thoughts about his ability to fight.

When he walked into the saloon, the place was already crowded. This was often the case when ships were in. There was little else for the sailors to do. Tomorrow many would go into New Orleans to spend their money but this night they would have a few drinks, some would have a woman, and all would sleep on a bed that didn't sway with the sea.

He saw the blonde girl the moment he stepped through the door. She was sitting at a crowded table but appeared to be alone. Up close she was much prettier than he had previously thought. Her hair was curly and tied on top of her head, and her dress fit tightly across her tiny waist. He tried desperately not to stare but couldn't help himself.

He walked in and headed toward the bar but couldn't keep from sneaking peeks back at the girl. He felt somewhat foolish but just couldn't help himself. Then he spotted Bowie at the bar and walked over to him.

"Hello, Jim," Lucian said as he motioned to the bartender for a beer.

"Lucian," Bowie acknowledged. "How's business out at the Temple?"

"Good for now, but the Governor is out to shut the Bos down," Lucian answered.

"It was bound to happen," said Bowie. "The brothers and me are headed to Galveztown in the morning. We're going to start bringing slaves in from Lavaca. You're welcome to come with us. We could always use a good hand."

The bartender handed Lucian a beer. He took a drink and glanced over his shoulder at the girl and then looked back at Bowie.

"No thanks."

"Slaves are just part of life here, Englishman. Get used to it," Bowie remarked.

"I doubt that I could ever get used to that," Lucian said as he glanced a second time at the girl. This time, Bowie noticed Lucian's wayward eyes and looked at her also.

"You like the little ones, do you?" Bowie asked.

Lucian tried to ignore the comment but suddenly felt a sense of anger. Until that moment he hadn't thought of her as anything other than just another girl. He definitely didn't look at her the way Bowie just had. He quickly cooled his rage. He'd heard the stories and knew that it was not smart to get in a fight with Jim Bowie.

It was odd, he thought, that the work that had brought her to Grande Terre had not even entered his mind. He looked at her the same way he did Rosanna Blackburn back in Tenbury Wells. He hadn't thought of Rosanna in a very long time. He and Ephraim were both in love with her. They would get in trouble for looking at her during Communion. Of course, neither of the boys ever spoke to her. Her father saw to that. The Bradford brothers were not up to his standard. Lucian always regretted not ever speaking to Rosanna.

"I do like the small ones, Jim. Have a good trip," Lucian said as he walked away from Bowie and over to the girl.

#

Charlotte had been sitting there alone for about an hour when the large man walked through the door. Until that moment all she had done since entering the saloon was stare at her wine glass. She detested the taste of wine, but Dianna told her that wine was the drink of a lady. The "Lovely Ladies of Cheri Royal" were always to look like ladies.

The large man stopped at the door and looked at her for a long moment before going over to the bar. Even then he kept glancing at her. She had learned in the past two weeks that some men did it that way. Most were just shy and needed a drink or two to get up the courage to come over to her. She really didn't understand that. Surely they knew that the only reason she was there was for men like them, but some men were just that way.

She watched him closely. She was learning how to judge a man. Some men were frightening, and she tried to avoid that kind. Some were loud and self-confident. She didn't like those either. But some, like the large man, were just lonely. As long as she had to do this sort of thing, these were the men she preferred. Men like this one were usually kind and not too rough.

Then, in an instant, her opinion of him changed. She hadn't noticed the other large man at the bar, the one with the knife. She knew his face. That was a face she would never forget. More importantly, she knew the knife he carried on his belt. A cold chill ran from her head to her toes as she remembered that terrifying night and the other man's hand dangling from his arm. She had hoped that she would never see that man again.

What frightened her most was that the man who kept looking at her walked right to the man with the knife, and the two immediately began to talk. They seemed to be well acquainted, and Charlotte didn't like that at all. If this man and the man with the knife were friends, then this was not a man that she wanted to be alone with. It then occurred to her that this was not the Cheri Royal. Jeth wasn't behind the bar with his club. This was a pirate island. It may not be what she expected a pirate island to look like, but it was still a pirate island and as such there was little, if any, law. If a man like the one with the knife felt free to do what he did in a city like New Orleans, then what would he do in a place like this?

She reasoned that if someone decided to kill her here, that would be it. No one would ask any questions. She had no family to miss her. Mr. Hamilton would, of course, expect to be paid for his loss, but aside from that they could toss her body in the bay. She would be forgotten within hours.

Suddenly her fright gave way to the empty loneliness that she had hidden in a corner of her heart. She fought off a tear and took a sip from her glass of wine as she thought how she was simply a vessel sitting in a saloon waiting to be used and tossed aside. If she disappeared tonight, no one would remember her, and no one would care.

Ephraim's face entered her mind, and she began to smile. Then she realized that if something happened to her, he would sit there next Tuesday at the Pearl Café waiting, and he would never know why she hadn't come. She pictured the little boy look on his face and how he had smiled when she said that she would meet him for lunch. He would be so hurt. It was then that she realized how badly she wanted to see him again.

She took another sip and then noticed that thinking about Ephraim had made her feel at peace inside. She also realized that thinking about him made her smile. It seemed almost comical that in the middle of this awful place and surrounded by all sorts of dangerous people she couldn't keep herself from smiling.

Then as quickly as the calm came to her heart, it vanished when she saw that the large man was walking over to her.

#

MEMORIAL HOSPITAL:
NACOGDOCHES, TEXAS
September 2002

Jeb sat in a miserable, uncomfortable chair in the corner of a darkened hospital room watching as his daughter slept. He wondered why they couldn't put a decent chair in these rooms.

Of course, as soon as he found himself angry at the uncomfortable chair, he would look at his baby, and any discomfort he felt would disappear from his mind.

The Coopers from next door had come and taken Hannah and Missy home, which helped a great deal. The night was impossible enough; the little ones would have only made it more difficult.

The surgery had taken most of the night. First, they had placed a bone graft in the vertebrae and then installed something to keep her vertebrae from any further damage when she moved. Once those were in, the bone would begin to set, and hopefully the healing process could begin.

The next several hours would be critical. If there was no further damage, meaning no movement or no mistakes during surgery, then her body could possibly heal, and hopefully, she could return to a normal life. If not, well, Jeb refused to think about that.

Kay had finally gone home for some sleep. Jeb had wanted her to go home earlier and get some rest, but she refused to leave until Rebecca woke up, which wasn't until late the next afternoon, and then she barely opened her eyes. By the time Kay had left she was exhausted, both physically and emotionally. Jeb was as well, but he felt that Kay needed the rest more than he.

Still, fatigue was beginning to set in, and he wondered how much more of this he could take. He constantly found himself staring at the wall, not thinking about anything, just staring.

"Daddy," Jeb heard softly from his daughter.

Startled from his numbness, he instantly jumped to his feet and to her side. His heart was pounding as he looked down at his little girl.

"Hi, baby," he said.

Her eyes were barely open, and she was groggy from the various drugs.

"Where's Mommy?" she mumbled.

"She's getting some rest. She'll be back soon," Jeb promised in a feeble effort to be comforting.

As the words came out of his mouth, Kay came quietly through the door, followed by Uncle Louie. She walked directly to her little girl's side and gently kissed her on the forehead.

"I'm here, baby," Kay said softly.

Rebecca's eyes opened wide with delight for a brief moment, and then she fell back into a light sleep. Louie came to the child's side and took hold of her hand.

"Let's go outside," Kay said softly to Jeb.

Jeb knew that this meant that there was something important to discuss; otherwise a bulldozer couldn't have pried Kay from that room. The two headed to the door, leaving Louie holding Rebecca's hand. As he was stepping out, Jeb glanced back to see Rebecca's eyes open briefly and look at the old man. For a brief moment, a hint of a smile played on her little face.

Kay stopped outside the door and explained, "I stopped by the home to let him know what was going on. He insisted on coming by for a minute. I thought that you could take him back."

Jeb just nodded. He had thought about Uncle Louie and had planned to stop by the home after he got some sleep.

"He and Rebecca have grown really close. She thinks of him as a grandfather," Kay continued. "Also, my mother is coming to help with the girls. She'll be here tonight."

Jeb was prepared for that one. He didn't like it, but he was prepared. Kay was right, of course; they needed help with the girls, but the thought of living with Kay's mother didn't enthuse him any. He fought the urge to ask how long.

"She won't be here very long," she said, clearly knowing his thoughts. "She'll drive me crazy too."

"But we'll need help. Who knows how long it'll take Becca to recover," Jeb heard himself arguing.

"I've got some thoughts on that. We'll talk about it later," Kay said and then turned and walked back into the room.

#

GRANDE TERRE ISLAND
September 2, 1814

Charlotte tried to remain calm as the large man came over to her, but deep inside she was terrified. When he got there, he looked down at her. His stature alone made him frightening, but there was something gentle in his manner.

"May I sit down?" He asked.

Charlotte smiled as politely as she could under the circumstances.

"Of course."

"My name is Lucian," he told her.

"I'm Charlotte."

At that, neither said a thing for quite some time. Lucian cursed himself for not having thought of something to say before he just walked over there like a fool. For the life of him, he couldn't think of a single thing to discuss with this girl.

Charlotte, conversely, was somewhat amused. She could see the bewildered look on his face, and she realized that he was not like his friend at the bar. He was just lonely, and he had come over to her because there was something about her that he liked.

Finally she decided to put the situation to rest. She knew exactly why he had come over, and up close he didn't look dangerous. It was going to happen anyway so it may as well be sooner rather than later. If he did turn out to hurt her, then it was better to get it over with.

"Would you like to go upstairs?" she asked.

Charlotte was surprised by his response. There was a hint of disappointment on his face. It was only then that she saw the extent of the loneliness in his eyes and understood that all he really wanted was someone to talk to. Dianna had told her that some men were like that but insisted that she always invite them up. Usually, they would come along. "You aren't paid to sit in the bar with them."

The large man finally nodded.

"It will be two dollars. Do you have that much?" she asked. Usually the business part was done in the room, but this time she felt that she should take care of it up front.

Lucian nodded again, and she stood and took his hand, leading him up.

All the way to the room Lucian kept asking himself what he was doing. He'd never been with one of these women, and quite frankly, the thought frightened him. All he could think was that this girl just didn't seem like that. She seemed so much like Rosanna Blackburn.

Charlotte could feel tension in his hand. It was even a little clammy. It was strange that she frightened him, but that sometimes happened. Dianna had warned her about that kind as well.

She had been told to use the second room on the right. When they got there, she was pleasantly surprised. The room was every bit as clean and actually better furnished than the room she had at The Cheri Royal.

When she had entered the room, she noticed that he had stopped at the doorway. She then looked up and saw that his demeanor had changed dramatically. He was no longer shy and gentle. He looked almost angry, and it frightened her. She froze for a long moment looking at him, not knowing exactly what to do.

"Why are you doing this?" he asked softly.

She stood frozen, not knowing how to answer.

"Isn't this what you want? You don't belong here. You're not like those other women."

Charlotte was now more frightened than ever. She had been playing a part. She did what she was told and acted as if she belonged, but this man saw through her, and she had no idea how to respond to him. If he hadn't been blocking the door, she would have run out, but it was impossible to get past him. Against her will, tears began to swell up.

"I'm more like them than you know," she said softly.

"No," he said. "You may become like them some day, but you aren't like them now. Why are you here?"

In the tension she tried but couldn't hold back as tears began to roll down her cheeks. She hated who she had become and hated all of the things that had brought her there. Most of all, she hated that she would someday be like the other ladies who treated each other so terribly.

She sat on the side of the bed and began to weep. It may have been anxiety or stress or possibly the fact that her life had taken such a terrible turn and she had no hope of change. The truth was that she didn't really know why she was crying. At this point it was unimportant. All she knew was that she couldn't stop. She briefly looked up to see him close the door. She knew what was next. She'd been through this part before, but this man surprised her. He simply sat down on the bed next to her and put his arm around her and held her.

The comfort of his touch almost overwhelmed her. Men had held her many times in the past two weeks, but not the way this man held her. They held her because of what they could get. He held her to give.

Soon, she was telling him everything. How her father had died, her mother's marriage to Mr. Rhodes. How Mr. Rhodes had come to her room at night and how she had come to be married to Mr. Whitechapel. She told about Mr. Whitechapel's death and how she had been robbed when she got to New Orleans. She told of the park and sleeping under the bench and how she finally even took food from trash cans. But she left out the part where she saw the man with the knife cut a man's hand off. She was beginning to trust this man, but not that much.

Lucian was overwhelmed. She was not only beautiful, she was exactly as he had expected. She was no different than Rosanna Blackburn. She was just a small town girl who had gotten caught up in a situation where she had no control. It pained him deeply that there was nothing he could do for her. She would leave the island and go back to that place and keep doing this because she had nothing else that she could do.

He began to tell her his story. He told of leaving the 85th Light Foot in England and the ship he was on being raided by the pirates. He explained that his friend had worked out a deal for them to join the pirates and work off their passage once in America. He even told her about killing the man while on the *Tigre*.

Then Charlotte realized that they had been in the room far too long and that she had to go back down stairs.

"We have to pay our boss at The Cheri Royal," she explained. "I can't come up short."

"How much do you have to pay him?"

"I pay three dollars a night."

Lucian reached into his coat and pulled out some coins, "Here. You don't have to go back down there tonight."

Charlotte laid her head against his chest, and the two just sat there until they fell asleep.

#

MEMORIAL HOSPITAL,
NACOGDOCHES, TEXAS
September 2002

Jeb and Kay were sitting across from one another in the hospital cafeteria. Kay's mother was at home with the girls, and Uncle Louie was sitting with Rebecca. She was awake now and watching television, but there would be at least one more surgery before she could go home.

Surprisingly, Jeb thought, the food in this hospital was quite good, and even better, there was no hint of a disinfectant smell to ruin his appetite. Even better than that, the price was quite reasonable. Under any other circumstance, he might actually like eating there. He doubted that it would go over well for him to take Kay there for their occasional "date night," as she liked to refer to it, though.

It had been a terrible couple of days. Kay was right; her mother was driving her crazy. Jeb would have thought that he would have been the one to want to kill the woman, but as far as he was concerned, she had been absolutely delightful. Kay, conversely, was at nerves' end. The two women had constantly been at odds. Jeb might have found the situation amusing, but he knew full well that so much as a smile would bring down his wife's wrath.

"Remember when Uncle Louie first moved here, and we talked about making an apartment for him out of the back half of the garage?" Kay asked.

One of the things that Kay used to get Jeb to buy-off on the house was the garage. The building was separate from the house and was exceptionally large. The back half was an enormous room to itself, and Kay had suggested that Jeb could have a workshop. In his mind that meant a room with a couch and television that could be locked to keep the four women he lived with outside. But of course, instead of his own private sanctuary, the room had become a place where Kay could store her unimaginable collection of Christmas decorations along with some of Jeb's dad's old stuff.

"I remember," he answered with a hint of caution.

"He and I talked about it, and we think that we should do it," Kay told him.

"Don't you think that you have enough on your hands right now?" Jeb responded.

"Just listen. It makes sense."

"No. We were stretched to the limit taking care of the girls before this happened. The last thing we need right now is to be taking care of him."

"Will you just listen?"

Jeb sat here patiently looking at Kay. If there was one thing he had learned about his wife, it was that she thought things through. In this case, like most, she had some twisted reasoning that, in her mind, made Louie moving in with them a perfectly reasonable idea.

"First of all," she began, "Uncle Louie is in perfect health, and he gets around really well for a man his age. Secondly, the girls love him and are constantly asking why he can't live with us."

"I've never heard that."

"You've heard it. You've just never listened," Kay said firmly and then continued. "You're right. We have our hands full, and when you're at work I'll need to be with Rebecca, but I'll also have the other two to deal with. And I'll need to run errands and go out to the home to check on Uncle Louie.

Mother would be happy to stay as long as we wish, but frankly, she's getting on my nerves," she said.

"Really, I hadn't noticed," Jeb added with sarcastic innocence.

Kay shot him a look that told him that this was not the time or the place for his humor.

"But if Uncle Louie was there, he could sit with Becca while I ran errands. He's great with her, and she loves him, and if he needs anything, I'm a phone call away."

"He's an old man. He needs to be in a place like that home," Jeb stated in what he was beginning to see as a losing battle.

"There is nothing there that we can't give him. He can have most of his meals with us, and, if he likes, we'll build in a kitchen. There's plenty of room. He's actually a pretty good cook," she told him.

"What about his girlfriend?"

"They broke up. She dumped him for a younger man. That's one of the reasons he wants to come to our house. I think that he's pretty down. He doesn't belong there. He belongs with us. He's part of the family."

"How are we going to pay for all of this?"

"We won't. He has plenty of money and wants to pay for it. Actually, he's insisted on it. He really wants to help. The girls mean the world to him," she said, quite confident that she had won another one.

"How long do you think the construction will take?"

"I talked to a contractor this morning. He's going to come by tomorrow at noon and make an estimate. His early guess is that it would take three to four weeks."

Jeb knew that he'd been beaten.

"You called a contractor before talking to me?"

"Yeah," she answered matter-of-factly.

"And your mom is leaving?" He asked.

"Absolutely," she answered.

Chapter 9

GRANDE TERRE ISLAND
September 3, 1814

L ucian woke early even though he had slept very little. He
spent most of the night trying to think of what to do. He
wanted badly to help this girl, and he hated the thought of
her going back to that place. But there just wasn't anything
he could do about it. Deep in the back of his heart, what he
really wanted to do was to marry her and take her to Texas,
but that would take making some arrangements. So for the
time being all he could do was let her return to the city.

Charlotte felt Lucian moving. The two had spent the
night fully clothed. Normally, she would have sent him
home, but he made her feel safe for the first time in a very
long time, so she didn't move.

She looked at him and smiled as he rose from bed.

"I don't know how," he said as he put his hand on her
cheek. "But I will take you out of this. I promise."

Then he walked out of the door, and she assumed, out
of her life.

#

It was Llewellyn's habit to get up at sunrise. He would dress and then go to the Bos' house for breakfast. The Bos, of course, didn't get up so early, but Llewellyn had no intention of arriving after Mr. Lafitte.

Most mornings he would sit on the veranda until the Bos arose, which was sometimes as late as eight or even nine. Llewellyn, quite frankly, didn't understand laziness. Any man who slept as much as Lafitte did not deserve the kind of wealth this man had accumulated.

This morning, however, when Llewellyn arrived, Lafitte was standing on the veranda looking out into the Gulf of Mexico. When he climbed the steps he could see that the Bos was looking at a ship anchored in the distance.

"Is there a problem, sir?" Llewellyn asked.

"I don't know," the Corsair replied as the Major walked out of the house, buttoning his uniform coat, concealing the two handguns that he carried.

At that same moment, to Llewellyn's annoyance, Louis arrived at the house. Breakfast was normally just him and the Bos. Occasionally, the Major joined them, but that was all. He didn't like the idea of Louis joining them, but then, since the man was leaving for Texas, it probably wouldn't hurt.

"It's the Union Jack, Captain," Louis said to Lafitte.

Suddenly the ship had Llewellyn's undivided attention.

"Is that a boat I see coming?"

"Yes sir," answered the Frenchman.

"To, I assume, demand our surrender?" the Bos asked.

"I doubt that, sir. If they wanted, they could have blown us off the island during the night. Those are officers coming to negotiate."

"And in your opinion, Lieutenant, exactly what do the British think that I have to offer?" Lafitte asked.

"They want your help planning an invasion. They need someone to guide them through the bayous. The way they see it, we're nothing but a bunch of criminals. They will make you a financial offer, which they won't pay, to get you to help them against the Americans," Rose explained.

"Arrogant British scum. I'm an American businessman. What good would it do me to help them?"

The three men watched as the boat came closer. They could now see the bright red uniforms.

"I suspect that the two of you should find a place out of sight. A deserter and a French officer are probably not the sort they are hoping to run into here," Lafitte suggested.

"We'll be at the hotel, sir," Rose said and turned to walk away, trailed by Llewellyn.

#

An hour later, Louis Rose, with Lucian and Llewellyn Bradford, sat sipping coffee on the second floor veranda of the island "Hotel" watching Lafitte and the British officers take breakfast.

"What does it mean?" Lucian asked.

"It means that the war has come to Grand Terre Island, gentlemen," Rose answered. "And you two will to need to decide just where your loyalties lie."

Lucian and Llewellyn looked at one another. Until now the thought of choosing a side hadn't entered either of their minds. Both had assumed that if the British invaded, Grande Terre would be ignored, but now it seemed that the war in Louisiana would begin, quite literally, on the doorstep of Jean Lafitte's house. The two of them, along with Ephraim, were now the enemy of both sides.

"What are they doing up there?" Lucian asked.

"Louis thinks that they are negotiating," Llewellyn answered.

"They're going to need guides through the bayous. Who better than professional smugglers?" Rose added.

Lucian thought about the situation for a few moments and then asked, "Will the Bos help them?"

"I don't think so," Louis responded.

"The Army will hang us," Lucian stated.

"We have to get out of here. I think we should head for Philadelphia right away. Today, if we can. The Bos will understand," Llewellyn said.

"Lafitte will not understand," Rose stated flatly.

"Sure he will. He knows that we are wanted. When the British take New Orleans, it will be only a matter of time before they find us," said Llewellyn. "I've discussed our situation with him. He thinks we will do well in Philadelphia."

"I'm not going to Philadelphia," Lucian said flatly.

"What do you mean, you're not going? We've sat right here and discussed it," Llewellyn countered.

"I don't want to go to Philadelphia," Lucian replied.

"Then we'll go to Baltimore or Boston or New York," Llewellyn conceded.

"I'm not going east. I think we should go to Texas with Louis," Lucian said emphatically.

"Don't be ridiculous," said Llewellyn. "There's nothing in Texas. The money is in the big cities. We'll follow the river north. There's a road that heads northeast to Tennessee and Kentucky. We could be in Baltimore in less than a month."

"I'm not going east," Lucian said, this time with conviction.

Llewellyn looked at his brother in shock. Lucian had never confronted him before.

"What about our plans?" Llewellyn asked in bewilderment.

"They're your plans. You and Eph can go. I'm going west," said Lucian.

Llewellyn just stared at him, but Lucian didn't flinch. His mind was made. He was going to find a way to get Charlotte away from that place where she worked and head west to San Antonio de Bexar.

"It doesn't matter," Rose began. "You two have proved to be too valuable. Lafitte isn't going to let you go anywhere until the relocation is finished. With that ship out there, the move is suddenly more pressing."

Ephraim and Cort walked out of the hotel and onto the veranda.

"Is that a British warship in the bay?" Ephraim asked.

Lucian looked at his little brother and answered, "The Bos is having breakfast with the officers."

At the house Lafitte and the British officers arose from the table, and the pirate escorted them to the dock. As Rose watched the British officers being rowed back to their ship, Reggie walked out of the Hotel and onto the veranda.

"The Bos would like to see all of you. He especially asked for you, Lieutenant," Reggie said.

"I expected as much," Louis responded. He then turned to Cort, "Sergeant, I believe you and I have just joined the American Army."

#

A few minutes later Llewellyn, his two brothers, Rose, Cort, Captain Youx, and the Major were all seated around the same table where Lafitte had only minutes before entertained the British officers.

"Well, gentlemen, it seems that the King has declared war on Louisiana," Lafitte announced.

They were all silent as they waited for the Corsair to continue.

"There is an Admiral Cochrane in Jamaica who wants to invade New Orleans."

"Alexander Cochrane. He is Commander-in-Chief of His Majesties' North American forces," Rose elaborated. "He's a very accomplished seaman and not to be taken lightly."

Once again Ephraim was amazed at the Frenchman's knowledge.

"He's coming with twelve-thousand troops," Lafitte said. "You were right, by the way, Mr. Rose. They need help planning and executing their assault. That Lieutenant Lockyer was quite cordial. He said that if I helped them, they would grant me amnesty, which is to say that if I help them, they won't hang me. Of course, that offer wasn't extended to any of my men.

They actually think I agreed to their outrageous offer. That fat Lieutenant 'ordered' me to continue operations. I should have cut his throat."

Fuming, he looked at Rose, "Lieutenant, how many men do you have trained?"

"About fifty," Rose replied.

"Llewellyn, I want all ships that come in to be inventoried and sent to Galveztown to unload. Sooner or later the British will take this island, and I don't want anything falling into their hands. Get word out that I want all ships to remain at Galveztown until we get a grasp of the situation."

He looked over at Reggie and Captain Youx, "I want all powder and weapons sent to Devil's Island immediately."

"Yes sir," the Major responded, quite militarily, Ephraim thought.

Lafitte then stood with a cup of tea in his hand. Ephraim watched as he sipped from the cup and looked out into the bay at the warship. Ephraim was seeing a different side of the man than he had previously seen. He was sometimes the dashing Prince of New Orleans. Other times he appeared to be a leader of this little band of pirates, but at that moment Ephraim saw a calculating commander planning his next move.

"Lieutenant, could I impose upon you to delay your trip to Texas for a while?" Lafitte asked Rose.

"Of course, sir," Rose responded.

"I need more men trained," Lafitte ordered.

"It will be done," answered Louis.

As the English ship's sails rose and it began to drift away, Lafitte took a long sip of tea and looked at Ephraim, Lucian, and Llewellyn.

At the same time Lucian looked to the north side of the island where Charlotte and the other ladies walked out to the dock and got back onto the boat that had brought them out from New Orleans.

"I suppose that I should ask - are you Englishmen, or are you Americans?" the Bos inquired.

Lucian looked at the Bos and then at Charlotte as she and the others sail away.

"Americans," Lucian answered flatly.

Ephraim and Llewellyn looked at one another, shocked by Lucian's sudden conviction. Then after a moment of thought, the two looked at Lafitte and nodded in agreement.

"Good. Ephraim, since you and the governor are such good friends, I have a mission for you. I want you to deliver some letters the British officers gave me along with one I'll write offering our assistance. I'll also explain that the English currently think that I am cooperating. Then I want you to tell him that I have nearly a thousand trained men available to the Louisiana State militia. All I request is that he drops any grievances against my men."

"Sir, I doubt that he will see me," Ephraim responded.

"The Major will go with you," Lafitte said and then added, "Come back here when you have his answer."

\#

Lucian, Cort, and Llewellyn walked with Ephraim and the Major to the dock. Jim and Rezin Bowie were also on the dock waiting to go to New Orleans. Lucian walked over to the Bowie brothers.

"It looks like we're about to be in the middle of a war," Lucian said.

"You, maybe," Jim answered. "We're headed to Lavaca. I still say that you should come with us," Jim answered.

"I told you before. I don't like your line of work."

"So what's the Bos going to do about the British?"

"I think that he may fight," Lucian said.

"What about you?"

"I'm an American for now, but I'm considering becoming a Texican," he answered.

Llewellyn overheard the remark and looked at his brother, realizing that Lucian was serious about his plan to go to Texas.

Llewellyn looked at Ephraim, "Be careful, Kid."

"Thanks, Llewellyn."

For the first time he felt like his oldest brother was treating him as an equal and not just the littlest brother. It seemed strange, but Ephraim felt like he had grown up in the past few months. Albeit briefly, he had served in the army. He was living on his own and running a business, and now he was carrying a message for Captain Jean Lafitte that could affect the outcome of a war. He was no longer the kid that left Tenbury Wells. He was now as much a man as Lucian and Llewellyn.

He looked over at Cort and asked, "I guess you will be staying a while?"

Cort smiled at his friend. "I'm a soldier, and there is a war coming."

"I told you before. Being a soldier isn't all that great," Ephraim answered as he stepped off the dock onto the boat.

#

NACOGDOGHES, TEXAS
September 2002

Jeb was in Kay's kitchen pouring a cup of coffee. Kay had relieved him an hour earlier at the hospital, and he had come home for a quick shower and a cup before going to class. It had been a week since he had been to work. The department had been great about the situation, but he felt that it was time to go back to class. It would be rough for a while, and he wasn't sure how he would stay awake. At least at the plant he could take a nap and no one would notice. But there was no way to snooze while giving a lecture.

The contractors were already pounding away in the garage. If there was one thing he could say for certain about his wife it was that when she set her mind to do something, she got on with it. Jeb wondered, however, if they could actually finish in three weeks like they had promised. He also wondered if he could stand three weeks of their constant hammering.

Kay's mother was upstairs getting Hannah dressed, and Jeb figured he had about fifteen minutes to quietly enjoy his coffee before heading off.

On the table was the past weekend's *Dallas Morning News*. Kay always liked to have the Sunday paper from Dallas. She claimed that the Dallas paper had great editorials, but the truth was that the Sunday paper was packed full of sale ads. Of course, Nacogdoches didn't have most of those stores, but nine years of marriage had taught him not to question the woman's thinking.

Jeb flipped through some pages and then noticed a lengthy article about the famed pirate Jean Lafitte. Scanning the article, he saw that the Texas State Archives were apparently in possession of some controversial diaries that were supposedly written by Lafitte himself.

Jeb sat there a moment and turned to the second page of the paper and looked for phone numbers. Then he stood and took the phone handset off the wall and dialed.

"*Dallas Morning News,*" answered an operator. "How may I direct your call?"

Jeb quickly turned back to the Lafitte article and looked at the byline.

"Could I speak to Brad Jutras, please? He's a reporter," Jeb responded.

A moment later a voice came on the line.

"Jutras," a voice announced.

Jeb almost spilt his coffee.

"Mr. Jutras?" Jeb began. "My name is Jeb Bradford. I'm a History professor at Stephen F. Austin in Nacogdoches. I just read your article on Jean Lafitte, and I was curious about something. Do you have a moment?"

"Sure Professor. What can I do for you?"

"Well, in the Lafitte documents, did you by chance come across an Englishman by the name Ephraim Bradford?"

"Lafitte's emissary."

"Excuse me?" Jeb replied in shock.

"He was Lafitte's emissary." Jutras explained. "Bradford was the young Englishman who arranged the meeting between Lafitte and Andrew Jackson."

Jeb sat silent for a moment.

"I take it you haven't read the diaries, Professor?" The reporter asked.

"No," Jeb said. "I've not seen them."

"I'm curious. Where did you come across that name? Are you related?"

At that moment, Hannah came running down the stairs and took hold of her father's leg.

"Daddy," she said loudly.

Jeb picked up his daughter.

"Mr. Jutras, I'm sorry, but I've got to go. My daughter just came in," Jeb said.

"You didn't answer my question," said Jutras.

"Yeah." Jeb thought a moment. "Well, I think he may be my ancestor."

"Daddy," repeated Hannah, in a demand for attention.

"I'm sorry I have to go. Thank you again," Jeb told Jutras.

"No problem."

Jeb put the handset back on its base and held his daughter close to his chest.

Then he mumbled, "That old goat did it to me again!"

Chapter 10

CANAL STREET, NEW ORLEANS
September 6, 1814

Charlotte stumbled twice as she hurried up the street. She was late, and there was simply no excuse. Well, none except that she had kept going back to the mirror to check her dress and her hair and to see if she should wear a bow and if she looked better with a shawl. Naturally she settled on both a bow and a shawl, but only after serious deliberation.

Honestly, she didn't know what she was doing. This was a nice young man. Sooner or later he would find out where she lived, and that would be the end of it. But as quickly as reason entered her mind it was washed away by the memory of how he looked at her. There was just something about him. She couldn't help herself. He was all she could think about.

A block away, Ephraim was sitting at a sidewalk table in front of the Pearl Cafe. He had begun taking most of his meals there. The café itself was much too nice for Ephraim with white table clothes and black-coated waiters, but the sidewalk was less formal, with just a few tables where Ephraim felt comfortable.

He had arrived early. He knew that he was early. It wasn't that he wanted to wait on her, and it wasn't that he didn't have anything to do. He just didn't dare have her show up and him not be there.

He had been up half the night worrying about that very thing. He had no idea how to find her, and the thought that she might not come terrified him. What would happen if the British did take New Orleans? What would happen to people like Charlotte? What would happen to him and his brothers? They hanged deserters. For Ephraim, though, as fearful of hanging as he might have been, the possibility of not seeing Charlotte again frightened him much more.

Late in the night he had realized that he was obligated to tell her about the British ship and that there would be war right in New Orleans. He was going to have to make a choice. Either fight or leave. Llewellyn had told him about the plan to go to Philadelphia. He liked New Orleans, but Llewellyn was right. The smart thing for them to do was leave. Ephraim didn't mind the idea of going to Philadelphia, but he wasn't going to run off without Charlotte.

They were Americans now. When they had gotten on *The St. Pascal Baylon,* they had turned their backs on England for good. But were they ready to take up arms against the King?

It was while sitting there waiting that he realized how deeply he longed to see her. She was all he could talk about to Cort, who must have gotten sick of listening to him go on. He remembered feeling similarly about Rosanna Blackburn back in England. But somehow that was different. For one thing, Rosanna ignored both him and Lucian whenever they tried to talk to her. Secondly, Rosanna didn't smile at him the way Charlotte did. Charlotte's smile gave him a feeling that caused a sort of chill to go all through his body, but it wasn't a cold chill. There was something warm about it, and it made his heart beat faster.

While thinking about her smile, he looked up the street and saw her coming. When their eyes met, he saw a smile in them which made him feel that strange chill again, and as she approached he sensed that she felt it too.

Charlotte tried to slow her pace as she came to the Pearl Café, but it was difficult to do so. The moment she saw him, she found herself speeding up.

Her heart was pounding when she came to the table. She told herself that it was because she had been practically running all the way from Bourbon Street, but she knew that wasn't the case.

Ephraim stood as she approached and suddenly realized that he had no idea what he was supposed to do next. If she was a man, he would just shake hands and that would do it, but she was not a man. Was he supposed to kiss her on the cheek? He'd seen people do that, but it sure didn't seem right; but then if he didn't, was she going to think that he was rude?

"Charlotte," he said. "I mean, Miss Fuller."

"Hello Ephraim," she said as she put her hand out.

Ephraim took her hand and shook it like he would a man. When she drew her hand back, it suddenly occurred to him that she might have been expecting him to kiss her hand.

"And you can call me Charlotte," she said with a much more confident air than she actually possessed.

They both sat down, and almost immediately a waiter brought them coffee.

"Thank you Winston," Ephraim said to the waiter as he put two cups on the table.

"Will there be anything else, Mr. Ephraim?" the waiter asked.

Charlotte was impressed. Not only did the wait staff bring coffee before he asked, they knew him by name.

"Not right now, Winston. That will be all," he responded.

When the waiter walked away it occurred to Charlotte that Ephraim must be very rich. Only rich people got treated like that. He didn't dress like he was a rich man, but what else would explain it?

"You must come here a lot?" She asked while taking a sip of coffee.

"I have dinner here most nights," he said innocently.

That proved it. Only someone who was rich could afford to eat at a place like the Pearl every night.

For a moment they just sat there. Charlotte could see that there was something serious on his mind.

"Charlotte?" Ephraim asked and then paused.

His eyes told her that he was troubled.

"Yes?"

"Do you," he asked hesitantly, "like me?"

"Of course, I like you."

"No. I mean, do you," he paused, searching for words, "love me?"

Charlotte was shocked, and her expression it showed.

"No, that's not what I meant. Could you love a guy like me?"

Charlotte still didn't know how to respond. She wasn't prepared for something like this.

"Ephraim, we just met. I don't know," she said, knowing in her heart that she was lying.

Ephraim looked around to make sure that there was no one listening.

"The British are here. They have a ship in the bay. They are going to attack New Orleans."

Charlotte, of course, knew that the British were in the bay. She had seen the ship from the island, but how did he know?

There had been a great deal of discussion among the ladies as to what the ship meant. Everyone agreed that there would probably be an invasion, but no one knew just how that would affect them. Some welcomed the idea of soldiers coming. Soldiers were customers, and customers meant money.

Still, all of the women agreed to keep quiet. The men on the island were pirates, and since the British were talking to the pirate Bos, it meant that he had to be working with the British. More than likely, the pirates didn't want anyone in New Orleans knowing that they were cooperating with the British. The ladies knew that if they told anyone, they all might end up in the river.

The thought of a British attack had kept Charlotte up that night. The large man she had been with on the island, Lucian, had an English accent. He told her that he had been a deserter, but she worried that he may have been a spy, although he didn't seem like a bad person. There were probably lots of Englishmen in New Orleans who weren't spies. Ephraim was English and he wasn't spy.

"Are you sure?"

"I'm positive," he told her. "If they take New Orleans, I'm going north. I'm English, so I'd be branded as a traitor and probably hanged."

He stopped short of telling her that he was actually a deserter and would definitely be hanged.

He paused for a long moment, looking at her and thinking about what he was going to say. Finally, he decided to just say it.

"Will you come with me?" He asked her.

Charlotte's heart stopped. Was he asking her to marry him? He couldn't be. But the way he was looking at her. And he'd just asked her if she loved him. Her heart felt like it was leaping with joy. She almost said "yes" before she even began to think clearly about it. Then she saw in her mind the Cheri Royal. What was she thinking? This nice, rich young man would never marry her.

Still, she was about to say, "Yes," when a tall man in a military uniform walked up behind Ephraim.

"Mr. Bradford," he said to Ephraim.

Ephraim jerked his head around. He had left word at the warehouse that he was at the Pearl, but he hadn't expected Reggie so soon.

"Reggie," Ephraim said, standing.

"Am I interrupting?" the Major asked.

"We were just having coffee," Ephraim explained. "Oh, I'm so sorry. Charlotte Fuller, this is my friend Reggie, Reginald."

Ephraim paused, realizing that he forgot Reggie's last name.

"Reginald Blankenship," the Major told her with a slight bow. "How do you do?"

"Very well, thank you," Charlotte replied.

"Ephraim, I can come back," Reggie told his friend.

"No. We should go," Ephraim replied and turned to Charlotte. "Charlotte. I must go. I know that I promised you lunch, but we have business with the Governor that I must attend to. Will you please meet me tomorrow?"

Charlotte was fighting tears as reality interrupted her moment of fantasy. Young men who dine at the Pearl and do business with the Governor do not marry the "Lovely Ladies of Cheri Royal".

"I can't," she said, hiding her emotions.

"Then the day after?" Ephraim said with a plea in his voice.

"I can't," she repeated.

He looked at her with hurt in his eyes. Charlotte was now fighting to keep from crying.

"I just can't," she repeated softly.

"Then next week?" he pleaded.

She shook her head, not daring to speak.

The hurt in his face was now turning to real pain. He'd all but asked her to marry him, and she was breaking his heart.

"Please," he begged.

"The week after," she conceded.

His face lit up, and in an instant any sign of hurt had erased from his eyes.

"Two weeks from today. Right here?" he asked.

She couldn't help but smile at the enthusiasm that lit up his face.

"Right here," she replied, feeling in her heart that there was no way she should possibly come.

He started to leave with his friend.

"Stay here as long as you like. Winston will take care of you. The oysters are very good, and think about what we discussed," he told her as he and Reggie walked away.

#

A few minutes later, Ephraim and Reggie walked up Chartres Street.

"A lovely girl," Reggie said.

Ephraim remained silent but had a smile that told a story of its own.

"Clearly you think so," Reggie continued.

"I'm going to marry her," Ephraim said.

They came to a stop in front of the doors to The Cabildo. The old former Spanish Governor's mansion was an enormous remnant of Spanish rule in New Orleans and served as Governor Claiborne's office. Ephraim had walked past the place many times, since it quite literally bordered Pirate's Alley and overlooked the *Place d'Armes.*

The Major pushed open the huge door and the two walked in. Immediately inside was a large foyer with a wide staircase leading to the second floor. In front of the stairs sat a desk where a short, potbellied man sat shuffling some papers and appearing to be quite busy, although Ephraim knew better. Ephraim recognized the man from his frequent visits to the Alley. He, like many government officials, wasted large parts of his day searching for bargains among the "illegal contraband."

"Mr. Ephraim Bradford, here to meet with Governor Claiborne," Reggie announced to the man who had yet to acknowledge their presence.

"Do you have an appointment?" The man asked without looking up at them.

"No," Reggie responded with an angry tone.

"Well you can march right out the door because the Governor doesn't have time," the man said and then suddenly froze without finishing his sentence when he finally looked up and saw Jean Lafitte's notorious bodyguard standing before his desk. Then he hesitantly added, "Governor Claiborne doesn't see anyone without an appointment."

At that moment another man walked into the room. Ephraim recognized him from the day the Governor had come to the Alley. The man saw the Major and immediately walked over to the desk.

"I'm Farnsworth, the Governor's secretary. You're Lafitte's man, are you not?" Farnsworth asked somewhat belligerently.

"I am," Reggie replied.

"What is the nature of your business?" The secretary asked with a hint of condescension that clearly annoyed Reggie.

"Our business is between this man and the Governor," Reggie answered.

"Would you like to make an appointment?" asked the secretary. "Perhaps I can fit you in next week."

"No, we would not. Now tell him that we have urgent business that needs his immediate attention. We will not take up much of his time," Reggie demanded, clearly losing patience.

"The Governor doesn't see anyone without an appointment. Perhaps you can discuss your business with me, and if it needs his attention I can relay your message." the secretary said, trying to stand his ground.

The Major motioned with his head to the staircase, "The Governor's office is up there, is it not?"

"It is."

Without further comment Reggie, trailed by Ephraim, headed to the stairs. Farnsworth, unwilling to be ignored, ran around the two in effort to stop them.

"I can't let you go up there."

"Sir, at this moment there is a British warship in Barataria Bay. Perhaps you would prefer to discuss this when their troops arrive," the Major stated flatly and then walked on up the stairs.

Farnsworth followed Reggie and Ephraim to the second floor where they came to a large set of double doors. Without knocking, the Major pushed the doors open and walked into the Governor's massive and elegant office.

Governor Claiborne was leaning back in an oversized leather chair with his feet on a large desk, reading a handful of letters. He clearly recognized the large uniformed man standing before him.

The secretary hurried and circled around Reggie and Ephraim.

"Sir, Mr. Lafitte's emissary," Farnsworth said as an introduction.

The Governor sat upright.

"And what does Mr. Lafitte's emissary want?" the Governor asked.

Ephraim stepped before the desk.

"Governor, there is a British warship in the bay," Ephraim said. "They have twelve thousand troops and plan to invade this city."

Suddenly they had Claiborne's full attention.

"A ship arrived Saturday morning," Ephraim continued. "Some officers landed at Grande Terre and offered Captain Lafitte amnesty in exchange for aid in planning an invasion of New Orleans."

"What was that pirate's answer?" Claiborne asked.

"Captain Lafitte asked for twelve days to make a decision."

"Exactly why does your Captain Lafitte want me to know this?"

"Captain Lafitte instructed me to explain that he has no intention of helping the British and that he's simply buying time. He asked me to tell you that he has a thousand trained men who are willing to join your militia in defense of the city," Ephraim told him.

Ephraim handed Governor Claiborne a leather packet with Lafitte's letters.

"His offer is in here, along with the letters given to him from the British officers."

"What does the pirate expect in exchange for this generosity?" Claiborne asked sarcastically as he took the packet.

Ephraim looked at the Major somewhat uncomfortably.

"He simply asked for amnesty for his men," Ephraim said.

"In other words, he will sell his services to whichever side makes him the best offer?"

"Sir, Captain Lafitte is an American, and this city will need every man available to defend it," Ephraim argued.

"Lafitte is a thief and no different than the scum stealing purses in that alley you run." Claiborne said. "You can tell your Captain Lafitte that I am not interested in his offer."

#

Ephraim and Reggie hurried from Cabildo and back to Canal Street, neither eager to spend another moment in the presence of Governor Claiborne.

"What do we do now?" Ephraim asked.

"I suggest that we report to the Bos immediately," answered Reggie. "He genuinely expected that pompous fool to accept his offer."

"What do you think he will do?"

"First, I think he will move operations to Galveztown Bay on the Texas coast. We've always been prepared for situations like this. Aside from Galveztown there are hideouts on Cat Island and Devil's Island and another in the bayous. More than likely, we'll sit out the war in Galveztown, which is quite comfortable. The Bos likes his comforts," Reggie explained.

"My brother, Llewellyn, wants us to go north. He thinks that we can do well in Philadelphia," Ephraim confided. "But my other brother wants to go to Texas."

"And you?"

Ephraim just looked at his friend.

"Does she have family here?" Reggie asked, reading Ephraim's mind expression.

"I don't think so."

Reggie thought for a minute. "I'd go to Texas, if I were you. The British Navy has a blockade in the Gulf, so leaving by sea is dangerous at best. The trip to Philadelphia by land is long and very hard. If you ask me, Texas has more opportunity."

"When do you think they will invade?"

"I asked Lieutenant Rose that same question. He thinks that it will take a month or two to actually set up the logistics. Our people would have reported if there were troops already on the ground."

Ephraim thought that over for a moment. "Twelve thousand men. How many troops does Claiborne have?"

"There are fifty or sixty regular troops downriver at Fort St. Philip, and two or three hundred militiamen here in the city."

"My God! And that fool turned down a thousand men?" The young Englishman stated in bewilderment.

"He doesn't believe us," Reggie commented, "and he hates the Bos more than he fears the British."

Reggie stopped in the street and looked at Ephraim.

"Get that girl and leave soon. Once word gets out that the British are coming, it's going to be difficult to leave this town."

#

Governor Claiborne made a grand entrance into the Sala Capitular, the grand hall of the Cabildo that he used as a conference room. Immediately after the two pirates left his office, he summoned his advisors.

"I assume all of you have been apprised of the situation concerning the pirate Lafitte," Claiborne said as he seated himself.

"You mean, the British situation, don't you sir?" interjected John Blanque.

That was exactly the kind of response Claiborne expected from Blanque, the legislature liaison. In a region largely comprised of French and Spanish loyalists, Claiborne's popularity, and the popularity of the United States for that matter, was extremely low. When Claiborne was appointed territorial Governor, President Jefferson suggested, by way of an order, that the Governor have a local representative attend staff meetings in an advisory role. The territorial committee, soon to be Legislature, sent Blanque, the most annoying member of what Claiborne thought to be the State's most useless governmental body.

Claiborne personally thought that Jefferson should have minded his own business and allowed Claiborne to do his job as he saw fit. Claiborne didn't subscribe to the popular belief that Jefferson was a brilliant man. Rather, he thought of Thomas Jefferson as a simpleton and felt sure that history would someday show that the United States of America was able to succeed despite the foolhardy meddling of that Virginia farmer.

Then James Madison, who in Claiborne's opinion was no brighter than Jefferson, took the office. Madison's simple-mindedness would forever be memorialized in the "Bill of Rights" that he insisted be inserted into the Constitution.

Madison, like Jefferson before him, meddled far too much in Claiborne's Louisiana affairs. He, too, felt that the locals should be represented. Thus, in order to comply with the meddling of Washington City, Claiborne was forced to put up with the likes of John Blanque.

At first the Governor felt that Blanque would be quite suitable. He was from a wealthy family, and he was also educated, albeit in France. He had close personal friendships with a number of Congressmen, but as it turned out, Blanque was as much barbarian as any of the locals. Blanque's worst offense as Claiborne saw it was that he had close ties with the pirate Lafitte. Claiborne didn't know the nature of their relationship, but he did know that Blanque had ties with the man and would surely come to his defense even though Lafitte was attempting to blackmail The United States of America.

"About the British situation," Claiborne corrected, while glaring at Blanque. "I've summoned my Board of Officers to discuss our options."

"Governor Claiborne," Blanque interrupted, "if there are British warships in the bay, we should inform General Jackson immediately."

"He's right, Bill," added the State Treasurer.

Claiborne glared at his brother-in-law, the Treasurer, and then looked at Blanque, "Mr. Blanque, need I remind you that as the legislative liaison you are a guest at my staff meetings, and as such your opinions are not warranted?"

"Bill, can we not dispense with the politics until we deal with this crisis?" Blanque fumed. "My god, there are British warships less than sixty miles from here."

Rising to his feet, Claiborne became livid. "I will decide what is and is not crisis, Mr. Blanque."

At that moment the door opened and Farnsworth marched in.

"Your Board of Officers sir," Farnsworth announced.

Claiborne regained his control and took his seat as in walked Commodore Daniel Patterson of the United States Navy, Major General Jacque Villeré, commander of the New Orleans Militia, and Colonel George Ross of the United States Army, commanding officer of both Fort St. Leon and Fort St. Phillip on the Mississippi River.

The three men took their seats at the far end of the table with Commodore Patterson directly opposite Claiborne. Farnsworth took his seat at the Governor's right hand and took out his note pad.

"Welcome gentlemen," Claiborne said to the three soldiers. "I am to understand that my secretary informed you of the Lafitte situation?"

"Governor Claiborne," Commodore Patterson began, "it is time we do something about that island of bandits. Until now they have simply been a nuisance, but this threat from Lafitte makes it clear that he is not only a danger to the city of New Orleans but is also an enemy to this country."

"What threat?" Blanque interjected.

"I have to agree with the Commodore, Governor," Ross added, ignoring the comment from the legislative liaison. "Lafitte's smugglers know every bayou on the delta. I can deal with a British attack as long as they are forced to come upstream, but with Lafitte to guide them, there is nothing we can do."

"George, you don't have enough troops at that fort to keep the alligators out, let alone a war-hardened army. The British will roll over Fort St. Phillip and Fort St. Leon and then march right into this city," Blanque argued. "The problem, gentlemen, is not Jean Lafitte. It's the British we need to be concerned about."

"Mr. Blanque, I have had enough," Claiborne yelled, bolting to his feet. "This is a meeting of my Board of Officers. Your input is neither needed nor warranted. Now, if you will excuse us, we have a situation to deal with."

"I beg your pardon?" Blanque asked, somewhat shocked.

"This appears to be a Federal situation and not a matter concerning the state Legislature," Claiborne responded. "Now, if you will please leave us to do our job, Mr. Blanque."

Blanque stared at Claiborne for a long moment and then quietly stood to his feet and headed out of the room.

"Now," Claiborne said once Blanque was gone, "what do you have in mind, Commodore?"

"I've been working on a plan for months," Patterson boasted. "We build a flotilla of barges, loaded with General Villeré's and Colonel Ross' troops. I'll escort them in the Carolina. We attack the island in the morning with the sun to our back. We can destroy that sandbar and every bandit on it before they even know they're under attack.

Claiborne looked over at Ross. "Once the pirates are eradicated, in your professional opinion, what do you think the British commander will do, Colonel?"

"If they do attack, which I doubt, they'll simply have to come up river." Ross answered. "There is no way that they can march over land, and I don't care what that Frenchman says, with General Villeré's help, I can stop an attack from the two forts."

"General, how many troops do you have under your command?" Claiborne asked.

The General leaned back in his chair with a look of great pride on his face. "I have almost two hundred men here in the city, and in a month's time I can muster up another two hundred, maybe a few more."

"According to that contraband peddler, the British have twelve thousand troops," Claiborne told them.

Villeré's expression turned from arrogance to horror.

After a long pause, Ross finally spoke up. "Governor that simply cannot be possible. It would take an armada to move that size of force. It would not be possible to bring that many troops upriver, and besides, New Orleans is not that valuable. The British will come upriver with a couple of thousand troops at most. That pirate is trying to frighten you into giving him amnesty."

Claiborne sat back in his chair, contemplating the situation. After a moment he looked at the Commodore. "Mr. Patterson, implement your plan as soon as possible."

"It will be done, Governor." Patterson replied.

Claiborne then turned to his secretary. "Farnsworth, send the pirate's documents to General Jackson and draft a letter explaining that they came by way of Jean Lafitte, and as such, are unreliable. Also, explain to the General that Commodore Patterson is taking steps to eliminate Lafitte and the Baratarians once and for all."

"Yes sir," Farnsworth said proudly.

#

It was late the following day when Ephraim and the Major arrived on Grande Terre. They could hear cannon fire from the moment they entered the bay. They thought for a while that the island was under attack, but when they got close they could see that Louis was training his "troops" as an artillery brigade.

Reggie explained that Lafitte possessed a sizable arsenal. In all, Lafitte's "enterprise," as Reggie liked to refer to it, operated more than fifty ships. Each ship had between five and twelve cannons. More importantly, they often took cannons, powder, and other weaponry from ships that they raided. Currently, most of the cannons were being shipped to the hideout in Jacko Bay. In total, he had counted just fewer than two hundred cannons and about six tons of powder.

When they got off the boat to the island, they could see the row of cannons firing out into the gulf. Louis and Cort were in command, both wearing new blue American-looking uniform coats.

It occurred to Ephraim, as he and Reggie walked to the house, that this offer of Lafitte's meant much more to him than just helping the Americans defend New Orleans. There was something respectable, even honorable, about the gesture. No doubt the pirate saw himself as a Colonel or even a General. *General Lafitte, the hero of New Orleans.*

When they walked up the steps, Lafitte was standing on the veranda, proudly watching the training session. He reminded Ephraim of the commander of the old 85th Light Foot.

"Well gentlemen. What was Governor Claiborne's response?" Lafitte asked.

Both men hesitated to answer, then finally Reggie spoke up. "Not good."

Lafitte stood sternly looking at them. His face showed neither surprise nor anger.

"He made it clear that he doesn't desire your assistance," Ephraim said diplomatically.

"The imbecile," Lafitte commented.

He turned around and walked to the end of the porch and looked out to the sea and yelled, "Herman!"

A moment later a black man in a white coat walked out of the house and onto the veranda.

"Yes, Captain." The man answered.

"Would you be so kind as to summon Lieutenant Rose?" Lafitte asked.

"Yes sir," Herman said and then walked out to where Louis was standing.

"Did he say if he is going to send for the army?" Lafitte asked.

Ephraim and the Major looked at one another. Finally, Ephraim answered, "Sir, we talked about that. We just don't know. I gave him the letters. He has to take the threat seriously."

Lafitte thought for a long moment and then turned and looked at Reggie.

"Begin shifting the enterprise to Galveztown Island. I want off of Grande Terre within a month. The British fleet isn't going to let us sit here while they deploy troops to the mainland. They will either make us help them or they will blow us off this island. I'm not going to let them do that," he told Reggie.

Louis arrived at the veranda. "You requested to see me, Sir?"

"Claiborne turned down our offer. I want you to draw up your plans of how you think the British will attack. Our people can get you detailed maps of the terrain," Lafitte ordered.

"It will be done," Louis replied.

"Good. Plan an ambush. Two hundred cannons can do a lot of damage. I want every detail worked out. The Major here will assist you," Lafitte ordered. "Ephraim, go back to the city. You'll be my eyes and ears there. Make yourself visible. Spend a lot of time in the Alley. I want Claiborne's people to see you there."

#

NACOGDOCHES, TEXAS
October 2002

At the very first suggestion of building an apartment for Louie, Jeb knew exactly what it meant to him. Work. There was no way around it. Sooner or later he was going to be in that little garage with a hammer or a paintbrush or a saw or some other tool. Today it was a paintbrush. Or paint roller, to be completely accurate.

Kay had decided that they could save money by doing the painting themselves. Of course, it was Uncle Louie's money, and even though he didn't care, that point of reasoning was somehow lost on Kay. The truth, as Jeb knew better than anyone, was that Kay just couldn't stand to have those men working on the project and she not being in there getting her hands dirty. That, in and of itself, would have been just fine except, for some reason, it was every bit as important to Kay for Jeb to get his hands dirty.

The previous two weeks had been a miserable montage of hammering, crying babies, a complaining mother-in-law, stressful hospital stays, and worst of all, a wife with way too little rest. Kay was normally about as pleasant and easygoing a woman as any man could hope for. High maintenance, in his house, normally meant that he had to build a deck or some shelving, which was usually good for the property value, but for the past couple of weeks, she had been almost impossible. Jeb had attributed her warpath to her mother being in town, combined with the stress of Becca's injury. That was understandable. Even he had been on edge, but it seemed that she had been especially difficult the last few days.

It started, as best he could recall, the day they were in the hospital administration office discussing the cost of Rebecca's treatment. Thankfully, they had good insurance coverage, which was mostly due to Kay's foresight more than Jeb's, but still, even with the extra coverage, they estimated that with the surgeries, the hospital stay, and the upcoming months of therapy, there would be an outstanding balance of at least ten thousand dollars. Combine that with the eleven thousand they still owed after Jeb's father's strokes, and the two of them were right back where they had been a couple of years earlier.

Naturally, with that sort of news, she was a little on edge, not to mention the added stress of worrying about her little girl.

"You missed a spot," Kay said, pointing at the wall.

"I'll get back to it," Jeb told her, a little more snidely than he intended.

"You'll forget."

"I said I'll get it," he snapped.

Kay reached over with her roller and painted over the spot he had missed, causing Jeb to glare at her.

"I would have gotten it," he added snidely.

"You missed another one," Kay said pointing to the wall.

Jeb took his roller and slapped paint on the spot she was pointing out. "There, are you happy?"

"Jeb, don't start with me. I'm not in a mood to fight with you," she said flatly.

"Start with you? You're the one hovering over everything I do," Jeb argued, quite reasonably.

Kay shot a glare at him. "Go in the house."

"We're not finished," he said, feeling his temper rising.

"I'll finish. Now go!" she demanded.

Jeb looked at her for a long moment before deciding that this wasn't worth a fight. If she wanted to be that unreasonable, so be it. With that, he stormed out of the little apartment and into the house.

Chapter 11

GRANDE TERRE ISLAND

September 16, 1814

When Louis Rose, now most often referred to as Lieutenant Rose, was a boy in the Ardennes, the workday began at approximately five in the morning. Hard work was the way of life on the Rose family farm. When he left home at age fifteen to join the Grande Armée, one of his reasons for leaving was to escape his father's regimen. Only after joining the army did he realize that the lifestyle of the military was much more structured than anything his father could have imagined. Thus, order and regimen had reluctantly become his way.

Life on Grand Terre, though, was nothing like the Ardennes or the Grande Armée. The pace on the island would drive a sensible man insane. For Rose, a career soldier, this lazy attitude was almost intolerable. In Rose's world, a man woke with a purpose, and he served that purpose throughout the day. However, in Louisiana, Rose learned that a man's purpose in life was no more important than a man's enjoyment of that life, a concept that was lost on the officer of the 82e Regiment d'Infanterie de Ligne.

Nevertheless, there was one habit of this slothful society that Rose did learn to appreciate. The people of Louisiana loved their morning coffee. Prior to arriving at Grand Terre, he had never taken a liking to the taste of coffee, but after only a few weeks on this sandbar, he'd begun to enjoy a few peaceful moments in the morning with a hot cup in his hand.

Most mornings he would sit on the second floor veranda of the island "hotel" with a hot cup of coffee and watch the sunrise over the bay. This particular morning, however, he and the Sergeant had a fresh group of recruits to train. There were over twenty of Lafitte's ships in the bay, and Rose wanted each crewman to get some basic instruction before they relocated to Galveztown.

As was his habit when a ship came in, Cort would give a speech to the crew. The crew would, naturally, ignore him, but Cort had a way of eventually earning their respect. Rose thought that he would have made an excellent non-commissioned officer in a real army had he been given the opportunity.

Some of these crewmen needed little training. Captain Youx had arrived the previous day with the *Tigre*. This was the same crew that Rose had trained in route to Grand Terre. Still, as the sun was making its first appearance, Cort had the men of the *Tigre* marching in near perfect formation on the field south of Lafitte's house.

Rose watched for a few minutes with the interest of an officer in charge of new recruits. Then something caught his eye. To the southeast the U.S.S. Carolina was slowly sailing in the direction of the island. The ship had sailed past the previous day, confirming that it was a good time to evacuate Grand Terre. As he watched the ship draw closer, he clearly began to see along with the Carolina a number of river barges.

"We're under attack," Rose mumbled.

#

Unlike his employer, Reginald Blankenship never slept past five in the morning. This was especially true when he stayed at the island, which was all of the time now that his family was in Baton Rouge.

Reggie kept a room in the big house on the second floor, on the opposite end of a long hall from where the Bos slept. He always felt awkward whenever he stayed there. The room, actually a suite of rooms, was larger than an entire floor of the house where his family lived in New Orleans, and it was, without question, much more elegant.

This particular morning, like most, he dressed and went to the kitchen where Margaret, as always, had a pot of coffee brewed. Reggie then took a cup out to the veranda where he would relax until Margaret brought breakfast.

Reggie had been concerned, at first, at how the Bos would receive Claiborne's reaction to his offer, but as always, the Bos fooled him. Rather than reacting in pure anger, which was more than possible, he became invigorated. The Bos, Reggie decided, had become bored with life, and the idea of relocating and building an army was a bit of an adventure.

Of course, it wasn't adventurous enough to get the Bos out of bed at a decent hour.

As Reggie stepped out on the veranda, the first thing that got his attention was the sight of the Carolina. It was difficult to see because of the sunrise, but it was definitely the Carolina. The gunship was not an unusual sight. The Carolina often passed the island, but she usually did so later in the day when the winds were better and it was easier to spot the sandbars. The Mississippi delta was constantly creating sandbars that were treacherous to large ships such as the American Navy Gunship.

This morning though, the Carolina had only one sail up. Clearly the ship wasn't trying to get up speed, and she was really close, far closer than he had ever seen her. Then he realized that the gunship was, in fact, slowing down, and he saw why. Alongside of the Carolina was a flotilla of barges. This meant only one thing. A raid!

Instantly, Reggie dropped his cup and ran up to the second story of the house and onto the balcony. On the northeast corner Lafitte had hung a large bell. When he built the house, the Bos had it put on the second floor for this very purpose. If the bell rang, the island was under attack. So far, no one had ever heard it ring.

Reggie yanked the rope attached to the bell, and a deafening clang rang out.

He continued pulling the rope, but before Reggie could get the bell to ring a fourth time, a half-dressed Jean Lafitte was standing by his side, looking off into bay. Suddenly, cannon fire from the Carolina began to pound the island. Buildings along the street began to break into pieces as twenty-pound cannonballs crashed down.

Men began running frantically into the street. On the field south of the house, the crew of the *Tigre* began sprinting to the dock. A hundred yards from the island Captain Youx was on deck of the *Tigre* trying to make way.

"Get to the boats," Lafitte ordered. "Leave everything."

#

Lucian and Llewellyn had just awakened and were dressing when they heard Louis yelling that the island was under attack. A moment later the bell began to ring. Like everyone on the island, they were well aware of the meaning of the bell, but still they were startled by the sound of it. Just as they stepped on the veranda to see what was going on, a cannonball came crashing into the saloon across the street, and the real significance of what was happening came as a stark reality.

"Do we go to the boats, or do we head for the *Tigre?*" Lucian asked hurriedly.

"I don't know, but we had better do it quickly," answered Llewellyn as he ran into their room to grab what things they had.

Moments later the brothers, along with Rose, were running out of the hotel just as another cannonball suddenly hit the Bos' house. All three stopped and looked as the roof of the house burst into flames. Then they saw the Major running out toward them.

"Head to the boats," Reggie Blankenship yelled.

Suddenly, a barrage of gunfire came from one of the barges. The flotilla was still out of rifle range, but all four men dropped to the ground nevertheless. By now there were hundreds of men on the island running in all directions.

When it was clear that the barges were reloading, Llewellyn looked up.

"Now," he yelled.

Reggie jumped to his feet and began issuing orders. Most of the men began running to the west end of the island, but some tried to make it to their ships in the bay.

A few of the ships returned fire, only to be fired upon themselves. Other ships futilely attempted to get under way, but ran aground on sandbars.

Lucian and Llewellyn leaped to their feet and started running to the west end of the island, when suddenly they realized that Rose was not with them. Then something caught Llewellyn's eye.

"This way," he yelled to his brother.

Lucian followed him to the north side of the island where Cort and Louis were frantically shoving powder into the cannons that Cort had used to train the crews.

"Come on, leave these things," Llewellyn yelled at Rose. "You can't fight them off."

"We're not," Rose replied. "We're disabling the cannon. The Carolina will never make it around the island, but they can fire on us with these if they are useable."

Immediately, Lucian and Llewellyn understood and began helping. In moments, they had all twelve cannon stuffed with as much powder as they could get in them. Louis broke a flint and lit a torch.

"Head for the boats," he ordered.

"I should do it, Lieutenant," Cort replied.

"Just go," Louis said.

"No. If something goes wrong, they will need you more than they need me," Cort replied sensibly.

Louis stopped and thought for a moment. Then he looked back and saw troops beginning to come off the barge and wade onto the island. An officer was barking orders, but the militia rushed past him, apparently more interested in raiding the warehouses than responding to his commands.

Rose looked back at Cort. "Okay. Give us a five second head start and set them off one by one, and then run like you've never run before."

"Yes sir," Cort barked, and then jumped to full attention and gave Louis a salute.

Rose looked at the young man and returned the salute.

"Come on," Rose said to Lucian and Llewellyn and began running west.

Lafitte had long expected that someday there might be a raid. He had concluded, quite accurately as it turned out, that any attack would come from the east end of the island. The east end was closer to New Orleans and the delta. It also had a wide beach where shallow boats could easily put men ashore.

In anticipation of such an attack, he had forty boats lying bottom up on shore on the west end of Grande Terre. The boats were covered with tarpaulin and kept out of sight. Each boat could carry twenty men and had a keg of water.

Once the boats were at sea, they could cross through the narrow straights between Beauregard Island and Fifi Island. If a ship tried to follow, it would be forced to sail around those islands into deeper waters. Lafitte and his men would then catch the current to the mainland and escape into the bayous.

When the three men got to the beach, there were already five boats in the water.

"Flip that boat and get it ready," Rose ordered Lucian and Llewellyn as he pointed to one of the boats.

Rose looked back at the little town and could see fires breaking out. The men from the barges were running in and out of the warehouses with their arms full. The big house was fully ablaze, yet militiamen continued running into it. Had there been any military discipline at all, Rose thought, no one on Grand Terre could possibly escape.

To the north Cort began lighting the cannons. One at a time he lit each fuse, and when done ran at full speed toward the boats. Suddenly, the first cannon exploded, causing everyone on the island to halt what they were doing and look as a ball of flame and smoke shot up. Then there was a second explosion, and a third and so forth until each cannon was blown to bits.

As Lucian and Llewellyn pushed the boat into the water, Rose casually stepped in. At about that same moment Cort reached them and leaped in alongside Rose. Then off in the distance, they saw Reggie running out of the big house carrying something in his hands.

"Hold here a minute," Rose commanded.

With remarkable speed for such a big man, Reggie came running into the water. He tossed some things into the boat and climbed in.

"The Bos forgot his diaries," he said.

As they floated away, Rose looked forward to see Lafitte standing in the front of the first boat, barking orders to the helmsman. Margaret, Herman, and the other servants along with five crewmen were with him as he led the little fleet of about a dozen boats afloat toward the adjacent islands. Behind them Rose could see the raiders running like madmen. No one seemed to notice the two hundred or more people leaving the island; they were far too busy looting the house and warehouses.

Finally, Rose sat down and took hold of an oar, and, along with his friends, began rowing the boat. Eight months earlier he had been an aide-de-camp to General Jacques de Monfort who took his orders directly from Emperor Napoleon himself. Now he was on the run with a band of thieves, and the only reason that he was not dead was that the undisciplined and incompetent militia behind them was unaware that they had escaped. The irony of the situation was that those foolhardy soldiers were, in effect, committing the same crimes that these pirates were so often accused of.

#

TEXAS ELECTRIC PLANT,
KILGORE, TEXAS
October 2002

Jeb thought of his office at the plant as a filthy little box. The office, which he shared with three other engineers, was a freestanding room with glass windows at the end of a long wide-open generator room. The generator was precisely forty-four feet in length and looked like a long blue cylinder lying on its side and half buried. The room in which the generator sat was constantly being cleaned to keep dust from affecting the operation of the machine.

Jeb wondered just how the shop could be so pristine that you could actually see your reflection in the floor, yet his office hadn't been so much as dusted in the fifty years since it was built.

His desk was an ugly, steel monstrosity that had probably not moved an inch since it was brought in. With it and the two other identical desks, there was barely space to slip through the door and squeeze into a chair, which was so worn out that the cushions on the arm rests were long gone, and he dared not lean back too far or chance falling down. That, though, wasn't too much of a problem because the wall was less than a foot from his back. The thought had once occurred to Jeb that he was hired not so much for his experience but rather because he was thin enough to fit between the desk and the wall.

About the only thing in the room that was purchased after the Kennedy Administration was his computer. To be honest, he wasn't sure just how old even it was. It did manage to handle the constantly updated software that he used to monitor the generator, but it was painfully slow and crashed several times a day. He often wondered how long it would take to get electricity to the city if his computer finally gave up at the same time there was a generator problem.

Fortunately for him, that hadn't happened yet. The worst problems he had seen were the usual issues with the excessive demands due to the Texas heat.

Most afternoons Jeb had the office to himself. The daytime guys usually spent the afternoon either downstairs in staff meetings or filling out the seemingly endless reports. He normally came in around one in the afternoon and stayed until about six or six-thirty, when the night-shift engineer took over.

It had been a win-win situation. He bridged the gap between the two shifts and made sure that the night guy was up to date on all the issues that came up during the day. He was also there to cover for anyone who had to call in sick or go to a kid's little league game. The bottom line was that someone with experience had to be there to monitor the system.

Best of all, since there were few real issues that he had to deal with, he had plenty of time to grade exams and prepare the following day's lecture. In some ways this was the best part of his day. If it wasn't for the fact that the generator was as noisy as a dozen freight trains, he might have even found it peaceful.

Jeb was so absorbed in grading papers that, if not for the blast of noise when the door opened, he may not have noticed Burt Avery walking in. Burt and Jeb were old friends. The two had shared that same office back when Jeb worked at the plant the first time. Burt, of course, stayed on and eventually became supervisor over all engineering.

Burt was a big, barrel-chested fellow who looked more like he should be working on the shop floor than supervising engineers.

"Burt," Jeb said looking up at his friend.

"Jeb," Burt responded with no further need for greeting. Both men were old-school Texans - a nod of the head would have sufficed. "How's Becca?"

"Better," Jeb answered. "The worst is over, we think."

"You don't know how glad I am to hear it." Burt replied.

Then suddenly Jeb recognized the look on his old friend's face, and he felt an icy cold feeling in the pit of his stomach.

"Look, Jeb. I know this couldn't be at a worse time," Burt began.

#

PIRATE ALLEY,
NEW ORLEANS
10:30 a.m., September 16, 1814

Ephraim had one thing and one thing only on his mind - seeing Charlotte. Despite all that had happened since they last met, she was all he could think about. He had rehearsed everything that he was going to say over a dozen times. When they last met, there was no doubt that he had frightened her. The suggestion of love had certainly caught her off guard.

Ephraim, you are an idiot.

Of course it had caught her off guard. Only a fool would have said such a thing, but there was something in her eyes that said to Ephraim that she felt exactly the same way as he did.

The more he thought about it, the more he knew that she would go with him. During the past week, Ephraim had studied every map he could find. Llewellyn was set on going to the east. He wanted to get rich, and the money, he said, was in the big cities. That would be fine if it were just the three brothers, but like Reggie said, the trip was long, and he had no idea how Charlotte would handle it.

Lucian had mentioned Texas, but that option didn't seem so good either. Texas, Ephraim had been told, was a desolate place with few only a few towns, and the towns there tended to get raided by Indians. Land could be purchased cheaply, but Ephraim had no idea if it could be farmed. Frankly, he knew nothing about farming, so the price of land was of little relevance.

Ephraim had finally decided that the best option was to go upriver to either Baton Rouge or Saint Louis. Those cities were part of America and not Spain, so they spoke English, and flatboats traveled to both regularly.

The real problem would be getting a spot on a boat. That was something else that Reggie had been right about. Word had spread quickly about a British ship in the Bay, and people throughout the city were nervous. A horse and wagon were virtually impossible to buy, and every boat going up upstream was packed.

There wasn't a panic yet, but everyone was expecting the worst. The moment word got around that the British might invade, everyone started stocking up on things. Very few ships were coming in from the Gulf, indicating that they could no longer get past the blockade. Naturally, business in the Alley flourished. Flour, sugar, and wine were the first to go. Then house goods began to disappear. Ephraim reasoned that in a day or two at most, the warehouse would be completely empty.

Frankly, Ephraim thought, as he stood in the middle of Pirate Alley, it couldn't happen fast enough. Soon the Bos would complete his relocation from Grande Terre. Ephraim would then get word to his brothers that he had gone upriver. They could meet him in Baton Rouge. There just wasn't any time to discuss his plans with them. They would understand, he thought, especially once they had met Charlotte.

It was odd that he was suddenly thinking of going somewhere without them. Until now the thought of doing anything without Llewellyn to lead the way had never entered his mind. They were a family, and as such they stayed together, but sooner or later each would begin a family of his own. Ephraim had always known that this would happen, but he never imagined that he would be the first to take a wife.

For the first time in his life, Ephraim had been living on his own, and quite honestly, he liked it. He liked thinking for himself rather than just following along with whatever Llewellyn had decided, and he liked thinking about asking Charlotte to marry him.

He was still having trouble making sense of it. All he knew was that he loved her, and somehow he knew that she loved him. If he'd had the time, he would court her, the way his father had courted his mother. He would meet her family. He would even bring gifts, but there just wasn't time. He couldn't risk being captured by the British.

The wait was driving him insane.

Ephraim reached for his watch again but stopped himself when he suddenly noticed that the Alley had gotten quiet. Because the alley was walled on both sides, the closed-in nature of the place caused the noise to sometimes be deafening. He often wondered how the venders managed to make a sale, but now it was almost silent.

Ephraim looked around. At both ends of the Alley he saw armed soldiers. From one end an officer and two sergeants came marching directly toward him.

Ephraim, like everyone else, stood watching, not knowing anything else to do as the officer passed everyone else in the Alley and walked up to him.

"Ephraim Bradford?" The officer asked.

"Yes," Ephraim replied.

"Come with us. You are under arrest," the officer said as the two sergeants took hold of Ephraim's arms.

"Arrest?" Ephraim asked, suddenly realizing what was taking place.

The officer turned and motioned to the soldiers standing at attention at the south end of the Alley.

"This illegal operation is now closed by order of Governor Claiborne. Everyone is under arrest," the officer shouted.

In an instant the Alley was in a state of chaos with vendors and shoppers running in every direction. The rest of the soldiers rushed in, some grabbing vendors while others started looting. Fights began to break out between the vendors and customers. Soon, soldiers, vendors, and customers were all grabbing things and running.

The two sergeants holding Ephraim suddenly let go and started to take part in the mania. Ephraim stood silent next to the officer who was shouting orders to his men and trying to take command of the situation.

In moments, people from the other streets began running into the ally and started stealing what merchandise the soldiers were unable to grab. In just a few minutes time what had been a normal day in "Pirate Alley" had turned into a full riot. The officer, who had been futilely shouting commands to his men, climbed up on a table, and in what Ephraim thought to be an amazing display of stupidity, fired his pistol into the air. Suddenly, gunfire rang out from all directions. Ephraim dropped to the ground to avoid being shot just as the officer fell, wounded, next to him.

Then, as quickly as the mania began, the Alley emptied. Within moments of the first shot, almost every person who had been in the alley was gone along with all of the merchandise and all of the soldiers save the officer lying next to Ephraim.

Slowly rising to his feet, Ephraim thought for a moment about making a run for it. The soldiers were nowhere in sight, and the only person to stop him was this young officer who was badly bleeding and not going anywhere.

Then he saw that the officer was trying to get to his feet. Ephraim reached down and helped him up.

"Sit down on the table," Ephraim told him.

The man sat down, and Ephraim took some torn cloth that had only minutes before been part of a bolt of red and white gingham and pressed it on the officer's wound.

"What's your name?" Ephraim asked him.

"Henderson. Lieutenant Henderson," the officer replied.

"Well, Lieutenant, it looks like I'm the only arrest that you're going to make today," Ephraim told him.

Lieutenant Henderson took a deep breath. He was obviously in pain. "If you want to run, I can't stop you."

At that moment one of the sergeants ran back into the Alley. When he saw Ephraim and the officer, the sergeant knelt to firing position, pointing his rifle at Ephraim.

"I guess I missed my chance," Ephraim said to Lieutenant Henderson.

Henderson looked at the sergeant, "Put down the rifle and come help me, you idiot."

#

A few blocks away Charlotte had just finished getting ready to see Ephraim. She had awakened shortly after sunrise, which was quite unusual for her since she had come to the Cheri Royal. Here, work began at about the time decent people went to bed, and it didn't end until almost morning.

She disliked sleeping into the day. It went against everything she had been taught, but then everything she did at the Cheri Royal went against what she had been taught.

But this day was different than any since arriving in New Orleans. There was an excitement in her heart that spread out to every pore of her body. It was an odd feeling for her. It was a feeling that she had never felt before. All she really knew was that she couldn't keep herself from smiling, and for the first time that she could remember, she knew exactly what she wanted for her life. Ephraim had asked her to leave with him ahead of the British. He hadn't exactly asked her to marry him, but he did use the word "love," and deep in her soul she knew that buried in his awkward shyness, marriage was exactly what he wanted. She didn't know why she knew this. There was just something about Ephraim that told her exactly what he wanted.

She wondered if there was something in her that said the same thing to him. Normally, such a thought would have been terribly embarrassing, but, for some reason, she hoped that he knew what was in her heart. For the same reason she was sure that he did.

The truth was that she and Ephraim were not much different. He was a small town boy living a long way from home, and she was a small town girl a long way from home. The only difference was that she was a girl doing something that would deplore him.

In the past few days she had spent plenty of time thinking about that. She had decided that she had to tell him everything. How she came to be married. How Mr. Whitechapel died. How she had lost everything she owned the day they met. How she had lived under the bench in the park. She would even tell him about seeing the fight and seeing that man get his hand cut off. And finally she would tell him about the day that the church had no food and how she came to work for Mr. Hamilton.

Ephraim would probably turn and walk away. He certainly had the right. What man would want to marry a girl like her?

Regardless, she had to tell him. There was no way that she could go through life keeping such a secret. More importantly, she wanted him to know the truth.

Honestly though, she didn't think that it mattered. When he had asked her if she loved him, her heart had almost leaped out of her chest. The thought of love frightened her to the core of her soul, and the mere thought of him mentioning it made her smile. He was so much like a boy in love. He wanted her with him, and he just didn't seem like he would let her past stop that from happening.

As she strolled up the narrow sidewalk of Bourbon Street, her heart felt so full that she almost floated. She was nervous, but her fear was overcome with the excitement. She was going to tell Ephraim that she would go with him anywhere he wanted to go, and not only could she love him, she did love him.

Charlotte had planned to arrive at the Pearl just after eleven. She fully expected Ephraim to be waiting, but when she got to the café, Ephraim was not sitting on the sidewalk like last time.

The black man Ephraim had called Winston walked up to her and asked, "May I help you, ma'am?"

"I'm meeting a friend," Charlotte replied.

"Mr. Ephraim?" he asked, smiling broadly.

"Yes," she said, trying to conceal her excitement.

"He usually likes this table," Winston said as he directed her.

She sat down, and a moment later Winston brought her some coffee.

"This is our best."

"Thank you. Have you seen Mr. Bradford today?"

"No ma'am, but I'm sure that he will be here presently."

#

An hour and a half after she arrived at the Pearl Café, Charlotte was still sitting at that table. There was a hint of moisture in her eyes. Her worst fear had come true.

Two weeks before she had sat in that very chair, and he had all but asked her to marry him. He wanted to take her away. He was a knight who would rescue her from the dungeon walls of the Cheri Royal.

For some reason her knight had chosen not to come. Instead of being rescued, she would make that long walk back down Bourbon Street to the bedroom prison that was, she knew, her permanent home. She would spend the rest of her evenings in that smoky saloon growing old before her time and hating the world around her. Ephraim had been her only escape, and he wasn't coming.

At first she had hoped that maybe he had just been delayed, but as the morning crawled by she began to realize that Ephraim was not going to come. Winston had stopped by the table many times and told her that Mr. Bradford was a busy man and perhaps business had delayed him, but the expression on Winston's face betrayed the lie on his lips. Ephraim wasn't going to come.

She had given herself a dozen explanations for his not showing up. It could be anything, really. It could be his business or his family. He may have been hurt. But she kept remembering the excitement on his face at the prospect of seeing her. She knew if it had been because of any of those things, he would have gotten word to her. There was only one reason for his absence. He knew what kind of girl she was.

His friend, the one he called Reggie, must have recognized her. Even though she hadn't recognized the man, she felt sure he that he must have been to the Cheri Royal. Many men came into the saloon. She tried hard not to remember their faces, but, of course, he would remember hers. Naturally, he had told Ephraim. That is the sort of thing a friend would do.

A multitude of thoughts ran through her head. The things she wanted to tell him, the feelings that she wanted to share. She wanted to tell him all about Randallstown and about her father, and about Mrs. Whitwell. She wanted to hear about England, and his little town, and his father, and his family. Most of all she wanted to feel his touch and the warmth of his arm around her. But those were things she would never share, and the warmth of his arm was a feeling that she would never feel.

With her knees quivering beneath her dress, it took all of the strength Charlotte had within her to stand. As she began to reach into her purse, Winston came to her table.

"Please ma'am, Mr. Bradford's table is always on the house," he said.

Charlotte looked at Winston and smiled.

"Today, this is not Mr. Bradford's table," she said as she laid down some coins. Her knees trembling and her heart pounding, she held her head up as she made her way back to Bourbon Street and the Cheri Royal.

Chapter 12

October, 2002

When Jeb pulled his pickup into the driveway, Hannah was on the porch with Uncle Louie. The old man turned out to be great around the house, and just like Kay had said, the kids loved him and treated him like a grandfather. *That woman is always right.*

As he pulled to a stop, Hannah leaped from the porch and met Jeb before he was able to get out of the truck.

"Daddy!" she yelled cheerfully.

Jeb picked her up in one arm, and with his free hand managed to gather his books and assignments and walk over to the steps.

"What have you been doing today, sweetheart?" Jeb asked Hannah as he set her down on the porch.

"Uncle Louie was telling me stories. Does he tell you stories?"

"Sometimes. What story is he telling today?"

"Ephraim is in love," she answered with the tender sweetness that only a six-year-old girl could possess.

"I've heard that one. Charlotte dies."

Hannah whipped her head around and looked at Uncle Louie, who just smiled and shook his head. She then looked back at her father with an angry scowl.

"She does not," she said scolding.

"What brings you home so early, Jeb?" Louie asked.

"Oh, I just wanted to have dinner with my little girl," Jeb said, looking at Hannah.

Louie could see that there was more to the story but also could see that this wasn't a conversation for a little girl's ears.

"Where's mommy?" Jeb asked Hannah.

"She's in the kitchen with Missy. Becca's asleep."

"Thanks honey. Stay out here and keep Uncle Louie company for a while, will you?" Jeb asked, but she knew that it was more of a command.

As he walked into the door, he could hear Hannah whispering to Louie, "That's what he says when he wants to talk to Mommy."

Jeb put his papers and things down on the dining room table. Kay hated it when he did that, but with the news he was about to give, he doubted a small offense like this one would be noticed. When he stepped into the kitchen, Kay had her back to him mixing something in a bowl. Missy was swinging in her little mechanical swing. She immediately held her hands up for Daddy to pick her up.

"I thought I heard you drive up," Kay said without turning around.

Jeb picked up the baby and walked over to his wife.

"Prepare yourself."

Kay turned around and looked at him. She had an uncharacteristic appearance of alarm on her face. For once she had no clue what was coming.

"Burt laid me off."

Kay looked at him for a long moment, letting the news settle in before she spoke.

"Good," she said flatly.

"What?"

"Good."

"You want to explain that?"

"You're overworked and stressed to your limit. I was thinking about asking you to quit that job anyway."

"Are you crazy? That job is the biggest part of our income." Jeb argued.

"We'll be fine. Uncle Louie is demanding to pay rent."

"Pay rent? He built the apartment."

"I know. But he wants to help out, and I think that we should let him. Anyway, he's still paying half of what that home was costing him, so with his rent and your income from the school, we should do okay." She told him. "And besides, you've been a complete pain the last few weeks. The two jobs were killing you even before Becca's fall. Now, you're impossible."

"I'm impossible?" Jeb countered in disbelief.

"Yes. I know it's hard for you to believe, but you've been somewhat less than cordial," she said sarcastically.

Jeb began to get a little agitated.

"I'm less than cordial. The other day you threw me out of Louie's apartment," he defended.

She turned around and went back to work on dinner.

"Jeb, I've had a long day, and I'm not going to fight with you. Take Missy upstairs to see Rebecca while I finish dinner," she ordered.

Jeb just looked at her a moment, fuming. When he came home, he was just a little dejected from losing his job. Now he found out that his wife, who had spent the past three weeks on the warpath, was happy that he'd been fired because she thought that he'd been a pain in the butt.

#

DEVIL'S ISLAND, LOUSIANA
October 20, 1814

Louis Rose surveyed the current situation with a clipboard and paper in hand. There were nearly three hundred men on the island, with more expected, and four of Lafitte's ships sat in the little straight between them and the mainland. The plan was to train as many men as possible and send most of the ships on to Galveztown with skeleton crews where they would wait out the war.

That was all well and good except for two problems. First, there were three hundred men and housing for less than thirty. Until the past few days, Lafitte's brigade, as Rose had begun to think of it, didn't even have materials to make tents, and since it rained almost every night, most of the men had to row out to their ships in order to have a dry place to sleep.

Secondly, and more importantly, was the issue of food. Supposedly, Napoleon had once said that an army marched on its stomach. Rose doubted that it was Napoleon who actually said it, but it was true nonetheless. Napoleon's supply train had been as long as the army itself.

Twenty-two ships were lost in the raid along with much of their crew and all of their cargo. Most of the ships had never gotten underway, and those that had got hung on sandbars. The men, they learned, were taken prisoner and were currently held in the Calaboose. The cargo, naturally, had been looted.

Of course, the food problem became apparent as soon as they arrived. When finally one of Lafitte's ships got to the island, the commander, Captain Gambi, was not at all interested in giving up his valuable cargo to feed Lafitte's private militia. It took quite a bit of negotiating, but the Bos eventually convinced the captain to leave half of his cargo and take the rest to Cat Island to be smuggled into the city. He would then go to Galveztown for more supplies.

The plan worked for both sides. Lafitte needed to keep his captains happy, and business was business. This was a loose-knit organization, and he hoped to continue operating after the war. Secondly, he had to feed these men, or they would start disappearing.

Supplies and logistics are two of those aspects of the military life that the average civilian can't quite grasp. Little Bonaparte, as Rose liked to think of Lafitte (though never verbally), was one such civilian. When he had sent Gambi for food, it had never entered his mind to send for utensils. Displaying his extraordinary incompetence, he seemed to think that there was nothing wrong with that. Even though as commander he had a private shack and Margaret to prepare his meals, it seemed perfectly reasonable to him that his men eat raw potatoes and shrimp with their hands in a drizzling rain. It had taken Rose most of a morning to convince Little Napoleon that this was a volunteer army, and like all armies, they would eventually grow disgruntled. The most fundamental rule of command is to keep your men well fed.

Of course, feeding three hundred men was not easily done. Rose had designated Llewellyn as supply officer, to which Lafitte readily agreed. Llewellyn was a natural for the job. He had a brain that was geared for organization and supply. For similar reasons, Rose assigned Lucian as housing officer. Like his older brother, Lucian understood organization, but more importantly, he also worked well with the men. Within a week he had enough materials for a mess and latrines, and it was Lucian who'd pointed out the most important problem facing this army.

Lafitte had been using the Devil's Island hideout for years to stash less marketable but nevertheless valuable items such as powder and flint. But the buildings over time had decayed to the point that they were barely standing. One good storm and the powder would be completely destroyed. Lucian had fortunately finished constructing the armory only hours before they had two straight days of heavy rains.

It had taken a little over two weeks to get to the island from Grande Terre. They'd hit shore about forty miles east of Grande Terre and walked through endless marshes, swamps, and forests before finally getting to this barren little piece of swampland so aptly named Devil's Island.

The place was barely habitable. There were channels of water everywhere, and the ground was little more than marsh. When they arrived, the grass was waist- deep and had to be patted down in order to walk, and of course, there were the ever-present snakes and alligators.

But the fact that the island was such a miserable place made it a perfect spot for them to train. No one would purposely go near there. Lafitte may have known nothing about supplying an army, but he knew precisely how to hide one.

The island, as it turned out, proved more than adequate for training purposes. It was open in almost every direction and had a wide flat plane for the men to drill.

That, of course, was Captain Cort's department.

The command structure was one of the hurdles that Rose was forced to deal with. Frankly, he thought later, it was even more important than getting the men food. No army can survive without structure and discipline, as they'd all learned during the raid on Grande Terre.

Upon arrival on the island, Rose met with Lafitte to discuss a chain of command. Lafitte, of course, was the supreme commander. He assumed the rank of Colonel. "The Major," Reggie, was his aide-de-camp and served as third in the command structure. Rose was commissioned at the rank of Major and would be second in command but shared his duties with Reggie who, Rose decided, was a natural officer. His very countenance demanded respect, and, unlike the Bos, Reggie quickly recognized the issues involved in building this militia.

Since each ship had a command structure, the men from these ships were organized into individual units. The ship's commander served as the leader of that unit. Cort, now given the title of Captain, served as training officer and helped coordinate the units.

It was somewhat more difficult to persuade Little Napoleon to go along with that particular commission rather than the others. Lafitte argued that a black man, not yet twenty years of age, was hardly equipped to serve as a captain. By merit of age, Rose had to agree. Most captains that he knew were over thirty, but Rose argued that Cort had demonstrated on Grande Terre that he was more than capable. Secondly, Rose needed someone to coordinate with the unit officers, and Cort had developed a rapport that made him ideal for the task. If they had designated him as a sergeant, the ship officers would understandably be reluctant to take his orders.

Rose made his way with his clipboard of notes toward Colonel Lafitte's command center. It was actually four poles with a tarpaulin suspended to provide shade. The accommodations were certainly not elegant, but then again this was an army in exile.

Ahead, he could see Lafitte climbing down off of his horse. Rose had no idea where the horse had come from. There were a few farms nearby, and Rose suspected that Lafitte had purchased the filly from some happy farmer for several times what she was worth. Still, she was a fine animal, and Rose had to admit that with his uniform coat and riding crop, Jean Lafitte looked as impressive as any general Rose had ever seen, save Napoleon Bonaparte himself. However, Rose recalled, although Bonaparte might have looked impressive in uniform, he wasn't a particularly good general. It was Rose's opinion that if the Emperor hadn't been so good at choosing his commanders, he might have been a complete failure. Napoleon, like Lafitte, was led by his ego.

As he approached the tent, Rose saw Llewellyn and Lucian already seated at the table along with some of the ships' captains. It was obvious that the captains held some resentment for him, Cort, and the two brothers having so much status in the newly formed Lafitte militia, but little of that resentment was vocalized. Although most of the captains had previously served in some actual naval capacity, none had any experience in ground warfare, and they soon learned to respect the ability of Major Louis Rose. Since few, if any, understood anything about supply logistics or construction, there were no real issues where the Bradford brothers were concerned. Cort's role was the only one that came under question. This was mostly because of his youth and the color of his skin, but those issues were quickly erased by the young Spaniard's uncanny ability to communicate with the captains. Rose suspected that it came from Cort's years on board ship that gave him an understanding of how to deal with the extraordinary ego that ship captains often possessed.

There was also a bit of consternation among the captains and the men as to whether or not to help the Americans, especially after the raid. Lafitte eventually won the debate by arguing that their business depended on an American New Orleans. Because of their history of raiding British and Spanish ships, they would be put out of business if the British won the war. He also reasoned that before they could make the move to Galveztown and become established as legitimate importers, they would first need to secure amnesty.

Rose took his seat at the table. The table was something else that he wondered about. Where could a table like it have possibly come from? It was one of the most ornate tables Rose had ever seen, and he had been inside European Castles. It was hand-carved mahogany and was at least fifteen feet long. In fact, one end of the table hung out of the makeshift tent. It was the sort of thing one might expect to see in a king's palace. The likes of Napoleon and the Tsar of Russia no doubt had dined at such a table while entertaining monarchs and queens.

The two brothers, Rose could see, were already out of sorts with one another. They had been at odds since Lucian first introduced his plan to go to Texas. Llewellyn, conversely, held steadfast to his idea of going north.

What concerned all of them, however, was Ephraim. There had been little word from New Orleans since the raid on Grande Terre. They had not anticipated the attack, and therefore, there was no plan of action. Ephraim surely knew about the raid by now, but he had no way of knowing where to find them. Rose doubted that it mattered. He hadn't mentioned it to the brothers, but Rose suspected that Ephraim had been murdered before the raid. At the very least he was probably in the Calaboose with Captain Youx, but the discipline of the New Orleans militia told Rose that arrest was unlikely. They'd probably raided the warehouse and killed anyone in their way.

Cort approached from behind and took a seat next to Rose.

"The count is three-hundred and twenty-two men, sir." he told Rose.

"Thank you, Captain," Rose answered.

Lafitte wanted an exact count, though Rose had no idea why. At this point the difference between three hundred and three hundred and twenty-two was of little consequence. But Lafitte was the commander, and quite frankly, needed something to do since there was virtually nothing to occupy his time except to ride the horse and act like a General. So he ordered an exact head count.

Lafitte seated himself at the head of the table, the end that was under the tent. Though he dared not laugh, Rose couldn't help but find something terribly comical about a pirate in a military uniform seated in an ornate chair at an ornate table under a makeshift tent on a barren, snake-infested island.

"Now that we're all here, gentlemen, your reports?" Lafitte asked as he looked at Cort. "Captain?"

Rose wondered if Lafitte knew Cort's name.

"Three hundred and twenty-two men, sir. All have begun both infantry and artillery training. Currently, I have the better shooters assigned as infantry and the rest manning the big guns," Cort reported.

"The better shots meaning the men who can hit a house if it doesn't move," Lafitte said lightly.

There was a round of obligatory laughter.

Lafitte looked at Lucian. "Lieutenant?"

"The armory is completed. The mess will be completed by the end of tomorrow," he said. "We have a limited supply of materials for barracks, though."

"Thank you Lieutenant. We'll have to keep some of the ships here for the men to have shelter. I doubt that this little paradise will draw any attention," Lafitte said and then turned to Llewellyn. "Lieutenant?"

"There's food and water for the next week available on the island. I would like to go with Captain Gambi to Galveztown to inventory the supplies. There are a number of things that we need, and I think we can do a better job if I'm there to supervise," he answered.

"Excellent idea," Lafitte answered. "The sooner the better."

"I have already made the arrangements, Monsieur." Captain Gambi told Lafitte.

"At your earliest," Lafitte replied. "Major Rose?"

"The Captain has training going according to schedule," Rose answered. "I would, with your permission sir, like to travel to New Orleans and study the terrain."

"You've decided that the British won't attack from Barataria Bay?" Lafitte asked.

"The route north from Barataria would be long and difficult. The British won't attempt it without guides. Napoleon would, but not the English. I suspect that they will establish a base somewhere on Lake Borgne from which to attack."

"The same thought occurred to me," Lafitte replied. "Lake Borgne seems the most likely route. Can you leave today?"

"Yes sir," he replied, surprised that Lafitte had come to a similar conclusion.

"Good. One of our smugglers, Broussard, has a farm near here. He'll guide you," Lafitte told him. "Is there anything else?"

"Sir?" Lucian asked.

"Yes, Lieutenant?"

"I'd like permission to go with Louis to New Orleans to look for our brother."

Lafitte thought for a moment and then asked, "The construction?"

"It's well under way, sir. I'm sure it can be completed without me," Lucian replied.

"I'm hesitant because quite honestly, I don't think that your brother is alive," Lafitte said and then paused to let that sink in.

Once again Lafitte's instinct caught Rose by surprise.

"The New Orleans militia acted like barbarians at Grande Terre, and they call us pirates? I'm sure that they did the same thing in the city, but if you wish to go, I certainly won't stop you," he said.

"Thank you," Lucian answered.

"There's a lawyer named Moreau. He has an office on Canal Street. If your brother is alive, Moreau will know where to find him," Lafitte added.

Chapter 13

FORT ST. LEON
October 24, 1818

State Legislative Representative, John Blanque, had been waiting weeks for an opportunity to pay a visit to the garrison. Of course, it wasn't a real garrison. It wasn't, in fact, a garrison at all. It was actually a collection of stonewalls and buildings constructed years ago by the Spanish to protect their horses from Indian raids. Later the French added a few more walls and called it Fort St. Leon.

Officially the "Garrison," as Fort St. Leon was known, was the last defense against any hostile ships approaching New Orleans from the Gulf, the first line of defense being Fort St. Philip some sixty miles to the south. The "Garrison" only housed a small contingent of soldiers whose only real function was to carry the flag during the annual Independence Day celebration, a celebration that was ignored by the eighty percent of the city's population who knew nothing of the significance of that day.

The city was on the edge of panic. As a result, a number of businessmen, led by former Congressman Ed Livingston, had organized under the title of the "Committee for Public Safety," though most of the members were far more concerned with the economic impact of a British-owned New Orleans than the security of the public. Nevertheless, since no one had any confidence in Governor Claiborne's ability to deal with the crisis, they were in the process of framing a letter to send directly to General Jackson, circumventing the Governor. Blanque agreed in concept but convinced the group that before taking action, they should know the nature of Lafitte's meeting with the British. Thus, he was elected to have a discussion with the prisoner in cellblock A. Blanque's problem was finding a way to see the prisoner without Claiborne knowing, especially since there officially wasn't a prisoner in cellblock A.

The raids on Barataria and Pirate Alley were shaping into a legal nightmare, with state, local, and federal officials arguing over just who had jurisdiction. The prisoners arrested at Grande Terre were currently held at the Calaboose, thus in the hands of the State, but everybody was fighting over who got to bring official charges.

The young man arrested at the Alley, though, was mistakenly taken to the garrison. It was rumored that the Lieutenant in charge of the raid had been injured, and the Englishman had saved his life. The officer had not been given orders regarding prisoners and therefore had brought the Englishman back to the garrison. This put the young man in the hands of the Army, and Colonel Ross, displaying his overwhelming incompetence, chose to hold the prisoner in his custody without charges until the jurisdiction issues with the prisoners from Barataria had been resolved.

Blanque could, of course, go to the Calaboose for the information he needed. Surely the famous Captain

Dominique Youx would know what had happened, but Blanque knew that it would be impossible to see Captain Youx without half the city, especially Claiborne, knowing.

The young Englishman was another matter.

All Blanque needed was to find a way to get in and out of the garrison without running into Ross, who would surely want to know what he was doing there and undoubtedly would report the visit to Governor Claiborne who would immediately attempt to take some sort of action against the Committee for Public Safety.

Fortunately, as it turned out, one of the committee members was able to provide a solution. Winston, the restaurateur who owned the Pearl Café, took Blanque to the side and explained that Claiborne held a weekly lunch meeting at the Pearl with his Board of Officers, Commodore Patterson, General Villeré and Colonel Ross. The luncheon usually lasted about two hours, but Winston was able to guarantee that this particular luncheon would have exceptionally slow service, ensuring that Colonel Ross would be unlikely to make the long ride to Fort St. Leon.

As Blanque rode in his carriage out to the garrison, he wondered if Lafitte or any of his men had survived the raid. He had heard several different stories as to exactly what had happened that morning. The only thing that the stories had in common was that the militia was more interested in looting Lafitte's warehouses than capturing any pirates. The official story had Lafitte killed in a fire after a cannon ball hit his house. At least, that is what was printed in the newspapers. A second version had Lafitte killed in gunfire, but since his body was not found, neither of these stories could be confirmed. A third story had a number of small boats escaping to the west. To Blanque this version made the most sense. Jean Lafitte was no fool. He would have had an escape plan.

What really made Blanque believe this version of events was Claiborne's reaction the day after the raid. The Governor was furious with Commodore Patterson and General Villeré and Colonel Ross. Claiborne wanted Lafitte either dead or behind bars. If he had thought for a moment that Lafitte was dead, he would have been celebrating. The fact that Claiborne was so angry suggested to Blanque that Claiborne knew that Lafitte had survived.

He really expected more difficulty getting into the garrison than he actually had. He should have, he thought, been questioned about his business as his driver drove his team through the gate. But they didn't raise so much as an eyebrow until he marched into the brig, where he approached a nappy little sergeant seated behind an enormous Spanish desk and requested to see the young Englishman arrested in Pirate Alley.

The little sergeant was dumbfounded by Blanque's presence - not so much at having an unannounced visit from a member of the State Legislature, but by having a prison visitor at all. Apparently the sergeant wasn't accustomed to having civilians request to meet with inmates and had no idea how to proceed. Blanque was in the process of passing the sergeant a ten-dollar gold piece when a young Lieutenant with his arm in a sling stepped out of one of the adjoining offices.

"Excuse me, sir. I'm Lieutenant Henderson. Did I hear you ask to see the Englishman?" The Lieutenant asked with a look of suspicion.

"Yes," Blanque answered trying to appear impatient.

"You're Mr. Blanque, are you not?" The Lieutenant asked.

"Yes, I am, and I'd like to speak with the Englishman right away, if you don't mind."

The Lieutenant turned to the sergeant. "I'll take care of this, Sergeant Evans."

Henderson walked out from behind the desk and motioned with his free hand for Blanque to follow.

The two men began walking down a long, dark hallway. There were cells on either side. All were empty.

"You're here to ask Ephraim about the British ship, aren't you?" The Lieutenant asked.

Blanque stopped in his tracks. He knew that his mission would raise some suspicion, but he had no idea that anyone would suspect the actual reason he was there.

Blanque looked at the Lieutenant and answered, "Yes I am."

"I'm guessing that the citizens are trying to decide what to do," the Lieutenant stated.

"Something like that."

"Ross is acting like a fool. He thinks that this is his golden opportunity to make general. He and General Villeré and the Commodore all think that they'll be heroes. The Commodore is already considering a run for President."

Blanque looked back at Lieutenant Henderson with a new respect, although he never expected to hear a lieutenant question the good judgment of his colonel.

"Lieutenant, this is important. Do you know if the Governor sent word to General Jackson of the possible invasion?" Blanque asked.

The Lieutenant looked down the hall at Sergeant Evens to make sure he didn't overhear the conversation.

"He did," The Lieutenant answered, "but he emphasized that the information came from pirates and therefore was not reliable."

While Blanque was taking that in, the Lieutenant added, "Sir, with twelve thousand troops, they will roll right over Colonel Ross and General Villeré."

As the two continued down the hall, it occurred to Blanque that the lieutenant not only knew about the British ship, which was common knowledge, but he knew just how many troops the British were allegedly bringing. Even Blanque didn't know that.

He looked back at the Lieutenant. "Were you wounded in combat, Lieutenant?"

"I was shot when we were closing down Pirate Alley," he answered.

They stopped at a cell. The door was open, and the Lieutenant put his head in.

"Ephraim, you have a visitor," the Lieutenant said.

Blanque stepped to the door. Unlike the other cells, this one had a bed with a cushion. There was also a cushioned chair where a tall young man sat with his legs crossed, reading a book.

The young man looked up from his book. "Ah, thanks, Johnny."

"I'll leave you two alone. The Colonel won't be back for a while, so take your time, Mr. Blanque," the Lieutenant said and walked away.

The young man stood and put out his hand. "I'm Ephraim Bradford."

"John Blanque," Blanque said, looking around the room. "I see that they are treating you well."

"Johnny got the chair and some books."

"Johnny?"

"Lieutenant Henderson," Ephraim explained. "He thought it would be okay since the Colonel never comes down here. You're not going to tell the Colonel, are you? I'd hate for Johnny to get into trouble."

"Of course not. I need to ask you some questions."

"Okay. Please, sit down. Would you like some water?" Ephraim offered, motioning to a table where there was a pitcher and a glass.

"No, I'm fine son," Blanque said as he sat down on the chair. Ephraim sat on the bed across from him. "I'm going to get right to it. Jean Lafitte was an old friend of mine. You know that they raided the island and probably killed him, don't you?"

"I know about the raid, but I don't think that he's dead," Ephraim answered.

"You seem confident."

Ephraim clearly looked uneasy.

"I mean it, son. I consider Jean a friend."

"Johnny told me that some militiamen saw boats escape to the west. He said that they didn't kill anyone. They could have captured everyone, but the militia was more interested in raiding the warehouses than taking prisoners. He thinks that they all got away. He said that one man told him that he definitely saw Captain Lafitte leaving," Ephraim explained.

"Good," Blanque said, a bit relieved. "Jean is probably relaxing in Mexico."

"I don't think so."

"Why?"

"Captain Lafitte was in the process of moving off Grande Terre. They were going to a hideout to train his army. He is planning to attack the British as they land."

Blanque smiled. Only someone as arrogant as Jean Lafitte would consider attacking a seasoned army of twelve thousand with a few hundred pirates.

"He'll be destroyed," Blanque said, amused at the idea.

"I think that they will have a good plan," Ephraim said confidently. "His military advisor is Lieutenant Louis Rose of Napoleon's eighty-second infantry. He's a real soldier. Louis is planning hit and run attacks with cannons. Captain

Lafitte has a lot of cannons. They will take out a lot of British troops."

"You really believe that the British are coming, don't you, son?" Blanque asked.

"Yes sir, I do. I saw them."

Blanque's eyes widened. "What happened?"

"We woke up, and their gunship was sitting just off shore. They could have blown us off the island if they had wanted to. After sunrise some officers came ashore and had breakfast with Captain Lafitte. They offered him amnesty in exchange for his assistance with their attack. He was furious when they left. He immediately sent me to warn the Governor and to offer to help."

"Jean was always a bit of a hothead."

Blanque stood up to leave.

"I should be going," he said. "Is there anything I can do for you?"

"Can you get me out of here?"

"Probably not, but there is a lawyer in town who does some work for Lafitte. I'll see what he can do. Is there anything else?"

"I have two brothers who were on Grande Terre. If you hear anything of Captain Lafitte and his men, will you let them know that I'm okay?"

Blanque suddenly realized that the young man he was talking to was no more than a teenager.

"I know some of the people who live in the bayous. I'd bet that there are a lot of people out there who know where Jean is. I'll see what I can do," Blanque promised.

He shook Ephraim's hand and turned to leave.

"Thank you, sir."

Blanque could see that there was something on the boy's mind. "Is there something else?"

"Ah. Sir, I don't know how to ask this."

"Try me kid. I'm in a good mood," Blanque said, suddenly aware that he liked the boy.

"Sir, there's this girl. I was about to go see her when I was arrested. She probably thinks that I'm dead or something," Ephraim said.

"What's her name?"

"Charlotte Fuller, sir. Johnny's been looking for her but hasn't had any luck."

"I'll ask around. I promise."

"Thank you, sir. I really appreciate it," Ephraim said humbly.

#

STEPHEN F. AUSTIN UNIVERSITY
Nacogdoches, Texas, 2002

Jeb Bradford sat in his office munching on a cold ham and cheese sandwich. It had been months since he'd had lunch in there. Of course, using the word "office" was a bit of an exaggeration. The room was barely more than a closet. He had a desk and two chairs, one for him and one for a student to use while trying to justify spending a night before an exam partying instead of studying.

His desk was a cluttered mess of papers and books. The little room, which wasn't more than five feet by ten feet, was lined with stacks of books and old exams. Jeb had long-since intended to throw the exams out but had neglected them to the point that he hardly noticed their existence.

It occurred to him that what he really needed to do was to call Kay. She would have a field day with the place. There was little she liked more than throwing out his things.

Jeb sat back in his chair and propped his feet up on his desk and took a long sip of his Coca-Cola. That was a treat in itself since Kay only allowed sugar-free soft drinks around the house. All things considered, he was enjoying his first day away from the plant.

Today all he had on his agenda was a couple of lectures and one student meeting, all of which had already been completed. And really the students weren't that bad. Most were bright and energetic kids who wanted to learn. Granted, there was the guy with a dozen lip rings and the girl in his nine o'clock who not only had her head shaved but also had some sort of mystical dragon tattoo on the side of it. But Jeb had noticed over the years that some of those kids were the brightest and showed a lot of promise.

Quite frankly, Jeb was having the most enjoyable and relaxing day he had experienced in recent memory. Since going back to the plant, teaching was just something he had to do every day before going to work. He had forgotten that he actually liked teaching. He even took a walk through campus and got a sandwich at the snack bar. He couldn't recall the last time he'd walked in there. In fact, the Student Union had undergone a complete remodeling a few years ago, and this was the first time he had seen it.

Just as he was getting really comfortable, he glanced down the hall and caught Rob Skinner's eye. Rob, in Jeb's opinion, was the perfect stereotype of how a college instructor was supposed to look. The reason, as Jeb realized some years before, was that Rob wore the uniform. In the business world a professional wears a suit and a tie. But in academia the professional wears a pair of well worn dark slacks, a shirt that needs ironing, a mustard-stained tie, and most importantly, a corduroy jacket with patches on the sleeves. Jeb, of course, was the rebellious sort and had always worn jeans and whatever shirt Kay had picked out that day.

Rob, though, pulled the look off because he was, in fact, a professional educator. Jeb always felt like an intruder on this sacred ground. Frankly, most of the professors treated him as such, but Rob didn't. Rob had gone out of his way to mentor Jeb in the early days. That was long before Rob had become chair of the History department.

Rob saw Jeb looking down the hall and came into Jeb's office.

"Hi, Jeb. Got a minute?" Skinner asked.

"I've got all afternoon. Sit down,"

Rob took a seat and asked, "Did you get hit in the layoff?"

Jeb was instantly reminded of the last time he'd had a boss come to his office and ask to talk. He felt something in the pit of his stomach and wondered if this meeting would end like the last.

"Yeah. I take it you heard?"

"Just what I read in the paper. You guys going to be okay?"

"Kay says that we are. I have my doubts. I don't miss that job, though. I have to tell you, I could get used to being a full-time educator," Jeb replied.

"Good, we'll like having you around. You know, we have a faculty basketball league. The History department team stinks. We could really use you."

Jeb smiled, "Thanks Rob. Give me a few days. I have a feeling that Kay's got a list of projects for me now that I have some 'free time'."

"About that," Rob hesitated for a moment. "Remember that staff meeting where the Dean suggested that everyone try to get published?"

"Yeah, but I don't recall it being a suggestion."

"I had a talk with the Dean and, well, don't feel obligated right now."

Jeb was somewhat taken aback by the statement. "Excuse me?"

"I know that you're under a lot of stress with your daughter and all," Skinner answered. "How is she doing?"

"Better. With time and a lot of therapy, she should have a fairly normal life, but what about this book thing?"

"Jeb, you've been on edge for weeks. I'm just saying that you don't need to feel pressured."

"You think I've been on edge?"

"You've been holding down two jobs. You've got three small kids and one of them just had life-threatening back surgery. Pressure like that would get to anybody," Rob explained.

Jeb sat silent, processing his boss's statement.

"Being a dad isn't easy. Things like what happened to your daughter - that's what life is all about," Rob earnestly added.

Jeb stared at his friend a moment and then asked, "Rob, did you ever feel like...like you missed something? Like you should have done something more with your life?"

"Every father feels that," Rob told him as he stood up to leave. "Anyway, don't worry about a book right now."

"Actually, I started something. I think I'm going to try to finish it, now that I have more time."

"What are you working on?"

"I've got this old uncle with a load of stories. I used to think that he was full of crap, but some of his stories seem to have some merit. I'm not sure, but I think that I've got this great grandfather, once or twice removed, who had something to do with Jean Lafitte."

"I'm intrigued. Lafitte was a fascinating character. You know, Jim Bowie was one of his cronies."

"That's what my uncle tells me. To be honest, I don't really know where to start. It's going to take a ton of research."

"There's a guy named Parker over at Louisiana Tech," Rob told him. "He's done some stuff on Lafitte and Bowie. He's got some letters and documents. Give him a call. He's good guy. Probably has a bunch of stuff you can look at. Come by my office later. I've got his number there someplace."

#

CANAL STREET, NEW ORLEANS
October 24, 1814

Lucian was tired, sweaty, and dirty. The trip from Devil's Island was longer and a lot more difficult than he had anticipated. For most of the trip they were on small boats poling up endless miles of bayous and marshes. Louis was troubled from the outset, realizing that it was clearly impossible for them to move several hundred men and cannons over that sort of terrain.

Lucian though, was not concerned with the war. He had come to New Orleans for two reasons: to find Charlotte and to meet with this lawyer, Moreau.

Reggie had warned Lucian not to trust Moreau. He said the man was as crooked as they come. "He's afraid of the Bos, but be careful. He'll turn on you if he thinks that the Bos is out of business. Don't trust him. Tell him that the Bos wants him to look for Ephraim. Then get out of town."

Lucian didn't know the Major well, but he wasn't going to question his assessment of Moreau, and he didn't intend to waste time in New Orleans. If he was recognized as one of Lafitte's men, he would surely be arrested or even shot. His plan was to meet with Moreau then go to Cheri Royal and see Charlotte. Right after dark he would go to the river road where he'd meet Rose and Broussard, their guide. They would then follow the river road south and return to Devil's Island on Captain Gambi's ship.

Lucian had no trouble finding Moreau's building. It was exactly as Reggie had described, a narrow red brick building that looked like it was squeezed in between two other buildings. In fact, the building had been built in what was previously an alley and looked from a distance like someone had pushed a building into a narrow gap.

He did just as Reggie had told him. "Go up the first flight of stairs. Moreau's office is on the second floor under the steps leading up to the third floor."

Sure enough, up one flight he walked through the narrow hall around the stairs and found a door with Moreau's name upon it.

When Lucian reached the door he was suddenly perplexed as to what he should do. He'd never been to a lawyer's office before. Was he supposed to knock or was he supposed to just walk in? He stood there for a moment pondering when he heard voices from inside. The lawyer was meeting with someone. Now Lucian really didn't know what to do. He thought for moment or two and finally came to the conclusion that he should wait outside the door for the lawyer's customer to leave.

Then as he was just about to walk away he heard the name "Lafitte" come from inside. Previously he hadn't really listened to what was being said. Frankly, he was too busy trying to decide what to do. Now, though, they had his attention. Then he heard a man's voice say, "Ephraim Bradford".

#

Blanque had rushed back to his office from the Garrison. The last thing he needed was to run into Colonel Ross along the road. He despised the Colonel. Blanque had studied at Ecole Polytechnique in Paris, one of the most prestigious military institutions in the world. He had dined with Napoleon and any number of his Generals, and if the Emperor had not been desperate for cash and sold Louisiana to Thomas Jefferson, Blanque would, no doubt, have become a Colonel or possibly even one of the Emperor's Generals. The truth was that Blanque knew a real soldier when he met one, and Colonel Ross was not a real soldier. Blanque had always thought of Ross as a short, fat bureaucrat in uniform. That, in Blanque's reasoning, was probably why Claiborne and Ross were such tight buddies. They were both fat, little bureaucrats.

The boy held at the Garrison had confirmed that the British were definitely coming. He also confirmed that Jean Lafitte was not only alive; he was planning to take a few hundred men and mount his own private campaign against the British. Lafitte's plan would be comical if not for the fact that he was the only thing stopping the British Army from burning New Orleans to the ground.

Blanque waited until late afternoon to meet with Moreau. He knew from previous dealings that the man could not be trusted. But Moreau was probably the only person in New Orleans who would try to help the boy in cellblock A.

Blanque was standing in Moreau's little office telling him to get Lafitte's man out of that Garrison when suddenly the door opened, revealing an enormous Englishman.

"Did one of you say the name 'Ephraim Bradford'?" Lucian asked.

Moreau, for a moment just stared at the huge man, not knowing if he should be angry or afraid.

Blanque realized immediately from the thick English accent that this man had to be one of the boy's brothers. There was even a strong family resemblance.

"You're his brother?" Blanque asked.

Lucian just nodded, looking at the two men. He didn't trust either.

"Come in, quickly," Blanque said. "Close the door."

Lucian stepped in. With the desk and the law books there was hardly any room for the three men in the tiny office.

"I'm John Blanque; this is Edward Moreau," Blanque told him. "I'm a friend of your Bos. I've just come from seeing your brother. He's being held at the Army Garrison."

"I'm Lucian," Lucian said.

"Look, if this kid is out at the Garrison, there's nothing I can do about it," Moreau argued, not interested in getting in a fight with the Army.

"Just go and find out what he's charged with. We'll meet later and find a way to get him released." Moreau countered.

"Who do I say that I'm working for? The Army is going to ask," replied Moreau.

Blanque was growing impatient with the man. "Tell them the truth. Tell them that you work for Lafitte. Everybody in town knows that you work for Lafitte."

"But Jean Lafitte is dead," Moreau argued.

"Jean's alive and we both know it," Blanque answered. "He's at his hideout on Cat Island."

Blanque and Lucian locked eyes. Lucian had to think about it for a moment but realized that this Blanque fellow didn't trust this crooked lawyer either.

"I just left him. He told me to send you to get Ephraim out," Lucian said.

Moreau looked up at Lucian, not wanting to start an argument with the man.

"I'll go out there tomorrow afternoon, but I can't promise that I can get him out," Moreau conceded.

"Go tomorrow morning. I want you to be sober," Blanque replied.

Moreau glared at Blanque, but the Legislator ignored him. Lucian decided that, though he wasn't sure if he trusted

Blanque, he definitely liked the way the man handled himself.

"Lucian, you and I should go for a walk. Do you have any more business with Moreau?" Blanque asked.

"No. Captain Lafitte said that he'd get my brother free. That's all," Lucian replied.

"Moreau, I'll be back here tomorrow," Blanque said to the lawyer as he led Lucian out the door.

#

Lucian followed Blanque out of the building and on to Canal Street. He started to speak, but Blanque motioned for him to keep quiet. They walked to the Pearl Café where Winston greeted them.

"Monsieur Blanque. Welcome," Winston said. "How was your day?"

"It was quite interesting. Thank you for making it possible. I hope you didn't anger any customers," Blanque replied

"Unfortunately, those four patrons will return," Winston said with a smile.

"Can we have a private room? This gentleman has come from the bay and has news of our friend who used to live there. As you can guess, it would not do for him to be noticed," Blanque asked.

"Certainly. This way," Winston said.

Lucian, not understanding a word of the conversation, followed them into the restaurant. It was essentially a long, narrow room with booths along one side, some tables in the middle, and a bar along the opposite wall. The place was almost empty. Winston took them to a door in the back. Lucian looked in and saw what appeared to be a large booth that closed for privacy. Lucian and Blanque stepped in and sat down while Winston closed the door and left.

"I come here often. This room allows us to speak without worrying that we may be overheard," Blanque said. "First things first. Your brother is well. He's made a friend out of the lieutenant in charge of the garrison. The lieutenant is making sure that he's reasonably comfortable."

"Who are you, and why are you helping my brother?" Lucian asked.

"I'm sorry. I'm John Blanque. I'm in the State Legislature," Blanque said. "I consider your Bos a friend,"

There was a soft knock on the door.

"Yes, Winston," Blanque said.

The door opened and Winston sat two cups on the table and filled both with coffee.

"Thank you Winston," Blanque said.

"Will there be anything else, sir?" Winston asked.

"No, that will be all," Blanque told him, and the man closed the door and left.

Blanque took a sip of coffee and looked at Lucian. "Were you at the island during the raid?"

"Yes," Lucian replied. "Most of us got away."

"I thought as much. The papers said that everyone was killed, but Jean's too smart for that. Claiborne's a fool. He hates the sight of Lafitte. He thinks of Jean as nothing but a common criminal," Blanque explained and then asked, "Forgive me for asking, but you look familiar to me. Have we met?"

"I don't think so," Lucian replied. "I ran Mr. Lafitte's Bazaar. Did you ever come out there?"

"Of course. I remember now," answered Blanque. "You should be careful while you're in the city. If you're recognized, you'll end up in the Calaboose. What are your plans? Are you going back to where Jean is training his men?"

There was surprise look on Lucian's face.

"Your brother told me that Jean is putting together a militia," Blanque explained.

"I'm leaving tonight," Lucian said.

"Good. I need you to take a message for me to Jean," Blanque explained. "Tell him that I'm going to send word of the British plan to General Jackson. He's in Mobile. Tell him that Jackson is much more level-headed than our Governor."

"I will," Lucian answered.

"Also tell him that Moreau is trying to help Captain Youx and his men, but, frankly, it's a legal nightmare. It's going to take a while," Blanque added.

"Is there anything else?" Lucian asked.

"Yes. Your brother asked me to get a message to his girl. Do you know where I can find her?" Blanque asked.

Again there was surprise on Lucian's face. "He's never said anything to me about a girl. I really don't know."

"Too bad. I was hoping you could help me," said Blanque, looking at his watch. "I need to get back to my office. When I leave, wait a few minutes. Winston will lead you out the back way. Try not to be seen."

"I will, and thank you for helping Ephraim," Lucian responded.

Blanque stood and the two men shook hands.

"Be careful, Lucian. I mean it," Blanque said warmly and then exited.

Lucian sat there a moment and thought about his little brother having a girl. He thought how nice it would be if they all went to Texas and settled together.

Then his daydream was interrupted by a knock at the door. Winston opened it and put his head in.

"Come with me, please, sir," the waiter said.

#

Charlotte walked slowly up Tchoupitoulas through the warehouse district. This was the first time she had been along this street since the day she first saw Ephraim and thought that he was a thief. Actually, she avoided this street for the very reason that she feared ever seeing him again, but at the same time she wanted badly to run in to him.

She had made a habit of taking long walks in the afternoon. She did so partly for some exercise but mostly to get out of the Cheri Royal. Those were just excuses. Inside she longed to see his eyes once more. Even if all she got was a glance from across the street, she desperately wanted just one more time to see him.

Most of her walks took her through places like the River Front near the Place d'Armes, but always her walks wound up on Canal Street passing the Pearl Cafe. As always, she walked on the far side of the street to avoid "accidentally" running into Ephraim if he sat outside having coffee with some other young woman. She always walked slowly, never actually admitting to herself but secretly hoping that he would be sitting at that same table all alone.

Even now the thought of that day brought a tear to her eyes. She had expected that she would be past tears by now, but apparently the heart had its own timetable.

When she came to the corner of Tchoupitoulas and Canal she looked at the spot where she was attacked and remembered the look on Ephraim's face when that man had tossed him so easily to the ground. The memory brought a smile to her face, and then the memory of him stumbling over the little lady on Royal Street popped into her mind and she saw him smile again. She fought back the tears this time. Still, she refused to let go of the memory. She was growing to cherish that picture of his smile. Smiles were far too rare on Bourbon Street, and a genuine smile was almost never seen in Cheri Royal.

She crossed Canal and headed up the street opposite the Pearl like she did every day. As always, Mr. Winston was there to greet customers. And, as he did whenever she passed, he nodded her direction with a consoling expression as if to say, "I'm sorry, dear. I haven't seen him today."

She then turned the corner and headed up Bourbon Street and back to her little prison.

Charlotte entered through the front door as always. Usually there would be one or two of the "Ladies" sitting somewhere in the saloon. Today Dianna was there alone. Charlotte started to go up to her room, but as she entered Dianna stood and came to her.

"Charlotte, there's a gentleman here to see you," Dianna said, motioning her to the bar.

Charlotte hadn't noticed the large man standing at the bar. That was probably because she had no reason to expect anyone. On those occasions when someone did come in the afternoon, they usually didn't come in to drink. They just headed directly upstairs with whoever happened to be available.

When her eyes adjusted she recognized the man. He was Lucian, the man from the island. She didn't usually remember names here. Names were the sort of things she tried to forget, but he was different.

"This gentleman asked specifically for you," Dianna continued. "He insisted on waiting."

Charlotte instantly switched on her work smile. It really wasn't a smile, though. It was just a face she made to get her through another night.

"Charlotte," he said with a sense of excitement in his voice.

"Lucian, it's so good to see you again," she said with a sincerity that she had trained herself to show.

Lucian was clearly uncomfortable.

"Can we go somewhere? I haven't much time." He asked.

"Of course," Charlotte replied. "I wish I had been here when you came in. I wasn't expecting you."

She took his hand and led him up the stairs. His hand was warm, but she could feel it trembling, reminiscent of that night on the island. He had held her so tightly all night long but hadn't asked for anything from her. He was the only person she had met since coming to New Orleans who was genuinely nice to her, with the exception of Ephraim, of course. She felt the muscles in her stomach tense up. She tried hard not to think of Ephraim while in Cheri Royal. For some reason it was more painful in there.

Perhaps, she thought to herself, that was why she liked so much to take her afternoon walks. It was okay to remember him outside of those walls.

They walked silently up the stairs and then down the hall to the third door on the left. When she opened the door and they stepped in Lucian, took her into his arms and pulled her to him. At first she tensed up again and started to resist but then realized that he just wanted to hold her.

As he held her she tried very hard to relax the way she had that night on the island. But weeks of coming into this room, pretending to be someone that she wasn't, had made it difficult for her to simply be herself.

He slowly let go of her, "You're all I've thought about."

She stood for a moment not knowing what to say. Finally she said the only thing that really came to her mind. "We thought that all of you had been killed."

He looked at her, somewhat taken back.

"When they raided the island, the paper said that all of the pirates were dead," she explained.

Lucian smiled, "They didn't kill anybody. They just looted the warehouses. A few people were captured, but the rest of us got away."

Charlotte smiled at him. She was genuinely happy that he was okay. When she had read the account in the paper, she was saddened that he may have been killed.

"I'm so glad that you're all right," she said and took hold of him and hugged him again.

"Charlotte?" he asked.

She let him loose and looked up at him.

"I'm going to Texas with some friends. I want you come with me," he told her.

Charlotte smiled patronizingly at him but suddenly saw Ephraim's little boy sweetness and disappointment in his eyes. She wondered if her memory of Ephraim was that strong because Lucian really did seem to have that same boy-like look.

"Lucian, I can't," she said.

"Why not?" He asked with bewilderment.

"Lucian, you know what I am," she said sensibly.

He took hold of both her hands. "I know what you do, but this place isn't who you are. Come with me. Become my wife. I'll take care of you. I promise. I'll always take care of you."

As she looked into his eyes she felt a tear beginning to build. She was hearing words that she so longed to hear, but with the wrong voice.

Lucian took her back into his arms. This time it was Charlotte that began to tremble. A million thoughts were going through her mind, and she tried desperately to sort them out. Her first instinct was to tell him that she could never go with him, but then she realized that Ephraim was not ever coming back and would never love her. Lucian was a good man who wanted desperately to love and care for her. He was standing there asking her to let him take her from New Orleans and Cheri Royal forever. Even though she thought she might never have the feelings for him that she felt for Ephraim, she knew that he looked at exactly who she was and still found a way to love her.

Charlotte slowly pulled away from his chest and looked into his eyes. "When do we go?"

Chapter 14

DEVIL'S ISLAND, LOUISIANA
November 7, 1814

The *Petit Milan* had long-since lowered her sails and begun to drift with the Gulf current below the south side of the island. Captain Gambi ordered that the anchor be dropped, and Louis Rose felt a strong tug as the ship held-to and then turned until her nose pointed against the flow of the warm Gulf-stream waters.

For almost an hour they could hear the constant burst of cannon fire along with small arms. Early on, Rose had questioned the wisdom of using so much of their ammunition on training purposes, but Lafitte assured him that they had near endless resources. The pirate had learned early in his career that he could sell almost anything in New Orleans without raising any eyebrows. The governmental officials, though, would be considerably less accommodating should he be marketing cannons and powder. Thus over the years his stockpiles had become quite substantial.

Rose kept a keen eye on the island as he, Lucian, and Broussard, led by Captain Gambi, climbed off of the ship onto a small boat to take them ashore.

Broussard, in contrast to Rose's first impression, proved to be an exceptional guide. He looked to be at least seventy years old, but as Rose decided later, he was probably no more than forty-five or fifty at most. He was a short man with dark skin that had been so weathered from hard work and harsh sunshine that it looked more like boot leather than human flesh. His hair was long and gray, and he had a gray-white beard that was matted in some places and tobacco stained in others.

By simply looking at the man, Rose would never have imagined that that he owned a plantation, nor would he have imagined that Broussard was one of the wealthiest landowners in the state. Born and raised in Louisiana, he descended from some of the very first French settlers. Unlike most of Lafitte's men, he had used the money he'd earned smuggling and his knowledge of the area to purchase some of the best parcels of land in the region.

His familiarity of the terrain proved invaluable to Rose. He not only moved through the bayous with ease, he knew every spot on the map where an army might land. And equally important, he understood military tactics having spent much of his life fighting Indians and serving as a scout for both the French and the Americans.

When they stepped off of the boat and onto the island, the first thing Rose saw was Lafitte in uniform riding his horse past a line of cannons. He couldn't help but think that this smuggler was, without question, the most egotistical man he had ever met. To presume that just putting on a coat and mounting a horse made him a soldier was the ultimate in arrogance.

As that very thought was passing through his mind, Rose realized that the man on the horse was not Lafitte but was rather Cort, the young black Spaniard. To his surprise, at the cannon nearest them, he saw Jean Lafitte, sweaty and shirtless, lighting a fuse.

A moment later his shot hit his target, a group of barrels. He and the three other men manning the cannon immediately cheered and celebrated. Rose concluded that Cort had made a competition of the firing exercises, and by the look of things, Lafitte's team seemed to be winning.

As Rose, Broussard, Lucian, and Gambi walked to the command post, Rose couldn't help smiling once again when he looked at the ridiculously long table sticking out of the canvas tent. Broussard apparently saw his expression and said in his heavy Creole accent, "Only Jean would put a king's table under a canvas tent on a desert island and act as if it is perfectly normal."

It was Gambi who first lost control and began to laugh. Soon all four men were laughing as they took seats at the table, realizing that they all had been thinking the same thing.

There was still a jovial mood when Lafitte, now in his uniform tunic, along with Cort, Reggie, and two of the ship captains, entered the tent. Cort took his seat next to Rose while Lafitte took his usual position at the head of the table.

"I apologize that I wasn't able to meet your boat, gentlemen, but the young Captain had me manning one of the guns," Lafitte told them.

Rose looked at his junior officer, who remained motionless in his blue officer's coat.

"I decided that it was ridiculous for the men to be trained soldiers while their officers remain nothing more than civilians," Lafitte told them.

Lafitte looked at Rose and waited for a reaction. Only then did Rose realize that the man wanted his approval.

"I think that is an excellent idea, sir," Rose responded.

"It is foolish," Lafitte continued, "for our men to be trained and the rest of us not. I want each officer to be capable of handling any position on a heavy gun team, and if possible, to receive a perfect score with a rifle."

Listening, it occurred to Rose that he might have badly underestimated this man.

"Score sir?" Rose asked

"The Captain can explain," Lafitte replied, indicating for Cort to speak.

"I needed a way to evaluate marksmanship," Cort explained. "We have targets set at different distances. For a perfect score the soldier has to hit each from a standing, kneeling, and prone position."

Rose was again reminded that this was a very bright young man beside him.

"It has been quite effective. The men are enjoying the competition," Lafitte said. "What are the results, Captain?"

"Sixty percent of the men have scored perfect," Cort said. "The rest are at various stages. I expect at least ten percent more to have a perfect score within the week. Another five percent should have what we deemed to be an excellent score. The rest are at various levels because of poor eyesight or other handicaps."

"One of my men is missing an eye. You cannot expect him to be a perfect shot," Gambi interjected.

"Actually that's not true, is it Captain?" Lafitte responded.

"There are two one-eyed men who have scored perfectly," Cort told them.

"And the others?" Lafitte asked with a proud smile.

"One man with a missing arm got a perfect score, and there are two men with only one leg who scored perfect standing and prone," Cort answered.

"We gave them an overall perfect score. We decided that they would probably have scored perfect kneeling, if they were, in fact, capable of kneeling," Lafitte said, bringing more laughter around the table.

Lafitte allowed the laughter to die and looked at Lucian. "Did you learn anything of your brother?" He asked.

"He's alive," Lucian told him. "I went to see the lawyer, Moreau. There was a man there named Blanque. He told me that he knows you, sir."

"John Blanque. He's in the State Legislature," Lafitte replied.

"He knew of Ephraim. Apparently Eph was arrested by the army in Pirate's Alley the day we were raided," said Lucian. "He's being held at the Garrison. Blanque went there to talk to him about the British attack. He said that Eph is in good shape and being treated well. He put a lot of pressure on Moreau."

"Blanque is a good man," Lafitte said. "He will do his best to help your brother. Did he say why he was interested in the British?"

"He doesn't see things the way the Governor does. He said that he is going to get word to some General named Jackman in Mobile that New Orleans is going to be attacked."

"Jackson?" Broussard asked.

"That's right," Lucian replied, realizing that he had forgotten the general's name.

"You know him?" Lafitte asked Broussard.

"I met him a few months ago," Broussard responded. "He was a politician and they made him head of the Tennessee Volunteers. When he won the Creek Indian War, the Army made him a General."

Lafitte thought for a moment then asked, "What do you think of him?"

"He's tough," Broussard replied, "and there's nothing he would like more than a chance to beat the British."

"What about us?" Lafitte asked. "Is he a man I can negotiate with?"

"His Tennessee militia was nothing but a bunch of possum-eating backwoodsmen, and I would bet my plantation that most of them had bounties on their heads."

"Good," Lafitte said and then turned to Rose. "What did you learn?"

"There are at least ten usable routes into the city," Rose began to explain. "But after seeing the roads and landscape, there are only three that are really likely: Lake Pontchartrain to the north, the west-river road from Barataria Bay, and Lake Borgne. Lake Pontchartrain is too shallow for their ships and much too visible for unarmed shallow-draft boats. Barataria is the best place to land troops, but it would be difficult to move through that terrain. And they would still have to cross the river before entering the city."

Lafitte looked at him, "Lake Borgne?"

"There are plenty of places where Admiral Cochrane can land his troops. The road is passable, and his men won't be cut off from their supply lines," Rose explained.

"And your plan?" Lafitte asked.

"Independently, we can only harass the British as they take the city," Rose said.

"But?"

Rose paused to choose his words carefully. "There is a place called Rodriquez's Canal."

"Above the Chalmette Plantation," Lafitte said.

"If I were this general, I would build an embankment along that canal. I measured it to be just under a thousand yards," Rose told them.

"Put our guns on the high ground and let them march into us?" Lafitte asked.

Once again Lafitte's intellect surprised Rose. "Exactly. It's possible that a couple of thousand men could hold off the attack if not defeat them entirely."

Lafitte leaned back in the massive chair and contemplated the news. "You really think they will land at Lake Borgne?"

"I have alternate plans, but my experience tells me that this is the route that Cochrane will choose. The British will know that there isn't a significant army presence in New Orleans, so they will expect little resistance."

Lafitte stood from his chair and turned his back to the men at the table.

The men silently watched him as he looked out at the water surrounding the island. As he watched, Rose realized that he had been wrong about this man. Jean Lafitte was not a pirate pretending to be a general. Lafitte was a general who lived the life of a pirate.

Standing with his back to them, Lafitte said, "That will be all, gentlemen. Major, will you remain and show me your plans on a map?"

"Yes sir," Rose said, with a newfound and unexpected respect for the man that everyone on the island called Bos.

#

CABILDO, NEW ORLEANS
Nov. 12, 1814

John Blanque was not sure why he had been summoned into the Governor's office. All he knew was that he and four other Legislators had been called to a secret meeting. The meeting was secret, of course, only in that there were a few drunken sailors passed out in Vieux Carré who had not yet heard about it. Like bureaucracies throughout the world, in the Louisiana State Government, the fastest way to get information to spread was to imply that it should be kept secret.

When he walked into the room, he was a little surprised by the group assembled. There were two other Legislators, four of the Governor's advisors, General Villeré along with his adjutant, Commodore Patterson and his aid, and Colonel Ross who was accompanied by Lieutenant Henderson. Blanque recalled that important officers had assistants with them at all times to take notes and run errands. Clearly, if a militia leader like Villeré had an assistant along, a regular Army Colonel like Ross couldn't show up without his attending officer.

Blanque took a seat next to another legislator just as the governor marched in, followed by his immediate secretary whose name Blanque could never remember.

"Gentlemen, I'm glad you are all here," Claiborne said as he hurriedly took his seat. "The British have been sighted in Lake Borgne."

Blanque sat silent. He glanced around the room at the other faces, seeing that their expressions were as emotionless as his.

Finally, the State Treasurer said, "Sir, didn't we get this report from Barataria a couple of months ago?"

"Yes, but this information comes from a reliable source," Claiborne said somewhat smugly as he nodded to Villeré.

"Two of my slaves spotted a British ship in the lake offshore from my plantation this morning," General Villeré reported. "I immediately sent my adjutant to confirm the report."

While you, Ross, Claiborne, and Patterson had gumbo, Blanque thought to himself.

"The question, gentlemen, is what are we to do with this information?" Claiborne asked.

"Governor, my men are ready and eager for a fight, and with Colonel Ross' troops, I am confident that we can defend the city," Villeré said proudly.

Lieutenant Henderson glanced at Blanque.

Blanque did the math in his head. The militia had between two and six hundred, depending on who was sober, and Ross had sixty regular soldiers. *Surely that would be sufficient against twelve thousand war-hardened troops*, he thought sarcastically.

"Thank you, General Villeré," Claiborne said, obviously having heard Villeré's petitions before. "I appreciate your confidence in your command."

Claiborne paused as if he expected agreement from the others present, but he got none. Everyone, with the exception of Ross, Patterson, Claiborne, and Villeré had concluded that Lafitte's report of a twelve-thousand-troop army was a possibility.

"Sir," the State Treasurer said, planning his words carefully, "I don't want to suggest that the militia is not capable, but if the British were to succeed?"

He paused to think a moment.

"Go on, Jefferson," Claiborne ordered.

Then, suddenly uncomfortable, the Treasurer continued, "Would we be capable of taking it back?"

Blanque watched as even Villeré seemed to take in the nature of the situation. Unexpectedly, the Governor looked at him. "Blanque, you've been quiet. What is your opinion?"

Blanque thought about playing it safe but then decided to put all his chips in. Claiborne had asked for his opinion, so he might as well give it. "Governor, you need to send an urgent plea for General Jackson to come immediately. If the British come, and it appears likely, they will come with a sizable force."

He turned to Villeré, "General, the British are just off victories against Napoleon, and I apologize if this offends you, Jacques, but you are no Napoleon. They bombarded Baltimore and burned Washington to the ground. They got pushed out of the Chesapeake because we had an army and navy there to do the job. There is no army or navy here. As we speak, Massachusetts and the rest of the New England states are debating secession because of this war. If they take this city, gentlemen, the New England states will secede, and that will be the end of the Union. The Republic that Washington and Jefferson and Adams and Hamilton gave us, and the men of Valley Forge fought and died for, will be no more, and all of us will become subjects of the King."

Everyone in the room was silent, taking in Blanque's statements. Of course, Claiborne had the same smug look on his face he always had when Blanque spoke, but then just as Blanque was about to open his mouth to make one more plea, Claiborne shocked him by asking, "Who do I send to Mobile?"

"Obviously, I should go," Colonel Ross said.

"No." Claiborne said flatly. "I want you and General Villeré to remain here and make preparations. Jackson may choose not to come, and we will need to defend this city ourselves."

"I'll send my adjutant, Colonel Clark," Villeré interjected.

"Governor," Blanque interrupted. "Might I suggest that you send Lieutenant Henderson? He's army, and as such, Jackson might be more inclined to listen to the opinions of an army officer than that of a militiaman."

"Agreed," said Claiborne, in a tone that ended any debate. "Henderson?" Claiborne asked, looking at the Lieutenant.

"I can leave immediately, sir," Henderson replied.

"Thank you, gentlemen. If you don't mind, I have a letter to draft. Lieutenant, you can wait outside," Claiborne ordered, ending the meeting.

\#

Blanque exited with the others but lingered a few moments outside Claiborne's office, speaking idly with Villeré while a few feet away Ross was giving orders to Lieutenant Henderson.

"As soon as the Governor gives you the letter, return to the Garrison. I want you to travel light. Take two soldiers with you and return with the General's answer as soon as possible," Ross ordered, making it clear to everyone in earshot that he was in command of this young officer and not the Governor.

He then turned to Villeré and Blanque. "Gentlemen, I'm going to Fort St. Philip to take inventory of my munitions," he said with way too much self-importance. "General, if it fits your schedule, I think we should meet at the end of the week and begin planning our strategies."

"That would be excellent," Villeré said. "Perhaps you could come out to my plantation for breakfast."

"Agreed," Ross said as he left the room.

"I'll be enlisting every able-bodied man in the militia. Can I count on you John? You'll be an officer, of course," Villeré asked Blanque.

"Certainly, Jacques, but I suspect the Legislature will be quite busy for a while."

"As long as you are available for the fight."

"Absolutely," Blanque said as the General reached out to shake his hand.

"Good. Now I must go. I have a war to plan," he said and then turned to Henderson. "Godspeed, Lieutenant."

When Villeré had left, Blanque turned to the Lieutenant. "Make sure you tell Jackson everything you know. Everything. Tell him about the early sighting. Tell him about the number of troops reported, and make sure you tell him about how weak our militia is."

"I will, sir," Henderson answered, and thank you for suggesting that I go to General Jackson."

"I've met Jackson, son. You may not be thankful after you meet him," Blanque said with a smile. "How's the wound?"

"Better. Thank you for asking, and Ephraim's doing fine too."

"Good."

"That lawyer is there every day demanding to see the charges," Henderson said.

"And Ross?"

"He keeps putting him off. I think that he'd let Eph out, but he's afraid of Claiborne."

Just that moment the Governor's door opened and the Governor's secretary put his head out.

"Lieutenant Henderson, you can come in now," Farnsworth ordered.

"His majesty is ready for you," Blanque said to Henderson in a tone loud enough for the Secretary to clearly hear. "Good luck, Lieutenant."

"Thank you, sir."

#

NACOGDOCHES, TEXAS

November, 2002

As he walked in the door, Jeb wondered just how long it would take him to get accustomed to coming home at three in the afternoon. He almost felt guilty, as if he was skipping work.

Sooner or later he would get over it, he thought. But he'd prefer if it was sooner. The feeling of guilt just compounded the stress around the house. Jeb had expected Kay to adjust to the circumstances, but, if anything, it had only gotten worse with time.

Of course, it was understandable. Kay had her hands full. The baby alone would have been enough, but then there was also Hannah. Not to mention Rebecca, who needed around the clock care, and if all that didn't overload her, there was Uncle Louie.

Jeb had decided early on that she just needed him to give her space. The best thing for him to do when he got home was to stay clear of Kay and help out with the girls. When the time came, Kay would begin to deal with the stress and she would become less difficult. That or they would have the fight to end all fights.

As soon as he got home, he would take his things up to his "study" and then head down to Rebecca's room to sit with her for a while. She had always been "Daddy's girl," and his being in there served two very important purposes. First, it took some pressure off Kay, who definitely needed it, and second, it kept him out of range of anything Kay might suddenly decide to hurl at him.

Every time he walked into Rebecca's room, his heart broke. They had moved her pretty little canopy bed out to make space for this mechanical monstrosity that the insurance company had rented. It wasn't as tall as a normal hospital bed, but it had all the motors and such to allow it to be positioned just right, which had, until just recently, been flat on her back. Now she could lie at a slight incline for a few hours at a time.

The part that was heartbreaking, though, was the tinker-toy looking frame-work wrapped around her. They had a harness contraption with rods attached that were designed to keep her relatively motionless except for when the therapist was around.

The therapy sessions were as much torture for him as for Rebecca. Fortunately, the therapist usually came while he was in class. He had experienced a few of those sessions at the hospital. It almost killed him to watch. Though she rarely complained, the expressions on Rebecca's face revealed the pain. Jeb had torn his meniscus playing high school basketball and knew full well about pain. But there was something so much more agonizing about watching his little girl go through it.

"Daddy," Rebecca said cheerfully as he came into her room.

He leaned down to kiss her forehead. "Hi, sweetheart. How have you been today?"

"Janice came," she answered cheerfully.

"Janice?"

"My therapist," she said as if he was the biggest dummy on earth.

"Oh."

"She drives a Jeep. And you know what?"

"No. What?" He answered, enjoying their little game.

"She brought her dog. He's a big Golden Retriever named Flannel."

"She brought her dog in here?" Jeb asked, wondering if that was a smart idea.

"Mommy said that it was okay," Rebecca explained as he made himself comfortable in the armchair next to her bed. "Daddy?"

"Yes, sweetheart?"

"Can we get a dog?"

"I think that's probably the kind of decision your mother would want to make," he replied.

"She said that it's up to you."

Jeb bit his tongue trying not to curse. How dare that woman. Now he had to be the bad guy.

"I don't know, baby. Hannah and Missy are awfully little for a dog," he answered as diplomatically as possible without giving an outright "no".

"But they loved Flannel, and Janice said that Goldens are real good with children," Rebecca pleaded.

Jeb leaned back in the chair as if he was deeply thinking about it. He, of course, was thinking more in terms of firing a therapist. If Kay was going to make him the bad guy, then so be it. Someone had to make the decisions in this house. This family had enough problems with a baby, a five-year-old, a grouchy old man, and a little girl confined to bed. The last thing they needed was a dog.

"I don't think so, Becca," he said.

"But Daddy…"

"No," he said a little more harshly than he intended.

Rebecca immediately got the quiet, pouting look on her face that had the same effect on a daddy as a spear to the heart.

"Honey, it's just not a good time," Jeb told her, defending his decision. "Maybe when you get better."

The two sat silently for a long, uncomfortable moment. Jeb knew that he had disappointed his girl, but there were times when a father had to make tough decisions. Finally, he reached for the television remote control.

"Let's find something to watch," he said, in effort to change the subject.

"Daddy, I'm sorry I fell off the swing," Rebecca said softly, catching Jeb unprepared.

"Honey, that was an accident," he replied. "You don't have to be sorry."

She looked tearfully at her father. "Then why are you mad all of the time?"

"Sweetheart, I'm not mad," he said as sincerely as he could possibly manage to be.

"You were mad at Mommy. I heard you downstairs arguing," she replied.

"Honey," he said tenderly, "parents sometimes do that, but it had nothing to do with you."

"Mommy said that you have a lot of stress," she told him.

Jeb got out of his chair and sat halfway down on the bed, putting his arm around his daughter as best he could under the circumstances.

"Baby, I love you. I could never be angry with you, and I'm not mad at Mommy," Jeb told her as reassuringly as he could.

"You promise?" She asked with her eyes pointed right through him.

"I promise."

"I love you too, Daddy," she said. "I need to pee-pee. Can you get Mommy?"

"I can help you, Baby," he told her. "Where's your pan?"

"Daddy!"

Jeb looked at her and realized that although she was his little girl, she was no longer a baby.

He smiled at her. "I'll get Mommy."

#

A few minutes later Jeb was in the den, half sitting and half lying on the couch, with a TV remote in his hand searching for ESPN. It occurred to him that Uncle Louie was right; there were too many channels.

About the time he found the channel, Kay walked in and parked herself on the chair across from him. Out of the corner of his eye, he could see that she was not happy. Of course, that was no surprise. He would have ignored her, but he knew from years of experience that there was no chance that she would let that work.

Finally he turned off the television and looked at her.

"Why did you tell Rebecca that we can't get a dog without talking to me first?" She said evenly, but Jeb was familiar with the tone and knew that there was a lot of anger behind it.

"Because you wouldn't," he said, standing his ground.

"I think that we should have discussed it," she said with a little more anger.

Jeb was getting tired of this. The woman obviously just wanted to fight.

"Don't you think you have enough on your hands?"

"Of course, I have enough on my hands," Kay replied. "I'm thinking of the girls, and you should have come to me before telling her that she couldn't have one."

"Kay, we can't get a dog!" Jeb said a little too loudly.

"Hush. They can hear you."

"Have you completely lost your mind?" He said a little more softly. "In Becca's condition, you want a dog running around here?"

"It's good for her," Kay said. "The therapist and I talked about it. You wouldn't believe how much that dog cheered her up, and the other two fell in love with it."

Clearly the woman had lost it.

"We're not getting a dog, and that's it. No more discussion," Jeb said firmly, proud of being the voice of sanity in the situation.

Jeb could tell that Kay was fuming, and he braced himself for an attack. This time, though, she was not going to win. There is just no sense in getting a dog.

Kay calmly stood and headed toward the kitchen but stopped at the door.

"I don't know what has gotten under your skin the last few weeks, but it's time you got over it," Kay told him calmly and then walked into the kitchen.

#

FORT BOWYER, WEST FLORIDA
November 21, 1814

Lieutenant Jonathan "Johnny" Henderson was tired. He had no reason to be tired. He hadn't done a single thing for two days except sleep and eat, yet for reasons he didn't understand, he was sleepy. He had just finished his noon meal and was now on his way to take an afternoon nap even though he didn't need but just wanted one. He simply had nothing else to occupy his time, so he headed back to the Officer's quarters to take a nap.

The trip from New Orleans had taken five full days, at least two and half more than it should have taken. Much of that extra time was spent at the plantation home of one Mr. Alan Shepherdson, who Lieutenant Henderson considered to be nothing more than a roadside thief.

The mission, though, had gotten off to a terrible start even before encountering Mr. Shepherdson. Normally the quickest route from New Orleans to Mobile would be to ride to South Point on Lake Pontchartrain and then take the ferry across the lake to the Mobile road, but just as they were boarding the ferry some fishermen had arrived with information that they had sighted a British frigate in the Mississippi Sound.

The ferry master, ignoring Lieutenant Henderson's pleas, refused to leave until nightfall despite the unlikelihood of a vessel of that size entering the lake. Thus it was well after midnight when they had arrived at the east bank.

When morning came and they finally got started, some heavy rains blew in that slowed their progress to little more than a walk. Then Sergeant Ferris' horse threw a shoe, slowing them down even more and forcing them to stop at Shepherdson's plantation.

As it turned out, losing that shoe was somewhat fortuitous because just as they were about to continue on their way, the most horrific storm Lieutenant Henderson had ever witnessed began to blow through. He had heard about hurricanes. Everyone along the coast had heard about them, but he had never witnessed one. Though Shepherdson argued that it was too late in the season for a hurricane, it was still by far the worst storm Henderson had ever encountered.

The weather meant that they'd had to stay overnight at Shepherdson's, losing more precious time. Of course, Shepherdson, storm or no storm, saw no reason to let three soldiers spend the night at his home free of charge. A night in Shepherdson's leaky barn during a hurricane cost considerably more than Lieutenant Henderson had once paid for an evening at Cheri Royal, with companionship.

Because of the storm, the road to Mobile was a total mess. Many areas were flooded, and what wasn't flooded was so muddy that they often had to walk their horses, or more accurately, pull their horses along the way. Any place that wasn't flooded or muddy was cluttered with fallen trees, tree limbs, and the occasional dead cow. All of which slowed them down even more.

Then, when finally they got to Fort Bowyer in Mobile, General Jackson was nowhere to be found. Jackson, in anticipation of a British invasion along the Gulf of Mexico, was in Pensacola preparing his defenses. He believed, and quite soundly in Lieutenant Henderson's judgment, that the British would invade either Mobile or Pensacola and then head west over land to Baton Rouge, cutting New Orleans off.

The only problem with Jackson's version of the British plan was that no one had seen the British anywhere near Mobile or Pensacola, but they had been seen in Barataria Bay.

Fort Bowyer's officers' quarters were quite nice. His room was spacious and had a large comfortable bed. It was much better, in fact, than his quarters in New Orleans, which had a leaky roof and were rat-infested. It was so bad that he had quietly moved into the cell next to Ephraim in the brig. Colonel Ross, of course, would have thrown a fit if he knew that his only junior officer was sleeping in the brig, but the room was larger, the roof didn't leak, and there were far fewer rats. Quite frankly, Ephraim was good company. Besides, since Colonel Ross lived in a large house in New Orleans, he was unlikely to ever know where Henderson spent his free time.

Just as he was slipping out of his boots to lie down to take his nap, he heard a commotion outside in the garrison court. When he looked out the window, which was something else that his "official" room at the Garrison didn't have, he saw that the commotion was the fort getting prepared for the commanding General's return.

Jackson, like most generals, enjoyed what was known as "honors" when he arrived at his command and had sent a two-man guard ahead to announce his impending arrival. Thus the entire fort was a flurry of activity. Henderson quickly pulled on his boots and headed over to the commander's headquarters in hopes of intercepting the General as he entered.

He had just arrived in the headquarters when the General and his entourage rode into the Fort. The sight of the General's entrance was an impressive spectacle. He was at the lead with twenty men following. Every trooper was on horseback and in perfect formation behind him. If

Henderson hadn't known better, he would have thought that he was on the parade ground back at West Point, New York and not at a distant outpost led by a Congressman-turned-army general. "This man," Lieutenant Henderson thought, "is real soldier."

The Lieutenant had seen quite a few generals, but he had not, even in his academy days, seen anything like General Andrew Jackson. Most generals expected and even demanded the attention and respect of his men. Jackson got both by merely walking into the room. He was lean and tall with dark, slightly graying hair. When he walked into the Headquarters, everyone present was already standing at attention. Henderson noted that his coat was not the least ruffled or mussed even though he had been riding all morning long.

Jackson stooped his head as he entered. He looked at the Master Sergeant, an older, heavy-set man named Josiah Witherspoon who looked ridiculously out of place in his ill-fitting army uniform, and ordered, "Bring some tea to my office, Josiah."

"There's a cup waiting on your desk, Andy," the Sergeant replied.

Jackson stopped in his tracks and looked at the Master Sergeant Witherspoon.

"I'm sorry, Andy," the Master Sergeant said apologetically. "There's a cup on your desk, General."

Jackson heaved a sigh and continued toward his office and ordered, "Back to work, everyone. This isn't a holiday."

Suddenly he stopped and looked directly at Lieutenant Henderson as if he had just noticed something out of the ordinary. He stared at Henderson for a long minute.

The one most important thing that Lieutenant Henderson had learned at the United States Military Academy at West Point was that a lieutenant does not speak to a general unless specifically spoken to. Under the circumstances though, it was clear that Jackson was expecting him to speak even though the General hadn't uttered a word.

Henderson crisply saluted and barked, "Lieutenant Jonathan Henderson of Fort St. Leon, sir. I have an urgent message from the Governor of Louisiana."

"I suppose he has seen the British," Jackson mumbled and headed into his office. "In here, Lieutenant. Bring the Lieutenant some tea, Josiah."

"Yes sir, Andy. General," the Master Sergeant replied.

Lieutenant Henderson followed the General into his office. Jackson plopped down into a big leather chair behind a large cluttered desk and picked up a cup of tea that was waiting for him. It became obvious to Henderson, regardless of the impression Jackson had made moments earlier, that the man in the chair before him was clearly exhausted from a long hard ride.

Henderson approached and as per his training stood at attention approximately two feet from the front of the desk while holding out Claiborne's letter.

Jackson sipped his tea and took the letter from Henderson's hand. As the Lieutenant retracted his arm, his face showed some discomfort.

"Have you been wounded, Lieutenant?" Jackson asked.

"I took a musket ball in the chest a couple of months ago, Sir," Henderson replied.

"Sit down Lieutenant," Jackson ordered.

"Thank you, but I'll be fine sir."

"Sit down, Lieutenant," Jackson ordered firmly.

Henderson stiffly sat in one of the chairs opposite the desk and was clearly uncomfortable. Jackson watched him closely.

"West Point?"

"Class of 1810 sir," Henderson proudly replied.

"I doubt that Commandant Johnny Williams ever mentioned it, but officers are still people, and a wound is still a wound. Take care of that chest," Jackson said with surprising warmth. "There's going to be a fight with the British sooner or later, and I'm going to need good officers."

The Master Sergeant suddenly appeared and handed Henderson a cup of tea as the General read the letter.

"Lieutenant, a while back I got a letter from your Governor telling me that the British had been sighted by pirates, but he couldn't vouch for their reliability. Now I get this, begging that I come to New Orleans immediately. What has changed?" The General demanded.

Henderson was clearly uncomfortable with the question. His honest answer was that the Governor of Louisiana was an arrogant fool, but he could hardly tell that to a Major General in the United States Army.

"I've no idea sir."

"The hell you don't. The one thing I've learned from the army is that lieutenants and sergeants are the *only* ones who know what's going?"

Henderson suddenly found himself backed into a corner with no idea what to do.

"Boy, if there is truth to this letter, the enemy is at my doorstep. If you have something to say, say it," Jackson said, now more of an order than a request.

Henderson took a deep breath, "General, my opinion is that the Governor has been quite foolish. The original reports came by way of the pirates at Barataria Bay under Captain Jean Lafitte. Claiborne openly hates Lafitte and all but dismissed the information."

Jackson took another sip of tea, "And you believe this pirate's report?"

"Sir, in New Orleans, Jean Lafitte's word is considered much more reliable than that of Governor Claiborne."

Jackson, now looking relaxed and even sleepy, slowly rotated around in his chair and looked out the window while sipping his tea.

Henderson paused and then continued, "I have one of Lafitte's men in my brig and have spoken with him at length." He stopped short of telling the General that the prisoner had become a close friend. "He told me that the British landed on Grande Terre Island in September and met with Lafitte. They offered him amnesty in exchange for helping with their invasion. He, in return, sent a message to Claiborne warning of the invasion and offered himself and his men to fight in defense of the city.

"The Governor, along with my colonel and the general of the local militia, simply sent you a letter without further investigation because he didn't trust the source. Frankly, General, if someone tells me that I'm about to be attacked by twelve thousand troops, I think that it should be taken seriously."

The General quickly turned around in his chair and cut Henderson off. "Twelve thousand troops?"

"Yes, sir. That was the report," Henderson responded.

Jackson looked out the door and ordered, "Josiah, get Colonel Bright in here, now."

Jackson stood and walked over to a map hanging on the wall to the left of his desk. Henderson sat silently, unable to remember the protocol.

If a general stands should I stand as well?

A moment later a slightly ruffled Colonel Shepherd Bright came into the General's office. He was also tall and lean but not as distinguished. Suddenly, Henderson realized that was the word to describe Jackson. He was distinguished. He looked like a real leader, like George Washington.

"You sent for me, sir?" Colonel Bright asked.

Jackson continued to study the map. "Shep, what did those merchant seamen tell you about the Brits in Jamaica?"

"They said that the British are massing a large army on the island. They have approximately fifty ships under Admiral Cochrane, and somewhere between eight and twelve thousand troops," Bright replied.

"Lieutenant, how many British sightings have there been in New Orleans?" Jackson asked, still studying the map.

"The pirates saw them in Barataria Bay, and then a ship was sighted in Lake Borgne. I personally ran into some fishermen on the way here who reported seeing a British frigate in the Mississippi Sound," Henderson answered, getting a look from both General Jackson and Colonel Bright.

Jackson turned back to the map and studied it some more and then began to think out loud. "The British know that we are here, and they probably know that we have a division at Pensacola, and undoubtedly, they know that New Orleans is only defended by a militia."

Henderson watched as the General stood in silence contemplating his strategy. It occurred to the young lieutenant that the man before him was not just tired from a long ride. He was a man with the weight of the world on his shoulders.

"If they take New Orleans, they can go overland and take Baton Rouge and thus control all of the lower Mississippi River," Jackson said, again thinking out loud. "They could then invade from Canada and capture the upper Mississippi as well, taking control of all of our territory west of the river."

"Sir," Bright said. "If they do that we'll be in no position to take it back."

"Lieutenant, how strong is the militia at New Orleans?" Jackson asked, still staring at the map.

Henderson was again uncomfortable but was now aware that this was a man whom he had to be completely honest with. "Weak and undisciplined, Sir."

Jackson turned around and looked at Lieutenant Henderson and then fell almost lifelessly into his big leather chair.

"Colonel, prepare a detachment to take to New Orleans. You will be in charge here," Jackson ordered. "We have assumed that they would take West Florida first, but it is entirely possible that the Mississippi river is their primary objective. They then could land at either Mobile or Pensacola and control the entire Gulf coast."

Jackson looked at Lieutenant Henderson. "Lieutenant, go to New Orleans immediately. Tell your colonel that I will leave for the city within the week."

Henderson stood, crisply saluted, and said, "Yes Sir".

He then turned about and headed to the door, saluting to Colonel Bright as he exited.

"One more thing, Captain Henderson," Jackson said just as Henderson exited.

Henderson at once turned about, "Lieutenant, Sir." He hesitantly corrected.

"Tell your Colonel that when I get to New Orleans, I want you immediately assigned to my staff as my personal guide and liaison officer," General Andrew Jackson ordered. "As of this moment consider yourself a captain. You now work for me. Sergeant Witherspoon will bring your commission papers."

"Yes sir," Henderson replied and then turned to walk out.

As he left, Henderson realized for the first time that there might be hope in the situation. Coincidentally, for the first time in months the wound in his chest didn't hurt.

Chapter 15

NEW ORLEANS, LOUISIANA
December 2, 1814

Charlotte Fuller stood along with most of the city's citizens on the sidewalks of Canal Street waiting for the arrival of the American army. It reminded her of when she was a child, and her father had taken her and her mother to Baltimore for the Independence Day Celebration. The entire city had lined the street to see the parade. Charlotte had sat on her father's shoulders and watched as the veterans of the Revolution marched past.

Of course, that was a different time and a different world. That day, everyone was cheerful and festive. This day, no one was festive. Everyone in New Orleans was terrified. There were rumors of British troops behind every tree and scattered throughout the bayous. No one knew for sure if the enemy had yet landed, but they all feared the worst.

Like everyone, she feared the unknown, and thus she stood on the street to cheer for General Jackson, the hero of the Creek Indian War, who would save New Orleans from certain destruction.

When the General rode his large white horse down Canal Street and passed the crowd, there was an odd mixture of cheers and murmurs. The General himself was exactly what everyone expected. He was tall and commanding on his horse and in his blue suit, looking every bit the man the city was hoping would protect them from the Red Coats. What disappointed the crowd, however, was the army that followed him. Charlotte had heard that there were thousands of Red Coats, but no more than forty or fifty men followed the General. Charlotte didn't know much about war, but she knew how to count. Still, the cheers continued until the American army turned on Royal Street and on to the Place d'Armes.

After the army passed, the crowd started to disperse, and Charlotte began her stroll back to the Cheri Royal. Each day she hoped that it would be the day that Lucian would return to take her to Texas. Part of her feared that he would not ever come and another part was sure that he would.

She knew when Lucian did come, she would have to move quickly. Mr. Hamilton wasn't going to stand by and watch her leave. It wouldn't surprise her at all for Mr. Hamilton to try to kill Lucian.

According to Jeth, the ladies were free to leave at any time, but Mr. Hamilton expected compensation for the loss. Thus there were two choices. She could find a replacement to take her room, or she could pay Mr. Hamilton a flat fee of one thousand dollars. Charlotte, of course, had no option. She certainly didn't have a thousand dollars, and she would never, under any circumstance, bring another woman into the Cheri Royal.

Her hope was that Lucian would come, and the two of them would somehow get far away before Mr. Hamilton noticed her missing. She knew, of course, that it was unlikely, but she still had hope. Lucian was strong, not just in size but also in spirit, and when she had told him about Hamilton, he seemed to have no fear of what could happen to them.

Once again she strolled along Canal Street opposite the Pearl Café, and as always, Mr. Winston was out front serving coffee to customers on the sidewalk. Like almost every day, he looked up and smiled warmly at her, and as she turned off Canal and down Bourbon Street she promised herself to not ever take that route again, but like every other day she knew that she would.

As she approached her final destination, her pace slowed. It was just one of those things she did without thinking about it. The closer she got, the slower she walked. Finally, she came to the door and entered, once again hoping deep inside that this would be the last time she would walk through those doors.

As her eyes adjusted, she saw Mr. Hamilton and Dianna seated at one of the tables with a bottle of whiskey and a couple of glasses. She often wondered how much of his day was spent sitting there drinking. Some days, that was all that he did, but there were other days that she knew he walked the streets looking for other young women like her.

"I suppose you were out there with the rest of the city welcoming our savior?" Hamilton asked as Charlotte walked through to the stairs.

Charlotte just nodded, not really knowing how to answer. Mr. Hamilton frightened her, and she tried her best to avoid him. Fortunately, he spent all of his time with Dianna, who quietly made it clear to all of the "ladies" that he was her man and hers alone. It was rumored that she'd had Jeth, the bartender, kill a woman who'd made the mistake of getting too close to Mr. Hamilton. Charlotte didn't believe the story. Nevertheless, she had no desire to get on Dianna's bad side, or for that matter, on Mr. Hamilton's good side.

"I hope he brought plenty of customers with him," Hamilton said dryly.

At first Charlotte was confused but then realized that he was talking about the soldiers.

"I counted about fifty," she replied as she began up the stairs hurrying, as always, to get away from Mr. Hamilton.

Hamilton laughed out loud. "Fifty American against thousands of war hardened British soldiers. Anyone want to give me odds?" He looked over at Jeth, who was behind the bar. "Jeth get ready. Those fools in the militia will be back tonight."

Charlotte finished her climb to the stairs, remembering that a captain from the militia had been there the night before trying to get the customers to sign up to fight the British. After the captain had made his speech, Mr. Hamilton laughed at him and had Jeth toss him out on the street.

In her room, she took off her dress, let down her hair, and lay down on her bed to take a nap before another night of work. As she closed her eyes, she tried hard to set her mind on Lucian and a new home in Texas. But like every day, in the darkness behind her eyelids she once again saw Ephraim's smile. And one more time she felt that cold feeling in her heart, and tears formed as she fell off to asleep.

#

CELL 6, FORT ST. LEON
December 2, 1814

Ephraim was lying on his bed staring at the ceiling. He normally would spend part of his day in his chair reading and then spend part of his day walking the halls. The days had been boring from the moment he'd gotten to the brig but, they had become more so since Johnny Henderson had been sent to Mobile. At least when Johnny was around, he had someone to talk to. The desk sergeant, a balding little fellow named Evens, was a great card player when the Colonel was away, but he wouldn't risk playing when the Colonel was around. That, Ephraim decided, was the difference between a sergeant and an officer. A colonel wouldn't punish another officer for playing cards with a prisoner but apparently would punish a sergeant.

The only other person around was Master Sergeant Redenbaugh. The Master Sergeant had no fear of the Colonel, but Ephraim was afraid of the Master Sergeant. Redenbaugh was a big, barrel-chested, and extremely loud fellow who had a reputation for getting into barroom fights.

Just as Ephraim was about to doze off for his afternoon nap, he heard a familiar voice.

"Wake-up you lazy Englishman. You're leaving," Captain Jonathan Henderson said jovially.

Startled, Ephraim leaped to his feet recognizing his friend's voice. "Johnny, when did you get back?"

"Last week. I wanted to come out and see you, but I've been down at Fort St. Philip getting things ready for the General," Henderson answered.

"He's coming?"

"He's here," Johnny replied. "He got here around noon. You should have seen it. The whole city lined the streets."

"How many troops?"

"Not many. Get your boots on. I was serious. Your lawyer is out front. Ross released you."

"I don't get it. Why am I being released?"

"For starters, that lawyer has been making a stink."

Ephraim rolled his eyes. "That guy is an idiot."

"That's probably true, but he's getting you out. Well, he and Mr. Blanque," Henderson explained. "Colonel Ross doesn't want the General to find out that he's been holding a civilian in his brig for over two months without any charges. He told me to get you out of here before Jackson shows up. The last thing he wants is to have the General come and your lawyer be here demanding your release."

Ephraim finished getting his boots on, and the two of them walked out of the cell and headed up the hall.

"What do you think of this General Jackson?" Ephraim asked.

"He's good. He's really good. If there is anyone who can keep the British out of New Orleans, it's him," Henderson responded optimistically.

"But how many men?"

"Fifty to start with," Henderson answered. "He just doesn't have a lot of troops to bring. He sent to Tennessee and Kentucky for volunteers, but for the most part he's going to try to defend the city with the militia. He's on his way right now to inspect the garrison, but he already knows that there aren't enough men to do much good. That's why I'm here. I'm supposed to get the garrison ready for the General's inspection. I work for him now."

"Jackson?" Ephraim asked.

"I'm his personal guide and liaison officer," Henderson said. "You should have seen Ross when he found out. He's fit to be tied. He wants to write a formal letter of protest, but the only person he can protest to is Jackson."

They both laughed.

"And another thing," Henderson continued, "you need to show me more respect. I'm Captain Henderson now."

Henderson pointed at the piping on his shoulder. Ephraim smiled, pretending to understand what the piping represented.

"Will Jackson take Captain Lafitte up on his offer?"

Johnny Henderson lowered his head in disgust. "When Jackson got here, he made a speech in the Place d'Armes and then met with Claiborne in his office along with Ross and Villeré and Patterson. The four of them have him convinced that Lafitte and his men are nothing more than roadside bandits."

The two reached the end of the hall where Moreau was waiting at the desk with Evans and Master Sergeant Redenbaugh. It was clear that the Master Sergeant was growing impatient with the fat little lawyer.

"Well, it's about time you released my boy!" Moreau proclaimed.

"Moreau, if you don't shut up, I'm going to throw you into a cell," Redenbaugh said, growing angry.

"On what charge?" Moreau demanded.

"On the charge that I'm sick and tired of listening to you," Redenbaugh replied.

"Calm down, Mr. Moreau," Henderson said. "You can take your client."

"You people haven't heard the last of this," Moreau warned.

Ephraim smiled as Redenbaugh began coming around the desk. The Sergeant was known for his short temper.

Captain Henderson shot the sergeant a glance that stopped Redenbaugh in his tracks and then calmly turned to the lawyer and said, "Mr. Moreau. I've seen Sergeant Redenbaugh when he gets angry, and honestly, you don't want him coming around that desk."

"Perhaps we should go," Ephraim said, glancing at Henderson, who half wanted the sergeant to attack Moreau.

"Yes, we should," Moreau agreed, and they turned to the door, "but I will file a protest to Colonel Ross."

Ephraim smiled as he and Moreau walked out the door. Then while passing though the doorway, they stopped as Major General Andrew Jackson, along with Colonel Ross and forty soldiers, rode through the gate to the garrison. Henderson heard the commotion and came to the doorway.

"That's him," the young Captain said.

Jackson came to a stop at the building marked "Office of the Commanding Officer" and climbed down off of his mount. He looked almost awkward as he lifted his long lanky leg over the horse.

Ephraim watched the General and Colonel Ross while Moreau got onto his buggy.

"Come on, kid," Moreau said, paying no attention to the arrival of a general officer.

Ephraim looked at Moreau and then, on impulse, walked over to General Jackson.

"General, Sir," Ephraim said loudly.

Jackson turned and looked as the young man approached him.

"General," Ephraim said. "You need men, and Captain Lafitte has six hundred men training as we speak."

Jackson looked at Ross, who had stepped almost between Ephraim and the General.

"General, this is one of the bandits Governor Claiborne told you about," Ross explained.

Jackson looked Ephraim up and down.

"How old are you, boy?" Jackson asked.

"I'm seventeen, sir." Ephraim replied, sheepishly.

"Is that a British accent I detect?" The General asked.

"Yes sir."

"What brings a seventeen-year-old British pirate to this facility?" Jackson asked Ephraim.

"He's been in my brig," Ross interrupted. With an annoyed glance over at Henderson, "He was supposed to have been released. I frankly don't know what he's doing here."

Jackson's face clearly showed impatience with Ross, "I was speaking to the boy."

Ephraim stood silent for a moment and then answered, "I left the army in Liverpool to become an American, sir."

Jackson's eyes widened, "So you are a deserter, a traitor, and a banditti. Go tell your Captain Lafitte that I have no need for his sort."

As Jackson turned to go into the headquarters, Ephraim spoke out. "Captain Lafitte has powder and nearly two hundred cannons."

Jackson looked at Ross who just shook his head. He then looked at Ephraim, "I doubt that, son. Now be gone before I have you locked up."

Ephraim watched as Jackson, trailed by Ross, walked into the headquarters, and then he went to the buggy where Moreau was impatiently waiting. As he climbed onto the wagon, Johnny Henderson walked up and remarked, "Either you like that cell or you have more guts than any soldier that I've ever met."

"How many men does he have, Johnny?"

Henderson shrugged his shoulders. "Counting the militia, maybe four hundred."

They looked at one another.

"Take care of yourself, Johnny," Ephraim said with real emotion.

"You too, Eph."

Moreau whipped the horse, and the little buggy left the garrison.

#

Two hours later Moreau slowly drove the buggy up Canal Street. It was only dusk, but there were few people out, far fewer than Ephraim had ever seen. He looked over at the Pearl Café as they passed and wondered if Charlotte had ever been back. Surely not, he thought.

"The town is pretty quiet these days," Moreau said. "People are scared."

"They should be," Ephraim commented.

"Is there any place I can drop you?"

Ephraim sighed, realizing that there was no place he wanted to go. "Anywhere along here. I was living at Mr. Lafitte's warehouse."

"It's probably empty. They looted it, you know," Moreau replied and pulled the buggy to a stop.

As Ephraim climbed off, he stopped to shake Moreau's hand.

"Thank you for getting me out of jail, Mr. Moreau," he said.

"You just tell your Bos that I'm the one who got you freed," Moreau replied.

"I'll tell him."

As Moreau whipped his horse and drove away, Ephraim started walking up Tchoupitoulas Street and back to the warehouse, all the while wondering if there was a way he could find Charlotte or if she would even talk to him again. These same thoughts had haunted him throughout his stay at the garrison. Girls like Charlotte didn't marry convicts. Yet there was something in his memory of her that gave him hope. Of course, he would have to find her first and then tell her that he had been in jail, and then he'd have to explain that he was in jail because he worked for a pirate.

When he walked up to the warehouse, it was almost dark out. He could see just well enough to discern that the building was empty. All of the shelving he had built was overturned, and there was broken pottery and glass all over the floor. He climbed the steps to his little room. Fumbling around he found some matches and managed to light the little lamp.

Surprisingly, his things were still there. He smiled as he realized that thieves had been in his room and come to the conclusion that he had nothing worth stealing.

He sat down on the bed and began to think about what to do next when he heard a noise down in the warehouse. Noises in the warehouse were not uncommon. Almost every night he'd heard rats, but something made him tense up. This was no rat.

He stepped over to the door and slowly looked down into the huge room. There at the base of the steps was a dark figure. It was a man.

"Ephraim?" The voice asked in a heavy Creole accent that Ephraim instantly recognized.

"Al, is that you?"

"I got word from the Bos. When you get free, I'm to get you up river," Al said.

Ephraim paused a moment wondering what to do. What he really wanted was to walk the streets looking for Charlotte, but he knew that even if he did there was little hope of finding her. Finally he shrugged and asked, "Tonight?"

"Oui, Monsieur. That is the Bos' orders," Al answered.

"Give me a minute to get my things," Ephraim replied.

Ephraim grabbed the little satchel that he had hanging over the back of his little wooden chair. Aside from some clothes, the only real personal item that he owned was a Bible. He started to leave it and then remembered that the cook on the *Tigre* had given it to him. He didn't know for sure, but he suspected that it had been stolen from some ship in the middle of the ocean. He wondered if it was a sin to own a stolen Bible.

Ephraim smiled, stuffed the Bible into the satchel, and blew out the lamp.

Chapter 16

NACOGDOCHES, TEXAS
October, 2003

Jeb parked himself on the couch in Louie's apartment, beer in hand, waiting for the Monday night game to begin. Uncle Louie, also with a beer in hand, was seated in a reclining chair in the corner of the room.

Jeb was not in a particularly good mood. He'd been unable to motivate himself to write anything on the book that he was supposed to have been writing. He went home every day to a wife who was progressively becoming more difficult. His children were mad at him for being the only adult in the house sensible enough to see that this was no time to get a dog, and now he was watching football with a grouchy old man who was in a worse mood than his wife and kids.

Jeb finally looked over at his uncle, who hadn't said a word since he'd come in the door and asked, "So, you going to tell me what's got you so bent out of shape?"

"I just don't see why all I get is one beer. It's my home, I should be able to have all I want," Louie replied.

"You need to talk to Kay about that."

"There's a whole six-pack in that refrigerator in the garage. I saw her put it there. But there's a lock on it."

"That's to keep the kids out."

"Then why doesn't she give me a key?"

"To keep you out," Jeb said, somewhat amused.

The old man glared at him.

"So what's under you saddle?"

Jeb looked over at him. "The wife and kids are mad because I won't let them get a dog."

"The dog thing? They got over that a week ago," Louie replied. "You've been in a crappy mood for a month."

"Why does everyone think I'm pissed-off? First, it was my boss, then Kay, then Becca, and now you?" Jeb demanded, becoming agitated.

Louie just looked at him without saying a word.

"You really think that I've been in a bad mood, too, huh?" Jeb asked.

"You've been a royal pain in the butt. Back in Nam I had a Lieutenant under me that acted like you. Someone in his platoon shot him," Louie told him. "That wife of yours has been an angel. Most women would have tossed you out for the way you've been acting. I understand that you've had some stress, but boy, you have no right to act the way you have."

Jeb sat silently and took a sip of his beer.

"The only person in this room with a reason to be mad at her is me," Louie mumbled as he took a sip of his beer.

Jeb looked at his father's cousin, feeling the weight of the world on his shoulders. His stomach suddenly felt nervous, and he could feel tears forming. His heart began pounding, and his hands began to shake.

"I can't do it, Louie," Jeb said softly.

Louie sat silently watching the change on Jeb's face. In a just a moment's time his expression went from arrogant and angry to broken.

"The kids, the job, this broken-down old house. Hell, I'll never be out of debt. Every time I walk in and see Rebecca my heart breaks. What if something like that happens to one of the other girls?" Jeb said as he leaned forward, putting his elbows on his knees, cradling his beer with both hands.

"It's a hard road, boy," Louie said sensitively. "It is for everybody. There's nothing easy about being a father."

Jeb looked at him. "That's easy for you to say. You lived a full life before you settled down. You and dad both did."

"What do you mean by that?" Louie asked, a little heated.

"Nothing."

"You meant something, or you wouldn't have said it."

"I don't know," Jeb said and took a swig of his beer. "I keep thinking about those stories you tell: Ephraim, the Bonnie and Clyde thing. You know, I found a newspaper article that backed up your story."

Louie finished his beer. "You didn't need a newspaper. It was true."

Jeb looked over at his uncle, finished his beer, and set the can down on the coffee table. "Maybe I'm just missing my dad. Maybe I'm just wishing that I could have had an adventure or two like you guys did before getting tied down. Maybe I just wish that there was more to life than debt."

Louie sat forward on his recliner. "My God, boy. Are you that stupid? I miss your father too, but I'm not sitting here sulking. Your dad spent the better part of his life looking and praying for someone like your mother. All Ephraim wanted in this world was to marry Charlotte. Son, you have a beautiful wife and three daughters who live for you.

Ephraim, your Dad, Me, all any of us ever wanted was what you have right inside that house. Debt and all."

Jeb sat there a moment looking at Louie, who was visibly angry. He then stood and walked to the door.

"Where are you going?" Louie asked, clearly put out.

"I'm thirsty. And I've got the key."

#

Jeb took each step carefully as he walked into the bedroom. He wasn't drunk, but he could definitely feel the second and third beer. This was probably the first time since getting married that he'd had more than one.

Kay was already in bed with the lights off, but years of marriage had taught him the difference between when she was asleep and when she wanted him to think that she was asleep. After thinking about it, he sat leaning against the headboard next to her and began to softly caress her hair. She surprised him by responding to the affection and pressed against him.

"I've been an ass," he told her as he put his arm around her.

Kay was a little groggy, hovering in that world between being fully awake and fully asleep.

"I said, that I've been an ass," Jeb repeated.

Kay opened her eyes.

"I know," she said. "When'd you figure it out?"

"Tonight."

She leaned tight against him as he held her close.

"Can you get someone to sit with Louie and the girls tomorrow night?"

She looked up at him.

"I thought we should go out to dinner," he added.

"Are you asking me out for a date?"

Jeb looked down at her. "Yeah. I am."

"Okay," she said, "but I should tell you in advance that I usually don't let a man in my bed until after he buys me dinner."

#

NEW ORLEANS, LOUISIANA
December 20, 1814

Ephraim had an uneasy feeling as he, Captain Lafitte, and Louis Rose left the house on Dumaine Street. The way he saw it, the chances were quite good that at sunrise he would be holding Captain Lafitte's cloak as Lafitte, pistol in hand, walked off twenty paces against General Andrew Jackson.

The trip to Devil's Island had been nothing less than miserable. Al had led Ephraim to a shack about twenty miles upriver and left him there to wait for someone named Broussard. Two days later the most foul-looking and foul-smelling human Ephraim had ever come in contact with showed up in a small flat-bottomed boat, announced himself as Broussard, and said that he would take Ephraim to the Bos.

They then spent the next four days in almost nonstop freezing drizzle poling through endless bayous and rivers. Ephraim wondered how a place that could be so miserably hot in the summer could be no less miserably cold in the winter. All things considered, jail was a far cry better.

The island seemed almost vacant when he finally arrived. Llewellyn was at Galveztown, and most of the crewmen had finished training and were living on board their ships to stay dry and warm.

Immediately upon their arrival on the island, Lafitte called a meeting of his officers where Ephraim was to tell of the conditions in the city, of which he knew little because he had left the city only hours after being released from jail.

Of course, the only thing that really interested Lafitte was this General Jackson and Ephraim's impressions of the man. So in a cold rain, seated at the most ornate table he had ever seen, Ephraim told of his brief meeting with the man who was to save New Orleans from the British. Naturally, he chose not to tell Lafitte that Jackson called him a "banditti."

Then and there Lafitte decided that he needed to meet with this General as soon as possible. Thus, without his even getting to take a good hot meal, a cold, wet, and hungry Ephraim joined Captain Lafitte, Louis Rose, and Broussard as they began poling their way back to the city.

Lafitte's reasoning made sense, actually. The sooner he met with the man, the sooner he could get Captain Youx and the others freed from the Calaboose and, hopefully, join Jackson's militia. With that in mind he ordered the captains to slowly begin bringing cannons and powder to Barataria Bay starting the day after Christmas. If the Bos met them, they would begin offloading powder and flint. If not, they would assume that the Bos was in the Calaboose with Captain Youx.

The house on Dumaine Street was the home Lafitte kept in the city. Ephraim was aware that the Bos kept a house in New Orleans, but until now he had no idea where it was. The house was nothing like the one on Grande Terre Island. This house was much smaller, although equally well-furnished, and, by comparison, far larger than their little home back in Tenbury Wells.

When they arrived at the house, Margaret had already prepared dinner. How she had come to be in the city was a mystery, and how she knew that they were coming was even more mysterious. But as Ephraim was beginning to learn, the Bos had ways of getting things done.

Still, even though Margaret was a fine cook, Ephraim wasted no time eating while there was a bed available. For the first time in eight days he had the opportunity to sleep in a warm and dry bed. Twelve hours later when he awoke, Margaret had breakfast waiting. Louis had already been on a scouting mission. He had learned that the General was using a building at Royal and Canal Streets for his New Orleans headquarters. He and Lafitte came to a simple plan. They would wait at the Pearl Café until the General and his officers came out. Ephraim, having met the general, would then walk over and make the necessary introductions.

This certainly wouldn't be the most formal of meetings, but no one could think of a better solution, considering, of course, that Lafitte was a wanted criminal.

So that morning, Captain Lafitte, Rose, and Ephraim took the same table that Ephraim and Charlotte had shared some weeks earlier. A ping of sharp pain pierced his heart as Ephraim wondered if she had come to meet him that day he was arrested.

When he saw Ephraim, Winston immediately wrapped his arms around the young Englishman. "I am very happy to see you again, Mr. Ephraim. We were all worried," he said and then added, "It is so good to see you again too, Captain Lafitte."

"Thank you, Winston," Ephraim replied, realizing that Lafitte's and Rose's eyes were fixed upon him.

"Major Rose," Lafitte remarked, "have you noticed how our young Englishman always seems to impress?"

Rose was about to reply when he noticed something across the street and nodded his head. "I believe that we are about to meet the General."

Ephraim and Lafitte looked across the way to see four soldiers walking a group of horses to the corner building. The front horse was the brilliant white mare that Ephraim had seen Jackson ride into the garrison.

Winston saw what had caught the attention of the three. "The General is quite regimental. He takes a ride each morning at this time," he said.

Lafitte rasked, "Does he ever dine with you?"

"Each evening at six, along with all of his officers," Winston answered.

"Ephraim, you will lead the way," Lafitte ordered.

Ephraim stood and walked across the street. Well behind were Lafitte and Rose. Just as he arrived at the horses, the General and an entourage of officers came out of the building and began to mount up. Among the officers was newly promoted Captain Jonathan Henderson. Henderson watched closely as Ephraim boldly approached the General.

"General, sir," Ephraim yelled a little louder than he intended.

Every head turned his direction, including that of General Jackson, who stared down at Ephraim.

"You're that pirate, aren't you?"

A few feet away Lafitte froze at the mention of the word "pirate" and studied the General closely. Rose could see anger smoldering in Lafitte's eyes and prepared to restrain the man.

Ephraim hesitated, not knowing how to reply to the General. Finally as Jackson mounted his horse he said, "Yes sir."

"Well boy, you must have something to say," said the General.

"General, I'd like to introduce you to Captain Lafitte," Ephraim said somewhat sheepishly.

"Son, I told you before that I have no time for that banditti. I have enough trouble making a militia out of the rabble in this city without hobbling myself with that penny thieving pirate."

Across the way a now-fuming Lafitte began to storm across the street only to halt when Rose grabbed him by the arm.

"General, Captain Lafitte has men and cannons, and you need both," Ephraim yelled as Jackson and his entourage began to ride away.

As they left, Henderson looked at Ephraim and shrugged.

#

When Ephraim rejoined Lafitte and Rose in front of the Pearl Café, Lafitte was flushed with anger.

"The man called me a pirate!" he said, almost shouting.

Ephraim and Rose just looked at each other, knowing that they could not control Lafitte.

"He served in the House of Representatives, and he has the audacity to call me a bandit," Lafitte continued. "An insult like that demands action. I'll challenge him to a duel. We'll see who is a bandit."

"Colonel," Rose said.

Lafitte looked at Rose, red-faced with rage.

"Colonel," Rose began, "I'm a soldier. I was awarded the Legion of Honor from Emperor Bonaparte himself. When I met you I also thought you were little more than a bandit, but in the past few weeks I've seen you turn a band of merchant seamen into a quality artillery command. Their accuracy could match anything I've seen in Europe, and they are all dedicated to their commander. You are not bandit. You are, in fact, a colonel. We just need to show him that."

Lafitte was still steaming but regaining control. "What do you suggest?" He asked.

Rose looked at Ephraim, "Who was that captain you were looking at?"

"That was Johnny Henderson. He ran the garrison where I was held."

"Are you friendly?" Rose asked.

"I consider him to be a friend," Ephraim answered.

"Stay here until the General returns," Rose ordered. "Make contact with that Captain and arrange a way for us to enter the Headquarters when the General is having his evening meal."

"Offer him money, if you have to Ephraim," Lafitte added.

"I don't think that will be necessary."

"Meet us at the house when you've made the arrangements," Rose ordered.

"How do you know that the General won't go to bed after his dinner?" Lafitte asked.

"He's a general. Generals don't sleep. He will finish his dinner and then go to his office and work," Louis answered as he led Lafitte away.

#

After the encounter with General Jackson, Ephraim spent the afternoon at the Pearl waiting for the General and his officers to return. The wait took several hours, all of which he wished he could be walking the streets looking for Charlotte, but of course that would be futile.

It was when Winston brought the second cup of coffee that the man said, "Mr. Ephraim?"

"Yes Winston?"

"It is not my business, sir," the waiter said hesitantly, "but the young lady you brought here before your arrest often strolls past."

"You've seen her?" Ephraim exclaimed with excitement.

"A couple of times a week, sir."

Ephraim jumped to his feet with his heart pounding. "Did she come the day I was arrested?" he asked.

"She stayed a couple of hours, Mr. Ephraim," the man replied. "It was the next day that I learned what had happened to you, sir."

Ephraim's mind was swirling. For the first time in weeks he had hope. "Do you think that she will come by today?" He asked.

"It's hard to say," Winston told him. "She usually stays on the other side of the street. She walks slowly until she gets close, and then she passes quite quickly, but she always looks over this way."

"Thank you, Winston. Would you be so kind to do me a favor?" Ephraim asked while his eyes searched the streets.

"Of course, sir." Winston replied.

"I know that it is an imposition," Ephraim asked, "but if you see her again, would you please tell her that I'd like to see her?"

"I'd be happy to," the black man replied as they both looked up and down the street.

"Mr. Ephraim?"

"Yes?"

"Will you and Captain Lafitte be joining us in the fight?"

"We will, if the General will take us," Ephraim replied and then asked, "You've joined?"

"My militia has joined. I'm just waiting until they send for me," he replied.

"Your militia?" Ephraim asked.

"The Freemen of Color," Winston answered proudly.

"Freemen of Color?"

"It is the name of our militia," Winston answered with great pride. "We won our freedom in the Saint-Dominique rebellion in '91."

Ephraim was suddenly quite ashamed. He'd looked at this man's face daily for weeks but not seen him. He only saw a waiter. It never entered his mind to ask if Winston was slave or free. Not only was this man free, but he was soon going to take up arms and possibly die to protect his home.

"Perhaps we will be on the line together, Mr. Ephraim," Winston said.

Ephraim looked at Winston's face, seeing for the first time this proud, courageous man and replied, "it's just Ephraim," as he reached out and took Winston's hand. "Perhaps we will."

#

Three hours later the General and his officers returned, and Ephraim's mind was back on the business at hand. He tried not to be too noticeable as the officers rode up to the building. Frankly, that wasn't very difficult. Officers rarely noticed people like Ephraim. It occurred to him that the officers of this army behaved almost exactly as the officers of the 85th had behaved. They were all far too consumed with their own business to take note of someone like him. He was suddenly reminded how he had treated Winston.

Ephraim managed to catch Johnny Henderson's eye, and a few minutes later the two of them were in one of the private booths in the back of the Pearl. Johnny was initially uncomfortable with the arrangement, but after some thought he had no cause for concern. All he had to do was leave the back door unlocked, which was no real problem since, to his knowledge it wasn't ever locked. Other than that he just told Ephraim which office belonged to Jackson and that the back stairs would be open. There would be a sergeant at the front door, but he'd most likely be asleep. The only problem would be Jackson's personal aid, a crusty old sergeant named Witherspoon who rarely took an evening meal. He didn't take orders from anyone but the General, so it would be useless to send him out. But the man liked to drink. Henderson reasoned that if he suggested a good saloon, the sergeant might take some time off.

#

So naturally Ephraim had an uneasy feeling as he, Lafitte, and Rose left the house on Dumaine Street and headed to the U.S. Army Headquarters. Although he had never actually witnessed it, he had been regaled with stories of the Bos' legendary temper. Judging from what he had seen earlier that day, he doubted that Jean Lafitte would stand patiently while General Jackson called him a banditti a second time. Thus it appeared altogether possible that at dawn he would be holding Captain Lafitte's cloak as he marched twenty paces and pointed a pistol at Andrew Jackson.

The General's office was in a three-story brick building on the corner of a block. Rose and Lafitte immediately went into the alley behind the Headquarters while Ephraim casually walked over to the Pearl. As arranged, Winston was waiting at the front door and nodded to Ephraim as a signal that the General and his entourage were, in fact, taking their evening meal.

Ephraim quickly rushed back to the alley to rejoin his two companions. When he arrived, he couldn't help but smile at the sight of Louis Rose, a highly decorated French Lieutenant, holding his hands clasped together to boost the ever distinguished Pirate King of Barataria Bay over an eight foot wall like a couple of mischievous schoolboys playing hooky. Once on the wall, Lafitte held out his hand and helped Rose climb up. Then Lafitte dropped to the ground while Ephraim jumped to take Rose' hand, but instead of climbing over like Rose had, Ephraim swung his leg over like he was mounting a horse. Unfortunately, the wall wasn't a horse. The maneuver was more difficult and considerably more awkward than he had expected. Had it not been for Louis' quick reaction, Ephraim would have fallen flat on his back. Eventually he got onto the wall and the two dropped into the courtyard.

"Are you okay?" Rose asked earnestly.

"Yeah," Ephraim answered somewhat sheepishly as he felt the cold breeze on his leg. Looking down he saw that he had ripped the inseam out of his trousers, leaving a nine-inch long tear.

As it turned out, there was a reason that no one locked the building's back door. That door had long-since been wedged shut by the constant shifting New Orleans' soil. No amount of pulling was going to open the door even though Louis gave it his best effort.

On the second floor, Lafitte spotted an open window. This meant that Rose and Lafitte had to lift Ephraim on their shoulders as he climbed into the window, hoping that the General's aid had in fact gone to a tavern, and then sneak downstairs to open a first-floor window that his two companions could climb through. Of course this meant hiking his leg through a window, further ripping his trousers.

Luckily, there was no sign of a sergeant or anyone else. With the exception of Ephraim's ripped trousers, all three were able to get into the building and into the General's office without any difficulty.

The office was not very spacious but was, nonetheless, the largest in the building. There was a small desk with an oil lamp where the General had obviously been writing some letters. Aside from that there was no furniture except for a couple of chairs. Two walls had windows looking out to Canal and Royal Streets, and the other two sidewalls were cluttered with maps and notes.

Rose immediately went to the window to watch for the General and his officers to return. Lafitte made himself comfortable in the General's chair. Ephraim wondered if Captain Lafitte would have read the General's correspondence, had there been enough light.

"They're coming," Rose announced.

Lafitte stood and the three of them silently took a position against a wall. A few moments later Major General Andrew Jackson walked into his office followed by another officer. Out of habit the General went directly to the desk where he took a match from a tin matchbox and lit the lamp.

"Sergeant!" the other officer shouted.

The General jerked his head in the direction of the officer only to see the three men standing against the wall. He looked closely, sizing them up.

Recognizing Ephraim the General calmly remarked, "Young man, you are becoming a bit of an irritant."

At that moment a sergeant rushed into the office.

"Sergeant, escort these men out of the building and then come back and explain to me how they were able to get in here," the other officer ordered.

"No Sergeant," General Jackson said calmly as he continued to look over the three men, "but we could use some tea, if you would be so kind."

"General," the officer protested.

"That will be all, Colonel Winslow," Jackson said to the officer.

"Yes sir," Winslow said reluctantly. "Should I leave the door open?"

"That won't be necessary," Jackson answered, not taking his eyes off the three men.

As the officer left the room, Ephraim stepped forward and announced, "General Jackson, I would like to present Captain Jean Lafitte."

"I assumed as much," Jackson said, looking at Lafitte. "Oddly, you don't appear the barbarian you have been described."

For a long moment the two looked at one another. Ephraim could feel the tension. At first he thought that Lafitte's temper would get the best of him, but then he sensed something else entirely. Looking back and forth between the two, he realized that they were of similar temperament and character, and most importantly, they both instantly realized it.

"My adjutant, Louis Rose," Lafitte said, motioning to Rose.

The General nodded to Rose and sat down behind his desk.

"Have a seat, Gentlemen," the General said with a wave of his hand.

Lafitte and Rose took the two chairs while Ephraim stood in the back of the room. Jackson looked at the boy, noticing his torn pants.

"Did you have a problem getting in?" Jackson asked.

Ephraim stood back, awkwardly trying to hold his trousers closed.

"Well gentlemen. What can I do for you?" Jackson asked.

"You are about to fight a war, and you desperately need men," Lafitte said. "I have cannons with powder and flint, and a militia trained to use them."

The General looked at Lafitte, and then Rose, and then back at Lafitte. Finally, he said, "I'm told that your men are a rabble. Bandits."

"The people who told you that," Lafitte countered, "said the same thing about me. Do I look like a banditti to you?"

Ephraim watched as Jackson studied Lafitte.

Jackson hesitated but then answered, "It would appear that I have been misinformed."

"Some time ago," Lafitte began. "A group of British officers approached me at my home and informed me that they intended to invade New Orleans with twelve thousand troops. They offered me amnesty in exchange for providing intelligence services. I immediately passed this information on to Governor Claiborne and offered my men and myself to help defend this city. For my efforts, my home was destroyed, and my warehouses were raided by the rabble this state calls a militia."

Jackson snorted. "We apparently have similar respect for the militia, and for what it is worth, since I declared martial law, Claiborne and his legislature have written a formal letter to the President demanding that I be relieved."

There was a knock on the door.

"Enter," Jackson ordered.

The sergeant walked into the room holding a tray with four cups of tea. The sergeant sat the tray on the desk.

"Tea gentlemen?" Jackson offered.

Rose shook his head, but Lafitte took a cup.

"Will there be anything else sir?" the sergeant asked.

"No, that will be all. Have you seen Sergeant Witherspoon?" Jackson asked.

"Not since stepping out for dinner, sir." The sergeant answered before leaving the room.

"I must apologize for that, General," Lafitte said. "My man, Broussard, is in a Bourbon Street saloon buying your master sergeant whiskey."

"Well, then. If I know Josiah Witherspoon, your man Broussard will lose a lot of money, and I won't see my aid before noon tomorrow," Jackson said showing a guarded sense of humor that produced a chuckle among the four men.

Then as quickly as it appeared, the moment of levity vanished.

"Tell me. Where did you get powder and cannon?" Jackson asked.

"My shipping enterprise often commandeers powder and heavy guns. It would be unwise to leave such on the ships we encounter, and it is equally unwise to sell them." Lafitte answered.

Ephraim watched Jackson's eyes widen as the General realized for the first time that Lafitte might actually have a stockpile of powder and cannons.

"I've kept these munitions on island hideouts for just such an occasion."

"Again I have been misinformed," replied the General. "What is it you would like in exchange for your generosity?"

"The munitions are yours, General." Lafitte began, "but it is clear that the local government considers me to be a criminal. I simply request that any of my men who are willing to join your militia be granted amnesty from all past crimes and that the men who are currently in the Calaboose to be released to serve in your command."

Jackson looked at Lafitte as he sipped from his tea and asked, "Your men know how to use these cannons?" Jackson asked.

"Lieutenant Rose was formerly aid-de-camp to General Jacques de Monfort of Emperor Napoleon's 82e Regiment d'Infanterie de Ligne," Lafitte said proudly.

Jackson looked intently at Rose with a new respect. The two, Ephraim saw, were real soldiers who had seen battle.

"You were at Leipzig?"

"Yes."

"How is it that you are now in my office?"

"I decided after Leipzig that I would never again order men into a battle that I know they cannot win," Rose said flatly.

Jackson's face stiffened as he looked at an officer who had clearly deserted after a defeat.

"Even if you were ordered to do so?"

"I obeyed that order once," Rose replied, "and I watched six thousand men die because their commanders were more concerned about their personal pride than winning a war. I was taught that an officer's job is to provide his men with the best opportunity for victory."

"And you feel that we can win this war?" Jackson asked.

Rose nodded.

"A few of weeks ago I had Lieutenant Rose scout the area for his expert evaluation of how the British may attack," Lafitte explained. "Perhaps you may be interested in his assessment?"

"Please," Jackson answered.

Rose stood and walked to one of the maps mounted on the wall.

"Mon General," Rose began, "the problem for the British is logistics. They must land men *and* supplies. There are no suitable options, and only three are even reasonable - Lake Pontchartrain to the north, Barataria Bay in the South, and from Lake Borgne to the East. Lake Pontchartrain is shallow. They could enter the lake with shallow-draft boats, but they would be slow and vulnerable, and they would be cut off from their supply line. Barataria would provide a less vulnerable landing, but it would put them on the wrong side of the river. I doubt that they would attempt such a trek without Captain Lafitte's men to guide them.

Rose looked at the General, whose stern face revealed nothing.

"This leaves Lake Borgne as the only suitable option," Rose concluded. "The British could use one of the islands southeast of New Orleans as a staging point and have a short march up into the city."

"What would you suggest we do to defend against such an attack?" Jackson asked.

Ephraim looked at Lafitte who was smiling broadly with pride.

"There is a small canal running a little more than a quarter of a mile between the lake and the river at a place called Chalmette," Rose said, pointing at the map.

"Rodriquez's Canal?" Jackson asked.

"Yes. If you built an embankment along the side of the canal and put cannon and infantry along its length, I think that you could hold off a vastly superior number of troops almost indefinitely," Rose stated.

Jackson sat back in his chair and took a long sip of his tea.

"A few hours ago General Villeré's son reported to me that a British landing party had put in this morning at exactly that spot. Since then the General has been captured, and they are using his house as their headquarters," Jackson said. "Over dinner, I ordered my officers to begin the building of an embankment on Rodriquez's canal."

Ephraim could see that Lafitte was now practically beaming.

"Captain Lafitte, consider yourself a Brigadier General of your militia," Jackson commanded. "How soon can you get your artillery here?"

"I've already given the order. The first ship should be in Barataria Bay in a few days," Lafitte replied. "With your permission, we can come directly upriver."

"The sooner the better," Jackson replied. "If you don't mind, General, I would like to borrow Colonel Rose for a while."

"It is actually Lieutenant Rose, sir," Louis interrupted.

"It's Colonel. This command is made up mostly of militia. You are one of the few real soldiers that I have at my disposal and I will not have some cobbler-turned-colonel telling you what to do," General Jackson proclaimed. "I'd like you to oversee the construction of the embankment."

"As you wish, sir," Rose replied.

Jackson stood to his feet followed by Lafitte. The General reached out and shook the pirate's hand and offered, "All I can do is ask the President to grant your pardon, but for the time being Colonel Winslow can take you to release your men."

"Thank you, Mon General," Lafitte replied.

"Officer's call is at seven each morning," ordered General Andrew Jackson.

#

NACOGDOCHES, TEXAS
November, 2002

Jeb pulled the pickup to a stop in the driveway next to the house. He could see Louie on a rocking chair and Hannah sitting on the porch playing with her dolls. Since the dog incident, Hannah hadn't been the welcoming little princess she'd previously had been. As he got out of the truck, he looked at her playing and smiled. He then walked around to the back of the pickup and opened the tailgate.

As he opened it, a dog barked.

Jeb was careful not to look at Hannah, but he knew that he had her full attention as he untied the leash and the two-year-old golden retriever leaped from the back of the truck.

"Daddy got a dog!" Hannah announced to everyone in a two block radius.

Instantly, she leaped from the porch and ran to Jeb, but instead of taking hold of the dog, she wrapped her arms around her father's leg.

"Can we keep him?" she asked.

Jeb looked down at his little girl. "You'll have to talk to Missy and Becca about it, but if they say that it's okay then I guess that we can."

Hannah quickly hugged the dog and took the leash from her father's hand and led the canine to the house.

"I'll go see," she said as she headed up the porch past her great-uncle. "Look, Uncle Louie. Daddy got us a dog."

"I see," he replied as she passed. Then he looked at Jeb, "You're a tough one."

Jeb looked down at his uncle as he went into the house. "Hush!"

Just inside the door Kay met him with the baby in her arms.

"A dog, huh?" Kay said with cocky look on her face.

"Don't you have a date to get ready for?" Jeb replied.

The two of them headed up the stairs to Rebecca's room. Inside, the dog stood with its front legs on the bed while Rebecca and Hannah pet it.

"Becca says that it's okay, and Missy likes him. I can tell," Hannah assured Jeb as he and Kay came through the door.

"What's his name, Daddy?" Rebecca asked.

"It's a 'her'," Jeb answered. "At the shelter they called her 'Bessie'".

"Bessie?" Hannah asked like it is the dumbest name in the world. "She's not a Bessie."

"I didn't think so either," Jeb said. "I thought you two could come up with a better name."

Louie appeared at the top of the stairs and entered the room.

"I like Charlotte," Rebecca said.

"Me too," agreed Hannah.

Jeb glared at Uncle Louie.

"Charlotte it is," Kay said as she put her free arm around Jeb.

Jeb pulled his wife close and whispered softly, "You realize, of course, that your daughters just named their dog after a whore."

Chapter 17

January 7, 1815

Ephraim, Cort, and Captain Johnny Henderson were sitting on some empty beer barrels sipping coffee in front of the Maison de Macarty, the large Plantation home that now served as General Jackson's forward command center. About a hundred feet in front of the house stood the embankment, the first line of defense against the British Army that was now amassing less than a quarter of a mile downriver.

The barrels were delivered and promptly drained the previous night after Sergeant Redenbaugh "liberated" them from several New Orleans saloons. The men didn't know that the General himself had suggested to Henderson that if such refreshment were available and if such could be acquired discreetly, it would be good for morale. Johnny, in turn, relayed the suggestion to Sergeant Redenbaugh. The sergeant, who was familiar with every saloon in the city, delightfully held a few particular saloonkeepers at gunpoint while liberating their stock.

It turned out to be a brilliant idea, which seemed the case with most of the General's ideas, because for the first time in days, nearly all of the men were in a good humor. Ephraim couldn't see why the General wanted his role kept secret, however. He had already confiscated nearly every horse, rifle, flint, and most of the food in the city.

The war, and General Jackson in particular, were becoming more and more unpopular in New Orleans. Most of the people saw the fight as a hopeless waste of manpower that would eventually result in bringing the British wrath on the city's innocent residents.

The Louisiana State Legislature wanted to surrender and probably would have if not for the fear that Jackson would honor his threat to turn his cannons on the State House should they make any attempt to communicate with the British. Governor Claiborne, it was rumored, agreed with the Legislature but kept silent on the subject. Ephraim suspected that his silence was out of fear that Jackson would personally horsewhip him.

Over the past few days Ephraim had been witness to the now-famous Jackson temper and was convinced that the General would, in fact, whip the governor if he spoke out. Given the General's temperament, Claiborne most likely felt his chance of survival was far better with the British than with Jackson.

The men on the rampart were more optimistic for victory than the citizens, although no one liked sitting there watching the British get ready to attack. At first the men resented Jackson's order that they build the embankment, arguing that they had volunteered to fight, not pack mud and dirt. Then Jackson brought in slaves to assist, and the militia's resentment worsened at the humiliation of working alongside slaves. Jackson simply answered, "You'll work together, and you'll fight together."

While the embankment was being built, the General had personally led an attack on the British camp. The raid, though successful, was very costly. That also was hard on the men who feared that Jackson didn't know what he was doing. Many of these men, like Broussard, had been fighting Indians for much of their lives. Indian fighting, Ephraim learned, was quite different than fighting an organized army. Indians fought in creeks and from behind trees rather than on an open field of battle, and most of the men on the line preferred to deal with the British in that same manner. To some extent, Jackson, who had tremendous success fighting Creeks, felt the same way, but he also knew that they were vastly outnumbered.

The General relied heavily on Louis' experience and knowledge of the British tactics. Louis believed that harassment, as he called it, would be only that. Sooner or later the British commander would march on the city, and the militia would be forced to face them on open ground.

Of course, the men didn't understand this. They felt that hiding behind this wall of mud and cotton bales was foolish and even cowardly. Ephraim mentioned this to Louis an hour earlier as they ate breakfast.

Rose simply replied, "The men will feel differently when they hear a thousand English musket-balls pound the mud embankment that they're standing behind."

"What do you think, Johnny?" Ephraim asked while cuddling the warm coffee mug in his cold hands. "Do we have a chance in this thing?"

Captain Henderson thought for a moment and replied, "I don't know, Eph. I've never really been in a fight, and they didn't teach fighting from behind a mud wall in the

Academy. But if Cort's artillerymen are as good as Colonel Rose says, we might be able to slow them down."

Cort looked at Henderson as he held tightly to his cup and shivered beneath his blue uniform coat and said confidently, "They will hit their targets."

"Do we know how many men they have?" Ephraim asked.

"It's hard to tell. But it's a lot," Henderson answered. "Yesterday I went down the West River Road with the General. We could see the Red Coat camp. It's big - eight thousand, maybe ten."

"And us?" Ephraim asked.

"Around five thousand all totaled," Henderson replied. "A few are spread out on the West side of the River along with a few cannon in case they try to flank us. We have a few hundred men on Lake Pontchartrain, and there are a couple of hundred slaves building us a fallback position a mile north. I estimate that we will have about thirty-five hundred on the wall."

As he finished speaking, they heard a rumbling sound echoing down the road leading from the city.

"They're here," Henderson said as he got off the beer barrel and stood at attention. A moment later General Jackson, followed by General Coffee of the Tennessee Volunteers, Louis Rose, Captain Lafitte, Captain Youx, Colonel Ross, and the rest of the senior officers, walked out onto the porch.

Ephraim and Cort stood as a long line of men marched in perfect precision past the house. Some wore uniforms like Cort, but most were dressed like the average citizens they were. Some were businessmen, wearing finely tailored coats and silk shirts. Others were farmers with scruffy coats and tattered hats. All had black skin.

The command marched with shouldered muskets around the house and formed four columns facing the front porch. As Ephraim watched he remembered how difficult such precision actually was. The 85th Light Foot drilled endlessly and never looked as organized as these men.

The formation stopped and came to attention. Winston was standing proudly in the front row. He, along with the other men in perfect precision, took his rifle from right-shoulder-arms to port-arms.

"General Jackson, The Freemen of Color are at your service sir!" shouted the man who had taken position in front of the rest of the command.

"Welcome, Major Lacoste," Jackson said. "If you would be so kind as to join me for some refreshments, I'll explain the current status. Captain Henderson will show your men to their emplacements."

"Yes sir!" Major Lacoste shouted, then crisply saluted and marched up the steps to the porch.

As Henderson led the Freemen of Color along the newly built road running the length of the mud wall, Louise Rose stepped off of the porch and walked over to Cort and Ephraim and said, "Cort, see if you can round us up four horses. General Lafitte wants to take one last look at cannon placement on the lake."

"Last look?" Ephraim asked as Jean Lafitte joined them.

"The General and Colonel Rose think that the main attack will take place tomorrow," Lafitte replied. "Ephraim, let's take a walk up the hill while they get the horses."

"Yes, sir," Ephraim replied, having become Lafitte's aide-de-camp.

The hill, of course, was the mud and dirt wall. All along the embankment Louis had ramps built for horse and wagons to haul up powder, cannonballs, and other supplies. The dirt ramp was steep, and the hike took some effort. The wall itself was between six and ten feet high, depending on just where along wall you stood. It was designed to be just high enough that a man couldn't climb it easily without a ladder. The side facing the British was almost straight up, with the canal running along its length. Jackson had ordered that the canal be widened to eight feet and deepened to four feet so that the approaching army would be slowed significantly when they got to it.

The top of the wall was just wide enough for a wagon to pass. Along the side facing the British, the men had built up the mud so that they could kneel behind it. In many places they had put up fences, wagon parts, cotton bales, and just about anything else that they could find that might stop a British musket ball.

Every so often they came to cannon batteries. As Ephraim and Lafitte walked along the wall, most of the men were repairing damages to the embankment while a few stood looking off to the South where the Red Coats could be faintly seen in the distance.

There had been several cannon bombardments. The previous day had seen the most lengthy cannon battle. To everyone's relief the embankment suffered little damage. Most of the Red Coat cannon balls had fallen far short of their target, and those that hit made almost no impact. The men were easily able to make the necessary repairs. The British, on the other hand, were not so fortunate. Their intention was obvious. They wanted to inflict as much damage to the wall as they could and at the same time intimidate the Americans. The result was quite the opposite. The British commander had no respect for the American cannon and placed his artillery positions where they were visible from the wall. Cort's men never missed a shot.

Most of the British artillery positions had been destroyed, and a number of their soldiers were injured or killed. Yet on the wall, not a single American was scratched. Even General Jackson was impressed.

Lafitte and Ephraim walked up to Reggie, who was standing next to a cannon and looking toward the British camp. Lucian and Llewellyn were there as well, repairing the stockade.

"Reggie," Lafitte began, "we're going out to the lake. The General thinks that we need more men. I want you to take a detachment into the city. Bring back anyone you can find. If he can hold a rifle, bring him."

Lucian spoke up. "We'll go with you Reggie."

#

Twenty minutes later as Ephraim, Lafitte, Cort, and Louis rode away, Lucian turned to Llewellyn and Reggie and said, "Reggie, I need a favor."

"What's that?" Reggie asked.

"There's a girl that I want to see while we're in the city," Lucian replied. "I'm going to marry her."

"You're what?" Llewellyn said in shock.

"I'm getting married, Llewellyn," Lucian explained. "I know that I should have told you earlier, but it doesn't matter. I'm going to do it today."

"Look, Lucian..." Llewellyn began.

"No," Lucian said, cutting his brother off. "You can't talk me out of it. I'm going to do it."

"Can't you wait until after this war is over?" Llewellyn protested.

"No, it can't," Lucian retorted. "She has no one, and if I get killed on that pile of dirt tomorrow she will be left all alone, but if I marry her today I know that you and Ephraim will take care of her."

Llewellyn studied Lucian's face, moved by his brother's statement. He knew that Lucian was headstrong, and once he'd made up his mind there was no changing it. In truth, up to that moment the thought of any of them dying had not entered Llewellyn's mind.

"You really love this girl?" Llewellyn asked although the answer was obvious.

"Yeah," Lucian answered.

Llewellyn studied the conviction on his brother's face and then said warmly, "I'll stand by you, little brother."

"Reg, I need somewhere I can take her to be safe. Do you have any ideas?" Lucian asked, looking at the Major.

"We can take her to my place. She can stay with my housekeeper," the large man replied.

"I appreciate it, Reggie," Lucian said warmly.

"I think that we'd better hurry, boys," the Major suggested. "We're going to a wedding."

#

NACOGDOCHES, TEXAS
November, 2002

Jeb and Kay strolled slowly down North Street of the little old college town. It was homecoming weekend, and the normally sleepy village bristled with activity. Like at universities all over the country, there was an atmosphere of excitement at homecoming.

They had just finished dinner at the Clear Springs Cafe, the one decent steak house in town. Just off Main Street an old warehouse had been turned into a rather nice restaurant, and was one of the few that didn't have a drive-through window. It was not fancy by any means, but they served a truly good steak. That was probably because the beef they served was most likely still standing on the hoof only hours before being charcoal-broiled and covered with mushrooms.

As the couple walked along the street, they could hear the school band playing at a pep rally in the stadium a few blocks away. Jeb instinctively took Kay's hand, and they turned down Griffith Blvd. toward the school. It occurred to Jeb that he couldn't remember the last time that he strolled down a street holding Kay's hand. Oddly, he recalled that the first time he had ever held her hand was the night of Aggie Muster, eleven years prior. Muster was a unique Texas A&M tradition, which called for Aggies, past and present, to gather in cities around the world to "answer the call" and honor Aggies who had passed.

"Do you remember the first time you held my hand?" Kay asked.

"Yes. Muster, your junior year," Jeb replied, feeling proud that he knew the answer.

"Do you remember the last time?"

"No," he said sheepishly.

"Your father's funeral."

"I'm sorry, Kay," he told her, holding her hand tightly. "I've been such a fool. You were carrying this family even before Becca got hurt."

"You've had a lot on your plate," Kay said, genuinely understanding.

"That's not it. Well, maybe that's part of it," he told her, trying to frame his thoughts. "Kay, every day I wake up with the same worries, the same debts, the same lousy job, and every day the only thing that changes is that the debts get worse."

"You love your job," Kay interjected.

"I did, but for a while it has just been a way to keep paying the bills."

They walked through the main campus. Banners and ribbons were hanging from the buildings, and they could hear the cheering from the pep rally.

"For weeks I've been listening to that old man."

"Uncle Louie?"

"For weeks I've been listening to Uncle Louie," Jeb corrected. "He tells his stories, and I keep feeling like there should be more, like I missed something in life. I wonder who my father really was, and I fear that my life is an endless string of bills. Now I'm constantly afraid of another of the kids having an accident."

He stopped walking and took Kay into his arms.

"Look, I really love you, and there is nothing in this world I want more than what I have right here. I guess that I'm just afraid that I can't carry the load."

"The load is mine too, you know," Kay added as she hugged her husband.

"Kay I really love you," he whispered softly in her ear.

"I know. I love you too," she murmured and then looked into his eyes, "but there's something I need to tell you."

It was clear by the look on his face that he had no idea where she was going. Men always seemed to miss the obvious.

"Remember that night I came up to the study?" Kay asked.

"The attic. Yeah."

"You got one past the guards."

Again, he had a look of bewilderment.

"Let me try to explain this where you can understand it, Professor," she said mockingly. "You knocked me up."

Jeb froze, not sure whether to be happy or to run away in terror.

He finally smiled and asked as he pulled her tightly to him, "Can we afford another one?"

Kay kissed her husband lightly and replied, "We can't afford the three we have."

"Not to mention the dog and the grouchy old man," Jeb said and then added, "Will you at least give me a boy this time?"

"I was hoping for a girl. We could name her Charlotte," Kay said jokingly.

"No," Jeb said firmly. "And if it's a boy we're not naming him after some damn pirate, either."

#

CHERI ROYAL, NEW ORLEANS
January 7, 1815

It had been almost a month since Lucian had asked Charlotte to marry him, and she hadn't heard a word from him since. For all she knew, he was in jail. He was a pirate, after all. Or he may have been captured by the British. Or he might be out with the rest of the men building what Hamilton called "the Jackson line."

Hamilton enjoyed mocking the men who had joined to fight the British. He considered them all fools, saying, "Everyone on that wall is going to die."

Off and on for days they had heard the distant rumble of cannon fire. The first time they heard it, Charlotte was sitting downstairs with Dianna. Dianna insisted that they remain prepared for business even though there were no customers. So every evening they sat, all dressed up, in that big empty saloon. At first, Charlotte had no idea what the noise was. She felt it more than she heard it. There would be a distant rumble that shook the glass in the windows. It wasn't until Hamilton joked, "The Red Coats are coming," that Charlotte realized that the noise was cannon fire.

It was even more frightening when the rumbling stopped because everyone knew that at any moment the

British could come marching up the streets. When it ended, Hamilton remarked, "Get ready girls, business is about to pick up." It didn't, of course, and so he had a few drinks, cursed, and threw things at the wall.

Every night was the same. They would come down and sit at the tables waiting for patrons who never came while Hamilton would sit drinking and working up his anger. Some nights he would be mad at General Jackson, others he would be mad at the Red Coats. Once after Lee Anne, one of the ladies, remarked that she hoped that Jackson beat the Red Coats, Hamilton drained his whisky glass and threw it into her face, breaking her nose and lodging a sharp piece of glass into her cheek. After that no one said much around Mr. Hamilton.

Each night Charlotte sat there with the "Lovely Ladies of Cheri Royal" hoping and praying for Lucian to return and take her away. Surely he would come. He didn't seem the sort to just disappear, but then neither had Ephraim.

As she sat there on her bed waiting for the day to pass into evening, she felt that pang once again at the back of her heart. It wasn't often that she thought of Ephraim any more. She had come to the point that she managed to block those thoughts from her mind, but now and again she let them slip in. Slowly his smile was becoming faint, and his image was becoming hard to hold, and deep in her heart, she began to fear that it would soon slip from her memory entirely.

Charlotte felt moisture build in her eyes, and for the first time that she could recall she cursed out loud. It wasn't because she had begun to cry but rather because she had let her thoughts dwell on him.

Suddenly there was a knock at her door, and she heard Dianna say, "Charlotte there is someone to see you."

Immediately the thoughts of the past few moments were erased as the reality of life at Cheri Royal returned. It had been awhile since she had heard Dianna say those words, but they always meant the same thing - customers.

Quickly, Charlotte checked her face and hair and stepped out into the hall leading to the stairs that took her from her safe little room and into the ugliness that was the world in which she lived.

As she rounded the corner and started down the stairs, she heard Hamilton say mockingly, "You look like you've been on the line with our brave heroes. How goes it? Have the Red Coats surrendered yet?"

"Not yet," Lucian said with an impatient tone.

Charlotte's heart burst with excitement at the sound of his voice.

Lucian looked at her as she came to the landing, smiled broadly, and told her, "Get your things, Charlotte. We're going."

Charlotte froze as she looked at him and then at Hamilton who was sitting at one of the tables with Jeth drinking.

"What are you talking about?" Hamilton asked, no longer jovial.

"Do it, Charlotte," Lucian said, smiling calmly.

Hamilton leaped to his feet, "She's not going anywhere unless I tell her that she can."

Suddenly, two men holding muskets came in the door. Charlotte recognized one as the large man who had met Ephraim at the coffee house.

Hamilton looked at the two men. Clearly he recognized the large one and said, "Major, I don't know what this is about, but it's not any of your business."

"Hamilton, why aren't you on the line?" The large man asked.

For the first time since she had known him, Hamilton was obviously afraid.

"I have a bad arm," Hamilton replied. "I can't hold a rifle."

"We'll give you a handgun," Reggie said as he pointed the musket at him.

"I'm not going out on that line, and that girl isn't going anywhere," Hamilton stated angrily.

"Get your things, Charlotte," Lucian repeated.

Charlotte hesitated for a moment but then saw the confidence in Lucian's eyes and turned and ran upstairs.

As she headed up the steps she heard Hamilton yell, "Charlotte if you try to leave with these men I'll kill you!"

As she reached the top of the stairs she heard a crashing noise and stopped and looked back down. Hamilton was lying on his back on the floor. He was holding his hand to the side of his face, which was streaming with blood. Lucian was standing over him holding a broken beer mug, having just crashed it against the man's head. In a flash the two men at the door came rushing in. One stood over Hamilton holding his musket pointed directly his face. The other pointed his gun at Jeth.

#

A few minutes later Lucian was waiting at the base of the stairs when Charlotte descended holding Mr. Whitechapel's bag. She probably could have folded her dresses and packed them neatly but she wanted out of that place and wasn't about to waste time packing.

She tried to hold her emotions and walk down the stairs with dignity, but as soon as she got to the bottom, she broke into tears, dropped the bag, and leaped into Lucian's arms. With tears streaming down her face, she looked up into his eyes as he leaned down and kissed her gently on the mouth.

For the very first time since leaving Randallstown, Charlotte Fuller felt truly safe. Let the war rage and let the British come. She now had a reason to live. At that moment she swore that she would give her heart to this man. He may not have the smile that made her heart pound, but he loved her knowing just exactly who she was and walked in willing to give his life to save her.

As she clung to him, one of the two men walked up and said, "We'd better get moving if we're going to get you married."

Charlotte pulled back and looked into Lucian's eyes.

"Will you marry me, Charlotte?" Lucian asked.

With tears still streaming, Charlotte tried to speak but words couldn't come out. All she could do was nod.

Lucian turned, still holding her tightly and said, "Charlotte, this is my brother, Llewellyn."

Charlotte reached out her hand and said with a break in her voice, "Hello, Llewellyn."

"Welcome to the family, Charlotte," Llewellyn replied.

#

By late afternoon Ephraim had decided that he was no more suited to be a dragoon than he was a foot soldier and quietly thanked God that this long day on horseback would soon be behind him. After riding most of the day, his backside was raw, his thighs were chaffed, and his legs were scratched from the brush, and the worst part was that they were just now entering the city and were still a few miles north of the Rodriquez's canal.

The Bos had insisted upon riding along the lakeshore north of the city to examine all possible landing sites and to inspect every artillery position. No one, not even Lafitte, expected the British to land on the lake, and there were plenty of spies positioned to warn them if any British ships did happen to move that direction, but General Jackson feared that the Red Coats would either send a small landing force down either from the lake or across the river. Both possibilities would mean disaster for the Americans. If the main force attacked from the south as expected and a smaller force came either from the lake or circled through the city from the west bank, the militia along the canal would be caught in the middle.

The only solution was to leave small companies of men in both places with just enough cannons to slow such an attack. If the American main force on the canal heard cannon fire from north of the city, the militia would fall back to a second, much smaller mud wall currently being built on the edge of the city. Half of the militia would remain at that position and hold off the main British assault while the other half took positions north of New Orleans.

The plan had only one problem, as Ephraim saw it. It had no hope of working. Actually, Ephraim had no idea if it would work or not, but Louis assured him that such a retreat in the middle of a battle would mean disaster. The only hope the Americans had was to hold the wall, and thus far, Louis Rose had been right about almost everything.

"One breach," he explained, "would guarantee a Red Coat victory."

Lafitte and Rose agreed that the positions were capable of holding off a small force should an assault come from the lake. The General had placed six cannons in three positions covering a mile of shore. He, of course, would have loved to have several times that, but the supplies were just not available.

The problem wasn't that there weren't enough cannons or even men. The problem was getting them into position. Right after Captain Gambi got to New Orleans with the *Petit Milan*, the British had put a blockade on the River. For about a week Lafitte's smugglers had moved weapons up bayous, but the General soon ordered that process halted, not wanting the supplies to fall into the hands of the enemy.

They ended up with a little over twenty heavy guns spread over three fronts with the heaviest concentration on the Rodriquez's Canal. That, Rose said, was spreading them way too thin.

The four men rode through the hauntingly quiet streets of New Orleans. As they turned onto Esplanade Avenue, Lafitte remarked to Cort, "Captain, if these buildings are here this time tomorrow, it will be a testimony to the accuracy of your artillery."

Then up ahead Ephraim saw something that he didn't expect. Reggie was sitting on a horse holding a musket across his lap while watching over two wagonloads of disgruntled but quiet recruits.

Lafitte spurred his horse and trotted up to the Major, who looked over his shoulder at the sound of his approach. Ephraim quickly followed with Cort and Rose behind.

"What do you have there?" Lafitte asked.

"These are a few volunteers for the Militia, General." The large man replied. "There aren't many people on the streets, but it's amazing what you can find in the saloons and bordellos. If you don't mind, sir, we could use some help getting them to the Canal."

When Ephraim caught up with Lafitte, he suddenly realized that Reggie was sitting in front of the church he and Charlotte had walked to that day they met at the Alley. It occurred to him that this was the first place he should come to look for her.

Hamilton, who was sitting with Jeth in one of the wagons nursing a bloody knot on his forehead, looked at Lafitte and demanded, "Lafitte, your man has no right to take us like this, and I expect full payment for that girl he stole."

Lafitte looked at the man with disgust.

"Hamilton," he said, "the Major is under orders from General Jackson himself to bring any able-bodied man that he can find to the battlefield. I suggest you come along quietly, unless you would prefer that I shoot you now and save the Red Coats the trouble."

Hamilton glared at Lafitte who, Ephraim thought, would prefer to shoot the man than take him all the way back to the Canal.

Lafitte then looked over at Reggie and asked, "What's this about one of his girls?"

Reggie hesitated. He was clearly uncomfortable as he looked at Lafitte and then Ephraim and finally said softly to Lafitte, "One of the boys decided to get married."

Ephraim strained to hear. About all he caught was the word "married" when Lafitte asked, "Married? Who?"

Still softly the Major replied, "Ephraim's brother."

Lafitte caught the message in Reggie's tone and looked over at Ephraim who could barely hear what was being said from the clatter of Louis' and Cort's horses.

Finally Ephraim asked, "Did you say that my brother got married?"

"Yeah, Eph," Reggie answered reluctantly. "They're inside."

Ephraim began to get off his horse.

"Don't, Ephraim," the Major said catching Ephraim by surprise.

"I should go in there." Ephraim protested.

"Don't!" Reggie said a bit more firmly. "They'll be out in a minute."

Ephraim hesitated as he looked at his friend. He felt that he should go in the church but realized that there was something behind the cold expression on Reggie's face.

A moment later the door of the church opened, and Llewellyn came out followed by Lucian and Charlotte. Ephraim's heart leaped at the sight of her, but suddenly an icy chill ran through him as he saw that she was holding Lucian's arm. Her face glowed as they came down the steps, having not yet seen him. Her smile, he thought, was larger than he'd ever seen it.

Ephraim's eyes darted over at Reggie, who was expressionless. He looked back at Charlotte as Lucian saw the four newcomers.

"Ephraim," Lucian shouted cheerfully.

Charlotte suddenly looked up to see Ephraim on a horse with Lucian's friend and four other men. Their eyes locked for a long moment as the smile on her face disappeared.

Llewellyn climbed aboard one of the wagons, taking the reins as Lucian, full of excitement, took Charlotte over to Ephraim and Lafitte.

"Charlotte," Lucian said motioning to Lafitte, "This is Captain Jean Lafitte, Louis Rose, our friend Cort, and my little brother Ephraim."

Charlotte's eyes were fixed on Ephraim as she and Lucian approached. She then glanced over at Lucian's large friend, the one he called Reggie, who smiled down at her. There was something strong in his expression that gave her strength. She looked up at Ephraim on the horse. He had that hurt little boy expression that her mind had kept seeing all these months. Her heart pounded within her, knowing the pain that was behind his eyes. Then, as she clutched Lucian's right arm, she remembered that Ephraim had disappeared. For whatever the reason, he had not come to the coffeehouse that day. Yet standing beside her was a man who had shown no hesitation to fight and even die to save her.

Charlotte looked at Reggie one more time and smiled. She then stood as tall as she could, and still clutching her husband's arm, she reached out with her right hand and said, "Hello, Ephraim, I'm Charlotte."

Chapter 18

RODRIQUEZ'S CANAL
1:45 a.m., January 8, 1815

Ephraim had given up any hope of sleep and decided to take a walk along the embankment. Throughout its length, scatterings of men were curled up against the low stockade with muskets in hand, snoring away. Most however, like Ephraim, were unable to even think of sleep. Intelligence reports were supposed to be secret, but everyone on the wall knew that at first light if not sooner, the sky would be filled with rocket fire, musket balls, and cannon smoke.

The British had tried to conceal their maneuvers, but Broussard and the other scouts had been returning with reports of troop movements since nightfall. The General had ordered an officers' call at midnight, and Louis explained what they could expect, given the troop placement.

"They'll attack," he explained, "hitting simultaneously at two different positions with enough reserves to follow with at least two more waves. They have had great success with this type of attack.

"The key for them is numbers. They know that we are militia, and they expect us to be undisciplined. They are assuming that we will fall back when we see the size of the initial assault."

The briefing had gone on for almost an hour. Ephraim heard almost none of it. Instead, all he could think about was the image of Charlotte holding on to Lucian and introducing herself as if they were strangers.

As he walked along the ridge, the image of her looking up at him kept flashing in his mind. Each time he saw her face, he felt a grueling pain in his stomach and a weight on his chest that made it hard to breathe. It was as if the war had already begun, and he had been shot a thousand times in the heart.

How could it have happened?

The ride back from the city had been long. Cort, who instinctively knew exactly what was wrong, had taken one of the wagonloads of recruits while Lucian took his new wife to Reggie's house where she would be safe. Reggie rode alongside Ephraim, not saying a word. He most likely thought that Ephraim was angry with him, but in reality there simply was nothing to say. There were a million questions running though Ephraim's mind, but no words came out from his mouth. His brother had just married the woman he loved.

All along the ridge were small groups of men. Some of the men were sleeping; others were telling stories. A few had small fires to make coffee and to provide a little warmth against the cold damp night air.

Then out of the corner of his eye, Ephraim saw a man stand and hold out a cup.

"Coffee Ephraim?" a familiar voice said.

Jolted out of his daze, Ephraim recognized Winston. His first impulse was to say "no" and walk on, but upon looking at the kind gentle eyes of his friend, he had to concede.

"Thank you, Winston," Ephraim said as he took the cup from the man's hand.

Seeing the troubled look on Ephraim's face, Winston asked, "Your spirits are down, my friend?"

Sipping his coffee, Ephraim smiled and answered, "We're about to have a war. Haven't you heard?"

Winston looked closely at the Englishman and then led Ephraim over to a couple of powder kegs and the two sat down.

"Your eyes cannot lie as easily as your lips."

Ephraim shrugged, not knowing what to say.

"I think it is about your girl. I think you've seen her?"

Ephraim clutched his cup of coffee as he looked out over the field toward the British camp. In the distance there were plumes of smoke from campfires. His heart felt heavy, and he sensed the making of tears in his eyes. He swallowed hard, trying not to show the pain swelling in his chest.

"She got married today," he said softly as he looked in the distance, fearing that Winston would see his tears.

"I'm sorry, my friend," Winston said warmly.

After a moment Ephraim looked over at Winston and asked, "Are you married, Winston?"

Winston smiled broadly, "I have a good wife and five sons."

Ephraim stared as he realized shamefully that, until now, it had not entered his mind that Winston might have a family.

"Why are you here?" He asked.

"We were slaves in Saint-Dominique," Winston explained, "but here we are free. My children are free. We are Americans. I fight so that my children may have a good life here."

Ephraim looked over his shoulder toward the city. He could see the glow of fires at the second mud wall. Late that day General Jackson had issued weapons to two hundred slaves who stood ready in case the Red Coats breached the line.

"They're not free," Ephraim said motioning to the other wall.

"No, but perhaps someday," Winston said confidently. "We, the Free Men of Color, choose to fight because this is our country where we can own our businesses and own our land, and we can choose to fight for those things. In Saint-Dominique I did not have that choice. Perhaps someday they will have that freedom. Why are you here? You are English. You should be on the other side."

"I don't know, Winston," Ephraim said as he finished his coffee. "This morning I was here for the same reason as you, but tonight I don't know."

Ephraim stood, handed Winston his cup, and said, "Thanks for the coffee Winston."

Winston stood and looked Ephraim in the eye. "That girl loved you, Ephraim. I saw it. Every day I saw her walk past, looking for you."

"Then why did she marry my brother?" Ephraim asked.

"Many are the plans in a man's heart, but it is the Lord's purpose that prevails," offered Winston. "Proverbs 19:21."

#

RODRIQUEZ'S CANAL
5:15 a.m., January 8, 1815

At four in the morning there had been one final officers' call. Broussard had returned with information that the enemy troops had amassed in attack positions. He claimed that there were units of the 44th Regiment followed by Scottish Highlanders forming in the center with other British units forming on the left and right flanks.

After the briefing Ephraim walked away from the Headquarters with Cort and Reggie. Cort's artillery had been split into three batteries, positioned at the right end of the Jackson line nearest the river. Cort commanded the first battery. Captain Dominique Youx commanded the second battery and acted as overall artillery commander, and Captain Gambi commanded of the third. This put Lafitte's militia unit at the right flank protecting the river road into the city.

Cort had his best teams on the big guns. The rest of the Lafitte men were divided into rifle units, one unit for each cannon. The various militias under Colonel Ross, General Coffee with his Tennessee militia and Choctaw Indians, and Major Lacoste's Free Men of Color would man the rest of the quarter mile line.

"What do you think?" Ephraim asked, just to make conversation, not because he cared the least about the war.

"I think that we will see their red suits at first light. I also think that you shouldn't be here," Cort replied.
Ephraim looked at his friend.

"Every man on this line has to do his job. Right now you don't care if you live or die," Cort explained. "That can be dangerous for everyone. I'm putting you with your brothers in Reggie's rifle group. General Lafitte gave him orders. If you can't do your job, he's to shoot you."

Reggie looked at Ephraim empathetically and said, "Eph, I'm sorry about the girl."

"Would you really shoot me?" Ephraim asked dryly.

The large man looked at his friend and then shrugged. "Yeah."

"Then do it now and get it over with," Ephraim said as he turned to walk away.

Suddenly, Llewellyn appeared on the rampart just above where the three of them stood and shouted, "It's starting!"

Cort ran up the mud ramp followed by Reggie and Ephraim. They came to a halt between two of the cannons. Every soldier on the American line was on his feet with his rifle ready, looking across the rampart. A thick morning fog had settled over the open plain before them, making it impossible to see more than a few yards. Eerie sounds echoed across the vast open field. Though it was faint, Ephraim could hear the orders being barked out by a British Sergeant-Major followed by the muffled rumble of marching troops.

"Eph," Llewellyn called, breaking the silence.

Ephraim walked over to his two brothers who were standing together looking out over the fields.

"Boys, if we stick together we just might get through this thing," Llewellyn said.

Ephraim and Lucian looked at one another and nodded in agreement.

Three horses loped up the ramp and came to a halt behind the brothers. Louis Rose and Jean Lafitte climbed down off of their mounts.

General Jackson remained on his white horse and barked out as the men on the line looked up at him, "It looks like they're up for a fight today, boys. Not far across that field stands a British army intent upon taking the city of New Orleans and making it part of Great Britain. Yesterday, the Louisiana State Legislature sent me a letter insisting that we surrender immediately. They're convinced that we will not win this war, and they think that we should give up this fight lest we anger our enemy."

The General paused, having the full attention of every man within earshot.

"Well, boys, the British have angered me!" Jackson continued. "I told that Legislature that I will burn every shack in that city before I surrender one inch of American soil to these invaders."

Ephraim stood in awe as every soldier within earshot began to cheer. It may have been the sight of the old Tennessee soldier on his white horse or possibly the relaxed self-assured tone in which he spoke. It could also be that he, as everyone knew, was terribly ill from influenza yet remained strong and defiant. Regardless, a sense of power and confidence spread throughout the line. They were a disorderly collection of Spanish and French settlers, Tennessee and Kentucky woodsmen, Choctaw Indians, professional soldiers, businessmen, slaves, former slaves, and pirates, but at that moment they stood together as Americans. Across the plain marched an army that was vastly superior in every respect, yet there was not a man on the wall doubting who would win the day.

General Coffee along with Captain Henderson loped up the ramp and came to a halt behind General Andrew Jackson.

"Men," the General continued, "if the British win this city, they will win this war. The future of the Union lives or dies on this pile of dirt. Keep your heads down and hit what you shoot at."

The General spurred his horse, and with Coffee and Henderson behind began to trot casually along the ridge.

With each step of the hoof, the cheers of the American militia echoed across the plain to the waiting British Army.

When the General had gone, Rose and Lafitte, muskets in hand, sent their horses down the ramp and walked over to Cort. Louis crisply saluted and said, "Where can we serve you, Captain?"

Cort looked somewhat uncomfortably at Rose and then Lafitte.

"It's your command, Captain," Lafitte said as he saluted the young Spaniard.

Cort returned the salute, nodded, and told them, "Reggie's infantry troop could use a couple more guns, Sir."

The two men took positions along the low stockade with Reggie, Llewellyn, Lucian, and Ephraim and looked across the dark, fog-covered meadow before them. In the distance to their left, another round of cheers broke out as the General made his speech on down the line.

#

FRENCHMEN STREET,
NEW ORLEANS
5:50 a.m., January 8, 1815

Charlotte Fuller Whitechapel Bradford lay motionless on top of a large iron-posted bed. She still wore what was now her wedding dress. It had been a long sleepless night. Just after dark, Maria, the housekeeper, had told her that word was spreading throughout the city that the big battle was about to begin. The two women had spent the night nervously keeping one another company.

Maria was much older than Charlotte. She was both white and black and had, she explained, been what the people of New Orleans knew as a quadroon when she was younger. Though the years had been hard on her, she was still quite beautiful.

Charlotte knew of the quadroons. They were essentially beautiful young women given by their families as mistresses to wealthy white businessmen who kept them in the little houses on Rampart Street. It was murmured, but never in the presence of Dianna, that Mr. Hamilton kept a quadroon in one of those little houses.

Maria had come to live with the Blankenship family after the businessman she so deeply loved suddenly stopped coming by. Her heart was broken when she learned that he had a family and had moved to Savannah without even leaving her a note to say goodbye. Like most of the quadroons, she believed him when he told her that he was not married and hoped that she would someday become his wife.

She said that she was lucky to have found the Blankenship family. They had been good to her. Most of the quadroons who lost their men ended up working in the brothels. Charlotte understood that Maria had told the story to let her know she was not at all unlike Charlotte.

As morning approached and they had not yet heard cannon fire, Maria fell asleep. Lying next to her, Charlotte was still wide awake with her thoughts. Late in the night had she lost control of her emotions and begun to weep. She told Maria everything. How she came to be in New Orleans. How she had met Ephraim, and how, by a twist of fate, she was now married to his brother. She told how he had looked so completely broken when she'd reached up to shake his hand. And now, she explained, both men could die on that wall standing against the vast British army.

As the two women lay next to one another clutching each other's hands waiting for the British to come and destroy the city, Maria whispered softly, "You are a very lucky woman to be so loved by two men."

With Maria now asleep, those words kept echoing through Charlotte's mind. Though they gave her comfort, her heart ached as she kept seeing the heartbroken expression on Ephraim's face.

How could this have happened?

Finally, as the first rays of sunlight hit the windows, Charlotte began to fade off to sleep only to be jolted back awake by distant rumble of cannon fire.

#

RODRIQUEZ'S CANAL
BATTERY ONE
5:50 a.m., January 8, 1815

There was silence from one end of the Jackson line to the other. The euphoric mood of the militia had long since faded away as Ephraim and his brothers stood motionless and looked into the darkness. The fog had thickened to the point that no one knew exactly how far away the British troops were or how many marched toward them. For a while they could hear the sound of boots in the mud, but as the fog thickened, the sounds had stopped.

Ephraim clung to his musket as he peered over the low makeshift stockade and waited for the first sign of the enemy, yet in his heart the enemy stood beside him. Horrible thoughts passed through his mind: thoughts of Lucian falling to a musket ball and even thoughts of shooting Lucian himself. These things shamed him, but he couldn't help letting them pass through his head, just as he couldn't hold back the image of Charlotte's face as she had reached up to shake his hand.

How could this have happened?

"There," Lucian said as he pointed.

A faint glow of sunlight was beginning to break on the Eastern horizon, and movement could be faintly seen in the distant fog. Ephraim and the others readied their muskets as the entire American line held steady, waiting for a target to appear.

Then suddenly they saw the flash of a rocket overhead, creating a red glow in the dark foggy morning sky, followed by the boom of cannon. Somewhere to their left they heard the cannonball pound the wall and stockade.

"Hold steady boys. They're just trying to wake us up," Reggie said just loudly enough to be heard by Ephraim and his brothers.

Then there was more cannon and rocket fire in rapid succession. Each shot pounded the wall, but not a man along the American line so much as flinched.

Behind them, Captain Youx appeared on horseback and looked down at Cort.

"There is a heavy concentration of troops directly in front of you about two hundred yards out. Cut down their infantry but wait until they commit their troops before you take out their artillery," he ordered.

"We will sir," Cort replied and then saluted crisply as the pirate spurred his horse and rode away.

In the distance Ephraim suddenly heard someone order, "Fire!"

Quickly, Louis, followed by Lucian and Lafitte, knelt down. Ephraim was at first puzzled and then ducked just in time to hear musket balls whistle over their heads.

Louis stood back up and, followed by the others, took aim. As he got back into position, Ephraim began to hear drums and bagpipes. Then Cort shouted, "Fire one"!

There was a deafening boom from the first cannon to Ephraim's right followed a moment later by screams and moans from across the field. Ephraim then saw what Cort had seen. Faintly in the distance there was a thin line of red, green, and white uniforms.

"Fire two!" Cort ordered

There was a second boom, and Ephraim then saw a small group of red coats fall as moans echoed across the meadow.

The cannon fire from across the field began more rapidly but seemed to be concentrated to Ephraim's far left, near the swamp. Then another volley of musket balls whizzed over their heads. This time no one heard nor saw from where they came. Then Louis pointed to their left. There was a mass of green coats marching toward them.

"It's the Scots. They're going to take out this battery," Rose observed.

"We're going to get busy. Hold until I give the order," Reggie demanded.

Suddenly a cannonball hit the canal in front of them. Ephraim, startled, fell backwards on his seat as water and mud splashed all over him.

"Fire at will," Cort ordered, and there were instantly a half dozen cannon blasts shaking the ground.

Ephraim stood, realizing that he had lost his musket.

As he knelt to look for it he heard Reggie yell, "Fire."

His musket was on the far side of the wall. He ran over to pick it up, checked to see that the flint was still in place, and returned to his spot on the line only to find that he was alone. The others had knelt to reload.

Just as Ephraim was about to fire his first shot, Reggie stood and ordered, "Hold."

As the others took their position on the line, Ephraim pointed his musket out across the field and saw the British for the first time. The sun was rising quickly, and the fog had already begun to clear. Ahead and slightly to the left were hundreds of the green coats of the 93rd Scottish Highlanders. Next to them were twice that many white coats of the British 44th Infantry, and directly ahead of him Ephraim could clearly see a familiar banner.

"It's the 85th Light Foot," he heard himself say as a volley of musket balls pounded the wall.

"I know," Llewellyn answered.

"Fire!" Reggie ordered.

Ephraim shot into the center of the field of red. He stood motionless as he saw a man fall, knowing that it was his shot.

At that same moment a blast from one of Cort's cannons mowed down four of five of the Scotsmen marching near the man Ephraim had shot. He froze, looking out into the battlefield as the others knelt to reload. The booming of cannon and musket fire was deafening, and smoke began to fill the air. Across the plain, British soldiers kept marching. A sergeant would shout, and the line would halt, kneel, and fire. A wave of musket balls would whiz past with some thumping the stockade.

Ephraim quickly knelt to reload and arose to point his weapon just as he heard Reggie shout, "Fire at will!"

As he fired his weapon, another cannonball pounded into the wall. This one hit just below Ephraim, and he and his brothers all fell hard to the ground. As he fell, Ephraim's head hit on a stack of cannonballs, and the world went black.

#

FRENCHMEN STREET,
NEW ORLEANS
6:20 a.m., January 8, 1815

Charlotte and Maria clung to one another as they looked out of the second story bedroom window of the little house. Neither knew what they hoped to see. All they knew was that the cannon and rifle fire had been continuous for over fifteen minutes.

The streets that were normally becoming alive at this hour were empty as everyone huddled in their homes, waiting for the British troops to march in and burn their city.

Charlotte listened to the constant booming of cannons and wondered if a person could survive such gunfire.

#

RODRIQUEZ'S CANAL

"Ephraim!" the voice shouted.

Ephraim's ears rang as he opened his eyes to see Lucian's and Llewellyn's faces.

"Wake up Eph," Ephraim heard faintly over the incredible noise all around him. He instinctively tried to sit up.

"He's okay, get back on the line," Llewellyn ordered Lucian.

Lucian nodded, and Ephraim saw him take his rifle and kneel next to a broken piece of stockade.

"You are okay, aren't you kid?" Llewellyn asked.

Ephraim nodded although he wasn't really sure. His mind was a little dazed, and his ears were ringing as he got to his feet.

"Grab your gun," Llewellyn said as he turned and took his spot on the wall.

Picking up his musket, Ephraim saw that the blast had knocked down part of the stockade. He ran over and knelt next to Lucian, who was leaning over the stockade firing his musket. Hundreds of soldiers from the British 44th and 85th were trying to wade the chest deep water of the canal. A few made it across and were trying to climb the wall.

Ephraim fired down into the crowd just below and saw a red coated soldier fall backward into the water. He immediately knelt down to reload. As he did, he looked down the ridge. As far as he could see along the embankment, the militiamen were frantically firing. Billows of white smoke plumed from each rifle. In the far distance he saw Winston and the rest of the Free Men of Color. In perfect precision one row of men would fire, then kneel as a second row stood and fired. Further down the line, General Jackson, still on his horse, waved his saber wildly as he shouted orders.

When his musket was ready to fire, he stood and looked out into the field before him. A morning breeze was blowing the smoke and fog to his right, and for the first time he got a clear sight of the army before him. Thousands of British and Scottish soldiers marched in perfect precision. In the distance a cannon fired, and a twenty-pound ball pounded the wall to his left. A moment later that same cannon exploded as one of Cort's big guns found its target.

Again he looked down and fired his musket into the crowd entering the canal. This time he clearly saw the face of the man who fell. It was a face he knew. This was the 85th, and the soldier he killed had been one of the deserters who stayed on The St. Pascal Baylon. Ephraim froze as he realized that had he and his brothers not come with Louis on the Tigre, he would at that moment be trying to cross the canal.

He paused and looked into the oncoming army. Hundreds of soldiers were falling. Through the deafening rifle and cannon fire he could hear a sergeant major shouting as soldiers kept marching over the dead before them. In the distance an officer on horseback fell, clearly hit by one of the Tennessee sharpshooters. Suddenly, a dozen British soldiers fell as one of Cort's cannons fired grapeshot into the mass marching toward them. He could hear screams of agony, yet the army kept marching. Below, a group of British infantrymen were climbing out of the water.

As quickly as he could, he knelt again to reload and again took his position between his two brothers. Lucian fired his shot and started using his rifle butt to push away soldiers who were trying to scramble up the mud embankment.

Ephraim aimed and fired and hit a soldier Lucian had just bashed with his musket.

As Ephraim leaned back to reload, he saw Lucian hit with a musket ball and fall forward through the gap in the stockade. Immediately, Lucian tried to get up, but the embankment gave way and he slid off the wall onto the small sliver of dry ground between the wall and the canal.

"Luc!" Ephraim heard himself yell as he, without even thinking, leaped off of the wall after his brother.

"No Eph!" Llewellyn shouted, but it was too late.

Quickly, Llewellyn fired a shot into the troops crossing the water and then flung himself over the stockade. Lucian was trying his best to get to his feet, but movement was difficult with a musket ball in his chest. Ephraim stood and fired his rifle into a soldier coming out of the water. Suddenly, there was rapid fire from the wall as Reggie, Louis, and Lafitte all fired into the crowd of British soldiers in the water. A dozen more fell as one of Cort's cannons blasted grapeshot into the mass of white and red coats rushing to the canal.

"Help me," Llewellyn yelled as he tried frantically to lift Lucian to his feet. On the wall above, Reggie leaned over the broken stockade, trying to reach down and pull Lucian up. Ephraim dropped his rifle and began to help his brother push Lucian onto the embankment just as a dozen or so musket balls hit the wall next to him.

Reggie, leaning as far as he could, got a hold of Lucian's arm and along with Rose pulled him up as Cort and Lafitte fired a volley into the oncoming British troops.

As Lucian was being pulled up, Ephraim and Llewellyn dropped to their knees. Both managed to find British muskets and fired a round into the oncoming soldiers.

Once Lucian was up, Reggie reached over the wall and shouted, "Come on!"

Both Llewellyn and Ephraim looked up and then at one another. Then Ephraim suddenly leaped forward into the water with the musket in hand and stabbed a soldier with the bayonet.

"Go," he shouted to his brother, who hesitated and then scrambled up and took the Major's arm.

On the wall above Ephraim, Winston and a dozen of the Free Men of Color took position and fired into the oncoming army. More and more British soldiers began falling as they approached the canal.

Ephraim, chest deep in water, flung the bayonet madly into soldier after soldier. Another volley of musket balls and grapeshot rained down from the wall, and soldiers fell all around him. He looked up and saw that Llewellyn was safely up the embankment and quickly crawled out of the canal and leaped as high as he could, just catching Reggie's arm. The big Englishman pulled Ephraim up with one forceful whip of his massive arm as if Ephraim were no more than a child's doll. When Ephraim got on top of the embankment, he and Reggie both fell to the ground.

After the young Englishman sat up, he saw that Reggie wasn't moving. He quickly leaned over his friend.

Reggie's eyes were open, but he was gasping for air. Ephraim looked down to see blood almost pouring from his chest.

"Reggie!" Ephraim shouted loudly enough to be heard by Louis and Lafitte over the rumble of cannon and rifle fire. He took the large man into his arms.

"Reggie," he said again as Lafitte knelt beside them.

The Major looked at Ephraim and painfully whispered, "I'm sorry, Eph. I'm sorry about the girl."

"That's not your fault, Reggie."

Ephraim could feel his friend gasping for air.

"I'm sorry Eph," Reggie said softly as Ephraim felt life flow from the man in his arms.

Slowly around them the cannon and rifle fire began to taper off.

Ephraim, shaking and in tears whispered, "It's not your fault," to the Major's lifeless body.

The young Englishman looked up into Lafitte's eyes as both of them realized that the battlefield had grown eerily silent. With Reggie in his arms, Ephraim looked out at the plain though the broken stockade. The sun was now high, and the heavy cannon smoke was drifting across the river, leaving a clear view of the battlefield. With the exception of an occasional rifle shot, the only sounds that could be heard were the moans of the thousands of British soldiers who lay on the ground in a bloody field of red and green and white coats. As far as he could see, there was not a soldier standing. The British force had been decimated, and the field was littered with the dead and dying.

Chapter 19

NEW ORLEANS
January 23, 1815

Ephraim walked slowly from the warehouse on Tchoupitoulas Street toward the riverfront. It was a brisk sunny morning, and he had his coat buttoned tightly to his neck and his satchel slung over his shoulder. This was a day he had been dreading.

Ephraim had just risen from his first night of sleep on something other than cold ground. It had been over two weeks since that bloody morning that the newspapers were now calling The Battle of New Orleans. Almost thirty-five hundred British Soldiers were either killed or seriously wounded on that field. Among the dead were the British commanding general and many of the officers. The Americans had fourteen wounded and eight killed. Ephraim and Captain Jean Lafitte placed one of those eight in a tomb at St. Louis Cemetery the afternoon of the battle.

After the smoke had cleared Louis, Cort, Llewellyn, and Ephraim carried Lucian down to the makeshift infirmary in the Macarty house. Llewellyn stayed and took care of his brother while Ephraim and the Bos buried Reggie.

That night Ephraim returned to the line where he stayed with Cort and Louis for almost two more weeks. Lucian eventually went to Reggie's house where Charlotte nursed him.

Despite the lopsided appearance, the British had come much closer to victory than any of them realized. Just as General Jackson feared, the Red Coats did move up the west bank of the river. They even managed to capture the American artillery, but, fortunately, they were too late. By the time they captured the American guns the British general had been killed, and the army on the Chalmette battlefield had been destroyed.

Still, that was far too close of a call, and since they really didn't know the extent of the British defeat, Jackson remained prepared for another attack. So with the exception of those caring for the dead and wounded, no one left the wall for over a week.

There continued to be a few skirmishes to the south, but it was becoming more and more clear with each passing day that the war had been won. Then finally, Broussard brought word that the last of the British troops had left the peninsula. It was over.

News of General Jackson's victory was spreading throughout the country. He was now a hero, as was Captain Lafitte. Crowds lined the streets and cheered when the little militia marched back into New Orleans. The General, naturally, led the procession, followed on horseback by his senior officers and then the long ribbon of proud soldiers. Cort and Ephraim had slipped out of the parade just as they entered the city, as did most of the Baratarians. They, of course, felt as deserving of honor as anyone, but there had not yet been any formal pardon which meant that they, heroes or otherwise, were still wanted criminals, and though everyone expected the General to be a man of his word, no one expected the same from Governor Claiborne.

Cort had come along with Ephraim and spent the night at the warehouse, but only after they had stopped by the Pearl Café for a good hot meal and to take part in the festivities. Winston's family hosted a victory celebration, and half of the Free Men of Color were in attendance. Cort was the toast of the party as everyone knew what role his cannon batteries had played in winning the battle, but every man who had taken a spot on the wall was a hero on that night. Celebrations took place everywhere in the city. Even late into the night when Ephraim and Cort finally arrived at the warehouse, the noise of revelry echoed through the streets. It was the grandest of times for all.

But for Ephraim Bradford, this morning would not be so grand. He was dreadfully solemn as he approached the gangplank to Captain Gambi's *Petit Milan*. Llewellyn had made the arrangements several days before. Gambi's schooner, now flying an American banner, would first sail to Galveztown to pick up cargo and drop off Cort and Louis. Llewellyn still harbored hopes of talking Lucian out of the ridiculous idea of going to Texas. Surely his wife, who came from Baltimore, would be able to talk him out of this foolishness. Nevertheless, Lucian or not, Ephraim and Llewellyn would sail on to Savannah and then make their way to one of the large cities in the north where they could make their fortune.

At least, that was Llewellyn's plan.

Llewellyn, along with Cort, Louis, and Lucian, was on the deck when Ephraim arrived. All watched him closely. Llewellyn was simply impatient to set sail and was angry that the ship was waiting on his little brother. Cort, always the insightful one, had surmised Ephraim's plans and shared his thoughts with Louis. The two watched and wondered how he was going to tell his brothers.

Lucian saw his brother through entirely different eyes. His little brother had not been the same since the wedding. He had noticed it from the moment Ephraim and Charlotte met. There was just something about the way they had looked at one another. Then when Charlotte came out to Chalmette, he overheard her ask someone if Ephraim had been hurt. She didn't ask about anyone else, only Ephraim.

"You're late," Llewellyn scolded as Ephraim walked up to them. "Captain Gambi has been waiting on you."

"I'm not going, Llewellyn," Ephraim said flatly.

"What do you mean, you're not going? We're about to set sail," replied Llewellyn.

"I booked a spot on a keelboat to Baton Rouge," Ephraim replied.

"Baton Rouge? What are you talking about? We have plans."

"I'm going to see Reggie's wife. She should know how her husband died."

Llewellyn and Lucian looked at one another and then at Ephraim. They both knew that this was no longer the kid brother who had followed them from Tenbury Wells.

"You're going to join me in Baltimore, aren't you?" Llewellyn asked in a tone that suggested that he already knew the answer.

"I've had enough of big cities, Llewellyn," Ephraim explained. "You're the business man. You don't need me."

"I guess that I can't talk you out of it," Llewellyn said with both sensitivity and admiration.

Ephraim just shook his head. Then Llewellyn, with both arms, reached out and pulled his brother to him.

"Somewhere between here and Tenbury Wells you grew up," Llewellyn said, letting go of his brother.

Ephraim then turned to Lucian who was still bandaged and looked pale. The two men hugged.

"You saved my life on that wall," Lucian said.

"No, Luc, I think you saved mine."

The brothers looked intently at one another. Somehow Lucian knew exactly what Ephraim meant.

"Take good care of your wife, Luc," Ephraim told him.

"I will, Ephraim."

When they let go, Ephraim walked over to Louis and took his hand.

"You're not the boy I met on the fields of Shropshire," Rose told him.

"I feel like I owe you something, Louis," Ephraim said as if searching for words.

"All I did was get you to America, son."

"Well, thank you," Ephraim said warmly.

Ephraim turned and looked at Cort. Somehow he knew that saying good-bye to Cort would be the hardest. As he looked at his friend, the Spaniard handed him a book.

"It's the one about Julius Caesar. I know you liked it," Cort explained.

Ephraim took the book with a tear swelling in his eye.

"I wish that I had something to give you," he said and then suddenly added, "Wait...."

Quickly Ephraim rummaged in the satchel hanging off of his shoulder and pulled out the Bible given to him by the cook on the *Tigre* and handed it to Cort.

"I never got around to reading much of it, but what I read was interesting," he explained.

"Thank you, my friend," Cort replied.

Ephraim turned and headed down the gangplank just as Charlotte walked up from the lower deck. For a brief moment she and Ephraim locked eyes. Ephraim paused, nodded to her and then turned away, tears again beginning to build.

News had spread quickly throughout New Orleans of the victory on the morning of the big battle. Around noon Charlotte and Maria received word that there had been only a few American deaths. When they got news of Mr. Blankenship, Maria wept terribly and immediately left for Baton Rouge to be with his family. That evening Charlotte went to the church on Esplanade Avenue and prayed thankfully with hundreds of other women.

The following morning, after Charlotte learned that Lucian was among the wounded, she went out to Chalmette. Two different Army checkpoints tried without success to stop her from going to the battlefield. General Jackson might be able to defeat the British, but he and his army were not going to keep from her husband's side when he needed her.

When she got to Lucian, he was lying on a bed with a bloody bandage on his chest. The musket ball had gone in deep but missed his lung. The doctor had managed to dig it out and assured her that he would live so long as he got plenty of rest. That, naturally, was her job, and she was not about to fail him.

He'd insisted that they take the *Petit Milan* to Galveztown. They easily could have waited a few weeks, but he refused and, so long as he promised to be a good patient, Charlotte conceded. She really didn't want him on the cold deck as the ship prepared to set sail, but he wanted to say good-bye to his little brother. She wasn't really sure what he had meant by that. Llewellyn insisted that they would all sail to Galveztown together, but Lucian was confident that Ephraim wasn't coming.

Charlotte hadn't asked any more questions. She knew that Lucian suspected that there was something between her and Ephraim, but neither she nor Lucian spoke of it.

When she stepped onto the deck, Ephraim looked at her with the same little boy look in his eyes that he had the day they met. There was a ping of pain in her chest, but it lasted only for a moment. She stepped up to Lucian and took hold of his massive arm and watched as Ephraim walked off the ship and wondered how two brothers could be so different. Lucian seemed to love her all the more because of her past. Ephraim...well he remained a mystery.

They all watched Ephraim walk up the dock. He didn't even look back as the gangplank was pulled up and the schooner began to drift away.

Finally, Ephraim gave in to the tugging of his heart and turned around to watch the *Petit Milan* slowly give in to the flow of the Mississippi River. All of his friends stood motionless and watched as he tearfully raised his hand to wave one last time. Charlotte stood next to Lucian, holding tightly to his arm. There was no emotion of any kind on her face. For a brief moment on the ship, he had seen the beautiful warm eyes that he had dreamed about each day that he sat in that jail cell, but the girl looking back at him was not the girl with whom he strolled on Royal Street. This was a different woman. This was his brother's wife.

The ship then turned and pointed into the flow of the river. He watched for awhile, feeling as if it was his heart sailing away. He then turned to head up the docks but stopped when before him he saw a familiar white carriage. Herman, the houseman from Grand Terre, was driving the team where Reggie had once sat. But in the back seat, wearing a broad-brimmed hat and with a bright smile on his face, sat the Pirate King of Barataria Bay and the hero of The Battle of New Orleans, Captain Jean Lafitte.

Ephraim walked up to the carriage unable, despite the pain in his heart, to keep from smiling back at the great Corsair.

"Hello, Captain," Ephraim said.

"Climb aboard, my boy," Lafitte said, smiling broadly, but it was more of an order than an offer.

Ephraim stepped up and took a seat on the carriage, and the driver began to walk the horses slowly along the riverfront.

"I see that you didn't go to Galveztown," Lafitte remarked. "The girl?"

Ephraim looked at him, surprised that Lafitte had any idea about Charlotte.

"Yeah, I guess so," Ephraim replied.

"The Major was quite troubled by that," Lafitte said. "He felt responsible. He thought that he should have done something."

"There's nothing that he could have done," Ephraim replied.

"I know, but he was still troubled. He liked you. You're going to Baton Rouge, are you not?"

Ephraim nodded, again surprised at Lafitte's insight.

Lafitte took a ring off of his finger and handed it to Ephraim.

"Sell this and give the money to the Major's wife. Don't take less than five thousand dollars," Lafitte ordered. "Tell her that I'll see to his estate."

"Did he have anything to leave her?"

Lafitte nodded, "Unlike I, the Major invested his money wisely. She'll be well cared for."

The carriage stopped next to a keelboat that was being loaded with supplies to head upriver.

"Your vessel?" Lafitte asked.

"Yes," Ephraim replied and stepped out of the carriage. He'd given up wondering how Lafitte knew such things.

"You played an important role in what happened here, you know," Lafitte said.

"I doubt that, Captain."

"Life takes one down many paths, young Ephraim," Lafitte said as he offered his hand. "Look at me. I was a blacksmith's son from the Pyrenees, but today I'm the Prince of New Orleans. You cannot always control which path you step on, but you can always control what you do on that path. Without you, Jackson may never have accepted my men into his army, and without our cannons, Jackson would have lost that war. You may have lost the girl, but what we did on that canal may well have saved a nation. Your children's children will honor what you did here."

Ephraim reached up and shook the hand of the great Corsair said, "Thank you, Captain Lafitte."

"Let's go Herman," Lafitte commanded.

Ephraim watched as the carriage drove up the docks and turned onto Canal Street and out of sight. Then he walked over and stepped on board the keelboat.

#

NAGODOCHES, TEXAS
November, 2002

Jeb was in the garage digging through some boxes. One of the drawbacks of having only one job was having free time to do Kay's projects. One such project had been hanging over his head for weeks.

When Jeb's father had passed away, most of his belongings were boxed up and put into the storage room in the back of the garage. When Uncle Louie moved into the storage room, the boxes found their way into the garage which, frankly, suited Jeb just fine. No one put a car in the garage anyway, but Kay's sense of organization could not possibly tolerate such clutter.

So on this unusually warm November Saturday, afternoon, instead of watching Texas A&M play Baylor, Jeb was waist deep in papers, books, and photographs that he vaguely remembered from his childhood.

In the apartment, formerly the storage room, Uncle Louie sat, beer in hand, watching his beloved Texas Aggies. The door from the garage was open to let fresh air into the apartment, and more importantly, allow Jeb to hear the game.

Digging though the old things, Jeb noticed something in the bottom of one of the boxes. It was a tattered old book. The spine was almost gone, and the outer boards were faded and worn, but faintly the words "Holy Bible" were still legible.

Jeb reached into the box and pulled out the testament that was so tattered that it could hardly still be defined as a book.

He opened it gently and stared at the words written on the first page and said to himself, "It couldn't be."

He sat down on one of the boxes as he stared with amazement at the words written in fine calligraphy. Finally, he read the words out loud,

> "To Ephraim and Charlotte.
> Whoso findeth a wife findeth
> a good thing and obtaineth
> favour with the Lord.'
>
> Cort."

"My, god, could it all be true?" he mumbled to himself.

Stunned, he read the words a second and third time, finally softly said, "To Ephraim and Charlotte?"

"Louie!"

THE FACTS

Most of the fundamental information in this story is historically accurate. Many of the characters were loosely based on real people such as Captain Youx, John Blanque, and Governor Claiborne. There were actually two Lafittes, Jean and his brother Pierre. Originally I wanted to include Pierre in the story, but I quickly realized that having two Lafittes was somewhat confusing, and therefore I dropped Pierre and created Reginald Blankenship in his place.

The British landing at Grand Terre took place very much as it did in the book. Lafitte's offer of help to Governor Claiborne went just as it does in the story, with Claiborne dismissing the information. The raid on Barataria Bay was very real, and Lafitte along with many of his men escaped just as described. The Battle of New Orleans also took place very much as it does in the book, although there are some who question if Jean Lafitte was there during the fight or if he was still in the process of smuggling weapons into the city. Without question, several hundred of his pirates were on the dirt wall taking part.

What happened to Lafitte and his men after the raid on Grand Terre Island is somewhat up to speculation. Clearly they were in hiding, but there is no evidence that he was training his men for battle.

ACKNOWLEDGEMENTS

First I must say a special thank you to Lynda Lively for taking on the challenge of editing this mess. Without her hard work I would never have been able to complete this story.

Secondly, I have to express my appreciation to Dawn at Austin Design Works www.austindesignworks.com for her cover and website design. She did a masterful job and I can't begin to express how proud I am of her work.

I would also like to thank Deanna Darr for going through the book for a final edit.

Finally, I have to thank Lori Martin Thompson who, for way too long a time, patiently listened to my whining about how difficult this was. She never failed to be the encourager and, quite honestly, I doubt that I could have finished without her.

I hope you enjoyed this yarn. I'm hard at work on the next one. For more information and updates come to my website www.LDWatson.com.

ABOUT THE AUTHOR

I'm a Christ Follower and I make no apologies for the reflections of my faith in my writing. Those values define who I am and how I see the world. I am also a Texan to the core. I own two types of shoes; flip-flops and cowboy boots. And, yes there is little I enjoy more than sitting on the back of a horse, but don't for a second confuse me with a cowboy. I don't dip snuff, I've never owned a pair of Wranglers, and I refuse to listen to country music (unless you count ZZ Top as country, of course).

I have a Bachelor's Degree from the University of Texas at Arlington where I studied Film and Television Production. For well over twenty years I've run around with film, video, and now digital cameras shooting everything imaginable including music videos, commercials, feature films, and television shows. Like everyone in my line of work I've written a few screenplays. One earned some awards but none ended up on screen. I was a blogger ten years before anyone thought up the word "blog." I'm also a photographer. You can see some of my work at www.LDPix.com .Please feel free to waste some time looking at the galleries and don't hesitate to comment on my photo blog.

L.D.

Made in the USA
Lexington, KY
24 August 2016